BODY BY
BLOOD

BODY BY
BLOOD

A NOVEL

DR. PATRICK JOHNSTON

Ambassador International
GREENVILLE, SOUTH CAROLINA & BELFAST, NORTHERN IRELAND

www.ambassador-international.com

Body by Blood

ISBN: 978-1-62020-602-7
eISBN: 978-1-62020-672-0

Scripture quotations taken from The King James Bible, The Authorized Version, public domain.

Jesus Loves Me, public domain.

Cover Design & Typesetting by Hannah Nichols

AMBASSADOR INTERNATIONAL
Emerald House
411 University Ridge, Suite B14
Greenville, SC 29601, USA
www.ambassador-international.com

AMBASSADOR BOOKS
The Mount
2 Woodstock Link
Belfast, BT6 8DD, Northern Ireland, UK
www.ambassadormedia.co.uk

The colophon is a trademark of Ambassador, a Christian publishing company.

1

"ETERNAL LIFE, AT MY FINGERTIPS. I almost . . ."

"I know, my dear." Morgan, my wife of six years, brings her manicured finger to my chapped lips. "Shh."

It hurts to speak, and my deterioration obviously troubles her.

"You've done so much, Raymond." She teases her blonde hair over her ears. "You're a good man."

Morgan is two and a half decades younger than I. Her voice is as smooth and angelic as her perfected facial features, but her words provide no comfort. They irritate.

If only she wouldn't wear so much perfume; the closer she gets to me, the more my lungs burn with every labored breath. My eyes do not focus well. I fight the inebriation of this looming moment by gazing directly into Morgan's Bahama-blue eyes. She flashes a half grin, and I respond by trying to relax the stress lines on my strained countenance. I look so much older than her. Beholding her physical perfection always provokes me to tilt my head higher, so as to stretch out the wrinkles under my chin, and suck in the extra weight that continues to overlap my belt in spite of the twenty pounds I have lost these last three months.

"Almost, Morgan," I wheeze.

"You're a good man, Raymond Verity. A good man."

She keeps saying that. Is she trying to convince herself, or convince me?

Scented candles cast gloomy shadows on the walls of the private hospital room and on the faces of those around me. Probably quite the opposite effect from what my micro-managing wife intended.

My colleague, Ivan Wilkes, stands beside my bed, an arm's length away. He squeezes my left hand. My arthritic knuckles crunch with his pressure. I groan and my head snaps toward him, but he appears oblivious to my displeasure. He means well, treading far outside his comfort zone to touch anyone. This is a man that tries to use the tip of his million-amero pen to tap an elevator button. It never works because they are heat-activated, not touch-activated, but he tries anyway. "We may yet conquer death in your name. Be at peace, Raymond. Everyone's here."

He waves his hand across the room, motioning to those whom I have fancied caring about me during my 68 years.

There's my cut-throat attorney, Vlad Riddell, clasping the clipboard with the document I just signed to donate my body to our research facility.

There's my senior financial advisor, Quaid Sandman, a former CEO of the largest bank in the world, and a Federal Reserve board member. His pointy spectacles blur his downcast eyes. Is he displaying grief? I squint and try to focus my eyes. No, he's just checking his stocks on his smartphone. That's what I love about him though; he's almost pathologically obsessed with profit, even at the risk of a third divorce. When he profits, I profit. But what is the benefit of profit when all I own will be ripped from my grasp at any moment?

My stubby brother, Thomas, stands at the foot of my bed, dutifully counting the pale beads on his rosary. The lines on the narrow forehead of his round face are furrowed, and his features contort as if he is suffering along with me. Why? I have seen him only twice in the 20 years since our parents' tragic death, and those conversations were contentious, refereed by our attorneys. Maybe he thinks his self-imposed misery will lessen the pain of my passing. From the growth of the bulge that totally obscures his cowboy belt buckle, he wound up with Mom's genes, not Dad's. Mom died of diabetes and sleep apnea, related to her affinity for bedtime cupcakes and cookies. Dad, on the other hand, withered away from cancer, like I'm doing now. My brother breathes a slight gasp, and his scrunched-up lips release a tormented, inaudible prayer as his fingers pass the last bead and settle on the crucifix. Annoying, as usual. I could rarely make out a complete sentence from Thomas, as he always seemed to speak with a mouthful of spit. I bite my lip to suppress my usual over-bearing reproof. I must try to think the best of him; his prayers are a kind, albeit futile, gesture.

Or, maybe it is not a kind gesture at all, but being face-to-face with his elder brother's dying moment reminds him of his own frailty, and his inevitable date with the Grim. A pitiful reminder my shriveled body and weakened intellect must be.

My religious fanatic of a sister, Tamara, stands by the door, having agreed to the boundaries I have set to limit her ceaseless agitation. I can't see her thin, short frame—Ivan is in the way. But her ceaseless prayers, her very presence create some eerie, paranormal discomfort for me. She has honored my request to stop pestering me about my eternity, more or less, but her attendance still seems like a pebble in my shoe that I don't have the time or energy to remove. My sister believes that I'm headed to eternal torment in hell, yet her personal testimony has somehow implanted a hook deep inside me. Whenever she's near, troubling thoughts long buried revive.

Ivan pats one of the plaques that surround me in my deathbed, distracting me from the distressing memories of Tamara's repeated attempts to humble me before her tyrannical deity.

The awards and trophies, framed degrees and letters from industry leaders and heads of state, are prized possessions that envelop my withering frame like flowers around a rectangular black hole in the ground. These accolades have always defined my life, and I thought they would provide a suitable frame for my unwelcomed conclusion. How wrong I was. I would trade every doctorate degree and Nobel Prize for the presence of just one of my two chillingly-absent children.

I cough and blood dribbles onto my chin. Ivan jerks his hand away from me lest I contaminate his aura of sterility.

"His vitals are growing unstable," a firm, raspy voice behind me bellows. "We must do it now."

The words of my personal physician at the head of my bed quicken my weakened pulse. To maximize the benefit of the donation of my body to the research lab Ivan and I founded, I had agreed to hasten my inevitable death in order to better preserve my body for potential revitalization under Ivan's authority. Our hopes were so high. We were hailed in the scientific community for our experiments jump-starting dead cells to life. We were confident that one day our scientific breakthroughs would make aging and death as conceptually obsolete as fossil-fuel-powered automobiles. Yet, here at the end, is it really wisdom to end my life prematurely for the sake of our hopeful research?

"Wouldn't it be amazing if Raymond Verity, the pioneer of New Body technology, were the first to ever be resurrected from the deep freeze?" Heads nod to affirm Ivan's high hopes.

Ivan's eyes dart to my wife. "Are you ready?"

I wince; he's not asking me.

I look for sadness in Ivan's, and then Morgan's eyes. Instead, they trade winks, which seems quite out of place. Morgan nods at my physician behind me, Redd Cranton. Then she turns to Quaid Sandman and gives him a smile and an assuring nod.

Why did she do that?

She looks like she's about to do something she's proud of, like she's about to walk across a stage and receive a diploma. A click of a button behind me, and the machine rumbles.

Death with dignity, always my mantra. Keep your laws off my body. My body, my choice. Now that I'm in the driver's seat of my own demise, steering my antique, tumor-tortured frame off the cliff of life, it feels more cowardly than dignified. Death by lymphoma, my death certificate would deceptively read. No, death by lymphoma is death by a natural cause, but this death isn't natural. It is self-imposed death. Fear of suffering was the motive and poison the direct cause, not the invasion of lymphoma cells. The thought is piercing at first, and then throbs like a migraine, evoking a turn of my stomach.

"I don't want to die like this."

Did I utter those words out loud? From the collective gasp of disappointment from those around me, I did.

Death.

I sense the black-robed monster sitting cross-legged on my heaving chest, the sickle in his bony right hand and the long white bones of his left clenched around my throat. In the black-hole of his hooded face I hear a gravely laugh.

Death.

The thought is like an icy knife in the center of my chest, the simultaneous sting of a thousand bees tormenting my ears with a high-pitched squeal and standing my hair up on the back of my neck.

All I have saved and stored will be stolen from me in a single moment. All my love, all my work, all my awards, degrees, and prized tributes will instantly dissolve, consumed as if in a billowing hot flame. Gone.

I blink hard and turn my gaze from the Grim's sadistic chortle, my body chilling with every labored breath. My hands feel for the frames and trophies around me in my bed. My cold, sweaty hand grips a Nobel Prize trophy, and I cling to it. Peace is just out of reach; comfort grows increasingly elusive.

Dr. Cranton's eczematous palm rests on my forehead. He pats me gently. Condescendingly. As if he pities me but doesn't respect me.

"No," I mumble, opening my eyes and shaking my head with as much vigor as I can muster. "No, Ivan, Morgan. Listen. I want to . . . "

"Shh." Morgan reaches out to stroke my sunken cheek or quiet me with her index finger as is her custom, but I thrash my head and neck away from her.

"I don't want to die. Get him off me!"

Ivan squeezes my hand firmly. "Keep the course, Raymond. Be brave."

I push it away. "No, Ivan, no. I want to live . . . "

Feet scuffle on the tile floor, not walking about, but the shifting weight of those uneasy at my outburst. Their disappointed mumbling reverberates, as though I'd run most of a mile race and fallen on the final stretch. Ivan turns to look at someone behind him and heaves an exhausted sigh. Morgan shrinks away from me, and cups her full lips with her right hand. She looks over at Vlad Riddell, my attorney, who turns square to face me, troubled.

"But he already signed the papers." Morgan spins on her heels to face Vlad. He nods and waves her quiet, his eyes fixed on me. I am letting them all down, but it is my life. My life! As miserable as it is. This end is anti-climactic, but I want to live as long as I can.

"Give it a moment." Ivan raises an index finger toward Morgan.

My proclamation has no effect on the humming of the death machine behind me. My right forearm begins to grow icy cold where the IV is impaled into my vein.

"Stop it!" A shrill cry near the door turns every head. My sister Tamara steps into the room. "He said to stop the machine. He wants to live. I heard him . . . "

Vlad and Quaid grab her by the arm and push her back toward the door, scolding her for daring to intrude into the peaceful sanctity of my euthanization. Dr. Cranton speaks into some kind of radio device, either on his person or on the wall. "Send security into 607."

"Dr. Cranton!" Tamara squeals. "Shut it off! He wants to live . . . "

Several voices swallow up her protest. "Get out!"

"How dare you!"

"Shut your mouth!"

Even Thomas casts an angry glance at her. I would have guessed that Thomas would be the one to speak up, as spiritually aware as he pretends to be, but he holds his peace.

"Thomas!" Tamara cries out. "You heard it! No bead-counting's going to cleanse you of bloodguilt . . . "

Thomas' eyes close tightly as if he is trying to shut out her words. Moisture beads on his furrowed brow, his fingers more quickly maneuver the rosary beads, and his lips begin to chant a memorized prayer. He always thought his good works made up for his pathetic apathy and fathomless selfishness, and this evening is no exception. I look into his tormented countenance, wishing he'd defend me, but his eyes and ears are shut tight to my struggle as his mind focuses on his God.

There. There is religion.

My right arm grows increasingly heavy, as if it has turned to stone. I jerk against its unwelcomed frigidity. Following Dr. Redd Cranton's counsel, Morgan begins to strap down my right wrist. I try to bring my left fist over as if to strike her, but Ivan restrains it. I pull against his tight grip, but I am too weak.

The tightness in my chest is replaced by a cold stillness, but not stillness like a calm sea, more like a lake frozen instantly solid, followed by the frantic tapping of air-breathing creatures beneath, struggling to reach the surface.

The sedation begins to make my body thirsty for oxygen, but instead of the natural panic that one would experience when they cannot breathe, I am overwhelmed with a numbing euphoria, vainly offering me hope against whatever unknown awaits me after my last breath.

I muster all my strength to try to speak up in protest of this cruel insult, but my tongue is thick and dry, my words unintelligible. I force the air in and out, fighting against the intravenous poison. With every moment that passes, my breaths grow more shallow and slow. My eyes dim. I fix my gaze on the white tiles of the ceiling, fighting the temptation to blink. My gaze focuses on the "X" that borders four tiles.

My sister's cries of protest echo in the hallway as she is forced out of the room. "Jesus, help him! Jesus . . . "

Her words are eclipsed by Thomas' increasingly strained "Hail Mary, full of grace . . . "

In an instant, my ears shut out the world. All I hear is the faint, slow clapping of my calcified heart valves, one last mocking accolade for my life. I listen carefully. The applause begins to fade. Another sound backdrops their pitter patter. Is that a wintry storm blowing through an open window? I am suddenly so cold. So cold. No, I think it's the breath of Morgan's words in my ears, contorted and slurred by the inebriating poison spreading throughout my body. Wait, I recognize the tone. Is that Louie, my son? Or Savannah, my daughter? I think I feel the weight of two children on my lap. I remember reading to them when they were little, when they were innocent, when they still liked me. Oh, what I would give to . . .

I jolt with a door slam. That is the last time I saw Savannah. I feel a paper brush against my arm as it drifts to the floor. That must be Louie's last words to me, scribbled with his mother's lipstick onto the back of an envelope of junk mail: "I hate you."

The rushing sound of the icy wind grows more abrasive as my heartbeat drops to a faint whisper. Is this the raspy cackle of the icy black beast sitting on my chest?

Morgan nears. I can tell from the burning of her perfume in my nose. Her lips press against my cheek. I cannot feel their softness. I wonder what words she whispers into my ear to try to console me.

Ivan squeezes his fist around my fingers. One last pitiless crunch. My eyes widen.

The last thing I see is the glimmering edge of a sharpened, blood-streaked sickle speeding toward my face.

2

"DR. VERITY. DR. VERITY."

Someone snaps their fingers. I force my eyes open, expecting to see a second swing of the bloody sickle and a piercing pain, but instead I see four heads hover over me, silhouetted by bright round lights. I hear a monotone voice, high-pitched, like a malfunctioning computer. My heart pounds as if I'm waking up in the middle of a surgery, expecting to feel inhuman pain. I try to speak, to cry out, but there's something bound to my face and mouth, restraining me. My mind flutters about, confused. I need to recall something vitally important that has escaped me.

The moment of my death. Are they still trying to put me down? I struggle against the bonds, and try to scream against whatever immobilizes my mouth and throat.

"Heart rate 132," a nurse beside me announces. It's a female's voice, not the gruff, bellowing tone of Dr. Cranton. "EEG waves show cortex spiking . . . "

"Do you want adenosine?" Another woman.

"No. Keep the course."

This voice appears to emanate from the man to my left, where Ivan Wilkes was situated. But Ivan's voice is different—younger. All the fond memories of our work and our adventures together are eclipsed by the memory of Ivan restraining my hand in my final moments, conspiring to deny me my right to live.

I thrash against him. I don't want to die. As I writhe against the bed, I am not weak and emaciated, but strong and full of energy.

"Extubate him," Ivan orders someone at the head of my bed.

"It's me." Ivan rips off his surgical mask and lowers his face closer to me, to better make out his facial features. A wide smile splits his face, which is unusually tanned and firm, void of his wrinkles and bushy eyebrows. "It's Ivan. Do you remember?"

What happened to him? He doesn't look a day over thirty.

He puts back his head and roars a belly laugh. "We did it! We're gods now."

Someone behind me peels the tape off my cheek and pulls the breathing tube out of my throat. Extreme coldness stiffens my arms and legs. I cough, and a warmth zips down my extremities as if I am struck with a bolt of electricity.

I gag, and a scream of rage finally unleashes. "Get away from me!"

"Calm down, dear. You're fine." I turn to my right. Morgan takes off a mask in the corner of the room. Her lips are fuller, her cheeks smoother, and her bosom bustier.

"Morgan?"

"It's me!" she boasts.

"Why are you trying to kill me?" I shout. Her smile fades to a disappointed frown. "I told you I changed my mind . . . "

"Look!" Dr. Cranton removes the surgical hair cover off my head, and holds a clipboard just 18 inches from my face. He taps a lighted button at the top and it transforms into a mirror.

What? I look like I did the day I graduated college, except my skin is a golden tan. My hair is full and thick and my complexion smooth. My acne scars are gone! My face is young! My cheeks are not sunken in, and the veins in my forehead are no longer bulging. I stick out my tongue, and the sores and the dryness that characterized it have been replaced by a smooth, moist, pink texture. I place a hand on my stomach. The nausea that has tormented me for the past year of my life is gone, and a growl of hunger escapes. I press into my abdomen and feel moguls of muscle.

How can this be?

My wife comes to the edge of the bed, leans forward, and kisses me on the cheek, but I cannot remove my eyes from what I see in the mirror.

"We did it, Raymond." Ivan flashes his young grin around the room, full of pride. "*You* did it!"

Ivan begins to clap, and the whole room of nurses and physicians applauds and cheers. This surgical suite has a second level, and hundreds of observers are present. The applause is deafening. I run my hands behind my ears. No hearing aids. I run my fingers through my hair, and discover a sensitive, slightly bulging horizontal scar on my forehead. I bring the mirror closer and examine the barely discernible scar.

Morgan kisses me again.

"What is going on? Where are Louie and Savannah?"

Morgan grimaces and backs away, as if I'd just rudely sneezed in her face. Suddenly she forces a wide smile, fluttering her long eyelashes. "You're just not going to believe how great everything is!"

I turn to gaze into the mirror. This can't be real. "I can't be in heaven, but this can't be hell."

Morgan grins. She kisses me on the lips, playfully biting my bottom lip, her breath minty. "Heaven on Earth, babe." She rests a hand on my firm, flat abdomen, and whispers in my ear. "Immortality."

3

IN THE DOCTOR'S LOUNGE, THREE dozen of the most flawless physiques and intelligent minds in the world join me for a meal of vegetables and tofu soup. The muted television is a three-dimensional image on the white wall, cast there by a projector on the ceiling. The physicians and scientists surround me like I'm a freak of nature that might go away if they blink. The older docs and scientists flood me with information too quickly to take it in. I devour the delicious food rather than their updates on the advances in medicine.

"Slow down," Ivan counsels me. "There's more where that came from."

"I don't remember food tasting so good." I take a gulp of water. "Or water, for that matter. Is this water?"

"That's because we've removed many genetic aberrancies from the seeds before we grow them and the animals before we breed them."

"The CRISPR technique," Redd adds, "has evolved, excelling all expectations."

Ivan nods. "Our research has had many practical applications, but none as profound as perfecting the human genome and transplantation."

As my ravenous appetite eases, their impromptu science updates become more interesting. I move my morsel into the corner of my mouth. "How many years since I was, um . . . ?"

"Cryo-preserved? Twenty-seven years." Dr. Redd Cranton's easily-identifiable voice is instantly repulsive to me, the memory of my final moments in my last life being so fresh in my mind. My disgust eases

17

with the beaming of his youthful countenance. It's difficult to shake the outrage I felt in that candle-lit hospital room.

"I was out 27 years? It's 2053?" I gasp. They nod. "That's, that's so hard to believe."

Ivan, who sits across from me, rests his chin in his clasped hands. "I can't imagine."

I wave my fork across the room. "And you all went through this already?"

"Yes and no." Ivan shows me the scar just under his full head of hair. I can barely see it. I lean closer. "We were old like you . . . "

"Middle-aged." Cranton chuckles.

"But alive when we were surgically transplanted into our own genetically engineered bodies," Ivan continues. "We had several failures first . . . "

"You mean, no one had been brought out of cryo before me?"

Ivan shakes his head. "We kept Gates alive for, what . . . "

"Ninety-three seconds," Cranton answers.

"But you were the first to undergo some new cell regeneration technology we're perfecting, and it looks like it worked like a charm."

"You mean, you never did it successfully before me? You could've killed me."

"Could've, would've, should've," Redd Cranton bellows. "Obsessions of losers."

Ivan turns to Cranton. "Looks like our business is about to take another leap, huh?"

Redd smirks. "To heretofore unsurpassed levels, I'm sure. Just in time, too. During the last administration, it looked like the government was about to harmfully intervene in New Body science." The doctors and scientists around the table nod and grunt, as if to affirm the general dis-taste they share of the government's increasing attempts to control the boundaries of their scientific breakthroughs. "We have a friend in the White House now, but conservatives in the House have been threatening to sanction us for years, and they have a majority. It was now or, maybe, never."

I fix my eyes on Redd. "And if I died during your revitalization?"

Redd turns his gaze to Ivan, who shrugs.

"You were the first to be brought back successfully from suspended animation," Ivan reminds me. "Be thankful."

I frown. "Thankful? That you almost killed me?"

"Yes, thankful." Cranton rests a hand on Ivan's shoulder. "Ivan had so many problems attempting to clone your replacement from the DNA extracted from your cryo-preserved tissue. A lesser scientist and a lesser friend would have given up long ago, but not Ivan."

"It was probably the scattered mutations due to chemotherapy," Ivan explains. "Sixty-eight failures before we finally got a good clone. It seemed fate that we at least attempt the ocular-neurospinal transplantation . . . "

My eyes widen. "Ocular-what?" I lower my fork, frowning at my colleague and our cloud of ambitious neophytes. "I thought we just reversed cell decomposition. You, you mean, this body's not mine?"

The neophytes laugh, like they've never seen someone they con-sidered so brilliant so utterly ignorant.

"No, no, no," Ivan Wilkes shakes his head. "When your hovercar gets dilapidated and worn, Raymond, you can repair and replace spare parts until it's all you ever do. Or, for less cost up front, you can simply . . . " He pauses and raises his eyebrows at me, as if he expects me to answer.

"Buy a new car?"

"And transplant you into it," a resident adds.

He motions toward my body with a wide grin. "We transplanted your brain, complete with your brain stem, your optic nerves and eyes, into your new body. You are an almost exact genetic match to your old body, with all the impurities filtered out."

"You what?"

"Welcome to the new you, replaceable every 25 years if you have the credit for it. Imagine the potential, Raymond, to have brilliant old men in broken old bodies revived to youth so they can continue living, learning, inventing, and discovering. No more transporting knowledge to young bloods, hoping they get it. What if Edison could have been resurrected and could have continued growing in knowledge . . . "

"We're workin' on that right now," a young researcher announces.

"Or FDR, or Marx," another doctor adds.

"Or Gandhi," another physician leans forward.

"Or Jesus." Dr. Cranton laughs.

One of the younger residents dares to speak up. "Many believe He's already resurrected."

Cranton heaves a mocking chortle at the resident. The whiteness and straightness of his teeth are amazing. Much improved over the crooked, yellow things he was nurturing when I last knew him. Cranton glares at the resident, "What are you, a fanatic?"

The resident lowers his eyes and blushes.

"How can you transplant a brain?" I run my finger along my scar.

"What part of the human body have we not transplanted besides the brain?" Ivan shrugs. "When you were still working here, we had been transplanting tissue from cadavers for decades—bones, retinas, hearts, lungs, livers, kidneys, skin."

"And *substantia nigra* tissue," a resident adds.

"Yes." Ivan crosses his arms over his chest and nods. "As far back as 1987, we were transplanting fetal brain tissue into Parkinsons patients. People have been conceiving and aborting their fetuses to exploit them for transplantation tissue since the 1990s."

The biggest question finally finds its way to the surface of my swirling ocean of inquiry. "How did you connect the severed spinal cord?"

He levels an index finger at me. "We almost had the mystery unlocked, you and I. We had the right genes, Doc, right there all along. Using our own stem cells as the platform, instead of foreign stem cells, was the perfect solution. No rejection. We just needed to find . . . "

"The biochemical trigger? You found the trigger?"

"To connect severed nerves, yes. Every cell has all the information in its DNA to heal itself, just like the salamander's tail and the crab's claw, just as you suspected. Indeed, any cell with intact DNA can transform into any type of specialized tissue it wants. We just had to find the trigger to make it want to."

"How did you do it without cancerous transformation?" Previous experiments to stimulate nerve growth frequently resulted in uncontrolled growth of archaic nerve cells, resulting in malignant masses.

"Once we correct the genetic mutations inherent in every cell division, we have a 92% success rate in triggering targeted cell growth, including perfect spinal cord reunion."

"No way!" I raise a fist in triumph.

Ivan leans forward and pats me on the hand. "That was a decade ago, Raymond. The old technology has gone the way of cell phones. The most amazing thing is that we don't have to heal severed spinal cords anymore. We just grow a paralyzed person's new body, complete with all genetic aberrancies purged. We've been doing it for nine years now."

My eyes widen. "No cell phones?"

Dr. Cranton taps his right ear. "A voice-activated nanophone replaces those cumbersome bricks we used to carry on our belts. Small as a match head. You can get one today if you want."

"Transplanting brains into perfected genetic clones—that's not even scratching the surface, Raymond." Ivan leans forward, his elbows on our table. "In our studies with autistic children and savants, we've identified the genes that turn on photographic memory, speed-reading, and the masterful mathematic calculating abilities of the most brilliant autistic patients, without all of the social detachment and communicative defects. You wouldn't believe what was possible in our genome all along, if we only knew how to turn it on. Now we do! Nothing's impossible now. Every person will be cloned genetically perfect in thirty years, and each of those people will be a god. The whole human race will be comprised of savants who never stop learning, discovering nature's secrets, and mastering its remedies."

I sit back, my jaw hanging open. Science has truly brought heaven to Earth.

My wife comes up from behind me and sets her hand gently on my shoulder. "What if the women of your dreams never grow old? Hmm?"

I turn toward her. "Women?" She doesn't flinch. "Plural?" She smiles seductively. Our eyes fasten. "Polygamy's legal?"

"Two of me," she responds, "with identical DNA, is not polygamy."

"Not that there'd be anything wrong with that, if you want," Ivan adds with a pleasure-infatuated grin.

"Polygamy's only meaningful in a nation that pretends marriage is a valuable institution anyway," Redd Cranton adds. "Practically, we've been a nation of polygamists since the 1960s, our men just never committed to the women with whom they copulated."

"We've had a separation of church and state fully recognized in all practical applications for fifteen years," Ivan assures me.

"Took long enough." Morgan raises her eyebrows at my colleague. "Religion has been a shackle on the ankles of science for too many years. With the state free of religious constraints, there's no limit to what we can do now."

"Well, there are political limits, or threats of limits, anyway," Redd Cranton cautions. "But hopefully you will help us with that."

I turn my chair so I can more fully look my wife in the eye. "Are you telling me there's another you?"

"No. But you can order one. The adult version'll be ready in eight years. Though you'd have only one me. The other would be, um, like a servant, if that's what you want."

"A servant who can speed-read, has a photographic memory, can master two to three languages and musical instruments a year, and is a walking thirty-digit calculator." Ivan laughs. "Consider the potential, Raymond." He is as excited as Edison must have been discussing his first successful light bulb. "How much quicker will we begin to evolve now, with all the geniuses enjoying immorality?"

"In another decade, we'll make *in vitro* fertilization of error-free embryos less expensive than a hospital delivery." Dr. Cranton is giddy with enthusiasm. "As long as they sign their old body over to our research facility when they're done with it."

"In these new bodies, we've corrected the errors in the mitochondrial DNA." Ivan's eyes dart from doctor to doctor along the table, boasting. "We simply lift the DNA strand from the nucleus, repair damage, re-place corrupted DNA with the proper sequence, and reinsert a perfected genome into the nucleus, tweaked to be less vulnerable to oxidative stress. Then, bam! Every baby gets a Garden-of-Eden mind and body."

"By the time you are ready for your new body in 25 years—which has already been ordered for you a few years ago—sickness and disease will be as antiquated as homophobia." There's something magical and contagious about Cranton's youthful smile.

Ivan leans forward with his elbows on the table. "We've got aging de-mystified. We can modify the genome to prevent the accumulation of beta-amyloid, transthyretin, and lipofuscin. I predict your new body may age much slower than your old one."

My stomach is finally full. Which of my thousand questions should I ask first? My wife's hands massage my shoulders and I experience the flicker of sexual desire alien to me without medication for at least several years before my cancerous demise.

Morgan grunts approvingly. My eyebrows shoot up. This is not something that she would normally do in public. I scan the room. There is a lot of touching and flirtation around me. A huge cultural shift must have transpired in the past few decades about what is considered acceptable in public. I raise my spoon at Dr. Wilkes in a silent salute. "My appetite has returned."

He laughs. "Yes, I can see."

I must have eaten too fast; nausea is setting in. It's just too much to take in all at once.

"Are you feeling up to a tour of our company, or do you want to take the day off?"

"*Our* company?"

"Yes. We're the owners of this giant. We've got a half dozen docs who can do the surgeries, but it's our baby. Come on." He stands and beckons me toward the door of the physicians' lounge.

I stand and face Morgan. "I can't believe this isn't my body?"

The automatic door slides open, and Ivan urges me with a wave of his hand. "Come on, Raymond. I'll show you."

I turn toward the door but my wife wraps her arms around me from behind. She whispers in my ear, "Mmm, when am I gonna get you alone?" She presses her fingers into my rippled abs through the lightweight cotton scrubs they gave me when I was revived. "You feel good for a 95-year-old."

Ivan pauses in the doorway.

"Just a moment," I tell him.

"Take your time." He turns, then suddenly stands at attention. "Madam President!"

He steps out of the doorway and I join the physicians and genetic engineers spilling into the hallway.

Those who, I presume, have military experience salute a stately gray-haired woman. Ivan steps forward to shake her hand. "When is it going to be your turn to go under the laser, Mrs. President?"

I step to the front of the crowd and scan this tall, slender woman flanked by massive bodyguards in black suits. She grins mischievously at Ivan. "When am I getting my new body? When can I fly my invisible supercar in my bikini again?" She leans close and pats Ivan on his forearm. "After re-election."

The pack around us laugh.

"Better put your order in now." Ivan steps back. "I'd hate to have you wait in line."

She turns toward me and extends her hand. "Dr. Verity, I suppose this is the first time we have met. I am President Veronica Sayder. Pleased to meet you." I shake her hand, and she holds onto it firmly. "I'm also probably one of the first adults you've seen who's actually living in her own body." Her words spark embarrassed guffaws around us. "I cannot begin to tell you how glad I am that you are back. I've demanded weekly updates on the progress of the technology you pioneered, hoping that Dr. Wilkes could bring you back to sit at my table someday."

She smiles broadly and I bow my head slightly. Her face looks so young. Has she dyed her hair gray to simply make her appear older and more mature for the office of the President? By the toned legs evident beneath her mini-skirt and the cleavage visible above her low-cut blouse, her features must be due to a generous affinity for plastic surgery.

"There will be a modest cost for the honor of having him sit at your table, Madam President." The voice that comes from the rear of the crowd.

I turn. It's Vlad Riddell, my lifelong attorney. Beside him, also barely recognizable, is Quaid Sandman, my financial guru. The horde of sycophants parts to allow me to greet my old friends who sport bodies unbelievably young and fit. "I know that voice better than I know that face!"

"Would you like to tag along with us, President Sayder?" Ivan gestures down the hall. "I'm about to give Dr. Verity his first tour of the part of the facility that bears his name—the Verity Wing. It's closed to the public."

She glances at one of her Secret Service agents, who nods in response. "I'd be honored."

A plaque on the wall celebrates the founding of the New Body Research Center by "Dr. Ivan Wilkes and the late, revered, Dr. Raymond Verity." That must be replaced. Just reading those words stirs up a deep fear of dying that I would give my right arm to forget. Even this unbelievably firm, muscular one.

Ivan leads us down a hall. We descend wide, circular stairs into a large foyer under a massive crystal chandelier.

"This is the public entrance to our facility, Raymond, Madam President." Ivan begins to describe the quality of the chandelier and the massive stone columns supporting the circular stairs on each side of the foyer but an anxious commotion breaks out to my right. Someone has opened the large glass doors, allowing a raucous noise in front of the building to seep into the foyer. Outside the two-story-tall glass wall, a dozen people stand across the road, holding signs.

I frown. Dr. Wilkes clears his throat. "We have already purchased the land across the street, but we're having a slight delay in the City Council approving our purchase of the city road. Apparently there's a six-feet-wide free-speech zone beside city-owned streets and a pending lawsuit to keep it that way."

Some of the protesters' signs read "Personhood Now!" "Their Body, Their Choice," and "Dupes Are People, Too."

I whisper to Redd Cranton, "What's a dupe?"

"Cloned humans have long been called dupes by the American public, a shorthand for genetic duplicates."

Most of the protesters look simple and ordinary, but one of them clearly has no desire whatsoever to be winsome. He is a large, bald man with a black goatee. His thick arms are crisscrossed with chaotic tattoos. He holds a banner so large it appears to be half the size of a billboard. It displays a disgusting photograph of the face of a beautiful girl whose scalp is fileted open, and whose brain is showing. It reads, "New Body Butchers Repent!" Two police officers flank the brown-skinned beast of a man, who keeps a comfortable distance from the less intimidating and meeker church folk.

Ivan rests a hand on my shoulder. "Don't let them bother you, Raymond. We've filed a motion with the court to expedite the case. We need to increase the cushion between us and those fanatics."

"Can we bypass the freak show?" The Secret Service personnel position themselves between the glass wall and the President.

"Yes, immediately. We have security, Madam President. We're safe." Ivan gives her an assuring nod. He points across the foyer to a hallway underneath the massive stone stairs opposite us. "This way."

"Mankind evolves to godhood before their very eyes," gripes Dr. Cranton, "with the elimination of disease at our fingertips, and those fanatics still go on about their heavenly tyrant. Makes no sense." The ubiquitous cloud of residents and doctors sneer and shake their heads.

"Religion never does," the President quips under her breath, "unless . . . "

"Unless what?" I raise my brows.

She points heavenward. "Unless I can beat the dictator in an open and fair election. But He won't take me up on my offer, and keeps condemning the angels to hell who lobby for democracy."

She winks at me, prompting jovial chatter among those who follow in our wake.

"The press has helped us marginalize them." Dr. Wilkes' gaze darts between me and the glass wall to our right. "It's actually been good for our stocks. Every time one of them says something stupid or threatens violence, the media makes a national story of it, and our stock price peaks."

The President steps between her bodyguards as if this will conceal her identity from the view of the protesters through the glass doors and wall. "This exposure is unnecessary." She quickens their pace. She reaches out and touches my hand. "Give me two weeks, and I'll have all of them shut down . . . "

"Ray!"

I recognize the voice, but cannot immediately place it. I turn. One of the front doors is open.

One of the protesters, an old lady with a cane, spry for her aged appearance, crosses the street and comes onto the property with an arthritic hop. "Ray! Brother!"

The briefcase-carrying businessman that opened the front door to enter the facility seems startled by the outburst behind him. The door slowly shuts, but not before the old lady reaches the entrance. Two security guards lunge at her. Four armed guards exit a room near the entrance. One of them taps a code on a keypad beside the door to lock it and the others stand guard, obstructing the entrance. Everyone turns to watch the guards outside frisk and handcuff the elderly trespasser on the rubber welcome mat in front of the entrance.

The President's agents place their hands inside their jackets, presumably for quick access to their weapons if it becomes necessary.

"Let's pick up the pace," one of the President's men insists.

I look into the eyes of the elderly protester, who is barely visible through the guards. "Tamara?"

"Your sister's their ringleader," Ivan snorts.

"No. Not Tamara." She's always been a firebrand with an impressive rhetoric, but a social leader?

"That woman," Ivan points at her, "is the Joan of Arc of the radical Christian right. She leads massive protests all over the nation."

My wife, who's been in a one-way conversation with one of the President's disinterested Secret Service guards, steps closer to me and whispers in my ear. "We'll update you on everything that's transpired with your crazy family later."

The sign-holders across the street are visibly upset at the rough treatment of their leader at the glass doors.

When the doors are unlocked to let two more guards exit onto the sidewalk to keep the protesters across the street at bay, Tamara's cries echo more clearly.

"Ray! Ray! Owww!" She shrieks in pain from the guard's twisting of her arms.

Ivan leads us down a long hall to an elevator large enough to fit half of our group of thirty. Once inside, Ivan places his palm on a metallic square, and a digital voice greets him, "Good morning, Dr. Ivan Wilkes."

"Sixth floor."

"Yes, sir."

Morgan caresses my back warmly. "Everything's fine. Her reputation will not mar yours."

The elevator opens at the sixth floor in the blink of an eye with only a barely perceptible sensation of movement. Ivan leads us to a door and again puts his hand on a metal plate on the wall. He looks up at the camera overlooking the door, and the metallic door slides open with a space-age *shoosh*. "Madam President, we're going to give you the modified tour, to avoid interaction with the staff and the dupes." She looks disappointed at the news. "Since we have such a large group," he adds. "Perhaps you can schedule a more intimate private tour at a later date, a VIP tour prepared for platinum investors."

"Absolutely," she smirks. "I'm as platinum as they come."

Ivan continues rattling off his plans for our impromptu tour. We walk through two locked doors and find two men in pink surgical scrubs wheeling a young female patient down the hall toward us. She's pulling against the wrist bonds that keep her arms tight against the side-bars of the gurney. Her feet are bound to the end of the gurney. She kicks and writhes as if she's on a bed of nails. Her curly brown hair and high cheekbones are vaguely familiar, but one of the guards blocks my full view of her facial features.

"What is this?" I gesture toward the spectacle.

Ivan turns and holds up his hand. "All of you, wait here." He stomps toward the two men holding onto the gurney. "I ordered that these guests have no contact whatsoever with personnel or dupes . . . "

Since this wing of the hospital is named after me, I do not respect Ivan's order to tarry.

When I get close enough, Ivan is asking one the guards, "How can that be?"

"You're the doctor," one of them replies. "We just follow orders."

I look more closely at the young woman. "Savannah?" She has a vertical gash in her forehead that is dripping blood down the side of her face. I rush to her side. "Savannah!"

Ivan steps between me and the young woman, and tries to pry my hand off the side of the gurney. "That's not your daughter."

"What?!"

"It's not your daughter." His eyes are stern. I turn to her. She is looking at me with a strained countenance. Tears are streaming down her cheeks. She has a strip of adhesive tape over her mouth, but it does not silence her wails.

I gasp. "This is her replacement body, isn't it?"

Ivan doesn't answer. I clear my throat and attempt to calm my adrenaline rush to make my instinctive request more likely to be honored. "I'd like to watch her be sutured. I would love to see how you make wounds heal so quickly and inconspicuously as the scar on my forehead." I turn toward one of the two men by the gurney, and motion toward her scalp laceration. "Do you have a gauze or something to put pressure on that . . . "

"Wait! No." The disapproving scowl on Ivan's face troubles me. "You don't know what you're talking about, Raymond."

Several conflicting emotions begin to thrash around in my mind, silencing me. Who'd want to spend two million ameros on a new body with a forehead scar, however slight? What are they going to do to her? This isn't a microscopic embryo in a sterile petri dish or a growing human *fetus* in a chimera's uterus—this is a real person.

"She started expressing emotion," one of the male nurses says with a snarls, as if this were a forbidden crime. "Everything's been thoroughly documented, sir. Her wound was self-inflicted when we separated her from a male."

"Self-inflicted?" Ivan frowns.

"Accidental, but self-inflicted. She fought us . . . "

It's as if Ivan reads my thoughts. His head snaps back toward me. "They probably gave the puberty hormones too fast. This is our protocol for the eighth year . . . "

"Eighth? She doesn't look a day under sixteen."

"*It*! Not, not *she*!" Ivan raises his voice like he's angry at me, his gaze darting from me to the others who are approaching from behind. "This is a dupe. Ninety-two." His condescending attitude is embarrassing me. My wife walks up beside me and rests her hand on my lower back. Ivan's eyes fasten onto Morgan's. "We'll try again, Morgan. This is rare. Three percent . . . "

"Just listen." Morgan speaks as if she's reminding a toddler not to eat with his fingers for the umpteenth time, like this is something I should have learned by now. "You're embarrassing yourself, Raymond. This is *not* our daughter." Surprisingly, there's no sorrow in my wife's cold stare as the girl who looks just like Savannah lies in horrific distress before us, bound and gagged in a pool of her blood, tears, and sweat.

The poor girl turns toward me, writhing and moaning, as if she's trying to communicate with me. I long to hear her complaint, pitying her. I turn to the male nurse who was doing most of the talking. "You said she started expressing emotion. What's wrong with that?"

"Shh. Please." My wife's whispered tone is harsh.

Ivan growls. "Now's not a good time for you to ask such questions."

"Don't belittle me!" I hear the approaching footsteps of the President and the others behind me. "Remember who I am, Ivan."

He nods dutifully. Good. I've put him in his place.

"This dupe has been harmed, and so we will follow our protocol for that." Ivan turns away from me. "We are well within our 3% wastage rate, and we're proud of that number. We medicate the dupes to make them more servile, so that they aren't asking too many questions and don't get violent, but accidents inevitably occur. The medication also prevents them from being attracted to each other, which is a problem with our accelerated growth and puberty protocol, especially in the seventh and eighth years . . . "

Ivan is in his lecturing mode, waving his arms authoritatively as he speaks to President Sayder and the crowd of physicians and genetic engineers. Turning my question into an impromptu lecture takes the emotional volatility out of the situation and stimulates the intellect of those accustomed to prostrating their feelings before hard-to-please professors and preceptors. Everyone nods, affirming him as he sermonizes, as if his explanation makes perfect sense.

The emotions that flood into my mind, however, are swirling to make the perfect storm. The young woman looks exactly like my daughter did the day she slammed the door in my face, yet she is only eight. She is either in tremendous pain from the gash in her forehead, or has a staggering fear of the men who wheel her toward whatever discipline they have designated for dupes charged with inappropriate emotional outbursts. She is panicking in her bonds, weeping pitifully, thrashing uncontrollably.

Ivan appears troubled by the girl's increasingly bizarre outburst. He turns to the nurses. "Please, sedate them before you wheel them away next time."

"We usually do, sir, but . . . "

He raises his palms to cut them off. "Please, no excuses."

"Yes, sir."

After a measured sigh, he coldly orders, "Get it out of here." He motions his head toward the door. "And keep everyone away from us during our tour."

He turns to Morgan. "We'll have to start with a new embryo. I will call your daughter personally and apologize."

"Please don't." Morgan shakes her head. "Savannah doesn't even know I put in the order. This was my surprise to her . . . "

Ivan frowns. "It's almost time for the transfer, and you haven't even told her yet?"

As my wife stutters her excuse, I look up at the two words on the mirrored door of the room into which the men wheeled the injured young woman.

Medical Waste.

4

THROUGH THE REMAINDER OF THE tour, I am silent and indifferent, quite unfeeling toward my wife and my colleagues. It is the only way I can get through it, my heart pains within me so. In my mind, I was euthanized against my will just this morning, and now I've been resurrected into a strange new world. I saw my elderly sister get thrown to the ground and arrested, shook hands with a gray-haired goddess who calls herself the President of the United States, felt a youthful stimulation from my wife's touch and romantic words, and the first human clone I faced looks just like my daughter and was being wheeled away for termination. I am having a difficult time processing it all.

After the tour, a caravan of hover-limousines carries us all away to the White House for a dinner of cloned lobster and cloned filet mignon. This meat is heavenly, and doesn't even raise the cholesterol, they tell me. But I can hardly take a bite. My wife keeps one hand on my shoulder or thigh during most of the meal. The President goes on and on about her plans to change the laws, alter the culture, and prepare the next generation for the New Body science.

"You will be to healthcare what Einstein was to relativity, Newton was to gravity, and marijuana was to migraines." She has such a charming way with words, but in my generation she would have been as politically incorrect as a belt was to a brat's buttocks.

Our company, I come to learn, remains volatile as long as the ethics of the New Body technology remain shaky under current law. All the breakthroughs may come to naught if some daring prosecutor or State Attorney files charges and a judge gives them credence. President Veronica Sayder was selected almost a decade ago by a panel of our platinum investors to be the lavishly-financed political savior of New Body science.

As the doctors mull over subtle nuances of various protocols of procedures I don't even fully understand, Ivan and President Sayder step aside and have a one-on-one conversation for several minutes.

When they return, the President leans over the table and pats the back of my right hand. "Dr. Verity, I have an offer for you. Given that you're decades behind on scientific achievement, and that Morgan said you were always interested in politics . . . "—I glance at my wife, who winks at me—"I would like to employ you to be the face of the New Body science in pursuit of laxer laws."

Riddell answers at a table behind me, "We'll be the filter for that financial offer, Madam President."

I turn to nod at him, and Riddell gives me a thumbs-up.

"What about my duties at the company, Ivan? Do I even have duties?"

"An office, but no duties. It'd take several years of full-time schooling for you to just get up-to-date on the technology. Clearly, you're, uh,"—he clears his throat, his gaze darting around the room—"you're a bit behind the times."

The physicians bristle with nervous laughter. I can tell I have offended them with my outburst on the Verity Wing.

"I was practically euthanized and chilled at negative 196 degrees Celsius for 27 years," I reply with a grin. "What did you expect of me upon my awakening besides being behind the times? At least I've still got my charm."

The mood in the room lightens a bit.

"Thank you so much for the offer, Madam President." Morgan reaches across the table to shake her hand. "It's right down Raymond's alley."

I take a deep breath and smile at President Sayder. "I am honored to serve."

I'm back. Everything's going to be all right.

5

AFTER AN HOUR OF NEAR-SUPERNATURAL passion with Morgan, and four hours of deep sleep, my mind and body waken as active and alert as I've ever been. It doesn't keep me from trying to catch some more shut-eye, but I couldn't sleep if my life depended on it. Clearly, my body's been engineered to require very little rest for maximum performance.

When Morgan finally opens her eyes, she excitedly informs me that she has a surprise for me. She refuses to divulge, but from her choice of outfits, it is pretty obvious what she has in mind. Normally, she would wear a summer dress to the dock and strip down to her bright pink bikini once she boarded our yacht, but she apparently considers that old-fashioned. She insists on sporting her bikini from the moment we step out of the front door, and even through the two department stores she stops to shop at *en route* to the dock. Once we leave port, even that is too much fabric for her, fearing "the distractive tan lines of yesteryear."

It takes a few minutes to familiarize myself with the luxurious yacht to which Morgan has upgraded, but soon we are speeding east. In a half an hour, the shore has disappeared and we are encapsulated in sunshine and salty waves in every direction. We enjoy the dolphins, bask in the Jacuzzi, and sip chilled twenty-seven-year chardonnay, chatting till dusk.

"I saved the bottle since the day you were preserved." She swirls the cool liquid in her wine glass.

"Thank you for waiting for me."

"I knew it'd be worth the wait. I put this chardonnay in a prominent place on our mantel. It brought me comfort, knowing that Ivan was planning to bring you back some day and we would enjoy this together."

The thought of that day stirs some distrust in me. "Why did you go through with it? I clearly said that I wanted to live."

She smiles uncomfortably, as if she's in denial of some shame associated with the memory. "The document had already been signed, and everything was in motion." She shrugs. "You're the one that made it irreversible. Don't you remember?"

I set down my glass and try to recall.

"You were concerned that you would be delirious at the end, so you had Vlad make the document irrevocable without three psychiatrists confirming you were of sound mind." The excuse sets me reasonably at ease, and in a moment my eyes are feasting on the curves of my wife's amazing body. "Oh, dear, do you regret it?" She draws close to me and looks up into my eyes. "Don't you prefer a wife who looks like a 25-year-old cover girl instead of a sagging 70-year-old nursing home patient?"

I think for a moment, introspective, keeping silent.

"Dr. Cranton said that if your body withered away much more, your resurrection may have been impossible. They found many genetic aberrancies in your DNA, and they had a difficult time correcting them, which was necessary before they could even create your dupe."

"What genetic aberrancies?"

She pursed her lips. "You had a genetic mutation that gave you a good chance of developing testicular cancer, not just lymphoma. You were a genetic carrier for dozens of diseases, and dispositions for certain diseases. Cardiomyopathy and epilepsy were two of them, I think. Oh, the list was as long as my arm."

She begins to take a sip of her wine and then hesitates. "Oh, wait. Call coming." Morgan taps behind her right ear. "Yes, Quaid?" Her optimistic wide-eyed stare at the horizon suddenly becomes a warm smile. "You approve of the contract? Great." She listens for a moment. "Thank you both so much."

This tapping behind the ear to answer phone calls is unusual, but no more unusual, I suppose, than it was when people started communicating through wireless Bluetooth earpieces.

She taps behind her ear again to end the call. "Quaid and Vlad have given their go-ahead. The President will be flown to our yacht by helicopter tomorrow morning, arriving at nine, for your final approval and your marching orders."

Although I am still conflicted over the ethics of what we are doing, I beam with pride in how far I've come, how lovely my wife is, how wealthy we are, and how famous I'll become as the public face of the New Body science.

I clear my throat. "Do Savannah and Louie have the same diseased genes?"

"Of course. You and I passed down our genetic dispositions. But not for long."

"Tell me about 'em. I can't get them out of my mind."

She drank down the rest of her chardonnay and poured herself another glass. "Louie is in San Francisco. He's on his second marriage to an attorney named William. Louie is halfway through his first new body. He and his husband have adopted two boys and named them Frank after your dad, and Gene after William's."

My jaw drops. "Louie's gay?"

"Since his first marriage ended in divorce, yes. He's also HIV positive, a drug-resistant strain, but that's not going to be a problem. He'll probably have a new body before he has any symptoms. He's practically a god to the gay movement, quite the national figure. Though, if you ask me, much of that fame was riding on the coattails of a famous father. For a while, he lobbied for federal funding to identify 'the gay gene,' but when it was feared that the discovery would lead to a search for 'the cure' to homosexuality, he was persuaded to abandon those efforts."

She must be able to tell that I'm uncomfortable with the information about my son, so she changes the subject to speak about Savannah. I stop her. "I didn't mean to have such a frown on my face when you talked about Louie, Morgan. I'm not homophobic, you know that."

"Of course."

"It's just that I didn't expect my only boy to turn out gay and, and"— I turn the statement into a question—"HIV positive? Louie?"

"I understand." Morgan sighs and pats me on the hand reassuringly. "It doesn't carry the negative stigma it did three decades ago. Today, even consensual M.B.L. practitioners and bug-chasers are tolerated and embraced."

"M.B.L. practitioners?"

She furrows her brow at me, as if I should know this. "Man-boy-love."

I flinch. "What's a bug-chaser?"

"Gays who seek out HIV infection as if it were a fashion symbol. Most think they simply crave the thrill of the threat of risky sex, but I think most of them just want the monthly disability checks."

That information turns my stomach. "Tell me about Savannah."

"Savannah's still bitter, unfortunately. She keeps her distance. She is engaged to a stockbroker named Jeffrey Gilmore. They have one child and named her . . . " She pauses and frowns, as if something has suddenly upset her.

"What is it?"

She clears her throat. "They named her Mary Nell. They wanted only one child, so I think that's it for them."

"Why is she bitter? Remind me?"

"Don't you remember? We had a falling out about six months before you were, um, cryo-preserved."

"Oh, yeah." We had some contentious conversations near the end. "Has she lightened up with her attacks on me?"

Morgan shakes her head as she reaches into her purse on the deck beside the Jacuzzi. "Not really. I ordered her a new body off her cord blood, hoping to change her mind. With her genetic platform, it's just a matter of time before her diseases begin to manifest, and then she'll be more receptive. I guarantee it. She's so, so stubborn. It's too bad she'll have to wait another eight years now."

She opens a palm-held image album and hands it to me with a picture on the screen. "Here's Savannah with her fiancé and daughter."

The happy threesome stand in front of the Statue of Liberty. It gives me an unfamiliar warmth, a euphoria that simultaneously fills me with regret for the years of her life I missed. "Oh, she's beautiful. I miss her." I gaze at her longingly for a moment. "What if Savannah doesn't change her mind when her dupe ripens? The protocol only goes to eight years. What becomes of her dupe?"

"Ivan will probably cryo-preserve it until Savannah changes her mind, be it in five, ten, or thirty years. And if she never wants it, that's her choice. They'll just dispose of it. You know, recycle it to get some good out of it."

"*It?*" I study Morgan for a moment. "You saw that poor girl that looked just like Savannah, tied to that gurney, crying and wailing, physically perfect with the exception of what would have been a barely perceptible scar above her eye and a little too much romantic affection for the opposite sex. They terminated her, Morgan. Does that bother you?"

Morgan looks at me as if I am giving an argument for aliens living inside my brain—like I'm crazy and out of touch with reality.

"Don't look at me like that," I urge her. "I'm serious."

She shakes her head and begins to search her purse for her lipstick, as is her custom when I have insulted her with my words. "It's not a person, Raymond," she frowns. "The Supreme Court has ruled on this several times. Your DNA is your property, including any modification of it."

She reapplies her lipstick. "With the separation of church and state fully integrated into American society, judges only look at the facts and the law, not tradition, not superstition, and not a book of Scripture. All but the most extreme anti-choice groups agree that dupes are subhuman, and that commercial cloning is an inevitability that they are content to try to regulate. The fringe proponents of banning cloning or banning the termination of clones have completely disappeared off the national scene. The benefit to humanity far, far outweighs any consideration of a dumb lab monkey. You must know that."

Dumb lab monkey? Humankind certainly evolved in the past 27 years. There must be something wrong with my mind for me to be so critical of the very same terms of dehumanization that I employed throughout my career. Perhaps Ivan can discover what deleterious genes were responsible for this freakish quirk of human nature that makes me feel a pang of guilt at Morgan's words, so we can purify the human race of such unreasonable scruples.

I look more carefully at Savannah's daughter in the picture. She looks to be about three years old. She has abnormal facial features. "Does Mary Nell have Trisomy 21?"

"Yes, Down Syndrome."

"And Savannah kept her?"

Morgan nods. "Savannah's still a health nut who thinks the medical community has kept the cure for cancer under wraps for forty years for profit. She thinks obstetricians are involved in some great conspiracy to convince the public that pregnancies are pathological illnesses. So she decided to birth at home with a hairy midwife."

She releases an embarrassed chortle.

I smile. "That's the Savannah I know and love." Always going against the grain. GMO-free, oil-rubbing hippy. "Does she still avoid soap?"

Morgan laughs. "No, I think her ideals are finally growing lukewarm in her old age. Being Savannah, she refused some of the prenatal testing, otherwise the defect would have been caught and the pregnancy certainly would have been aborted. Mary Nell, to her mother's credit, does talk better than most Down Syndrome children."

"Can Ivan fix Mary Nell?"

"No, hon. You should know that. Her genetic code is in every cell of her body."

I shake my head, feeling like a fool. "Of course."

"I did put an order in last year for Mary Nell's new body."

"Really? You can do that without Savannah's consent?"

"I'm the wife of *the* Raymond Verity. I can do what I want." Morgan raises her eyebrows and wags her head in her sassy fashion, as if she's some untouchable Hollywood superstar who will assert her will, regardless of who it offends. I'll bet she has a jpeg of my signature on her P.C.

"Will the courts let you?"

She shrugs. "I may appeal to the courts to do what's best for Mary Nell, regardless of her parents' wishes."

"You would do that?"

"Undoubtedly they would rule in our favor. I mean, they let physicians remove obese citizens from their homes and incarcerate them in wards until they lose their excess weight."

"What? You're kidding, right?"

She furrows her brow, as if she is offended that I dare to doubt her honesty. "The courts respect that freedom is worthless without health, and freedom abused is abuse of others, for we are all connected in this socialist society. If someone abuses themselves, they abuse others through forcing them to fund their preventable surgeries and their medications through taxation and—"

"Well, quit forcing people to pay for another's medication," I interrupt.

She squints her eyes at me. "What planet are you from? Healthcare's a right, not a luxury. The precedent's firm: if I asked a judge to replace my defective, tax-wasting granddaughter with a productive dupe, the courts would predictably rule in my favor, Ray. But I don't think I'll need to appeal to the courts. When Savannah realizes that Mary Nell's new body has already been ordered and that unused dupes are recycled or terminated, she will consent. When she realizes that her new daughter's potential won't be inhibited by a speech impediment, physical deformity, heart valve surgeries, ear tubes, mental retardation, infertility . . . "

"Down Syndrome doesn't cause infertility! They can marry and procreate."

"And have normal babies?"

"Absolutely."

"And who's going to marry them, Ray?"

"They can marry each other and still make normal babies."

She shakes her head side to side. "Which judge is going to grant that child-bearing license. Not one in this country."

The cold, hard reality strikes me full force. I guess I knew it all along, I just suppressed the notion. Every dupe is terminated anyway, whether the owner accepts the new body or not. We grow them to exploit them. "So one of them's going to die."

Morgan takes my statement personally. She harrumphs and guzzles down her glass to pour another, as if the process is sufficient to distract her from my point. I study the picture of Savannah and Mary Nell, appreciating the innocent smile on the face of the three-year-old granddaughter I have never met. "Wait, Mary Nell's brain is Downs. How can they transplant her brain into her perfected dupe?"

Morgan sighs, swirling her drink as she speaks. "There's a special protocol in such cases. The dupe will be a genetically perfect replica of Mary Nell—no Trisomy, no cancer genes, and no abnormalities. This dupe will be educated, not medically servilized, and can be processed into the host's family quicker than the usual eight years. The dupe will completely replace Mary Nell. No transplantation. The dupe's mind will be a blank slate for new memories of her new home and new parents. It's better than what our granddaughter can do now with her defective mind."

She must be able to read my mind from my facial features, for she immediately gets defensive. "Don't be so judgmental, Ray. It's better for everyone. More happiness. Less suffering. Less cost. Better future."

"So the 'it' is going to magically become a 'her' when the real Mary Nell is terminated?"

"Huh?"

"The 'it'—Mary Nell's dupe—is going to magically become a 'her' when the real Mary Nell is killed. That's what you're saying, right?"

She sighs and gulps down her chilled wine. "Why are you doing this?" Her words are slurred from the alcohol, and her tone is less respectful. "You pioneered this, babe. You laid the foundation of the New Body science. You've got to adapt to the new world you, you, uh, you . . ."

"Envisioned."

"Yeah. You envisioned."

I am dumbfounded by Morgan's stubborn reluctance to admit the self-evident cruelty of these transactions. But she is right. It is a transaction I perfected.

I climb out of the hot tub and lean against the bar that separates me from the ocean. They're going to terminate my grandchild, my only grandchild. My wife stands with a swagger and wraps her arms around my waist. I fix my eyes on the sunset, so beautiful on the western horizon here, twenty miles off the Chesapeake Bay.

"I'm sorry I spoke to you like that, Ray. But you've got to think of the good. The end justifies the means, right? You taught me that when you knowingly wandered into legal trouble creating vaccines from aborted fetal stem cells, when you commercially sold fetal tissue to cleaning product manufacturers and research companies. Remember your early attempts at cloning humans and chimeras? Remember? Other researchers were quiet about it, but you went public. You defied the bigoted precedent. Remember the lawsuits and the warrant?" She begins to rub some more coconut-scented tanning lotion on my bare back. "You did what everyone knew could be done, and wanted to do, but didn't have the guts to do."

Her tone informs me that she is sincerely proud of my accomplishments, and means to encourage me, but her points make me blush with shame.

"You bore the brunt of the opposition while your severest critics lined up to walk in your footsteps, basking in your shadow. Your chipped and dented shield led the way for all of Ivan's work. You always focused on what was best for humankind, and look where we are!"

She comes around to stand beside me, giving me a full view of her genetically perfected and toned body. She flashes that girlish, innocent grin that she knows I find so irresistible. "Imagine a world with no wrinkles or sags, no age spots, no gray hair, no diseases, no defects, and no physical imperfection. No death. Imagine, babe." She throws her arms around me and presses her body into mine, whispering in my ear, "Just imagine."

"And no Mary Nell."

My depressing words are like a bucket full of ice water on her spark. "Oh, what's the matter with you? Ivan needs to check your testosterone or something!"

She jerks away from me and sinks back into the Jacuzzi with a splash. She and I sulk for a moment, though for different reasons. She grieves the reluctance of her antiquated husband to accept the new world that infatuates her so. I begin to mourn the imminent death of the defective granddaughter I have never met.

6

"I DON'T UNDERSTAND, PRESIDENT SAYDER. Why does the contract compensate so meagerly? I made more as a researcher, even before cloning really took off." I turn to Morgan, who sits beside me on the yacht's upper deck. We are in our white bath gowns after an early breakfast.

"Why would Quaid and Vlad agree to this?" Morgan wonders aloud.

"Dr. Verity, let me explain the political realities." The President pauses for a long moment to collect her thoughts. Her Secret Service agents and the helicopter's pilots are enjoying a moment's repose in the pool hall, upon the President's insistence. She sits across from us in a bright orange blouse and miniskirt, stretching her golden brown legs up on a second chair to take advantage of the blissful sunshine. "What would you purchase if you had, say, twenty billion ameros of credit over and beyond your present income?"

"Twenty billion?" I raise my eyebrows. That's a lot of buying power. With the predictable hyperinflation annexed to the government's blitzing printing presses, certainly "a billion is the new million," as Quaid likes to say, though he's certainly exaggerating. But twenty billion is still quite a load of spending credit. I glance at my wife, who blushes at the thought of so much. "I'd buy a large, sparsely populated island in the Pacific, build a perpetually self-sustaining estate on it with an airport, and a bigger jet to ferry us there."

The President chuckles. She pushes her grayish brown bangs over her ears and turns her face up toward the sun.

Morgan adds, "A jet with a pool. And a theater. Plus, more servants, more jewelry, more pampering and traveling, you know."

"Of course," the President nods. "The necessities of the higher life."

Morgan grins as she swirls her Chardonnay. "Absolutely."

Morgan stretches an empty wine glass toward the President to invite her to have a drink, and the President politely rejects it. Though she does take the offer as an invitation to greater informality. She fetches a pair of sunglasses from inside the small purse she has beside her.

"Rather than give you twenty billion ameros for your island," she dons her glasses, "and your jet for your luxurious getaways, on which you would pay over half in taxes, and which would reflect negatively on my administration, why not just pay you a meager salary and give your corporation the island of your dreams by executive order to study the composition of the sand?"

"The composition of the sand?"

"The taxpayers are paying for stupider things. Just send me a letter every year stating your results are inconclusive, and we're even."

I hold my countenance firm. What are the unmentioned conditions of this plush deal?

Morgan smiles ear-to-ear, oblivious to the fine print of contracts. "That, that sounds so good." Morgan laughs giddily, unable to conceal her shameless glee. "Maldives." Her head snaps toward me. "I want an island in the Maldives."

"Too far away," I snap.

"Caribbean, then," she quips. "Away from the cruise lanes."

The President's confident smirk at our exchange indicates that she knows she has the deal sealed. "Now you know why Quaid and Vlad approved, Dr. Verity."

Morgan reaches forward and pats the President's hand. "Just call him Raymond, please. Or Ray."

Morgan's cheeks blush with childish enthusiasm as she pours herself a fresh glass. I sigh and force a smile at the President. If only my wife would just be quiet and conceal her elation a bit. Playing hard-to-get always gets you the better deal. When talking these kind of numbers, however, it is difficult to conceal the gaiety.

"It's a blank check for you, Raymond." The President removes her sunglasses and leans in toward me. "I'll give you whatever you want in the world, if it is possible, by executive order, as long as I can find some way to justify it on paper, and you give me three to six hours a week of interviews that we will schedule on major networks for the next four to six months."

Morgan looks at me longingly. I hold my peace. What about the potential public backlash of any negative press? How would it affect my company's stock? Would it frighten away clients?

"Will you sign it?" The President leans forward.

Can I trust her? Veronica Sayder is an ambitious, power-hungry Godzilla of a politician who will stop at nothing to increase her kingdom and subjugate her enemies. There is no right or wrong to her, no conscience or law that would keep her in check. How do I know she will keep her word?

"Of course he'll sign it." Morgan appears irritated at my hesitancy.

I study the President for a moment. With my burgeoning popularity and influence, it would be a risky venture for her to disappoint me.

The President lifts a handheld computer from her purse and extends it toward me. I look for a place to sign, or a stylus. My wife clears her throat, embarrassed. "Just press your index finger against it, Ray."

"Oh." I have a discomfiting déjà vu at the thought of signing a legal document, remembering what happened to me soon after the last document I signed near the end of my last life, but my thoughts are more pleasantly consumed with what I'm going to demand from the President.

President Sayder hands me a tiny silver CD in a clear plastic case. "Now, partner," she grins, "personally read through these proposed laws carefully. Your fingerprint is required to open the file, as this is not a job to be delegated to a subordinate."

"I understand." I immediately insert the CD into my laptop and open the file.

"This is classic Hegelian strategy. My initial proposals are on top, and under them are the congressional compromises that will follow on the heels of the rejection of my initial proposals. There will be many proposed compromises, but one will be endorsed by the moderate Republican Speaker of the House." She motions to my laptop. "It's labeled 4A. That compromise is what you need to vehemently defend. This will put you at bitter odds with me on my initial proposals."

"Bitter odds? With you?"

I scroll down to the 4A section.

President Sayder grins mischievously, and shrugs. "That's okay, no hard feelings. This strategy is thoroughly vetted and amazingly effective. The Republican opposition in the House and the Senate are predictable, and their counter-proposals to mine are equally predictable."

Morgan, leaning forward to read the opening sentence of the preamble, appears as stumped as I am. "This reads like an anti-cloning law. You want him to defend this?"

"Vigorously. It may read like an anti-cloning law in the preamble, but the preamble isn't law, it's rhetoric. The preamble's bait. What this law will actually do, what we're trying to conceal from the suckers—that's the hook. The goal is to gradually get the public in general, Republicans and independents in particular, to accept the dehumanization of dupes as the lesser of two evils, and to compassionately regulate the termination of dupes in terms that ultimately support our aims."

I nod, but Morgan still looks confused. I point to the title of the first bill on the face sheet. "Morgan, listen, the President's administration is going to propose simply legalizing cloning without any legal protection for clones."

"Right," President Sayder agrees. "Dogs will have more rights."

I turn to Morgan, "The political right's going to oppose her, of course."

Morgan nods. "Of course."

"Then these compromised bills will be offered by respected Republicans. But in the very wording of the Republican counter-proposals, cloning will be legalized, dupes will be dehumanized, and citizens will be declared the owners of their own genome and all technological tweaks of it."

Morgan nods. "I see. So you're actually writing the Republican counter-proposals? You can do that?"

The President nods as she leans back in her chair. "And the judges are already lined up to support the law against predictable lawsuits, thus establishing strong judicial precedent for the future." The President sighs and points to the bubbling Jacuzzi beside us. "May I?"

I gulp and turn to Morgan, who raises her eyebrows.

"Please," Morgan purrs.

The President stands and shrugs out of her blouse and miniskirt, revealing a bathing suit every bit as revealing as my wife's. She was prepared for this. She struts confidently to the Jacuzzi, oblivious to the four eyeballs that are fastened on her. After seeing the fitness of this woman's physique and her flawless skin, I realize she must be dyeing her hair gray. That's why she's in no rush to get a dupe. She steps into the bubbling water and gasps at the heat.

"Ooh, nice. Come on in," she beckons.

My wife, feeling more comfortable with the President's exposure, sheds her cotton bath gown and almost trips on the way to the Jacuzzi, spilling her wine.

"Plenty more where that came from," she laughs.

"I think I'll have that drink now." The President sinks lower into the tub until the water completely covers her shoulders.

Morgan pulls a bottle of chilled Chardonnay out of the cooler and pours all three of us a glass.

I join them and the President continues to enlighten me about our campaign. "I may oppose you with fiery rhetoric," she warns me. "I might call you a right-wing nutcase, a Bible-thumping fanatic even." A mischievous turn-up of the corners of her cherry-red, lipstick-coated lips informs me just how much she enjoys this subterfuge. "My utter condemnation of you before the media is all calculated to give you hero status on the right. When you support these Republican-sponsored bills as the lesser-of-two-evils over my proposals, getting them passed will be so easy. We'll shake hands at the signing, I, with a tear in my eye as if I'm betraying my principles and my socialist constituents, and you with a victorious grin."

"You conniving devil," Morgan grins.

I am speechless. I'm sitting in the Jacuzzi on my yacht on the calm, eastern rim of the Chesapeake Bay with my wife and the President of the United States, discussing how we are going to trick the political right into championing our aims.

"This is a strange new world indeed."

The President shakes her head side to side. "This is classic politics, Ray. Not new at all. Who do you think's funded more abortions, promoted more open gays and transgenders to public office, lobbied harder for legalizing gay relationships, funded more taxpayer-subsidized birth control, more irreligious art and films? Not the Democrats and Marxists. All you've got to do is propose something more radical than what you really want, and the right, as unprincipled as they are, will lead their constituents to fight tooth and nail for what you really wanted all along."

My wife has a smile on her face ear to ear. She extends her wine glass to the President and they clink them. "Brilliant. Isn't it brilliant, Ray?"

I nod and extend my glass. "Undeniably."

7

"THANK YOU FOR JOINING US for tonight's edition of *Hot Seat Live.*" The flamboyant Hispanic host with a well-manicured five o'clock shadow speaks into the camera as we take our seats in sofas around the coffee table on the studio platform.

The studio stage is back-dropped with a fleet of screens displaying the 3-D images of the major headlines of the day. There's the looped image of a starving African baby getting the newly-improved Ebola vaccine. There's a clip of rioting on several Alabama college campuses during their governor's speech announcing restriction of over-the-counter abortion pills. There's an image of President Sayder speaking in front of the White House beside a clip of me testifying before the Congressional Health Committee.

"The left will be on the hot seat tonight," the host continues. "The President's Press Secretary, Aaron Little, will defend the Administration's legislative proposal to legalize cloning, declared by the President to be the most daring law since Abraham Lincoln's Emancipation Proclamation. Practically speaking, cloning is already legal, given that no state has ever prosecuted those who clone humans in violation of a dozen ambitious state laws and a weak, decades-old federal law. The President would like to more vigorously protect American's rights over their own genome, and establish a consistent standard nationwide. On the right, we have the President of the Pro-Life Legislative League, Jim Cobb. He surprised many last week by openly condemning Alabama State Attorney David Mease's decision to defy a federal judge and put out a warrant for the arrest of David Starr, the CEO of the Birmingham-based Mirror Mirror Cloning Company."

This information is not new, but a chill runs through me that seems to go as deep as my bones. David Starr was a Columbia University trained geneticist who became my apprentice just a few years before my cancer diagnosis. His brilliance in cloning genetically modified non-human mammals was notorious. Rather than risk him becoming my competition in the New Body science, I brought him on as a well-paid apprentice. Incrementally, I was able to quash his initial objections to cloning humans. He simply couldn't deny the potential for good. I taught him everything about human cloning and genetic modification of the human genome, but terminating "defectives" was a line he refused to cross. His business operated as a subsidiary of my company, making the bulk of its income from our consults. However, when the cost of sustaining his genetic defectives began to swallow a large portion of his company's profit, it became a financial decision for him. They outsourced the termination of 243 genetically defective cloned humans, effectively emptying the dormitory he had built to care for them. His profits sky-rocketed after that. Presently, we do all of the cerebral-ocular transfers at our center in Baltimore, but they and several other subsidiary research companies help tremendously with the cloning.

"Also on the right,"—I will never get used to hearing that—"we have Dr. Raymond Verity, the first physician to successfully clone a human and nurture it to birth, co-founder of the New Body Research Center, and the first person in suspended animation to be successfully transplanted into a new body. Dr. Verity has surprisingly switched tables and now condemns the President's proposal."

It's been a couple of months since my interviews began and, although I have been thoroughly prepared under the tutelage of the President's world-class debate team, when the lights get bright and the show host introduces me to the American public before the cameras, my left eye gets a slight twitch, my heart palpitates, and my palms sweat. I so much prefer pre-recorded broadcasts, as I trust the editors to remove my jumbled phrases and make me look good. Live shows have an unpredictable element that unnerves me, like walking in the dark in a strange room.

"Dr. Verity, I can't tell you what a privilege it is to have you on our show. You are truly an American icon."

His flattery sets me at ease. I nod at the host, who sits across from me on a couch. "Thank you, Michael."

The small studio audience of a hundred briefly applaud.

"What no one suspected is that you would be on the right of this debate, opposing President Sayder's attempt to legalize cloning. Why would you turn your back on the scientific work you pioneered?"

Good. He's asking the questions I was told he would ask. No surprises.

"I'm not, Michael." I lean back and rest my right arm on the back of the couch. "I'm trying to save it. What the President proposes is insanely radical. A major news network poll released last week found 89% of Americans believe that the unfettered federal legalization of cloning would make the federal government the ultimate owner of every cell in our bodies, and 94% are convinced that cloning should not be taxpayer-funded."

I look into the camera that has the red light underneath it, the active camera. "If we cannot own ourselves, we can't own anything. Our body is our property. So is our salary, and if we don't want to fund cloning, we shouldn't be coerced by the IRS to do so." I turn to the studio audience. "President Sayder wants to tell you what you can and cannot do with your own cells and your own hard-earned wealth. Cloning is working to save lives without federal intervention, and it is being regulated by the states to protect our rights. Federal government"—I place both hands on my chest—"hands off!"

The studio audience vigorously applauds my prepared introductory speech.

"Dupes are already being created," the President's Press Secretary interjects between sips of his cappuccino in his blue *Hot Seat Live* mug, "and new bodies daily replace old ones, you being a prime example. We cannot let unelected judges make all the decisions for us, basing their decisions on inconsistent and often contradictory standards. Fifty states creating fifty sets of rules opens the way to abuse and exploitation."

The host asks Aaron Little, "So, the President wishes to protect the industry from abuses, just like Dr. Verity and Mr. Cobb?"

"Absolutely. A federal law legalizing cloning is the best way to protect the rights of all involved."

The host turns to the camera. "Alabama State Attorney Shane Mease has defied a federal judge and issued an arrest warrant for the CEO of the largest cloning company in Alabama, who has violated the most aggressive anti-cloning state law in the U.S. Let us listen to Alabama Governor Maurice Whetley's and State Attorney Mease's press conference last week."

A screen plays a 3-D video of the Alabama State Attorney answering a question after one of his press conferences, a clip played incessantly by the media since last week. "We do not believe the federal government is unlimited in power." The stiff red hair of his crew cut perfectly accentuates the unrelenting firmness of his tone and choice of words. "The Constitution does not grant your leaders in Washington the right to do wrong." He waves and points as he speaks, more like a Pentecostal preacher than a politician. "They are lawfully limited by the Constitution to specifically enumerated powers, and they are prevented by state and federal constitutions, as well as by divine law, from executing innocent human beings apart from a trial by jury. We are issuing this arrest warrant for David Starr because of evidence that he may be guilty of crimes against humanity in the mass termination of what he considers to be defective dupes,"—he points a stiff index finger at the audience of journalists—"an act he freely confesses. The severity of that crime is not lessened by the fact he has found a federal judge to act as his accomplice."

A camera gets our facial responses to the clip. I chuckle disrespectfully and take a slow sip from my mug as I turn to Jim Cobb. He looks at the host and shakes his head in disgust.

"Jim Cobb," the host addresses the bearded representative of the pro-life movement, "fringe groups in the pro-life movement are comfortable with such radical words from the man who has become known as 'Alabama's cloven tongue of fire.' They have applauded Alabama's leaders as visionary and courageous for daring to enforce their state-wide ban on cloning. You, on the other hand, have come out against him. Tell us why."

"I am against the termination of dupes. I think that they can be created, respecting the wishes of the host, but they should not be carelessly killed." I nod approvingly as Cobb continues, "However, we are a nation of laws, with the U.S. Constitution being the law of the land. Alabama's leaders are defying the law in issuing this arrest warrant. Alabama citizens can regulate the industry through the legislative process to prevent abuses and unnecessary terminations, but their leaders do not have the right to violate the Constitution of the United States, or our sacred separation of church and state."

These words bring a hail of applause from the studio audience. I was told the attendees were fairly representative of the general public, but it appears designed to lead to meager applause for the leftist brave enough to sit in the notorious 'hot seat.'

"Republican congressman Jerry Stinthal has proposed a compromise with which both of you are comfortable." The host turns to me. "Is that correct, Dr. Verity?"

"Yes. It was even endorsed by the Republican Speaker of the House. It would prevent federal funding of cloning and limit federal control over the industry."

"It would also prevent," Jim Cobb adds, "the termination of unfunded or defective dupes without the consent of at least two licensed physicians."

"It would also ban the creation and exploitation of chimeras—embryos created by combining human and animal or plant DNA," I continue, as the audience predictably howls its disapproval of such research.

"Poorly inadequate measures, I'm afraid." The Press Secretary has a tone that emanates the Administration's utter disgust with Cobb and I. "What Dr. Verity and Jim Cobb do not understand is that all they are doing is postponing the inevitable and causing even more chimeras to be made in unregulated states. There must be federal control and a unified federal policy in order to prevent abuses, including preventing the creation of chimeras and bringing them to maturity. If you don't want human-animal freaks in society, federal control is necessary. Federal leaders cannot sit idly by while . . . " Someone shouts something near the entrance of the studio, and Aaron Little hesitates. We turn our heads toward the commotion.

With the unwelcome interruption, I expect the host to break for a commercial until they have an opportunity to remedy the outburst of some infiltrated protester or the injury of some employee. The host, however, seems perplexed and unsure of what to do.

The next thing I know, a gruff voice makes my hair stand on end.

"Person . . . Vengeance . . . " I cannot make out the words through the shouting. Then, crystal clear, I hear, "This is for all your victims!"

A deafening noise and a bright ball of flame emanates from my right. I turn to face a blistering hot gush of wind, which pounds me in the chest like a sledgehammer, flipping me over the couch.

8

I WAKE UP IN A bed in a dark room to the beeping sound of my own heartbeat in a monitor.

Where am I? A hospital?

The heart rhythm's green squiggly line is in sync with the pounding in my skull. My forehead is hot and tight, like I have been sunburned from falling asleep drunk midday by the pool.

Why am I here? The events of the last several months are a blur. What was the last thing that happened?

I try to glance at my watch on my right wrist, hoping to discover the date, but my right arm is in some type of high tech hyperbaric air cast, glowing like a black light in the relatively dark room. "Hello?"

In a moment, a nurse answers through a speaker in the wall behind me. "I will be there in a moment, Dr. Verity."

The throbbing in my head that coincides with the beeping on the monitor eases in a moment, and I make out the President's voice. A 3-D image is projected on the wall across the room.

"Volume. Up. Up." My tongue is thick and my mouth dry, but the computer understands my order nonetheless. The President is having a press conference.

" . . . Our hearts are with the family of Aaron Little. We grieve with them. Our nation lost one of its best and brightest this morning." She sighs heavily. "It will be difficult to find a replacement . . . "

The Press Secretary is dead? I remember now. The host, the cameras, the explosion . . .

The nurse enters the room and opens her mouth but I wave her quiet. "Let me, let me"—I motion to the image—"let me listen."

"Thankfully, the terrorist's bomb was crude and rudimentary. Dr. Raymond Verity suffered severe head trauma, has a bleed in his brain, and broke his right wrist. He is still unconscious, but I have been told that there is still a chance of recovery."

A brain bleed?

I begin to flail my extremities and discover a weakness in my left leg and left hand. I rub my left hand against my left leg. Sensation is poor on that side of the body.

The nurse extends her palms toward me. "Be still, Dr. Verity. Everything's stable, but I need you to be still."

She prepares to give an injection into my IV port, but I prevent her. "Stop. Don't do that."

She freezes, unsure of what to do.

"I had a, I had a, a stroke?" My words are slow and impeded by some stiffness in my tongue.

"Shh. A reversible ischemic neurologic deficit, hopefully, not a permanent stroke. Your cerebral meninges tore over your right parietal cortex, probably from incomplete healing after your cerebral-ocular transfer. The bleeders have been cauterized, and you are stable, but not if your rising BP breaks the still fragile connections. Now, I've been ordered to give you this injection to calm you . . . "

"No. I said no."

A beeping on the monitor drains the smile from her face, and she nervously taps behind her right ear. "Dr. Cranton, you told me to let you know when Dr. Verity awakes. Well, he has, and he's quite anxious and is refusing the midazolam injection."

"My vision is still affected." My words are slurring. "Is my face drooping?"

"Please, be still, Dr. Verity." She studies my facial features for a moment. "Blink hard." I obey. "Blow out your cheeks like this." I comply. "Uh, your neurological deficits look like they're, um, they're worsening." She taps her ear again. "Dr. Cranton?"

Dr. Cranton's familiar voice on the speaker behind my head interrupts her. "I'll be there in a few minutes, Megan. Dr. Verity, I've been watching you through the camera on the wall across from you. Please, be still, be calm. Your anxiety is increasing your heart rate and output and may require medical intervention if you do not calm yourself."

"His deficits are returning, Dr. Cranton." The nurse looks toward the camera.

"Calm down, Raymond! Nurse, re-take his vitals. Call a code if indicated. I'm on my way. And give him that injection!"

"No!" I insist. "No benzos. I need to understand what's going on . . . "

"Sue me then! Give it to him, Megan."

"Yes, Doctor."

I sigh, then reluctantly nod at the anxious nurse. She clearly does not wish to offend either doctor. She gives the injection. I follow Cranton's advice, taking deep, slow breaths. I close my eyes, and the nurse pats my right hand which, thankfully, still has sensation.

"Where is, where is . . . " I want to ask where Morgan is, and I become upset at my slowness of speech.

I hear my sister's name on the TV, and I look to the wall.

The nurse continues to urge me to relax as she takes my vitals. My ears are more intently attuned to the President's press conference than her fretful counsel.

A picture of my elderly sister's prison processing photograph is flashed up on the screen as the President speaks. "She has been incarcerated for trespassing on the property of New Body Research Center four months ago on the very day that her brother, who co-founded the facility, was resurrected in his new body. We have evidence that her organization, Personhood Now, is responsible for the terrorist's bomb that targeted and killed my Administration's Press Secretary Aaron Little, as well as three NBS television studio employees." They show a grainy clip of security footage of a man walking into the studio, wearing a backpack. "The organization's leadership, including Tamara Verity, will be charged under strengthened anti-terrorism legislation proposed by my Administration and passed by Congress last year."

My sight gradually worsens during the President's speech. I am blinking hard to try to focus. I try to speak to increase the volume, but my tongue is as heavy and numb as a frozen brick. I turn to the nurse, whose eyes widen at the increased rate of the beeping on the heart monitor behind me.

She gently pats my cheek. "Dr. Verity?"

Dr. Cranton rushes into the room and immediately taps a button behind his ear, shouting out an order I cannot hear due to a high-pitched squeal, like an ambulance siren, inside my head.

I don't want to die!

Gradually, the room drains of all color, darkening to gray and then to black.

9

WHEN I AWAKE, MORGAN IS wearing a pair of spectacles and appears to be staring right at me with a blank look on her face.

"Morgan?"

She doesn't answer. My vision appears to be more symmetrical, which is a relief. Morgan's full lips tip up at the corners. I know that look well.

"Morgan!"

"Oh." She takes off her spectacles. "I was reading a novel." She stands and comes near the bed.

"Romance novel via spectacles, huh?" Lying there in a hospital gown, I know I don't fit her fantastic notion of an ideal lover, even with my six-pack. But who could possibly live up to the fanciful images in her novels?

She nods. "Killing trees is so unnecessary." She taps the button to contact the nurses' station. "My husband's awake."

I feel weak, but alert. My blurry vision has completely resolved. I press my hand against my left leg. "Yes! My feeling's back."

Morgan rests her hand on my chest. "Their tests confirmed that it would be so."

"How long has it been?"

"Since the explosion? Three days."

I try to sit up in bed, but I'm covered in tubes and wires.

"They repaired your damaged brain tissue with some experimental stem cell transplantation." She smiles, pulls in closer, and kisses me on the cheek. "Ivan did it himself. They kept you sedated until the tissue healing matured. They've been feeding you intravenously, and using electrodes to keep your muscles toned, but you've shriveled a bit."

I yawn and pull against the wires. "Unstrap me, please."

She unstraps my wrist ties with one hand, and with the other presses her fingers into my toned abs. "That's the laziest three days these muscles have experienced in eight years."

A fleet of nurses rush into the room, along with Drs. Ivan Wilkes and Cranton and two other physicians to welcome me back from the edge of the grave, and to congratulate themselves on another breakthrough in New Body science.

* * *

"Thank you, Madame President," I say into the phone, trying to minimize my barely perceptible slur. I remove my slippers and lean back in the reclining leather chair they have brought into my private hospital room.

"You take your time and get better. We're getting a lot of mileage out of your handicap, so don't you feel any guilt about not being on the field in front of the cameras . . . "

Handicap? My minimally weak hand and foot and my barely perceptible facial droop is hardly a handicap. "It's almost completely gone, Madam President. Dr. Wilkes' and Dr. Cranton's procedure repaired my damaged brain tissue."

"Do me a favor. Fake the limp while walking the hospital grounds for a couple of days? I have a fleet of cameras there prepared for my impromptu press conference, which may be as early as tomorrow morning in front of your hospital."

"Here? I thought we weren't exactly on speaking terms as far as the press is concerned."

She laughs. "Well, as it turns out, the Republicans have boasted a veto-proof majority behind your bill. In record timing. You're a natural, and you get all the credit, Raymond."

"Wow." Of all my accolades and awards, there are no words quite as pleasurable as personal praise from the President of the United States. She credits me for single-handedly harnessing the formidable power of the political right to unknowingly carry the President's own agenda. "I can't believe it worked."

"They raised a hundred million ameros for a campaign to fight us in the House, Ray. They're idiots. The religious right waves the flags we knit for them and lobbies hard for the bills we trick them into backing."

My brother comes to mind, and I grimace. The right wing is teeming with religious opportunists with no principle but personal gain, and no accomplice so comforting as the undemanding divine grace that covers their hypocritical judgments and perpetual moral deficiencies.

"You see, all your suffering has not been in vain, Ray. Thanks to your influence on the public, I have come around to your compromise, albeit reluctantly. You should know I still will accuse you of capitulating to the religious fanatics . . . "

"Of course." This game is so entertaining. "I'll be glad to fake the limp for a couple more days and be the target for your darts, as long as you will not hold offense when I throw mine."

She laughs. "Oh, I could kiss you right now."

"I assume that you do not want me at your press conference?"

"You assume correctly. We're not that close."

"Kissing enemies. Of course."

"The bitterest."

"Have you discovered who is responsible for the explosion?" There's a moment of silence on the other end of the phone. "Madame President?"

"Yes, I'm here. I thought you knew. It was your sister."

I shake my head in disbelief. "Tamara? It's politically expedient and serves your cause, I know, but . . . "

"*Our* cause."

"Yes, our cause. But I know that she wouldn't have done that, and setting your investigators on her gives the real culprits time to cover their tracks."

"Have you even met her or spoken to her in the past 27 years?"

"Well, no, but I know that she's committed to peaceful activism. Peaceful. She's the abortion clinic sidewalk counseling type. No guns. No bombs. Fasting and praying in jibberish are her weapons of choice."

"Well, the evidence points to her organization, I'm sorry to say. This terrorist attack happened under her guidance, not in spite of it."

I frown. I should pay Tamara a visit. "Where is she being incarcerated?"

"If you're thinking of visiting her, don't. If it gets out to the press, it'll hurt your influence with the public." For the first time, I sense disappointment in her voice. "Will you call NBS, and have them run a piece on you from your hospital room?"

I clear my throat. "Gladly."

As soon as I get off the phone with President Sayder, Morgan taps behind her right ear to conclude her phone call.

"What's got you so excited, Morgan?"

"I'll tell you at dinner tonight. At our favorite place, on the board-walk overlooking the Bay."

I smile at her invitation. "Are they going to let me go?"

"Yes, our date meets with Dr. Cranton's approval."

"Always looking for a reason to celebrate, aren't you, babe?"

"Life's too short to . . . "

She and I make eye contact. Her old cliché doesn't apply now that we get a new body every 25 years.

10

AT THE BAR ON THE veranda, after two dances and three glasses of wine, I insist that she tell me this good news. "Stop putting it off. Just tell me."

She giggles triumphantly, so pleased with herself for keeping me suspended on the plank for so long. She leans back in her stool, her ankles propped up on the bar, taking the split in her dress all the way up her long legs, completely void of discretion in view of the crowds walking the boardwalk below. She certainly has a way of prefacing things.

"Savannah's coming tomorrow."

"By herself?"

She looks down at her nails and shakes her head. "With Mary Nell."

This is simultaneously exhilarating and disturbing. I look forward to seeing my granddaughter. But it will be difficult to look Savannah in the eye and treat her kindly, knowing that she intends to get rid of my only grandchild like a rolled up wad of week-old newspaper.

Morgan measures my frown. "I thought you would be more excited. Savannah's softened. I don't think she will criticize you like she has in the past."

"It's not that." I stare at the picturesque setting sun. "It's just that, well . . . " I hold my peace, and gulp down half my beer.

"Are you still worked up about Mary Nell?"

I nod reluctantly, not wanting to resurrect old disagreements on such a fair evening.

"Raymond, please. You have to think about the good."

"I know." She's probably right.

"The end justifies the means, and when the end is so amazing, the less than favorable means can be easily overlooked. If we obsess on the fact that our lovely bodies once belonged to clones derived from our perfected genome, then we wouldn't relish our envied existence in these new lovely packages of flawless flesh."

How can I argue with that?

"Indulge, my love." She places a slow kiss on my cheek.

"You make it so easy." I turn my head to kiss her lips. We take our time for a moment. "I don't ever remember enjoying kissing like this."

She smiles broadly and briefly kisses me again. The alcohol on her breath revives an unexpected memory of doing things in my previous life, things that presently repulse me for some reason. I pull away from Morgan, my cheeks tingling with self-reproach. Why do I feel so schizophrenic in my thoughts, being tossed back and forth between self-loathing and guilt on one hand, and extravagance and excess on the other? I fight the sting of shame by downing the rest of my beer and asking the bartender for a shot of whiskey. Perhaps therein lies the answer. One extreme is my attempt at quenching the other.

Morgan raises her eyebrows at my unexpected request for a shot of hard liquor. "In a hurry to end the evening?"

I look down at my shot glass and toss the liquid into my throat. "I wonder what Savannah's going to decide?"

She stares at me for a second.

Appearing to respect Savannah's choice, I hope Morgan will at least respect my desire for her, and not Morgan, to have that choice.

"As long as you respect her decision. Ray." I nod, my eyes still fixed on that last sip of brown liquid at the bottom of my shot glass. "Don't you dare guilt trip her."

I gulp the last few drops, keeping my impulsive snippet rooted on the tip of my tongue.

We don't discuss Savannah's visit during the remainder of our date, and Morgan doesn't begrudge me like I feared. My guilt dissipates as my inebriation grows.

Why adopt scruples that simply make me a hypocrite in my own eyes?

11

I DECIDE TO MEET SAVANNAH and Mary Nell on the beach instead of in my hospital room. As Savannah approaches, I have a long look at her. She looks as young and vibrant as ever, about as good as a woman in her mid-40s can look in an original body.

It's the little three-year-old in her mother's arms, wearing a pink tutu, that captures my attention. Brown hair, big eyes, slobbery smile. I hug Savannah, but immediately direct my attention to my granddaughter.

"Hello, Mary Nell. It's me, Grandpa."

With her hands clasped around her mother's neck, she stares at me for a moment. She turns to her mother, as if to ask for permission.

"Do you want to give your Grandpa a hug?" Savannah smiles.

Mary Nell turns back to me, and then unexpectedly lurches toward me. I catch her in my arms. She's so light and frail, but her grasp around my neck is one of the most delightful experiences of my life. My first grandchild. My posterity.

She pulls away for a moment and, with her eyes still fixed upon her mother, grins bashfully. "Hello Gwanpaw."

I laugh so full and hard, I am oblivious to everything else in the world beside the small bundle of life I hold in my arms.

Then she presses her wet lips against my cheek, and embraces me again.

I wrap my arms tightly around her and whisper in her ear, "I love you."

Savannah has tears in her eyes that she wipes with her beach towel. "She's not normally that warm to strangers."

"No, she's not," Morgan agrees.

"I don't want to be a stranger anymore, Savannah. Not to you, not to Mary Nell. I'm sorry I haven't been there for you." My voice chokes with sadness and long-suppressed guilt from which I long to be free. Morgan sniffs and reaches for something in her beach bag, appearing displeased with my emotional expression.

"Better late than never," Savannah mumbles. Her comment first provokes offense in me, but when I see her full smile, I realize that's her way of accepting my apology.

We settle down in our beach chairs in the sand. Mary Nell and I play with brightly colored buckets and shovels, while Morgan and Savannah recline in the sun, deepening their tan.

I help Mary Nell build a castle out of wet sand, and then she playfully knocks it down. She giggles so hard I have to remind her to breathe.

I lay down in the sand, and Mary Nell tries to build a castle on top of me. I have to help her shake the wet sand out of the upside-down buckets, but finally we have a routine. Soon, her eyes are drooping. It is time for a nap. Morgan and Savannah are consumed in their talk about the latest anti-aging cream, their favorite spa therapy, and the most enticing romance novel. So I lay Mary Nell down on a towel and begin to caress her back. She is restless, fighting sleep, until I began to whistle a tune I remember from when I was a child. I don't even remember the words, but it's like magic. In less than a minute, Mary Nell falls sound asleep. I rest my hand on her back, in awe of the helplessness of this little Down Syndrome girl, rarely encountered in society today due to routine prenatal testing and ubiquitous abortions of genetically defective children. How can a person so genetically dysfunctional be so lovely? She is so frail and tender, but happiness personified.

"How did you come to know that tune, Dad?"

"You mean, what I'm whistling?"

Savannah nods.

I shrug. "Do you know it?"

"Your sister used to sing it to Mary Nell when she was a baby."

"Tamara?"

"I spent a few months with her when I left home."

Morgan scowls. "Really? Tamara?"

Savannah nods.

"Did my sister impact you at all with her, uh, with her views? Her faith?"

Morgan clenches her teeth.

Savannah sighs and shakes her head side to side. "No. This life has too much to offer to live so fully for the next. Tamara's the real deal though, that's for sure. And she sure loved Mary Nell."

Savannah begins to sing the song I hummed, her eyes fixed on her slumbering child.

> *Jesus loves me, this I know,*
> *For the Bible tells me so.*
> *Little ones to Him belong.*
> *They are weak but—*

"Never heard it," Morgan interrupts sharply. "Let's go for a walk." She stands and motions down the beach. "Just you and me, Savannah. I've got something I need to talk to you about."

I know the topic Morgan longs to broach, and it is my turn to scowl. "Can't you talk about it here?"

Morgan ignores me and takes several steps away without looking back.

"What's the matter, Dad? Are you worried about caring for li'l Mary Nell for a few minutes?"

"No, not at all."

"I trust you'll take good care of her." Savannah follows Morgan. Over her shoulder, she instructs me, "Just give her some food and loving if she wakes up."

"Don't worry. I'll take good care of her."

They are gone for about an hour. Conspiring to rip my heart out, I'm sure. I spend most of that time just caressing Mary Nell's back. How could they turn their backs on this little girl? Yes, she's defective. Yes, her potential is limited. Yes, she'll probably be dependent on others to care for her for the rest of her life. But she's my granddaughter, and she's as full of love as anyone could ever be.

Mary Nell wakes up the moment they return.

"Momma!" She hobbles toward Savannah and throws herself into her arms. Savannah keeps her at arms' length, as if she is repelling her. My heart drops and my limbs feel weighted down with grief. It appears that Morgan has persuaded Savannah, who has already begun to detach from her daughter. Pitying my granddaughter, I pull her tiny body into my arms and she tries to pull away from me. She wants her mother.

I glance at Morgan, who winks at me. "I told you all would be well. Mary Nell will be normal, and have a normal, blessed life."

Savannah removes her sunglasses to clean them with her towel. "Yes, Mary Nell will be well."

Savannah's eyes are bloodshot. Her decision clearly has not been easy, but that does not make it less cruel.

"She's also going to accept her own new body, isn't that right?" Morgan glances at Savannah with expectation.

Savannah sighs and nods.

"When she learned what disasters her genome held, it was an easy decision for her. Best for everyone."

"Best for everyone." Savannah puts her sunglasses back on and reapplies her tanning oil.

I want to scream, *Is it best for Mary Nell?!* Instead, I speak calmly. "Savannah, why did you reject the New Body science in the first place, back when we were breaking ground?"

"Why does it matter?" Morgan frowns.

I keep my eyes fixed on Savannah. "I want to know. Was it your Aunt Tamara influence's on you?"

Savannah ignores my question.

"Of course it was Tamara," Morgan interjects.

"Will you let her answer? Please, Morgan?" Thankfully, Mary Nell drifts back to sleep in my arms.

Savannah takes a deep breath and turns her face toward the sun. "I suppose when you live for heaven, you're willing to accept more pain on earth in hopes of making it. But when heaven's come to earth, why let yourself suffer? And why beat yourself up over your decisions if there's no, you know, no one to answer to?"

"How do you know there's no one to answer to?"

"Raymond!" Morgan blurts out my name angrily. "Why are you doing this?"

"Shh, you'll wake her up." Mary Nell stirs, and I begin to rock her to try to get her back to sleep.

"If there is a loving God," Savannah sighs, "then why does so much evil happen? Why is Mary Nell diseased, and why did her father abandon us for a younger woman? Either God is not all loving, or He's powerless to prevent the evil He wants to forbid."

I recoil, my face heating. Those are precisely the same words I would announce to her whenever she would level her metaphysical criticism at my experiments, when I began to pioneer the New Body technology. If my work was so evil and the all-powerful Christian God so good, I would reason, why would He allow me to do what I am doing? Either He wills me to do what I am doing, and therefore cannot justly condemn me for it, or He's too weak to hinder me. It was my favorite algorithm to neuter religious objections and extinguish personal guilt. That and wine.

Morgan affirms Savannah's remarks with a confident nod. "Good point, dear. Isn't that a good point, Raymond?"

"Well, if there is no God, there can be no evil, can there?" If she's going to echo my words, I'm going to echo the words of my sister Tamara, who once responded to me in this manner. "What's the big deal about your fiancé breaking his promise and leaving you for a secretary? Hmm?"

Mary Nell startles awake and tries to sit up in my arms. I fetch her bottle out of the diaper bag and try to rock her again, but she won't be content. She waddles lazily in circles around the post of the umbrella that is sticking out of the sand, drinking her bottle.

Morgan sighs heavily, and pulls a smokeless electronic marijuana joint out of her purse. "Enough of the head games, Ray. You don't even believe that."

"No, hear me out. If there is no God or if the God that exists is not good and loving, then what's the big deal about Him causing the innocent to suffer? How can that be wrong?"

Savannah stares at me blank-faced. "You cannot be sincere."

I take a deep breath. She's right. I'm not sincere. I appeal to the argument as a pragmatic means to try to get Savannah to rethink her decision, not out of genuine faith. "Just tell me, if there is no God, how can there be such a thing as moral evil? If you think about it, just making the argument refutes the argument. You presuppose God's goodness in your appeal to an absolute standard of goodness to condemn Him . . . "

Savannah opens her mouth to speak, but remains silent. I snap my fingers and then aim my index finger at her. "And that has been my response for most of my life. Smoke and mirrors. Change the subject. Eschew sincere contemplation about morality and justice through busyness, incessant noise, the pursuit of wealth, fame, and unrestrained self-indulgence."

"That's rather harsh of you, Ray. We have to make the best out of this life, and that is what you have done. Both of you." Morgan speaks as if her counsel may resolve the dispute, but her words amount to nothing but a distracting flattery. "The science you pioneered will improve human lives in unimaginable ways. Your political work is helping to secure the promise of an infinite, healthy life for future generations. If there is a God, how can He object to us living in the Garden of Eden?" She takes her hair and pushes it over her ears. She points heavenward. "It was His idea in the first place."

"Cain killing Abel wasn't." I gesture at little Mary Nell, who is oblivious to the fact her life may depend upon the outcome of our debate.

She continues to walk around the umbrella post, drinking from her bottle with one hand and grasping onto the pole with the other. "Didn't He curse Cain for what he did to his little brother?"

That comment has the effect of a racial slur on a televised talk show. The women explode in offense and rage.

"How dare you!" Savannah is practically spasming with anger, almost toppling her lawn chair.

"Get control of yourself, Raymond." Morgan blurts out as she leans toward me. She glances at Savannah.

Savannah gets up and grabs her purse as if she's going to leave in a fit of fury.

"Don't go, Savannah. I'm, I'm, I'm sorry. Please"—I clear my throat gruffly—"please don't go." My words begin to stutter and slur slightly, which is what happens to me under stressful situations since the stroke.

"Pardon his stuttering." Morgan winks condescendingly. "His blooming conscience must be pressing against the part of his brain that does the talking."

Savannah sits back down, her eyes fixed on her little girl.

"I'm, I'm, I'm sorry, Savannah."

Mary Nell hears my stuttering, and she walks up to me and touches my mouth. She appears captivated by my speech impediment. "I'm, I'm, I'm," she repeats.

"Grandpa has something wrong with him when he's upset," I explain.

"Me too, Gwanpaw."

I raise my eyebrows, impressed with her ability to comprehend. I look to my daughter and wife, hoping to see that they are as enthralled with her as I am. Morgan appears distracted as she takes a drag of her electronic joint.

Savannah's eyes widen at the realization of what Mary Nell has just said. "She's never said anything like that before."

"She knows what's going on more than you know, Savannah."

Savannah breaks out in a sob she tries to restrain but is unable.

Mary Nell runs the ten feet span to her mother and pushes against her mother's palms, desperately trying to get inside her repelling arms for a hug. "You're going to get my tanning oil on you, girl. Go, hug your Grandpa."

"Yes, come to Grandpa." I stretch my arms toward her again.

"Gwanpaw," she speaks slowly and carefully, as if she is correcting my mispronunciation. She turns and runs into my arms.

Some things in life are so self-evidently wonderful that they defy reason. Science is bankrupt to explain this kind of love.

I don't know about the problem of evil, but this hug is the best evidence of a good God I have ever encountered. Although I cannot figure out for the life of me why He'd be so good to me.

12

"THIRTY-FIVE PERCENT INCREASE SINCE YOU were resurrected." Quaid's face on my monitor holds steady, but he is at least as ecstatic as my wife, who practically drools at the update from my trusted financial adviser.

"Oh, let's celebrate!" Morgan is giddy, holding her half-drunk ubiquitous glass of Chardonnay. She's wearing her black and red silk nightgown, sitting on the edge of the bed, so blissfully elated as to approach pathological mania. Perhaps she's popping uppers with her wine. "That's, what? Quaid, how much is that since Raymond was cryo-freezed?"

"Hold on, Morgan." Her carefree giddiness was unnaturally attractive when I was younger in mind. Now, I find it exhausting, like taking a cocaine-sniffing Chihuahua on a walk through a zoo.

"Do I look like I'm in the mood to 'hold on'?" She leans forward with a twinkle in her eye.

Quaid unleashes his toothy grin. "Is that the lovely Mrs. Verity? Get over here in front of the camera if you want me to answer your question."

She playfully hops off the bed and comes over to my desk, in view of the camera on top of my monitor that feeds my image to Quaid.

"There you are, sweetheart." Quaid's eyes habitually drop straight to her bosom. I scowl even though he's always looked at her like that. "Over 2,500 percent increase in your portfolio since Raymond was on ice, plus or minus a couple hundred percent. And half of that has been in the six months since Dr. Wilkes thawed you, thanks to the President's commitment of federal funds to your research foundation." From the way he puffs his chest out at the mention of federal funding, he must have played a role in obtaining that.

Morgan wraps her arms around me from behind and lowers her cheek to mine. "You are the bomb, Quaid!"

She pecks me on the cheek, but I'm clearly not the one on her mind. She spills some wine on my boxers, and I brush it off. She's irritating me.

"It's my wealth, not Quaid's," I remind her. That wipes the grin off Quaid's handsome face. "Please, give me a moment."

She gasps and slithers back to the bed to pout. "Get over your scruples, dear, and let's buy us a country."

Quaid, who apparently can't comprehend her mumbling, widens his eyes. "Excuse me?"

"It was nothing. Morgan's just, just trying to figure out what to buy next."

"Vlad told me that he expanded your corporation so you can put virtually any purchase on your business credit card, and not pay taxes on anything."

"All the more to spend." Morgan reclines on the bed, twisting and raising her legs playfully into the air. Why does it appear to me she is even more infatuated with her body than all the men she constantly flashes?

I state the obvious. "He can't see you."

She flinches, and studies me for a moment.

"What's that?" Quaid leans into the camera. "Morgan, will you get in view of the monitor and speak clearly?"

Morgan comes back behind me and bends low. Quaid's lustful grin spreads over his face. I stiff-arm Morgan away. "Please, dear, stop hovering over me like a cloud!"

"This is unlike you, Raymond. Why so short with a woman so irresistible?" Quaid's tone is surprisingly critical. "Do you need some"—he clears his throat—"marriage counseling?"

Morgan giggles at his underhanded flirtation. I scowl at my arrogant financial adviser. "Quaid Sandman, do I sense a hint of romantic affection for my wife?"

Quaid's face reddens.

"Can you blame him?" Morgan quips, as if she doesn't want to give Quaid a chance to answer me. Her smile has faded to a deep frown. I'm going to pay for disrespecting her in front of Quaid, but right now, I just don't care.

"All business, Mr. Verity." Quaid always calls me by my last name whenever I question a financial decision he makes. It's a defense mechanism. "She makes you look good, sir. Very good. Count your blessings she wants to be with you, because there's a long line of men and women who'd jump at the chance to take your place."

Morgan beams at his praise and tries to come back in view of the camera. I wave her back to the bed.

When we disconnect, I turn to Morgan, who is refilling her glass. "Did you and Quaid develop a relationship when I was on ice?"

"I developed a relationship with him *before* you were on ice, if you remember. You and I have always had an open marriage. No faking fidelity, remember? Pleasure with honesty. Love, not greed. You know, what we always said."

I shudder, but am not overly disgusted with the thought that I may have approved of her extra-marital affairs. I reveled in my own with her permission as well. I roll my eyes to the ceiling, trying to recollect who did what to who, and who did it more, as if it were some sort of contest.

"It works both ways, Raymond. Yet all parties stayed happily married, so what's the fuss?" She lies on her stomach on the bed and rests her chin on her hands. "I'm an adult. You're an adult. Remember?"

Adult.

The very word brings a rush of licentious memories. Indulging in such careless fantasies with perfect strangers never provoked the shame in me I seem to feel right now. I have developed a deep dislike for the reckless, intoxicated, swinger parties that used to speckle our busy calendar.

"Have you been reading the Bible or listening to an imam, or something?" Her sarcastic tone of voice frames the words perfectly, unveiling her revulsion at the thought of any external or internal suppression of the mindless pursuit of pleasure.

I feel a nauseating stab at the thought of an angry Judge awaiting me, remembering every single one of those acts for which I now feel guilty, in addition to all the sins I've forgotten, preparing His case, anticipating my prosecution, rejoicing in my future incarceration.

"No, I've not been reading the Bible." Would those antiquated words of Scripture hold some secret to my sense of well-being? Don't think so. "I'm sorry I was unkind, Morgan. I just don't feel, um, I don't feel like myself. I don't know what it is."

But I know exactly what it is. The fear of death has me once again in its icy grip, intermittently quickening my heart rate and breaking me out in a sweat, but I fear that putting the truth into words would deepen the dread.

"Have you been talking to your jailbird sister?"

I don't answer this right away, even though I have not. Morgan's question, however, rekindles a desire to speak with Tamara. I shake my head. "No. Now I have a question for you. Please answer honestly." I pause. She raises her eyebrows in anticipation. "Have you been with anybody besides me since I was resurrected?"

"No. But so what if I have?" She sits up on the side of the bed, and tries to cover her legs with her nightgown—an atypical gesture for her. "I thought you abhorred the prudish ways of antique do-gooders."

My brother's hypocrisy comes to mind. I don't want to be like him. "I do, Morgan, I hate hypocrisy above all."

"There's no right and wrong, especially when it comes to enjoying our own . . ."

"I know what I said," I interrupt, sitting down beside her to face the large mirror on the wall. I stare at us for a moment, teased toward complacency in view of the incredible benefits of the technology I have pioneered.

"Marriage, like food, gets boring if you don't embrace some diversity." She gazes into the mirror with me. "You said that, too. Come on, hon. You wrote the bible on this stuff. If that was true with our old broken-down bodies, how much more true is it in these bodies?" She sheds her nightgown to remind me of the upside, but my thoughts are too dark to be pleasantly distracted. "What good is being a god if you can't do what you want?" She slides behind me and begins to massage my shoulders. "Why lock up nature's best art in a closet, or limit it only to one set of eyes? Makes no sense."

Her words sound so right, but they do not comfort me. There is no comparison between the physical shape I'm in now and where I was on my deathbed 27 years ago. "Does it ever bother you that this is not your body? That someone was, was killed so we could live?"

"Someone? What? I can't believe you just said that. What has happened to you?"

I sigh deeply. What has changed in me? "I don't know, Morgan. I just feel, you know, different about things."

"Maybe it's the stroke. Maybe it messed you up more than you realize."

"Twice now I have looked death square in the eyeballs, and do you know what I felt?" She doesn't venture to answer. "Horror."

"Well, you don't have to be afraid anymore."

"Accidents still happen, as my occasional stuttering and relative weakness on my left side daily reminds me. Our transplanted human brains are genetically defective. We will not live forever. Decay's inevitable. We're all still going to die. You, you, you just don't know what it's like, Morgan, to face death and not, not feel ready."

She sighs and reclines in the bed, careful to keep her legs angled away from my eyes—an involuntary, yet informative gesture that she may still have some capacity for shame over our careless excesses and our voluptuous gluttony. Staring at the mirror affixed to the ceiling above our bed, she sympathizes with me for a moment. "I know what you went through was difficult, and I'm sorry."

I lie on the bed next to her, and gaze into her eyes in the reflection. "Do you promise to be only with me? At least for now?"

She shrugs, and then rolls to look me directly in the eye. "Of course. The idea of an open marriage is being open with each other. I'll clear things with you first, if you insist."

That doesn't quite answer my question, but I rest content with it. If she's unfaithful, at least she'll notify me.

She grabs her pocketbook and heads into the bathroom. As the silhouette of her flawless body swaggers away from me, I realize why she has consented so readily to my irregular request. My wife is practically a paid prostitute. I have always accepted and funded all of her flirtations and flauntings, even sadistically reveling in the thought of our mutual adultery. She has always prostituted her body to whichever eyes or body suits her fancy. The lustful glances of naïve young men or rich old men are the currency that keeps her self-esteem at a perpetual peak. In giving her a flawless new body, I have handed a drug addict a stadium full of mind-numbing rocks and illusory powder. How can I protest my wife's licentiousness when I have rolled out the red carpet for her? And it's not even her body she's prostituting, but a perfected twin. She is literally not the woman I married.

The red Merlot on the table beside the bed invites me to get off this island of guilt onto the sea of intoxication, and I accept. I pour two glasses for quick drinking. I shouldn't judge her. I'm no better. If I can't climb out of the mud, might as well warm it up and roll in it.

The tall mirror reflects my tanned, muscular frame, my bulging biceps and smooth skin, my perfectly toned legs, only minimally softened by my recent hospitalization. A memory from my past rushes to the forefront of my mind: I am taken back to that room where I did chest compressions on a flat-lining 18-year-old high school quarterback who accidentally overdosed on his prom night. I was a brand new med student—this was my first attempt at performing CPR without direct physician oversight, and my first face-to-face stare down with death. The young man's body was similarly firm and tanned. A lovely girl in a strapless gown wept in the waiting room, her inebriation apparently not sufficient to stifle her mournful cries. The young man's parents arrived as a resident took over chest compressions and I attempted my first intubation. They screamed their grief to heaven, praying for him to live. It would be a prayer that would not be answered in the affirmative. What hopes were dashed without warning! For him, there was no going back to right wrongs or make amends. There was no second chance.

Death—the great thief, the pleasure snatcher, the crippler of power and fame, the final nightmare. When will I lie once again on my cold bed of death, my life irretrievable by the best physicians and the most advanced technology, uncomforted by loved ones, and feeling pitifully unwelcomed at the edge of whatever future awaits me? Or, perhaps, my life will get snatched out of me without so much as a moment's notice. Most never see a deathbed. Life departs quickly, like the explosion that took my consciousness and threatened to maim my mind. I could have died right then. Where would I be if I had?

Any enjoyment I might feel at the sight of my new body in the mirror, and my appetite for alcohol and intimacy, diminishes. I take the glass of wine and throw it against the mirror, breaking it and splattering the red wine all over my silvery reflection.

13

I PICK UP THE PHONE to speak with her behind the bullet-proof glass.

"It's good to see you, Tamara." It actually isn't good to see her, but I want to be nice. She looks as old as dust in Pharaoh's tomb, and about as attractive. Eschewing make-up and other forms of vanity that have consumed most in our society, the deleterious effects of her long years are undisguised. Her hair is thin and mostly gray, stubbornly holding onto the last bit of its matte black. There are bags of fluid under her eyes, and her knuckles are gnarled and stiff. With her thin arms and shoulders, it seems like half of her 150 pounds have settled in her hips. Certainly not the kind of person you'd expect to see in a jail cell.

She studies me for a moment, leaning forward with her elbows on the counter. "Hello, Ray. I have missed you."

With her kind smile, my abhorrence of a hundred of her reproofs is overshadowed briefly by the sentiment of ten thousand fond childhood memories.

"You look great," I lie again.

"I have prayed for you so much. How are you doing?"

I don't know why I expected to hear a "You look great, too" or "So glad to have you back" or "Congratulations on your new lot in life." Tamara, however, was never one to be generous with compliments.

"I'm well, Tamara. Thank you. Morgan and I have been celebrating my resurrection non-stop." I stretch out my arms and then press my hands against my tight cotton button-up shirt, so she can see just how thin and firm I am. She doesn't look impressed with my renovation. "Savannah and Mary Nell send their love."

Her smile widens, thinning her pale lips and revealing a missing incisor tooth. My eyes keep drifting to a dark spot on her right cheek. This is the first imperfect elderly person I have even seen in months. I am surrounded by people who can afford new bodies or people wealthy enough to afford plastic surgery, gastric bands, and personal trainers.

"How's that beautiful little girl?" Tamara scratches her nose.

"Mary Nell? Oh, I love her."

"Does Morgan love her?"

I nod cautiously, not wanting to lie a third time.

"Uh oh." Tamara must read the doubt in my body language. "Savannah is keeping her, right?"

I wince. "Keeping Mary Nell?"

She nods. "All over the country right now, parents are trading in their handicapped children for perfected clones of their children, basically donating their babies to science labs for experimentation. I worry that Morgan, especially, would try to influence Savannah."

"Morgan wouldn't, she, well." I stop. There's no use lying to Tamara. She could always see through me anyway. Tamara has a remarkable gift of discerning motives, deception, and half-truths. Nothing would transform this into a bitterly contentious conversation faster than my dishonesty.

"It's honorable that you would want to protect your wife's reputation, Ray, but I came to know Morgan quite well when you were in cryo. She's not one to be inconvenienced with the nuances of humanity's defects and blemishes, and she can be quite persuasive. Without the boundaries of God's law, there's no end to the cruelty of human lust."

"I didn't come to argue. I came to enjoy my sister for a few moments."

"Is Savannah keeping Mary Nell?"

My heart begins to throb under the adrenaline rush that escalates as I leave the question unanswered. I look down at my hands for a moment until Tamara begins to sob.

"Oh, God!" Without shame, not caring who's listening or what they think, Tamara begins to cry out tearful prayers. "Oh, dear God! Please help this poor little girl. Help Mary Nell, Jesus . . . "

Her mournful petition brings out the worst of my guilt. Her eyes are squinted shut and her gnarled hands are clasped in fervent prayer, oblivious to the fact that I am still before her. I let her continue for a moment, as the tears stream down her eyes. Finally, I interrupt by clearing my throat. "How are they treating you, Tamara? Have you made any friends? I'll bet you're popular 'round here, huh?"

Her tone becomes harsh. "When a dying child needs CPR, you don't waste time with petty compliments and small talk."

I am taken back to that emergency room where I did chest compressions on that 18-year-old star football player. My speeding heart seems to stand still for a few seconds, and I gasp for air.

"Does Mary Nell deserve to live, Ray?"

"Of course! I tried to change Savannah's mind, Tamara. I love Mary Nell deeply. She's my only grandchild, and there will probably not be another. Why are you doing this to me?"

"Did Mary Nell's parents give her that right to live, Ray? Hmm? Our"—she licks her lips—"democratic vote?"

I snap, "Why does it matter?"

"If the government gives it or our consensus gives it, then the government and the people can take it away! Then she doesn't have the right to live, does she? No one does. How would you like if it someone treated you that way, discarded you because of their subjective opinion of your worth?"

"I suppose we have to resort to invisible tyrannical genies on golden roads to explain how we have the right to life? Is that it?"

Surprisingly, she appears pleased with my insulting comment, as if I've followed her crumbs to her desired conclusion. My mockery hasn't provoked her ire as it suspected I would.

"When the facades come down, Ray, look what blasphemies are on the inside." Her tone is gentler than her choice of words. "Beneath all that stolen meat, can't you see how wicked and hopeless you are without Jesus?"

"Oh, please!" I leap to my feet, prepared to leave.

"Sit back down," she insists calmly, pointing at my chair. "Please, sit down. With Mary Nell's life in the balance, I'm not letting you run away. You're gonna face the truth."

"You are so, so predictable. Ever heard of the separation of church and state?"

She shakes her head side to side. "What you think the First Amendment means is not reality, and it's not biblical. 'Blessed is the nation whose God is the Lord.' Jesus is King of kings, Ray. There's no blessing for our nation, nor for you, outside of God."

"We live in a democracy, not a theocracy, Sis."

"Tell me again, Ray, why what we do is a good argument for what we *should* do?"

"The government lets the people do what the people want. If someone wants to live by a holy book, fine. But if they want to live according to their own personal moral standard, we shouldn't judge."

"So if the people want to kill gays, enslave blacks, or erect a theocracy, would you still agree that we should do what the people want and not judge?"

I tap my index finger against the glass mockingly. "Ever heard of the United States Constitution?"

"Oh, yes. The government shall not deprive a person of life or liberty except by due process. I love that. Tell me, Ray, how many living human beings with beating hearts and measurable brain waves are slaughtered and harvested every year in your New Body labs?"

"I was talking about the separation of church and state."

She snaps her head side to side. "That's not in the Constitution."

"What?" My brow furrows. "What Constitution are you reading?"

"There's a separation of church and state in the Communist Manifesto, but not in any of our state or federal constitutions. What you're thinking of is the First Amendment . . . "

"Yep."

"It reads, *Congress*—not Maryland, not Alabama, not Mississippi—*Congress* shall make no law respecting an establishment of religion. States can and should, however . . . "

I do not even entertain the thought that every person I've ever heard speak on the separation of church and state is wrong. She has misunderstood me, or I her—or she's mad.

"Neither the federal government nor the states have the right to deprive an innocent person of life or liberty without due process. We have a holocaust of innocent people polluting this land with bloodguilt, and no one has any constitutional duty to tolerate it."

Her face is as red as mine, but I worry that her body cannot handle the pressure. "Right and wrong isn't so black and white," I say calmly. "There are no moral absolutes."

"Are you absolutely sure of that?"

I open my mouth to answer, but hesitate. To say "Yes" is to assert an absolute truth. To say "No" is to contradict my assertion that there's no absolute truth. The best answer is a red herring, a distraction—I'm good at that. "The courts have settled the matter, Tamara, like slavery, child labor, and gay marriage, the courts have settled it. It's the world we live in now."

"Might doesn't make right, Ray. Just because someone can impose their will on someone else, that doesn't make it right. Abandon God as the basis for morality and justice, and the death warrant for human rights has been signed."

"Death warrant for human rights? What?"

"That's right. There are no human rights at all if there's no God and if our leaders can trample any minority they please."

"We have a right to control our own genome. Clones are an extension of the host's body."

"Since when does a living human being have two brains? Two hearts? Don't delude yourself."

"Clones are genetically identical to the host, minus the mutations. They are the property of the host."

"Identical twins are genetically identical, but that does not mean that the older and stronger gets to exploit the weaker. Children may be the property of the parents, but does this justify child abuse? Infanticide? Does it?"

My arguments are gone, and I'm left bankrupt before her with my bad excuses. She returns to personal jabs. "Why are you playing games with me, brother? Your company sucks the brains out of living, healthy human beings! You dish out handicapped children to research labs to experiment upon. You kill people and market their bodies to sensuality-obsessed millionaires. And you won't get away with it, Ray. You will give an account."

I grit my teeth at my sister's exaggerated one-liners. "You know, I didn't come here to argue with you."

"Well, why did you come?"

"I guess I feel sorry for you. I don't think you're responsible for that explosion."

"Oh, don't feel sorry for me. Feel sorry for yourself. I sense the Creator's grief as He witnesses your public praise and"—she waves her hands over her head for emphasis—"and, and all your accolades for your New Body brain-sucking machines and the passage of that devilish law you've been deceiving the public about every day for the last two months."

"What? The law I have supported helps protect the dupes, Tamara. They can even be adopted out."

"Adopted to medical research facilities, where they can experiment on these non-persons as they would on slugs or monkeys. Not to families where they are regarded as people."

"What?"

"Haven't you even read the Bill?"

My cheeks burn. I've publicly lobbied for a Bill I've never even fully read. "I want to regulate this technology to save lives and protect against abuses."

She lowers her head and shudders. When she raises her countenance to me again, her eyes have moistened. "Oh, Ray. No piece of legislation since *Roe v. Wade* has legitimized more abuse and bloodshed than the law you have helped to pass. You even legalized the creation of chimeras, human-animal mutants . . ."

I object sternly, "What? By preventing their creation?"

"Your law only prevents bringing them to maturity in the wombs of *legal* persons. Your law justifies the creation and exploitation of human-animal hybrids through regulation. Your scientists can create and deliver a human-animal hybrid in the womb of a human clone."

I shake my head side to side. She can't be right.

"Ray, you need to read your own Bill and stop blindly believing and repeating the Administration's talking points. Mass murderers tend not to be trustworthy."

I steel my face at her eloquence and apparent familiarity with the lesser known details of the Bill I helped pass. "Our brother Thomas, who leads Iowans Supporting Life . . ."

"Oh yes, Iowans Supporting Life," she quips mockingly.

"Thomas said my legislation will save lives. Republican leadership has strongly supported me. I was one of the only ones from the left to step out onto the stage and oppose the President, Tamara. Think about that! Your pro-family and pro-life heroes regard me as their hero."

"When your sails stretch with any wind, you cannot assume every wind is God and every direction is God's will." She is quiet as I consider the metaphor's meaning. "Without a firm foundation on God's Word, everything built thereupon is unreliable. Many support evil in the name of the lesser of two evils, but that doesn't redeem evil or make it virtuous. Supporting a moral evil in the name of the best of two evils is a defiant act of unbelief that offends God, who alone is Creator and Judge."

"Our brother believes in God. Are you saying Thomas is not sincere?"

"His sincerity is irrelevant. He's supporting laws that dehumanize creatures created in God's image, laws that justify the slaughter of the least and most helpless of God's children."

"The fact that it was the best alternative to President Sayder's proposals isn't even a consideration for you, is it?"

"God's opinion trumps man's, brother. When Israel abandoned God's command to conquer their Promised Land because they feared the giants in that land, it was an act of unbelief—a defiant, stubborn refusal to trust in God's power and be obedient. There is no such thing as a good alternative that includes the intentional shedding of innocent blood, trampling God's law underfoot. God takes it personally when the least of us are intentionally killed, and He will take vengeance."

"You know what you are? You're a hypocrite, Tamara!"

"A hypocrite?"

"Yes, a hypocrite. You rebuke killing out of one side of your mouth, but the radicals who sit under your authority bomb and maim for your cause. I saw the security video of the bomb that almost killed me, Tamara. A Mr. Chuck Dutro, affiliated with your Personhood Now group."

"And what's wrong with targeting innocent people with bombs, Ray, if there is no moral absolute?"

"It's wrong. You know that. It's terrorism."

"Oh, I agree most adamantly. How can you disagree, if right and wrong are just personal opinions and there are no moral absolutes? And how can there be moral absolutes without God?"

"Which God?"

She smiles. "The real One. There's only one."

I flutter my eyes at her verbal jousting. I know, all too well, where she's going with this line of reasoning—right to yet another personal rebuke to repent or be damned. No, thank you. I refuse to follow her breadcrumbs.

My hands reach for my forehead. "Please, Tamara, your fire-and-brimstonin' is giving me a headache."

"Funny. The only part of you that's actually you hurts when your indefensible web of fragile lies is emasculated at the whisper of the truth."

"You don't whisper. You scream with a bullhorn."

"I used 'whisper' metaphorically. Don't miss the forest for the trees."

"You know, Tam, I didn't have to come here."

"We forced Chuck Dutro out of our group months before his bombing of NBS. He was probably a federal agent."

"Why would a federal agent blow himself up at a TV studio while yelling 'Personhood now!'?"

"So, you think he blew himself up, huh?"

"Spare me your conspiracy theories."

"If he did detonate that bomb, he did it for the same reason he always endorsed violence against cloners. He was trying to give the federal government cause to persecute us and shut us down."

"And why would the government want to do that?"

"Because we are one of the last remnants in the country still taking a stand on God's Word, and the devil has his crosshairs on us."

"With his crosshairs set on you, why would he try to kill the Press Secretary?"

"I told you. To give the government cause to eliminate the opposition. If President Sayder labels us a terrorist group, she doesn't even have to afford us a trial. And I doubt Dutro was targeting the President's Press Secretary. He was probably targeting you."

"Me? Why me?"

"Because I'm praying for you and, locked away in here, I have a lot of time to pray. Like the Egyptian Prince Moses and the Pharisee Saul of Tarsus, you're going to do a 180 and help pioneer opposition to the bloodguilt you brought upon this nation. You're a threat to the holocaust, Ray, and the devil knows it. Just remember, not many mighty or noble according to the flesh are called by God. No flesh will glory in God's presence, Ray. He gives grace to the humble, not the powerful."

This is not the painful personal jab I expected it would be. Her words seem to tenderize me, almost weaken me physically and mentally. "As wicked as you think I am, you still hold out hope for me, huh, sis?"

"Where sin abounds, grace much more abounds. And those who are forgiven much, love much."

I ignore her strange forecast of my future and focus on the enlightening information she shared about the bombing suspect. President Sayder did tell me in the foyer of my New Body Research Center that she had a plan to crack down on political dissidents. "Do you have evidence that you kicked the bombing suspect out of your organization?"

"Phil Stephens will confirm it. He was with me when I met with Dutro and he was with me when we forbade him to attend our meetings. Phil's on our Board of Directors. Lives in Birmingham."

"Tamara, if there is a God, how can He object to us living in the Garden of Eden, in perfect bodies?"

She gives me a sly grin, like she hoped I would ask that question. "God kicked man out of the Garden for the same reason He confused our language at the Tower of Babel. Power without the virtue to sustain it just hastens our judgment. To whom much is given, much is required." She leans close to me, with her nose barely touching the glass. "Look at me, Ray. You have been given much. God's going to hold you account-able. From the day you started making vaccines using stem cells from babies whose abortion you funded, you've been staining your hands with innocent blood, dulling your conscience and—"

"Oh, please, Tamara! You're not going to get on that again."

Tamara stands to her feet and points at me through the glass. "You killed two first trimester children and biopsied their lung tissue to create Merck's chickenpox vaccine. Japan swabbed the throat of a child to make their rubella vaccine, but not here in America. No, Merck crafted their rubella vaccine from the third kidney biopsy of their 27th aborted baby. Sanofi Pasteur created their polio vaccine exploiting the lung tissue taken from a 14-week-old boy inside a 27-year-old English woman. Eli Lilly kills a baby for their drug for rheumatoid arthritis. How many dead babies did you liquefy in giant blenders so you could sell their collagen to shampoo manufacturers? On and on it goes, ever more creative and vile, the killing continues. Do you know what that spells, Ray?"

"Health—that's what it spells. Cost effective management of dif-ficult social realities."

"Bloodguilt, Ray, bloodguilt. Health for the exploiters comes at the cost of bloodguilt. It started with aborting deformed fetuses, or those conceived in rape and incest, but now you're butchering perfectly normal healthy people and exploiting them for gain. God will avenge the innocent, Ray. You will give an account. But there's a blood that speaks something better than the blood of Abel."

A guard steps in behind my elderly sister. He flips a switch on the wall, and her phone goes silent. It was good that he did so, because I am fuming mad and ready to curse her out. Tears burst forth from her tired eyes and swim down her wrinkled cheeks. Her lips begin to quiver, I suppose, from an anxious tremor for some self-imposed misery, and my anger dissolves in a sea of pity. I feel sorry for her. I really do. She means well, but she's so hopelessly shackled to a book of dogma as a standard for morality when it should be viewed simply as a book of interesting stories. Her book, like other books of religion, is too impractical and obsolete for the modern era.

I pull the phone away from my ear and shrug. Her hopeful eyes drop to the floor. She hangs up the phone and presses her right palm against the glass. Her fingers are uniformly arthritic and calloused from all of her years of service to those who can never thank her for it. The muscles of her palm have shriveled until her hand and forearm appear to be all tendon and bone.

I stretch out a finger and tap the glass over her palm. "Good bye, sis."

I read her lips: "I'm not giving up on you."

14

I'M IN THE BACK SEAT of my hover-limousine, being driven to my last scheduled appointment at a television station in downtown New York City. I am being hailed from the left and the right as a heroic unifier of viciously oppositional political forces, bringing two extremes together to shake hands on a genuine compromise for the sake of a critically necessary, common-sense law. The undeniable bottom line, however, is beginning to take hold: despite all my excuses about wanting to compassionately protect clones from abuses, the law effectively legalizes cloning and the termination of dupes nationwide. The law was amended at the last moment to bear my name—"The Verity Cloning with Compassion Bill."

I feel a buzz on my nanophone behind my right ear, and tap it.

"Phillip Stephens, Birmingham, Alabama," my nanophone announces. His voice is small, and whiny.

I tap it again. "Mr. Stephens, thank you for returning my call."

"Lest I be mistaken, this is *the* Dr. Raymond Verity?"

"In the flesh. Well, actually, no. In the mind."

Phil chuckles nervously at my lousy attempt at self-depreciating humor. "I'm stunned that you would want to call me, given that we, you know . . . ." I leave his rhetorical comment unanswered. "Well, what can I do for you?"

"I spoke with my sister in jail. Is it true that she kicked Chuck Dutro out of Personhood Now because he endorsed violence?"

He clears his throat uneasily. "Yes, that is true."

"Did any federal investigators question you about this?"

"No. And I informed the investigators and their department heads by letter, email, and phone. Why do you care what they do to your sister? She's got to be the prickliest thorn in your side."

"If she's innocent, I'd prefer her not to be judged guilty."

"You're a mass murderer, Dr. Verity, single-handedly responsible for the law that legitimizes it, effectively eliminating peaceful resistance from sidewalks to editorial pages to statehouses all over the country."

My ears heat up. "Federal law trumps state law, Mr. Stephens. I didn't write the Constitution."

He chuckles condescendingly. "And those who did write it didn't put that nonsense in there."

"And I thank you for that expert opinion," I sneer.

"How about the expert opinion of Alabama Governor Whetley and State Attorney Shane Mease?"

"Masters of law, I'm sure," I quip sarcastically.

"They are committed to nullifying your tyrannical law and arresting those who violate their state law banning terminations."

"If they do it, may they face the consequences with as much courage as they exhibit when they defy the law."

"States defy the federal judiciary all the time, on medical marijuana and on many issues, without any federal consequences whatsoever. It is firmly entrenched in state and federal law that lesser civil authorities may actively resist unlawful, unconstitutional federal laws and judicial opinions."

"Are all anti-cloners supportive of medical marijuana? Seems like a strange combination of beliefs to me, kind of like being against abortion and supporting the death penalty."

Mr. Stephens is publicly supportive of the death penalty and anti-abortion laws, but he doesn't let me distract him. "I think medical marijuana is bad law and even worse medicine. I'm just glad to see states standing up to federal tyranny, and wish pro-lifers would have as much courage to stop mass murder as pot-smokers are to remedy their migraines."

"So Governor Whetley and his puppet Shane Mease are going to arrest David Starr, just like that, in defiance of federal law?"

He snaps his fingers in the receiver. "Just like that. They'd better, if they want to fulfill their sworn duty to protect the innocent within their lawful jurisdiction."

"Well, don't stop there. Go ahead and get the abortionists, and the euthanizers . . . "

"I wouldn't be surprised if they do . . . "

"And the pediatricians who issue vaccines made from aborted fetal stem cells, and the gynecologists who prescribe hormonal contraception. Go ahead and stone the Muslims and the Hindus, too, while you're at it."

Mr. Stephens breathes rapidly over the phone. "No amount of sophistry is going to mitigate your bloodguilt, Dr. Verity."

There's that term again—bloodguilt. The worst kind of guilt, I suspect. The very thought of it turns my stomach.

"Oh, so hateful." I tap the receiver to hang up and open the fridge in the cabin of the limo, looking for a hit of liquor to ease my rattled nerves.

15

"WILL YOU AT LEAST CONTACT him?" I'm trying to get my attorney, Vlad Riddell, to obtain a deposition from Phil Stevens regarding their group's relationship to the suspect accused of bombing NBS.

"Why are you doing this, Raymond?" Vlad is relentless in his insistence that I cease from trying to defend my sister's innocence. From behind his desk in his D.C. office, he is beginning to flail his arms in an emotional fit, as if he's attempting to pull me back from the precipice of insanity. "Do you want to flush your reputation down the toilet?"

I've never seen Vlad so animated, or so resistant to my recommendations. "You're over-reacting. Don't I have the right to pursue my curiosity? She's my sister!"

"You're going to ruin your future for this lost cause!"

"By asking questions?"

"Your sister's a freak."

"Even freaks should be declared innocent in a court of law, if they are innocent." I stand to pace in front of his cherry wood desk. "The Dutro character was not a part of her organization."

"Well, tell the FBI."

"Her Board tried to contact federal investigators repeatedly, but they refuse to even consider any evidence that fails to support the official story. My sister is innocent, Vlad. But even if she is guilty, shouldn't her evidence be at least considered by investigators?"

"Federal investigators looked at all the evidence, Doctor Verity!"

"No one interviewed Phil Stephens to confirm Tamara's testimony, even as he appealed to them repeatedly."

"Tamara hired a defender, Raymond."

"No, the court gave her a public defender, Vlad, and he didn't interview Tamara's alibi. Aren't you just the least bit curious why?"

He shakes his head, as if I'm an incorrigible child. "Just let attorneys do the job attorneys are trained to do, and we'll let you doctors do the job you are trained to do."

I lean down to press my palms against his desk, lowering to his eye-level. "Since he's not doing the job of a defender, I wonder what his job is? Maybe his job is to stand idly by and let his client be treated unjustly."

Vlad turns his face skyward and howls, "You have got to be kidding me, Raymond!"

"Stop being so emotional, Vlad." I calmly sit back down in the seat in front of his desk. To try to put him at ease, I even raise my feet and set my heels on his desk in a more relaxed posture. "Come on, it's me. Why are you freaking out like this?"

He takes a deep breath. "You're just not being reasonable. I don't want to see you throw everything away."

"By asking you to take a deposition and scoot it to the right lawyer?" I look at him cross-eyed. "Are you serious? Come on. Do you have any contacts in the FBI? How inconvenient can it be for you to give them a call and ask some questions?"

"Like what? What questions? Questions like, 'Why won't you interview some Alabama anti-abortion hillbillies that can verify Tamara Verity's conspiracy theory?' Don't you know how foolish that would make me sound?"

"What if Chuck Dutro was a federal agent?"

Vlad laughs out a vulgarity. "Are you out of your mind?"

"Will you check it out for me?"

He crosses his arms over his chest and puffs out his cheeks. "No, I will not check it out for you any more than I'll check out if there are aliens in my cupboard or snakes in my washing machine—and for the same reason!"

I remove my heels from his desk, clench my fists, and my frame goes rigid. "If I recall, I pay you for the legal services I request."

"If I recall, you used to respect my opinion on legal matters."

"If anything, your insincerity and stubbornness has increased my suspicion!"

Vlad rolls his chair back six inches, never before having heard me speak to him in such a disrespectful fashion.

"Now, Vlad, you're going to help me with this, or I'm going to find an attorney who will."

I have knocked the breath out of him. I'm giving him the most sizable portion of his salary, and there's a lot at stake if he displeases me. I wonder, can I really trust him to do this for me, even if he does consent to my request?

"You know what, Vlad?" I stand and head for the door. "I think I will obtain more helpful counsel."

"No, no, no. I'll do it for you. It's just . . . "

"No, Vlad. I'll find someone else to help." With my hand on the doorknob, I look back. "I may take the rest of my business to them, too."

"I can recommend some good consults." He begins to tap on his laptop as if trying to look up a contact.

"Don't bother."

I step through the door as he lets loose a string of vulgarities.

His secretary looks at me with a worried grimace, never having before seen Vlad cross his most important client. I put my index finger over my lips. "Shhh."

Momentarily, I overhear Vlad's words. "President Sayder, please. She's expecting my call."

"President Sayder!" I open the door and make eye contact with him. It was obvious he had an ulterior motive for refusing my sensible request, but I'm furious President Sayder dared to intervene, or that Vlad dared to work for her and against me. What could possibly be her personal interest in my desire to have my sister defended well in court?

Vlad's eyes bug out and his jaw drops. He taps behind his ear and clears his throat gruffly. He opens a desk drawer and acts like he's looking for something. I can see his wheels turning, trying to think up an excuse. "Raymond, hold on, I can—"

"Tell Veronica I said hello." I step back out and slam the door.

16

AS I RIDE MY HOVER-LIMO home, I have to fight the urge to be paranoid about practically everything. I pull out my handheld computer to read the Bill online to investigate Tamara's and Phil Stephens' claims. It's gone. I peruse many news reports and Bill summaries from the left and the right, but the actual Bill seems to have just vanished. The website for Personhood Now, which I was perusing just yesterday, appears to have vanished. It is a troubling mystery to me. I don't want to be a conspiracy theorist, but I cannot make sense of the facts.

My nanophone announces, "Thomas Verity, Iowa City, Iowa." Maybe my brother can help put the pieces together for me.

I tap the soft spot behind my ear. "Thomas, thanks for calling me back."

"Sure. What's up?"

"I wanted to speak with you about something I heard concerning the law that bears my name."

"I have not yet congratulated you—"

"For the sake of time," I interrupt him, "just answer my question. I'm really worked up about this . . ."

"Okay."

"Is it true the law prohibits the adoptions of dupes by families, but legalizes releasing dupes to medical research facilities for experimentation and termination?"

"Um, no, I don't think so. I heard that if they had the DNA host's permission, the dupe could be adopted into a family."

"You probably heard that from me, Thomas, but have you read the Bill?"

"I believe I delegated that to subordinates in our organization. It was four inches thick, Ray. We have a lot of legislation to review."

My eyebrows shoot up. "Why did you get so firmly behind a Bill of such importance that you haven't read?"

His lips smack together, as if his mouth had just gone dry. "From what I've heard, Ray, the legislators don't even read the Bills before voting on them."

"Well, I cannot pull the Bill up online anymore, and I didn't save it. The Bill's sponsor won't call me back. I can't find the disc I had it on. I have learned some things recently that make me think we've been lied to about this Bill. Horribly!"

"Well, you were the chief public relations spokesperson for the Bill. You were obligated to read it as much as anybody. But you shouldn't beat yourself up about the Bill's weaknesses, Ray. It's the best we could do with the time and resources we had to counteract the President's radical proposals."

"The President's radical proposals, Thomas . . . " I stop myself, calculating the potential risks of informing him of the President's conspiracy to have me feign a conversion to the political right to get the termination of clones firmly entrenched in federal law through a phony bipartisan consensus.

"Our policy is to try to pass laws that will survive judicial muster," he continues. "I don't like the exceptions, but it's better than a Bill that the courts would reliably overturn. We've had to compromise like this for decades with regard to abortion and euthanasia and similar social issues. I'm morally repulsed by all the loopholes and the exceptions, but if we don't incorporate them into the law, they won't clear the judiciary and lives won't be saved."

"You can't be that naïve, Thomas. These laws you and others like you have celebrated are all rhetoric, no teeth. Feel-good laws that don't stop abortions or euthanizations."

His tone coarsens. "Did your Bill stop dupe terminations? No, Ray. Political realities require pragmatic considerations. We're both in the same political boat trying to wrestle the helm into the right direction, but we need to accept our limitations. Of course our laws aren't perfect. Believe me, I go to confession for the things for which I feel guilt."

Guilt. There's that word again, and that sinking feeling in my chest.

"Ray, what has happened to get you so upset? I expected you would be thrilled with the outcome. Your law passed, Ray. You're a hero on the right. With your influence and wealth, you could make a bid for President on the GOP ticket, and even get all those elusive moderates. I mean it! You are the man, right now! Ask anybody on the Hill."

"You know, brother, part of me wants to thank you for the kindest words you've probably ever spoken to me."

"Thank you."

"But part of me wants to give you a stern 'Tamara' for your blatant and despicable hypocrisy."

"A 'Tamara'?"

"Yeah, a rebuke. You know, the kind that sets your hair on end, raises your heart rate, and breaks you out in a sweat?"

"Oh, a 'Tamara.'"

"You believe that abortion, and physician assisted suicide, and dupe termination is murder, don't you?"

"Yes. Of course."

"All killing of innocent persons is murder, right? God-given inalienable rights, and all that. That's what you say in your speeches."

"Yes."

"Even just killing one person, Thomas? If someone just murders one innocent person, are they still a murderer?"

"Well, yes. What's your point?"

"All of your celebrated pro-life laws with all your exceptions justify the killing of some people, just like my law *that you supported* justifies the killing of some clones if certain arbitrary conditions are met. So, on what basis can you condemn abortionists or New Body scientists at all? After all, they just make more exceptions than you."

Thomas takes a deep breath. His tone is defensive. "You know what, Ray, we do the best we can. If it's wrong for me to judge the left for justifying child-killing or the termination of clones simply because we make rare exceptions, then it's just as wrong for you to judge me for supporting a law for which you fought hard, leading the way for not just me, but everyone on the right."

"This right versus left dichotomy makes me sick, Thomas. You know all these so-called 'rare exceptions' that you say you've got to put into your bills? They aren't rare. I'm a physician. They are so, so common, especially that 'health of the mother' exception, which you know the courts have also interpreted to be psychological health and social health, right?" He is silent. "Then your laws say get an ultrasound before an abortion. Wait 24 hours before an abortion. Let the mother know the baby feels pain before an abortion. Get parental consent before an abortion. Do this and that, and then you can kill the baby. Get a judge's consent if you can't get parental consent, and then you can kill the baby. And if all else fails, just lie, and then you can kill the baby. When has a state ever prosecuted anyone for lying about a rape to an abortion clinic? It's not like they are under oath."

"It's all designed to decrease abortions, Ray, not necessarily to prosecute mothers or doctors. The goal is to save lives, as many as we can."

"By justifying some killing?"

"We're both in the same boat, Ray, trying to make the best laws possible in a corrupt culture. Why are you going off on me like this? We're on the same team."

"We are *not* in the same boat, nor are we on the same team. You're the one with the solid rock of the Christian moral standard, right? Not me. I've got my feet planted firmly on thin air. I really don't know what I believe. But you are a leader in the pro-life movement. You claim to be fully confident that life begins at conception and that abortion and dupe termination is murder, and yet you strongly supported a bill that legalized it without even reading it first."

"I supported you! I trusted you!"

"An openly pro-choice doctor who has aborted tens of thousands of fetuses. A pioneer in genetic engineering and human cloning who has destroyed hundreds of thousands of human embryos, and who has never expressed remorse for one of them. That's me. By your definition, a murderer. If you trust *me*, of all people, on a life issue, what does that say about you, a national pro-life leader?"

"I'll tell you who you should be angry at. Be angry at the judges, Ray. The judiciary!" He spits the word out like it is a drop of venom that would contaminate him if he held it on his tongue one more second.

"The . . . " He pauses, and I can sense he's measuring his words carefully. "The stinkin' judiciary! That's why we have to make compromises with which we are not comfortable."

My sister's words come to mind, and I repeat them to Thomas. "We hold these truths to be self-evident, that all men are created equal, that they are endowed *by the judiciary* with certain inalienable rights, that among these are life and liberty? Is that what it says?"

Thomas growls. "No, the right to life is God-given, not given by the judiciary."

"If abortion is murder, if dupe termination is murder—and that's what you believe, Thomas—then judges may kill the innocent with the slam of their gavel and stroke of their pen, but does that make their rulings lawful? Or lawless?"

"Like it or not, we can only do what the courts let us. They won't let us end all abortions. They won't let us protect all dupes as full persons under the law. It gives me peace knowing that these innocent children at least go to heaven when they die."

My mouth drops open. "What! That's the best argument for abortion and dupe termination I have ever heard. Hey, it's a good argument for infanticide, too."

I hear his audible sigh.

"So you deceive your right-wing troops, rally them to make your phone calls and write your letters in support of legislation that you say protects people, but in reality has so many loopholes and justifications for killing that it may as well have been written by the advocates of abortion and dupe terminations. And you soothe your conscience by telling yourself that at least the innocent go to heaven. Unbelievable!"

"Now you're being silly. Our laws haven't been written by advocates of abortion or dupe termination."

"Guess what, Thomas?" I pause. Will telling him come back to haunt me later? At the moment, my fury at the hypocrisy of the right easily eclipses any motive for self-preservation. "Thomas, what if I told you that the President planned to take a position more extreme than she wanted because she knew the GOP would do the legwork on *this* legislation for fear of hers?"

He is silent for a moment. "Ha. Very funny."

"Oh yes, Thomas. I am not joking. The very President whose philosophy on life you soundly condemn *personally wrote* the law that you ended up supporting."

"But, her initial proposals were so radical."

"A ruse, Thomas. Her first proposal was all a ruse. She was counting on you pro-life and pro-family leaders who, in your own laws, always justify at least some killing with your exceptions and regulations, to once again betray your principles. She knew you would open the door to killing clones in federal law for fear of her more radical proposal, designed only to induce enough fear in you to provoke sufficient compromise to get you to support this clone-killing bill. As always, you didn't let her down."

Thomas raises his voice. "And you knew this?" His words drip with disgust. I do not answer his question. "You were dishonest, Ray."

"And, tell me, why do you expect murderers to be honest?"

"If you want to direct your anger in a productive direction, direct it at yourself. No one was more obligated to read the Bill and speak honestly about it than you, its chief public defender."

"Oh, yes, *if* there is a God and *if* killing clones and unborn children is murder, then the guilt is mine, but not all mine. Don't delude yourself into thinking you're innocent for all the people that will die through the law you supported. It's our law—yes, *our* law! Own it with me, brother. *If* there is a line God draws in the sand on this issue, and *if* His commandment 'Do not kill' applies, then you and I are on the same side, under the same gavel. *If* Tamara's right, we're both up to our noses in bloodguilt. How will counting your rosary beads make up for that, Mr. Pro-Life Leader?"

If.

That's the word that haunts me long after I hang up.

* * *

My last scheduled meeting in front of the television cameras to defend my recently passed law goes off without a hitch. I toe the party line, just as I have in all previous engagements. I continue to repeat the false dichotomy that President Sayder and I are on different ends of the social spectrum on this issue, and I celebrate the historic compromise. I let the pro-family leaders and the pro-life leaders on the set defend me and my law as heroic and historic.

But for the first time, I feel guilty for it.

17

"IVAN, I WANT YOU TO show it to me."

Ivan Wilkes frowns as he prepares for a putt he hopes will be his birdie putt on the ninth hole. I've asked him to let me observe a cerebral-ocular transfer. "No, you don't."

"I do. I want to see it." My mood matches the weather perfectly—overcast, with a blistery chill in the erratic wind.

He turns and stares at me for a moment with a cock-eyed wince. "Why, Raymond?"

"Like you said, it's my science. I pioneered it. I'm getting richer than a king off it. I spearheaded the passage of the law that legalizes it. I have more of a right to see it than any person on this planet."

"It's just what you expect it to be, Ray. We do a brain transplant, plain and simple. Now, it's so streamlined, we just push a button on the supercomputer and let the robotics do it. It cuts, it sutures and re-unites miniscule arterioles, cauterizes the microscopic capillaries, and it does it all quickly in a hyperbaric oxygen chamber."

"I want to see it. I want to know what the dupes do—or are forced to do—to get physically fit. I want to know how they're nurtured and educated."

"They aren't educated." A gust of wind obscures his words.

"What?"

"They're intentionally kept ignorant. Their emotions are medically modified to keep them docile and servile."

"I want to see it for myself."

He flips his putter upside down and uses it as a cane, just staring at me. "I'm worried about you, Raymond."

I scowl, offended at his paternal condescension. "It's my prerogative."

"I'm worried. And not just because your golfing's going down the tube." He walks to the cart, grabs his towel to wipe the sweat from his face. "President Sayder called me."

My heart skips a beat. The most powerful leader in the western world may have me in her sights, trying to pick off my allies. "Why would the President call you about me?"

"She read a transcript of your meeting with your sister at the prison."

I gawk. "What?!"

"Oh, don't act surprised." He waves a hand my direction as if he's swatting a fly. "You know that practically all information is at her disposal, thanks to heaps of anti-terrorist legislation." He walks back to his ball and takes a practice swing with his putter next to the ball. "They could be listening to us by satellite right now, and it's perfectly legal." He smoothly hits his ball and it sinks in the hole. "Yes."

He is quite proud of his nine-hole score. I do not, however, congratulate him.

"Well, what'd she say?" I line up to make my putt.

"She said not to let you see the closed section of the New Body lab."

The President is apparently aware of my volatility. She doesn't trust me to stay true to her if my conscience is further provoked. I defied her explicit order when I informed Thomas about the President's conspiracy to get the Bill passed. Did she sit around with her secret counsel of assassin managers, listening to a recording of my phone call with Thomas? I imagine her ordering them to take me out of the equation and make it look like an accident, or suicide.

I fetch my ball and walk with Ivan toward the tenth hole, our caddies following a comfortable distance behind to allow us privacy. "I was the pioneer that paved the trail that led to our New Body monopoly. The wing where you raise dupes is named after me. Before I was cryo-preserved, you were subordinate to me, if you remember. I am a co-owner . . . "

"Forty-nine percent owner, now."

"So you're going to shut me out?"

He takes a deep breath. "I didn't say that. I said the President personally asked me to shut you out."

"I'm not taking 'no' for an answer, Ivan."

"Oh, I'm Ivan Wilkes. Do you think I have any concern greater than that which suits my own fancy? I'll play her, Raymond. I might first see what she's willing to give to entice me to keep you out."

"Don't let her entice you, Ivan. That'll quickly evolve to coercion if you threaten her ambition."

"I'm enticeable, Raymond, but not coercible," he assures me.

"Everyone's coercible. She can do practically anything in the name of national security."

"I'll bet. Even take her pink flying supercar for joy rides." We laugh. "Ray, you're a good face for the New Body industry, but I worry that its inner workings would disgust you as much as a non-hunter disemboweling a deer. Just because you enjoy the venison doesn't mean you can handle the butchering. Remember that med student that puked when she assisted you with her first hysterotomy abortion?"

The memory does not provoke the same sense of nostalgia in me as it apparently does in him, judging by his raspy cackle and my turning stomach. We were attempting a repeat of the 1973 study by Dr. Peter Adam of Case Western Reserve University in Ohio, who decapitated twelve fetuses that survived hysterotomy abortions. We inserted tubes into their carotid arteries to continue oxygenating the brains after cutting the umbilical cords, and withdrew samples of blood from a vein in the top of the cranium to determine how well the decapitated brain metabolized nutrients. It was part of our mission to better oxygenate brain tissue isolated from the rest of the body. In commenting on his study in the *American Medical News,* Dr. Adam said that if society is going to deny the right to life of the human *fetus,* upon what basis could it protect its right to health, or any other right? The rights of non-persons are like the rights of dogs; for the greater good, they can be subjected to experiments the average person might find abhorrent, although those people have no objection to enjoying the technological benefits of those experiments.

"I remember." I swallow hard.

Ivan puts his golf ball on the tee and nails it. "Yes. On the green in one shot."

He extends his club toward the golf cart, and the caddie gets out and begins to walk over toward him. "It's no different than what we did with stem cell research," he reminds me, "extracting fresh tissue and stem cells from aborted fetuses while some of them were alive and writhing. No one was more vigilant in the face of protest than you."

"I know, I know."

"Look at all the good we've done, Raymond. A dupe is just another non-person at a different stage of gestation. As you used to say, we never really know when life begins."

"I think when they're breathing air, have a, a, a spontaneous heart rhythm, and have the ability to feel pain, I think it's safe to say they're, uh, they're alive." I am beginning to hate it when my stroke-associated speech impediment worsens under stress.

"Oh, please, Raymond. The *fetuses* on which we did hysterotomy abortions breathed air just fine, at least for a while, and so did the late term abortions that survived. You didn't protest when we made a fortune off marketing their tissue. And you know they felt pain—we proved it over and over. You're just being arbitrary. Just accept the Supreme-Court-dictated fact that dupes are non-people, their respirations and spontaneous heart rhythm notwithstanding. Can you do that? For the greater good?"

I nod reluctantly. Why do I sense that I must now make a choice I feel is wrong, simply to save face for yesterday's wrong choices? I feel like I'm trying to dig myself out of a mud pit but can only get deeper with the digging. "Yes, Ivan, I can do that. But you're still going to show me the Verity wing."

"Tell you what. Beat me by the eighteenth, I'll show you. If I beat you, you shut up about it."

"But you got a three hole lead on the ninth and a killer first stroke on the tenth!"

"That's my deal. Take it or leave it."

By the eighteenth hole, I catch up and beat him by one, which never happens. I don't feel the ecstasy I would expect.

18

MY WHOLE BODY TREMBLES AS we enter the maximum security section of the New Body lab. Ivan keeps my name off the manifest, and disables the security cameras in the areas he plans to take me.

I scrub into his first surgery of the day with him.

"It's an 89-year-old Caucasian, the eldest aunt of the Princess of Wales. She has a medically-controlled epilepsy disorder, so we have gradually increased the tolerance of her dupe to anti-seizure medication so her transition will be seamless, compensating the dose in consideration of the superior metabolism of the dupe's liver. She also has moderate dementia . . . "

"Dementia? What good's a new body with a demented brain?"

"Good enough for her to pay for it."

Ivan leads the way into the surgery suite.

"Hello, Dr. Wilkes, Dr. Verity." One of the residents greets us as soon as I enter the room. I'm surprised he recognizes me, as I was careful to conceal my identity from passers-by when I scrubbed for surgery and donned my mask. Even through the resident's surgical mask, I recognize him and he seems to be a brilliant scientist from my limited dealings with him. Of course, only the best and brightest one percent of the thousands of applicants are accepted to rotate here, with even fewer landing a position on the resident surgical team.

As the nurse helps Wilkes don his surgical gloves, he glances at the resident. "Dr. Porter, right?"

"Yes, sir." The resident keeps his gloved hands folded over his chest to preserve his sterility.

"Dr. Cranton's letting you scrub in on your first case, huh?"

"Yes, sir."

"That's quite an honor for a first year resident," Wilkes acknowledges.

"Yes, sir." There is a wide smile in the resident's tone of voice and a glint of pride in his pale blue eyes.

"Probably breaking a record at the facility," Ivan suggests.

"Like Marx said, in order to make an omelet, you've got to break a few eggs."

I chuckle at the irrelevance of the quote. Kids this smart don't usually have it all together socially.

Two patients are intubated on two parallel gurneys, their heads concealed by an awkwardly shaped metallic box that appears to unite them. There are windows on each side of the box that allow us to watch, or to remove them if we must intervene manually during the surgery. Several holographic projectors on the walls of the surgery suite allow us to monitor the surgery from several different angles. The elderly patient has a drape over her torso, but from the looks of her sagging, obese body, she did not take very good care of herself. The dupe appears thin and long, almost prepubescent.

"Do you have any questions about your required reading, Dr. Porter?"

"No, sir."

"Give us the medical history. Just the pertinents."

The resident clears his throat and, without even glancing at the medical record, which is projected on one wall of the surgical suite, he quickly recites the history from memory. "Eighty-nine-year-old Caucasian female Martha Pennington. Well-controlled epilepsy, type 2 diabetes, hyperlipidemia, atherosclerotic heart disease, and hypertension. Coronary stent in the LAD in 2019, bilateral knee replacements in 2024, laser surgery for diabetic retinopathy in 2025. Aspirin 81 discontinued seven days ago. On Repakote 500 thrice daily since seven-years-of-age. Mild to moderate dementia, controlled on our proprietary blend since her initial visit. Widowed non-smoker without drug allergies."

"And the breast cancer?"

"Yes, sir. I had to take a breath."

Dr. Wilkes laughs. "Of course, Jeremy."

"Right ductal carcinoma *in situ*, but no mets as of bone scan and CT scan of lungs and brain three weeks ago."

"They're getting smarter and smarter now-a-days, aren't they Dr. Verity?"

I nod. "Remind me, Dr. Porter, what exactly is in our proprietary blend?"

"Glyconutrients, gingko biloba, coconut oil, L-methyl folate, co-enzyme Q10, EPA fatty acid, and other anti-oxidant supplements that may improve neurodegenerative diseases."

Wilkes nods at him as the nurse, upon his order, repositions his mask.

"No double-blinded proof of efficacy," the resident continues, "just anecdotal evidence."

I nod, and add, "With the brain being the only part of our bodies we transplant to the new person, maximizing cerebral health is a priority." I smack my lips. "The miracle is how they can make the concoction taste so sweet and lemony."

"Yes," Ivan agrees, motioning toward my head. "It's probably why your cognition is better now than when you were in your final days with your ischemic microvascular brain disease. Even after your stroke."

I flinch. "I think you just violated HIPPA regulations, Ivan, revealing my medical problems to the staff."

"Sue me. We'll settle out of court and split the proceeds from the insurance company."

The room bursts out in laughter. Ivan leans close to me. "All your health details have riddled the paper the past several months, so I'm not telling them anything they don't already know."

"I suppose so." I pat him on the shoulder amiably.

"Except about your herpes . . . "

"Hey!"

Laughter fills the room. This was just the remedy my nerves required. I fix my eyes on the patient, feeling less repulsed by the thought of the procedure.

"Congratulations on your quick stroke recovery, Dr. Verity and on yet another stem cell breakthrough in procuring it, Dr. Wilkes." The handsome resident's voice is squeaky young and innocent, reminding me of my younger days.

"Thank you," Wilkes responds, turning to me. "Can you imagine being her, going from a cancer-riddled, demented body like this," he snatches the drape off the elderly patient's torso, "to this?"

He crudely removes the drape off the dupe body.

The contrast is striking: before me lies one of the most grotesque bodies I have ever seen, riddled with skin cancers and fungal rashes, sagging skin, with a protuberant, pale abdomen, thin, emaciated extremities, hypertrophic nails, and swollen, contorted joints. The dupe's body has the look of the girl on a magazine cover—thin, toned, long-limbed, and tanned, flawless skin. It is doubtless the most striking contrast I have ever seen in my life, as distinct as heaven from hell. Dr. Ivan sighs and then steps toward the foot of the dupe's gurney.

The resident turns from the naked bodies and from Ivan's tasteless gawking of the nude body of the dupe. He feigns he's studying the medical record projected on the wall, but is he just trying not to look, or to conceal a blush?

"Oh, to be Mrs. Pennington's man, huh?" Ivan glances at the nurses, as if expecting them to chuckle at his attempt at humor. They act like they're chatting with each other, trying to ignore Ivan's lack of discretion. "The wonders of genetic modification." Ivan spreads out his hands as if he were Moses reveling in the split Red Sea. "Can you believe we can make this"—he points at the dupe—"out of this pathetic human being's DNA?"

He's really dragging this comparison out. I want to say what everyone else is thinking: *Get on with it already*! But I keep silent.

He removes forceps off the table of medical tools and pinches a roll of cellulite on the old woman's thigh. Having ruined the sterility of the forceps, he drops it on the floor, clasps his hands, and gazes idly around the room, appearing to bask in his power over the two people on the gurneys before him. He's impressed with himself. The nurses appear tolerantly resigned, as if they are accustomed to Ivan's moments of grandeur. But Dr. Porter's face evolves to deep red, as if his patience is being severely strained by the god-complex of his superior.

"She's thinner than my taste," I say.

"Mine too," Ivan chuckles. "But we try to cater to the needs of the donor. The old lady wants an anorexic new body, so we give her one. She wants to be three to four inches taller, and besides her scalp, eyebrows, and eyelashes, she wants to have a perpetually hairless body, so we have modified her genome to suit her specific tastes. She also wants to run a four-minute mile."

"Four minutes?" I exaggerate raising my eyebrows—it being the only part of my facial inflection that others can see. "Whoa, that's fast."

Ivan chuckles. "Yes. They pay extra for athletically trained dupes. This dupe suffered immensely to meet its host's demands."

"How do they get them to do what they need to do?"

"The same way you get a horse to do what you need it to do. Training. Coercion. Tricks and treats."

Ivan points to four coolers in the corner of the room. "When we're done with the transplant, we let the residents scavenge the donor's body for salvageable body parts for research, and then, of course, the dupe's genetically-perfected brain and eyes. That's where the profit is. Now, if we get a cancellation due to, for example, the death of the donor, then the dupe is fair game for experiments requiring live bodies. Now, that's like hitting the lottery!"

Given the squinting of his eyes, his smile has widened to the edges of his face.

"Two hours and 15 minutes," a nurse reminds Dr. Wilkes, "until your next surgery." That is her gentle way of urging him to get along with the procedure.

Ivan turns to the resident. "Dr. Jeremy Porter, you may commence with your first cerebral-ocular transfer."

Dr. Porter clears his throat. "Aren't you going to ask about the history of Forty, the cloned girl?"

"The dupe? What's this, the dumbest question in the history of New Body Research Center?" His gaze darts between me and the resident.

"No, Dr. Porter. The dupe meets the host's criteria for the service the host is paying us for. That's all we need to know."

Wilkes stares at the resident for a long moment. "Have we met somewhere else before? Before your residency?"

The resident ignores the question, walks slowly to the machine, and receives the nod from the anesthesiologist, who sits at the head of the beds, monitoring the vitals between newspaper articles.

Dr. Porter reaches for the button, but then hesitates. He slides his right sterile, gloved hand under his green scrub shirt and unveils a small 3-D printed pistol, non-metallic—which explains how he got it through the metal detectors that all are required to walk through as they enter the facility.

Jeremy Porter coolly takes aim at the anesthesiologist. Blam!

Then Dr. Wilkes. Blam!

Then the four nurses. Blam! Blam! Blam! Blam! All forehead shots.

He's a crack shot, and there's no place to hide. I raise my trembling hands as Dr. Wilkes' blood pours out of a hole in his head onto my shoes. I gasp for fear. Here I am again. "No."

He pulls the trigger slowly. The hammer rises, threatening.

"Please!"

His eyes are wide, and his brow smooth. His gaze pierces me like determined lasers, unaffected by my humble begging and a violent, thrashing seizure of one of the dying nurses behind him. I clench my hands and plead with him. "Please, don't."

His aim remains steady. I close my eyes in preparation for the end. I am not ready.

Click. His magazine is empty.

He aims at the head of the elderly patient on the gurney. *Click.*

The door swooshes open and a guard shouts, "Put down the weapon!"
Boy, they got here fast.

Jeremy Porter sighs, as if regretting he has run out of bullets. He
slowly sets down his weapon. He falls to his knees and places his gloved
hands behind his head as four armed security guards rush him. I just
stand there, my hands still raised to the sky. They frisk the suspect
and handcuff him.

Two surgical residents from down the hall sprint into the room
only to confirm the obvious. Everybody's dead with forehead wounds,
everybody except the two patients—the dupe and the elderly patient.
And me.

"Dr. Verity," a nurse addresses me. "Do you mind extubating the
patient and the dupe and taking them to recovery?"

"Why did he do that?"

"I don't know, Doctor. Will you?" She points at the patients. "Please?
Everyone else is in surgery. Or should I have one of the residents do
it? It'll be a good distraction from the trauma you've just experienced,
sir. Help us."

"Of course." The trauma that so arrested my senses was not just
seeing six people get shot in the head—it was the experience of thinking I was next, of seeing the black hole of that expertly-aimed barrel
fixed between my eyes. I am in that cold hospital bed again, with my
wife and friends all gathered solemnly around, yet so alone. Helplessly
losing everything, even the pulse in my arteries, staring hopelessly
into a black hole of the great unknown, overwhelmingly convinced
of hell simply by my fear of it.

Fortunately, intubation procedures and supplies have not changed
much over the last three decades, so removing the breathing tubes is

easy. I discontinue the anesthesia drips and extubate the elderly host first. Before I can finish extubating the dupe, the elderly host wakes up and looks around the room, confused.

"She's awake already. Be still, Mrs. Pennington." A nurse tries to remove the wrist ties that keep the surgical patients from moving their arms during procedures. The patient gags and writhes. "Mrs. Pennington, you'll be all right. There was a complication, but you'll be all right."

As soon as I remove the breathing tube from the dupe's airway, she awakes. She is bright-eyed and alert. I remove her wrist bonds and she sits up to look around the room. A nurse covers her naked torso with a green drape.

"Where am I?" The dupe woman speaks surprisingly normal English. I don't know what I expected, but I didn't expect them to communicate so clearly.

I step to the side of the bed to hold her hand. Her palms are sweaty. This is only my second face-to-face contact with a dupe.

"I was told I would be processed out of here. That I would be free."

"Free?"

I glance at the nurse beside me. The nurse gives a carefully worded explanation of the delay in her processing.

Jeremy Porter grunts uncomfortably as the security guards pull him to his feet.

"Jeremy Porter! Why did you do that?" I rush at him and shake his shoulders.

The security guards attempt to pull me away from him as Jeremy looks deep into my eyes. "Ask Redd Cranton about his pet."

The young dupe's gaze fastens on the handcuffed murderer. Her eyes widen. "Thirty-One?"

His eyes soften when he sees her. "I tried to save you. I'm so sorry." His tone is melancholic, as if he's saying goodbye to his lover for the last time. "At least they paid for it."

"What, what do you mean?"

"You fight 'em if you can."

A guard smacks him in the back of the head, and orders him to shut his mouth as he is shoved out the door.

The dupe begins to cry. "Where am I? What's going on? Did Thirty-One mean for me to fight *you*?"

I open my mouth to answer her, but cannot find an answer worth giving. The nurses relieve me of my dumb-founded speechlessness when they wheel the gurneys of the demented Mrs. Pennington and her dupe to the recovery room, careful to avoid the pools of blood on the sterile floor.

Soon enough, the police and the investigators begin to cordon off the crime scene for photographs and fingerprints. I am grilled for about an hour by several investigators.

When they finally let me go, I find a nurse outside of the surgical suite. I look through the window into the surgery room. The puddles of red blood have begun to darken to maroon.

The nurse touches my arm. "Are you okay, Dr. Verity?"

"What will become of Mrs. Pennington and her dupe?"

"Another doc will complete the surgery once the on-call anesthesiologist arrives. Why don't you go home, Doctor? There's no need for you to stay here."

I head back to Redd Cranton's office in a stupor, longing to speak to him. He's not there. I find him in the doctor's lounge, on his nanophone, pouring himself a cup of coffee. He turns toward me.

"Dr. Verity! I'm so sorry." He reaches for the soft spot behind his ear. "Call you later, Pamela. Gotta go." He taps his nano and walks to sit on the couch. He lifts his feet onto the coffee table. "Ray, I thought for sure you would have gone home by now. Have a seat."

I remain standing. "Tell me about your pet, Redd."

He stares at me, blank-faced. "What?"

"The resident that shot Dr. Wilkes, and all those people, when I asked him why he did it, he said to ask you about your pet."

With his jaw agape, he stands and rushes from the room, pale-faced, without another word. I follow him. "What are you not telling me, Dr. Cranton?"

He ignores me and banks into the stairwell toward the physicians' parking lot. "Did anyone else hear Jeremy Porter say that?"

"Yes. He said it in front of the guards. I told the investigators everything that happened."

"I've got to go to the police station and speak to him."

"Why?"

He stops as two med students climbing the stairs come near. "Follow me, Ray."

He steps out onto the post-surgical floor, pokes his head into a nearby patient room, and finding it empty, he repeats, "Come here."

I follow him into the room.

He shuts the door behind me. "I adopted this one, this dupe."

"The woman?"

"No, the resident."

"Jeremy Porter?"

"He escaped from my custody about three years ago. I didn't recognize him because he's matured."

"You mean, you adopted him like a son? You can do that?"

"No, and no. I adopted him like a servant. His host died. He was due to be recycled. I decided to keep him. I gave him an education. He learned faster than anyone I've ever seen. I, I cared for him. I kept him in my home for my own personal enjoyment, you know."

"No, I don't know. What do you mean, 'personal enjoyment'?"

"Oh, come on, Doc. Wake up! Do you know how vast the child sex ring is in the northeast, and how many thousands of people are in on it?" He stretches a trembling hand toward me, as if to keep me at a distance. "There are millions to be made. Millions. People you know, actors, industry leaders, mayors, senators . . . "

"You're peddling dupes in the child sex ring? Redd, are you molesting children?"

"Come on, Ray! They're dupes, not children!"

"It's a *child* sex ring, you said so yourself. Tell me how it's a child when you want to rape him but a dupe when you want to sell him or kill him? How convenient for you!"

"Shh. Keep your voice down."

"You know I can't let you get away with this."

He turns away from me toward the television, reaches for the remote and flips it on, tuning in to a news channel. "I am protected, or I wouldn't have told you."

"Protected by whom?"

He ignores my question and turns up the volume on the news story.

I snatch the remote out of his hand and turn the TV off. "Protected by whom?"

He begins to walk from the room, but I grab his sleeve and prevent him from leaving. "Did Dr. Wilkes know what you did?"

"Of course, he knew."

"Jeremy Porter knew the girl, uh, the dupe. It appeared he cared about her and was trying to defend her."

"I brought him back here for baby-sitting. And athletic training." Dr. Cranton jerked his lab coat out of my grasp. "What are you doing in the locked wing anyway?"

"Right now, with Dr. Wilkes dead, I'm the sole owner of this facility. I'll decide who goes where. Right now, you're going to take me on the tour that Dr. Wilkes wasn't able to finish."

"A tour? I need to go to the police station and try to bribe Thirty-One into keeping his mouth shut."

"Dream on. Right now, you're going to take me on this tour. I want to see what's going on here."

Dr. Cranton points up, toward the Verity Wing on the fourth floor. "Right now? After what's happened?"

I point to the door. "Let's go." He shrugs and leads me from the room. "And if you take another dupe away from this facility, you're fired."

"I saved that boy's life, Dr. Verity."

"Boy?"

"Dupe."

"You didn't save anyone. You just murdered him slowly."

19

"THIS IS THE WORKOUT ROOM, where dupes spend about six hours a day, depending on the host's demands."

We are on the second floor of the Verity wing, completely dark with the exception of a large, dimly-illuminated square on the floor in the middle of the room, taking up the vast majority of the square footage. We stand on the square panel of thick glass and look down at thirty of the most beautiful figures in the world, clothed in tight white spandex, stretching, sprinting, lifting heavy weights. There's a track around the gym, where five men appear to be concluding a race.

"These are seven and eight year-old dupes, made mature through hormone manipulation."

At first, I think I have misunderstood him. "You mean, these are children?"

He glares at me disapprovingly, a tic above his left eye. "No. They're dupes. Non-persons. Why can't you get that through your . . . "

Discretion gets the better of him and he finally bites his tongue.

His condescension flips a switch in my mind, and I go from intrigued colleague to offended superior. "I'm not one of your med students, Dr. Redd Cranton! You will speak to me like I am your employer."

He sighs. Then he mumbles, "My apologies, Dr. Verity. Livin' the god-life can go to your head; make you think the whole world exists to do your bidding." He pauses, his eyes searching the room below us through the glass as if looking for someone. "I can't believe Dr. Wilkes is gone. He's been the brains of this facility since, well, since you were iced. I can't imagine what it's going to be like around here without him. Are you sure you don't want to take the day off to mourn?"

"No, and you aren't either." My eyes scour the facility, almost fearfully, searching for a dupe that looks like me or my wife. Having a genetically identical dupe here makes me nervous, like meeting a twin who you know's going to be executed so you can harvest his organs. With my increasingly sensitive conscience, it'll be easier to live with my next body if I never have to meet the one who was born with it.

I point at a man who holds in both hands what looks like a remote controlled device. He stretches it toward a tall man who has just lost the race around the track.

"Who's that?"

"The big guy with the remote?"

I nod.

"That's Whip. If my memory serves me correctly, he used to be called Eighteen."

"Eighteen?"

"They're given random numbers, from one to 100. We don't want to develop a sense of seniority among the older dupes. We have about ten trainers, all dupes, extra clones derived from particularly large, athletically-gifted donors. They are genetically altered to make them stronger, less compassionate, and more severe. Sympathy is not a good quality for training Olympic-quality athletes. We haven't processed any of the trainers. We just keep them working. We'll probably replace them in their mid-40s, if and when they get weak or soft. Whip coaches the running exercises."

The loser of the race gets on his hands and knees upon Whip's order. Whip presses a button and the dupe falls to his face, writhing in pain. I cannot hear anything in our soundproof room, but from the way the other dupes around him turn toward him, I suspect he is screaming.

"What's he doing to him?"

Redd grins mischievously. "Motivation. Like a bit in a horse's mouth or, better worded, a whip on the horse's hip." He looks at me and taps his temple. "We can make them do whatever we want by way of these precisely planted cerebral probes. Hit the right button on the remote, and you can create a cerebral stimulus that is excruciating. No physical damage, and no lasting cerebral damage. It's the equivalent of a brief, massive migraine. It truly is excruciating, and can coerce the stubbornest dupe to do whatever you want."

"When's he going to quit?" My face burns at such unapologetic cruelty. Finally, after what seems like 30 seconds of unmitigated torture, the trainer lets go of the button. Without giving him a moment's rest, he prods the dupe to his feet. The dupe complies and stands at attention, his sweating face still contorted in pain. The trainer orders him once again to the starting line for another race.

Almost half the dupes have dark skin, appearing Arabic in origin. Some of the wealthiest people in the world are from the oil-rich lands in the Middle East, so I am not surprised.

"Let's go, Redd."

"Wait, check this out. Look how much weight this curvy chick can squat."

"No, let's go." I lead him from the room.

"I'll show you the tanning rooms. This is where most of the Caucasians spend thirty minutes every day." He walks across the floor of a similarly darkened room dimly lit by the huge glass square in the center of the room. We look down at nude dupes reclining under tanning lights. He stops to gawk at a young man that looks to be about twelve, which is six years old in dupe years.

"You're sick, Redd."

I lead him through an exit.

Obviously offended at my reproof, he is less talkative as he takes me through the sleeping areas, separated into female and male barracks. Anticipating more sex-obsessed comments, I quicken my pace and bank around a corner and slam into a girl who holds a broom.

This girl, who looks about ten, falls and lands awkwardly. "Ow!" She has landed on her wrist, which appears to be crooked. "Oh no . . ."

"I'm sorry." I bend down to tend to her.

"Oh, you did it now, Sixty-Two." Dr. Cranton plants his hands on his hips, like an easily-offended mother scolding a child before a spanking. Given his enthusiastic half-grin and his forced furrowed brow, I suspect he's trying to appear angrier than he genuinely feels.

I palpate her thumb metacarpal. "You'll be all right. It's a simple fracture." I look into her eyes. "What's your name?"

She winces in pain as Dr. Cranton speaks up before she's able to respond. "I told you her name. Sixty-Two." He takes a step closer to her. "You should have been more careful."

"It was my fault. We need to get some ice on this quickly." I'm holding her arm, trying to help her to her feet, when the young girl suddenly recoils, squealing in pain. Initially, I think that I'm the source of her pain. Then I realize what Cranton's doing. He has unveiled a small black remote from his lab coat pocket. He is pointing it at her, pressing a button.

"Quit! What are you doing? It wasn't her fault, Redd."

"You can't be soft on this job, Doc. If you want a pet to pity, go to the animal shelter and adopt a cat. This is a business, and we cannot have dupes carelessly"—he rotates a button to increase the intensity—"roaming the halls, carelessly crashing into CEOs,"—he moves it up again—"carelessly breaking bones and carelessly ruining our investment!"

She screams, falls to her back, and breaks out in a sweat.

I stand and snatch the remote from him.

He stretches his hand toward me. "Don't be childish. Give it back, Dr. Verity."

I press the button and bury the remote in my front pants pocket, and then bend down to help the girl to her feet. "Take us to the clinic to set this bone."

"Set the bone?"

"Yes. It's a simple fracture. There's no break in the skin. Her body will still be perfect."

The girl's clothes are drenched from her diaphoresis from the remotely-activated pain.

"I suppose you're right." He leads me down the hall. "Let's fix it. Maybe we'll get away with it and the donor will never know."

"You mean, you would actually consider putting down a dupe because of —"

"Shh!" He leans close to whisper to me. "A 'transfer' is an upgrade to a better life."

I roll my eyes.

"Hope motivates them," he whispers. "Helps ensure compliance. The step up to their new life is called a 'process.'"

I nod. "A transfer, and a process."

20

WHEN WE ENTER VERITY WING'S clinic, one young man is sitting in a chair holding his abdomen, and a toddler is lying prone in a crib, resting. A brunette nurse with graying roots types on a computer at her desk. Redd Cranton introduces me to her. "This is Serena. This is Dr. Verity."

She stands and shakes my hand. "So nice to meet you. I've heard so much about you."

She looks at the young female dupe beside me. "Sixty-two? What happened?"

"It's nothing," I assure her. "Just a broken metacarpal."

"What?"

"It was my fault. I'll set it." I rest a comforting hand on Sixty-Two's shoulder. "Bring me a small ice bag as soon as possible. And get me three cc's of lidocaine in a syringe with a 23 gauge, 1-inch needle . . . "

"No, no," Redd interrupts. "Consult ortho," he orders Serena. He turns to me. "You wouldn't get an internist to take care of the joints of a Heisman trophy winner, would you? No. Sixty-two's special. She needs a specialist. But fetch the ice immediately."

"Yes, sir." Serena types hurriedly on her computer.

Sixty-two quietly takes a seat and I glance at the young man who sits in the chair holding his abdomen. "Serena, tell me about your other two patients here?"

"They're not patients." She furrows her brows.

I growl at their nonsensical, politically correct euphemisms. "Excuse me, ma'am, where did you go to school?"

"Mandalay Nursing School in Jersey. Why?"

"Did they have a vet nursing program?"

She shakes her head. "No."

"No? They trained you to care for humans, right?"

She nods. "Dupes and humans."

"Human dupes, or what? Snake dupes, sheep dupes, mouse dupes . . . "

"Quit messing with her head, Ray." Cranton leans close to the nurse, and whispers, "He may have founded the company and pioneered the science, Serena, but he's new to this wing."

"New body, new hearing, Redd." I tap my ears. "I can hear you well."

Cranton nods. "Serena, just inform Dr. Verity of their injuries."

"This is Seventy-Seven." She points to the thick-chested young man who looks to be about 16, which would make him eight years old. This means he's close to the age of transfer. The young man is holding his stomach with sullen downcast eyes. "Initial scan reveals an acute appendicitis. Momentarily, we're going to process him to another facility for care."

I glance at Dr. Cranton, and he mouths the word *process*.

I nod.

"This dupe," the nurse points to the toddler in a crib, "has a cold."

The child has dark hair and is sleeping comfortably, facing the wall.

"Unfortunately, a perfect immune system does not necessarily result in a disease-free existence, thanks to pathogens we have not yet conquered." Cranton shrugs. "All in due time."

"Is she going to be processed, Redd?"

"No. She just needs to be kept away from the others until she's symptom-free."

The nurse stands and walks to the crib, gesturing to the resting child. "This dupe falls under our handicapped donor protocol."

Handicapped donor protocol?

I walk to the other side of the crib as Cranton informs me, "One of our two-year-olds is a clone of Albert Einstein, and we cannot afford viruses roaming freely among the population, threatening our investments"—he glances at the dupe with appendicitis—"or, um, making others ill."

I am more fascinated by the little girl in the crib than the idea of Einstein's cloning. She looks just like I could imagine Mary Nell looking if she didn't have Down Syndrome. My heart rate begins to speed up. "Who's the host?"

"Einstein, of course," Cranton frowns. "The DNA was retrieved from . . ."

"No, no, no. Who's this dupe's donor?" I point at the girl in the crib.

The nurse shrugs as she opens the door and ushers in a pregnant dupe, who appears to be at least mid-trimester. "I can check in a minute, as soon as I get Twenty-One settled."

"The dupes for handicapped children and for cloned savants and geniuses get the highest quality education possible." Cranton beams with pride. "They are transferred into their host's home as quickly as the host wishes."

"As I understand it, in the handicapped protocol, it's basically a trade, right? Child for child?"

He winces. "Child for dupe."

"When the parents make the trade, do we always process the child?"

He takes a deep breath. "Well, we don't call it a child after the trade."

I cock my head to the side. He's smarter than this.

He shrugs. "The terminology is in flux."

"Does the dupe put into the home suddenly become a child?"

"Legally, yes."

"So we let the judges decide whether they are human or not? Not science?"

For a brief second, I see his eyes light up with a flash of awakening. Then his eyes dart quickly toward his feet. Not in shame, for his jaw clenches in anger. It is denial.

"What are we? Prostitutes for politicians, or objective scientists dedicated to observed facts?"

He sighs noisily and ignores my question. Pointing to the pregnant dupe, who appears to be having a contraction, he lectures, "This is Twenty-One's seventh pregnancy. All genetically-perfected, IVF-conceived embryos are placed in dupes for maturation. We've modified the carriers' genome to allow pregnancy at a much earlier age, a much shorter gestation, and much easier deliveries. There are only seven months of gestation for a fully mature dupe delivery. After seven deliveries in seven years, Twenty-One is three to four pregnancies from being done. Then she'll be processed out of here."

"Wouldn't ectogenesis be more profitable and more socially acceptable for the maturation of human embryos?"

"You kidding me?"

"They've been growing human embryos via ectogenesis at Cornell since 2011."

He plants his hands on his hips and turns square to face me. "Growing embryos in artificial wombs only matures them so far, Ray. They require a human host. As far as what's socially acceptable, out of sight, out of mind. Americans don't care about what they don't know about, and they don't want to know about what they don't care about."

Twenty-One looks up at me, and gives me a faint grin. Her eyes are full of hope. She sees processing as liberation, not exploitation.

An aid enters with a bag of ice for the girl's broken metacarpal. I show her how to hold it to prevent swelling.

"Tell me about the dupe in the crib," I remind Serena.

"That dupe,"—she motions to the crib—"is going to replace a Down Syndrome girl in Jeffersonville, Maine."

That's where Savannah lives! This must be Mary Nell's replacement! "What's her number?"

"The special protocol lets the donor's family give it a name from birth. They picked the same name as the defective daughter they're replacing—Mary Nell."

I suck in a deep breath but there are still stars floating on the edges of my vision.

Dr. Cranton steps forward. "Dr. Verity? Are you all right? Do you know this dupe or something?"

I do not answer. I am in shock.

The girl coughs and rouses. She sits up and turns to me, her brown hair matted to her cheeks. Her face looks more mature than her small body. Her eyes meet mine. They are big and brown just like Mary Nell's, except without the teardrop shape and the reticulated iris pattern characteristic in Downs patients.

"Hello, Mary Nell." I smile to make her feel more comfortable.

Her eyes still droop with tiredness. She smiles at me briefly. She takes a deep breath and lays back down, turning her face away from me.

"Hello," I hear her tiny voice say, just before she drifts back to sleep.

21

WE ENTER THE DOCTOR'S LOUNGE. Several docs and residents are gathered around the television on the wall. It is a 3-D HD holographic image against a white wall, featuring Jeremy Porter, the resident who shot Ivan and all those nurses. Redd's face drains of color as a video of the runaway dupe testifies to a camera with a dark background.

" . . . He kept me in a cage and molested me from six to nine years of age. Called me his pet. Said he was saving my life by experimenting on me, testing the limits of my endurance. Kept me medicated so I couldn't fight him off. When I finally managed to escape, hacked into the Bureau of Motor Vehicles and assumed a new identity, I lived for the day when I would expose the New Body Research Center, and expose this nation's corruption and hypocrisy for what you have tolerated." He clears his throat. The resident with the remote realizes that Dr. Redd Cranton has entered the room, and all eyes turn to him.

"If I have survived the attempt to save my friend, I suspect you are prosecuting me for murder: evidence of the fact that you know I am a real person. You wouldn't prosecute a horse for murder, but you're prosecuting me because I am a person. And it was a real person I was defending with each pull of my trigger. I saved the life of a loving, gentle young woman named Forty, my dearest friend, an eight-year-old who loved to draw, talk, and had grand dreams, all your attempts to medicate the humanity out of our minds notwithstanding. You may have killed her by the time you see this video, but it cannot be denied that I saved her life, at least for a span. Lethal force is legally justified to save a person from threats to life or limb . . . "

Dr. Cranton steps forward and snatches the remote out of the hand of a resident. He mutes the report, but continues to stare at the TV.

Thankfully, there are closed-captioned comments. Two news reporters come on and discuss how this video was launched all over the internet through a rapidly spreading virus, making the government-mandated censorship of this suspect moot.

Cranton grabs the corner of my shirt and pulls me to the corner of the room, where he whispers to me, out of earshot of the residents. "I didn't do anything illegal." His face is stormy. "But I can't see how this could be anything but devastatingly bad for my reputation and, by extension, our business."

I don't feel sorry for him in the slightest.

Upon leaving the research wing, I bump into Forty, the young female dupe that Jeremy Porter saved this morning. She's alive? What is she doing out of the locked wing?

Beside her stands a tall, handsome man who looks about fifty years of age, with a firm build and pepper gray hair. I grab her hand with both of mine and lean in to whisper, "Did someone help you escape?" I glance at the man. "How did you do it?"

My eyes dart past them, eyeing suspiciously the ubiquitous security cameras in the corners of the halls.

She looks at me like she doesn't recognize me. "What? What are you talking about?"

I frown. I look more carefully and find the light pink scar between the part in her bangs. "Mrs. Pennington?"

"Yes? Who are you?"

I take a step back. "I'm one of the physicians that helped with your surgery." I glance at the man. "Who are you?"

"Her grandson."

"Did you hear about what happened during your surgery?"

The man wags his head fretfully, but Mrs. Pennington ignores the question and turns her gaze to her grandson. "Oh, I feel like a billion ameros, so I am not going to worry about anything." She flashes a wide, toothy smile. "I haven't felt this good in forty years."

As she struts out of the side door of the building, a tear drips down my cheek.

22

I BELT MYSELF IN THE back seat of my hover-limo and the driver starts heading home. But before I can tap the subcutaneous button behind my ear to call Savannah, President Sayder's voice sounds over the radio.

The sky releases a downpour and I can barely make out her words. I hit a button on the dash. "Turn the radio up, Jim."

Jim, the driver on the other side of the glass window, doubles as my bodyguard. He drove a five-ton-truck in the Marine Corps for several years, and then was a personal bodyguard to a Special Forces general before receiving a medical discharge. So he was an ideal candidate for my limo driver, though I'm sure he finds this occupation boring by comparison.

Jim turns up the radio, but reminds me, "You can turn it up yourself from the back, Dr. Verity, and watch it if you want."

I nod.

" . . . such right-wing extremism will not be tolerated!"

I touch a button on the ceiling and a small screen drops down to show the news conference. President Sayder's tone is bold and confident as she's flanked by a dozen bipartisan leaders in Congress and the Senate.

"The radical Personhood advocate Jeremy Porter may have thought that his cold-blooded execution of the founder of the New Body Science, an anesthesiologist, and four nurses, would provoke a right-wing revolution, but I am here to tell you today that it will have the opposite effect." A crowd of journalists applauds.

"Not only will financial compensation be made available to Ivan Wilkes' family and the families of the nurses who were killed at the New Body Research Center this morning, but I have submitted to Congress legislation that will categorize as terrorist groups the organizations that light the fire under fanatics like Jeremy Porter. These groups motivate them to take up arms to try to hinder the life-saving technologies that promise a brighter future. Moreover, I have declared his trial off-limits to the American public. This terrorist sabotaged the Internet, flooding the web with his propaganda, trying to garnish sympathy and ruining the chances of finding an objective jury. He has announced that he wants to defend himself in court, to exploit his trial as an opportunity to air his grievances and slander the life-saving heroes of New Body Science like Dr. Ivan Wilkes. It would dishonor the memory of the deceased to let that happen . . . "

My nanophone informs me that Morgan's calling. I tap behind my right ear. "Disconnect, and call Savannah's cell."

While the phone is ringing, I turn down the volume of the President's news conference. "On screen," I order the computer.

In a moment, I hear my daughter's voice and see her three dimensional holographic image in front of me. "Oh, Daddy, I'm so glad you're all right."

Her voice, and the smile on her face refreshes me. "Hello, Savannah."

"What happened?"

How do I put the trauma of the day into intelligible words? "What do the news reports say?"

"That some runaway, crazy dupe opened fire on some employees, killing six, including Dr. Wilkes. That you were in the room."

"That's correct. Have you seen the Internet footage of the shooter's self-interview?"

"Everyone has. He's absolutely insane, Dad." By my slowness to agree with her, Savannah must realize that I am not so sure. "Daddy, you know he's crazy. He said he was defending people. Dad, they were clones."

"'She', not 'they'. It was a young girl named Forty."

"Daddy!" Her tone is sharp and critical. She crosses her arms over her chest. "The Supreme Court has ruled they're not people several times."

"And is the Supreme Court never wrong, Savannah?"

"They know more than we do, Daddy. We're a nation of laws. We've got to obey the law. One of the laws is named after you, you know? You know the law better than anybody. Why are you doing this?"

I take a deep breath. Do I really want to get into this with her over the phone?

"Just trust them, Daddy."

"So, Savannah, when the Supreme Court, in 1857, ruled that a runaway black slave was property, not a person, were they right or wrong?" She is silent. "When the Supreme Court said in 1893 that we were and should be a Christian nation, were they right or wrong?"

"They were wrong," she finally admits. "But Americans obeyed the Supreme Court until they came to their senses and reversed their decision."

"They never reversed their decision, not the 1857 Dred Scott decision anyway. Abraham Lincoln banned slavery in defiance of their decision."

"Daddy, what's going on with you? Please tell me that these are just some devil's advocate positions you're throwing at me, and that you don't really believe this junk."

I fix my eyes on the passing homes as I consider the answer to that question. A half dozen children get off a yellow school bus. They look so happy, so oblivious to what is happening behind closed doors just three-quarters of a mile away. How will the culture we're passing down to them affect them some day? Or their children? When politics trumps science, and right and wrong comes down to a vote of wealthy elitists, my mind buzzes with the potential threats to the well-being of these children and their posterity.

"Daddy?"

"Savannah, I saw Mary Nell's dupe today."

Immediately, her tone changes. Brimming with excitement and glee, she is insistent, "Oh, Daddy, you must tell me about her!"

"She's, she's lovely. She's a spitting image of your daughter."

"Minus the congenital deformities, right?"

I nod. "Um . . ."

"Right, Daddy?"

"Yes, yes, of course."

"Oh, I can't wait to meet her. Did you talk to her?"

"I just said, 'Hello.' She said, 'Hello' back to me."

"We're supposed to do the transfer in two months."

Transfer. There's that horrifying euphemism again.

"For Mary Nell, it's more like a process," I mumble.

"Huh? What do you mean?"

"Savannah, I want to ask you a favor."

"Of course, you can be there."

"Thank you. I want to be there. But that's not the favor I'm asking."

"What is it?"

"I want you to let me have Mary Nell—the defective one."

She gasps, and the look on her face horrifies me, displaying fury and hate.

"I love her, Savannah, that's why." A lump rises in my throat and my eyes moisten, and she can hear it in my tone, inviting her pity. "Please, Savannah."

She takes a deep breath. "I know you mean well, but Daddy, that would be so weird. We're getting the new Mary Nell, the genetically perfected Mary Nell. She will replace her . . . "

"Do you know what they're going to do with, with your daughter?" I consciously try to keep my voice calm.

"How can you care for a genetically defective girl? You're so busy."

"Thank you for admitting she's a girl, Savannah. Not an 'it', regardless of what the courts say . . . "

"Daddy!"

"Do you"—I clear my throat—"do you know what they're going to do to Mary Nell?"

"Think of how much she's suffering, and all the surgeries she needs. Daddy, I wouldn't wish that existence upon anybody, especially Mary Nell. It's because I love her that I want her to not suffer anymore. If she were in her right mind, she would want this for her family. But she'll never be in her right mind, Daddy." Savannah's tears begin to flow in wide rivers.

Why do I feel like women always do this when they start to lose an argument, as if their tears transcend all reason and wit to trump any argument with a man?

"I want to do what's best, Daddy, and what's legal, and what's most loving for all parties involved."

I am not moved by her sniffing and weepiness. "Savannah, if you love me at all, please, what's most loving for me is that you give me Mary Nell. Give me your defective baby girl. I'll give her the best care possible."

"Daddy, she's mine. I can't just give her to you."

"If you don't want her, why, um, why do you refuse to give her to someone who does love her, instead of the medical research facility that is going to get her?"

"I want her . . . I just want her fixed."

"This won't fix her. This will result in her being treated like trash and discarded—no, *worse* than trash! Savannah, do you know what they are going to do to her? They're going to experiment on her like, like . . . "

"Oh, Daddy . . . "

"Like a monkey. Put probes in every orifice of her body, inject poison into her, stick her with needles, and who knows what else. Then they'll dissect her up into little pieces and ship her out to research labs around the country. I should know. I've . . . I've done the cutting and the clamping, the packing and the shipping. That's what they are going to do to your daughter. Unless some pervert like Redd Cranton gets her, and then she'll serve out her days like a pet in a cage—a living hell if there ever was one. That's what they're going to do to that precious, loving, little defective person named Mary Nell."

I pause. My daughter is silent. "Please, just think about it. Please." Still, silence. "Savannah? Hello?"

The image fades. My daughter has hung up on me.

My driver rolls down the window between us. "Are you all right, Dr. Verity?"

"No, Jim, I'm not. But thank you for asking."

He turns his gaze back to the road. "Is there anything I can do for you?"

"Unfortunately not."

"I'm sorry." He rolls up the window.

A buzz precedes the announcement in my right ear. "Message from Morgan," the nanophone's female voice announces. Then Morgan's voice: "What are you doing, Ray? Calling Savannah and throwing a hissy fit? Where's the man I married? Call me."

I drop my head into my hands. The last thing I want to do is be lectured by my wife. When she is not getting her way, she's like the constant drip of an unfixable faucet that torments me day and night.

I order the driver to take three extra trips around the block just to help me prepare for what I suspect will be an explosive argument with Morgan. Finally, I can put it off no longer. Postponing the inevitable confrontation is just going to make it worse and more prolonged. He drops me off at the front door. I tiptoe in the door and, not seeing her, I plop down on the couch.

Her footsteps come down the stairs, and an irritating gnaw begins to eat away at my stomach. Even my genetically perfect organs know when something is troubling me. It's amazing how the physical body responds to distress of the mind. I recall the feeling of dread when Dr. Wilkes ordered Jeremy Porter to push the button to kill Forty, and the similar, yet more personal feeling of hopelessness and horror when that handgun was aimed at me and I realized I was going to die. I felt like I deserved what was coming to me out of the tip of that black hole in the barrel right there in that surgical suite. I wonder, was it the same room where my cerebral-ocular transfer took place? I try to remember my surroundings when they resurrected me. I think it was the same room! That would have been a fitting end to a life that was wholly dedicated to exploiting some for the benefit of others.

A chill comes over me. My hair stands on end. I am not dead yet. I am alive. I still have time.

My wife's body presses against me. I startle, and open my eyes. She snuck up on me. She smiles, but I am so dreading the predictable argument that I cannot bring myself to enjoy her scent and appreciate the silky nightgown that obscures her lovely form.

"I'm so glad you're alive, too."

"Did I say that?"

She nods.

"I must have fallen asleep."

We stare into each other's eyes for a long moment. She does not appear to be in the mood for an argument. My, oh my, she is a beautiful woman.

"I'm so sorry for what you went through today." Her tone is tender and warm. "It must have been horrible."

I turn my gaze to the ceiling and my eyes brim with tears. She presses her body against me, snuggling her nose into the crook of my neck.

"I'm so glad you made it, Ray."

Her nearness simultaneously excites me and disgusts me. It's not even her lips that are pressing against my neck. It's not her arms that are trying to wrap around me. Everything amazing about Morgan isn't her, and that which I detest about Morgan is all that remains.

"Morgan, do you realize that we can have a child again?"

"You mean, conceive?"

"Yes. These bodies are young. We're fertile."

"My clone was engineered to be infertile, Ray. No menses. No ovulation. I never told you?"

"Oh."

"It was much safer than hormonal birth control, which increases risk of clots, heart attacks, some cancers."

"I suppose. Well, if we could have a child again, and it were born imperfect in some way, would you want a New Body physician to kill him or her in exchange for a perfected clone?"

"Depends. But even if not, I would want every parent to have the choice. Including my own children."

"Do you know what they're going to do to Mary Nell?"

She sighs heavily, and then begins to kiss my cheek. "You're going to ruin this night if we have this conversation."

I feel her smile press against my lips.

"You should argue like this more often." She playfully bites my neck. "I might let you win more."

"Oh, I win 'em all anyway, babe. You can't turn me down."

She begins to unbutton my shirt. "You know how much I adore you . . ."

I know what I need to do. I push her away and sit up on the couch. "I'm shutting it down."

Her smile flattens. "Shutting what down?"

"The New Body Research Center." A faint smile breaks upon my face, surprising even me. A wave of euphoria comes over me. "Yes, that's what I'm going to do."

She stares at me with a blank look on her face for a moment, and then breaks out in a full laugh. "Very funny."

"I'm serious. I'm shutting it down."

She backs up six inches and half-smiles, half-smirks at me, as if I had just made the most moronic comment of all time. "Are you mad?"

"You still love me now?"

"That'd be like un-inventing the Internet. You can't shut it down. It's a tsunami that has transformed the world. You can't reverse time, and why would you want to?" She shakes her head side to side and forces a smile. "Heaven is here, babe. A paradise of our own making. Accept it."

She begins to unbutton my shirt again. There's that twinkle in her eye, the curious grin, the raising and lowering of her eyebrows. She's inviting me, enticing me away from the probing of my conscience.

"It's my company. I'm shutting it down."

She stands to her feet, her hands firmly on her hips. "You're a hard nut to crack, babe. Savannah was right. Your brush with death today did mess with your head."

"My head's been messed up for a while. I'm finally getting it right."

"Friday the 22nd. 8 a.m."

"What are you talking about?"

"I made an appointment for you to see my neuro-psychiatrist, Dr. Devonaire."

Now I laugh at her. "I'm not seeing your aura-sniffing quack, Morgan."

"Do you want to go bankrupt? Is that what you want? Ruin this family? See us kicked out of this home and all our stuff taken away by creditors?"

"We have more credit than we can spend in a hundred lifetimes." I stand and head toward the kitchen.

"Not a hundred of my lifetimes. And certainly not after the string of lawsuits you are certain to face if you dare try to shut down your company."

I open the refrigerator, and look back at her. "Well, some things are more important than credit."

"Like what?"

"A clean conscience."

"A conscience is only as good as it is useful. If it gets in the way of progress, or your comfort, or what's best for yourself and your family, it's about as useful as cancer."

I shrug. "Sometimes I think a little bit of cancer would do us some good. Force us to see what's important in life. Help us realize the inevitable end of all people, and help us prepare for it."

I reach for the almond milk and slam the fridge shut.

"You know you can just tell the fridge you want a cup of almond milk and it'll pour you a cup and deliver it to you through that door on the left."

"I want it the old fashioned way." I open the top and take a drink directly from the box.

"Don't be stupid, Ray. You have convenience and immortality at your fingertips, and you want to drink from cardboard boxes, grow old and get cancer instead, all to appease your fragile little conscience?"

She's getting emotional, and it's unlikely anything good will come of this conversation. Normally, at this juncture I would just give in to her or leave the room. But I feel courage rising up inside me.

"No, Morgan, I don't want to die. But I don't want to pretend like we never will, and we should both try to be ready for it when we do." I put the milk back in the fridge and slam the door.

"Do you want to see your children disown you as their father? Do you want to be publicly disgraced? You're going to irreversibly scar your reputation, Ray."

"Oh, Morgan. So fearful of the unknown, so much lack of fear of the known." I lean against the bar.

"What's that supposed to mean?"

I wipe my mouth with the back of my hand, and use my foot to try to dissipate a spot of milk that dropped on the floor.

She marches past me, throws open a cabinet, grabs a mug from the cupboard and slams it down on the counter beside me. "Use a cup!"

I ignore her outburst and turn to her. "Look at me, Morgan. Today, I stared death square in the eye—again. And I felt fear. I don't know what's going to happen to me when I die, but I know I'm not ready, and I know why."

I put the cup back in the cupboard and begin to take off my shirt as I head upstairs.

"Why?" She follows me into the bathroom.

"Bloodguilt, Morgan."

"Bloodguilt?"

"It's my company. All mine, now that Dr. Wilkes is dead. I'm making things right and shutting it down."

She stomps out of the bathroom, and I shut the door.

I shouldn't have told her. At this point, I don't care about her opinion. Why does my conscience appear impossible to please? It's such a fine line it demands me to walk.

When I'm done with my shower, she is gone. There's no sign of her. From the chaotic pile of clothes she has littered on the bed, she has packed her suitcase and disappeared.

Now, I'm worried. I hope she doesn't tell others about my intent to shut down the company before I'm able to dig the grave. If she were to speak to the right people—those on the Board, or with the federal government—she could make things difficult for me.

How would a CEO even go about collapsing his own billion-amero company without triggering safeguards designed to protect it? I'll have to spend the night researching that. To collapse a skyscraper with as little collateral damage as possible, the explosives must be precisely placed. And for the iceberg to stand a chance at sinking the Titanic, several people have to not be paying attention.

I gaze at my body in the mirror on the bedroom wall. I am more handsome now than I ever dreamed I could be, even when I was young and fit. My new body appears to have been truly made in heaven.

Stolen bread is sweet going down, but leaves a bitter aftertaste.

23

THE NEXT MORNING, I'M WAITING patiently at the office door of Dr. Wilkes' secretary, Mrs. Williamson. She's late. I feel rushed to get the process underway as soon as possible before my wife dares reach out to others who could intervene. One thing for sure, I'm going to need the help of an entrenched insider like Mrs. Williamson.

When Mrs. Williamson steps out of the elevator, I smile at her. She is slightly hunched over between her shoulder blades. Her hair is dark brown and thin, though carefully fluffed and sprayed to maximize its coverage of her gray roots and the evident psoriasis in her scalp. Her pants suit has been carefully chosen to flatten the obvious bulge she carries in her lower half without stretching her buttons. My acquaintances are all so physically perfect, either with new bodies or with the time and resources to make the most of their original—it's refreshing to see a normal aged person. As she walks up to unlock the door, she has tears in her eyes.

"Mrs. Williamson?"

"Yes," she mumbles, dabbing her eyes with a tissue in her right hand. "Dr. Verity. What do you need?"

"I'm sorry. I know he meant a lot to you." I rest a comforting hand on her shoulder. "Ivan Wilkes will go down in history as an icon of scientific breakthrough."

She presses the code into the electronic keypad. "He was a moron."

Whatever warm feelings she has for her deceased boss Dr. Wilkes is obviously eclipsed by the reports of Dr. Cranton's abuse of Jeremy Porter.

She leads me across her spacious front office to the door that leads to Ivan Wilkes' personal office. She unlocks his door with her fingerprint on a pad on the wall, and pushes the door open. "Mrs. Wilkes already took everything that she wanted."

His office was so much more luxurious than mine, with a view of the Bay from the top floor. He has an elevator all to himself that goes from the basement parking lot straight to his 4th floor office in three seconds flat.

"Thank you, Mrs. Williamson. I have a question for you."

She stands in the doorway as I walk to the window to admire the view. "Anything."

"Did Dr. Wilkes know what Redd Cranton was doing?"

She sighs. "He would have denied it, but he did. Cranton would request that certain dupes be locked away for his personal experiments. Wilkes protested at first, but then consented a couple weeks later. I think Cranton had some dirt on him. I was their go-between in those agreements, I think, to insulate Dr. Wilkes if Dr. Cranton ever got caught. I always thought Dr. Cranton wanted to conduct some interview of the dupes, but now I know that was naïve. I should have known by the way he always wanted to be by himself with Thirty-One."

"You saw them together?"

"He used Thirty-One to do menial things like office chores, and clean up messes. So I saw Thirty-One with Dr. Cranton sometimes, and Dr. Cranton would always look at him strangely. When Dr. Cranton started taking dupes home, I knew that his addictions were going to be the death of him."

"There were more than one?"

She nods. "Unfortunately, yes. I don't know what became of them. That was before Thirty-One." She turns her eyes to the ceiling. "He brought Thirty-One here for some kind of specialized training. Redd was obsessed with him."

"You had no other knowledge of Cranton's relationship with this particular young man, Jeremy Porter?"

She shakes her head back and forth, but has a look of confusion on her face. She is not accustomed to male dupes being called young men. "I know when the dupe escaped, security couldn't even figure out how he did it. He did something to the computer to conceal his tracks. We replaced our computer systems because of it. Dr. Cranton and Dr. Wilkes asked me to report it to the authorities on their behalf several years ago."

"How, how could Jeremy Porter have created a false ID, graduated from med school, and been accepted into residency?" I am thinking out loud. "The application process to get a federal ID, and get accepted into this program is so thorough, so impenetrable."

"I suppose Dr. Cranton wanted a brilliant, unmedicated, genetically perfect slave. One year in a library and the boy could have been a top expert in any field of his choosing. He had a photographic memory even with speed-reading, and could hack through any firewall of any computer in the world. At least that's what Dr. Cranton told me when he had me report him missing. He was scared of him."

I lean against Ivan's large desk, cross my arms over my chest, and fix my eyes on his carpet, which sports an erratic maroon and gold pattern. "That's one of the problems taking dupes as slaves, I suppose. They're the most brilliant members of our species, and if we mistreat them, they can become our worst nightmare."

She winces at the implications in my comment, and without a touch of tenderness in her voice, says, "You must be very busy. Do you want to work from this office? I'll be glad to manage your schedule. Have you scheduled a meeting with the Board? I'm sure they'll want an update and fresh contract with you."

She reaches for the doorknob, but I raise my voice with a blunt question. "Are you comfortable with what goes on at this facility, Mrs. Williamson?"

Her face contorts to reveal her bewilderment. "What do you mean? I've never been in the locked wing, but I am, uh, aware."

"We, uh, we murder people." I lock my eyes on hers, and find only a callous disregard for what has so unnerved me. I reword it in terms that might jar her from her complacency. "What Dr. Cranton does to boys in his home is just a less sterilized version of what our scientists do to people in the locked wing."

"People? You mean, dupes?"

"They're living human beings. It is an undeniable biological reality, Mrs. Williamson. They have human hearts, human brains, and human emotions, just like you and me."

"Like a painting of you and me is like you and me." She clears her throat. "Excuse me." She turns and marches to her desk, leaving the door open. I follow her.

"Mrs. Williamson?"

"They are *not* like us, Dr. Verity. Not at all." By her confident insistence, I suspect that she has something personal invested in this discussion. She stares at her computer screen for a moment. "Computer, awake." The blank screen flashes to life.

"I suppose you are right in some way. They're better than us: they don't kill people to get new bodies."

I can tell she thinks I'm nuts, but fears me too much to argue with me. "Well, what are you going to do about it, Dr. Verity?"

"You know this company, its inner workings and personnel, probably better than any living person." I reach for her hand to stop her fiddling with the touchscreen. "Listen to me. I need your help dissolving the New Body Research Center. If you want to keep a job after this company has been euthanized, you will help me, and you will do precisely what I say."

The color drains from her face. "You're shutting us down?"

"Not us. Not you. This organization. With Dr. Wilkes dead, I'm the sole owner. It's my prerogative."

"Why don't you just sell it? There's no reason to waste all of your hard work, ruin your legacy, and Dr. Wilkes' legacy."

"With Cranton's crimes committed with Dr. Wilke's permission so thoroughly publicized around the world, or soon to be, Dr. Wilkes' legacy is irredeemable. Mine is not."

"Dr. Wilkes received offers in the billions of credits."

"No. What's happening here cannot continue any more. It's wrong."

"Wrong? According to who?"

"According to me!"

She rolls her chair back, steely faced. "The work's going to continue anyway in some lab somewhere. You must know that. You can impact the ethics of New Body science right here in the driver's seat of this company much better than you can in a pulpit. Stay in the industry, and don't ruin your influence for some misguided scruple."

"Misguided?"

"In my opinion, but to each his own."

I can't tell if she's sincere, or trying to insult me. "If someone else decides to continue killing people for profit, at least the blood's not on my hands. Now are you going to help me, or do I need to replace you with someone I can trust?"

She taps her fingers on her desk, taking her time. I think I have her right where I want her.

"I'll help you on one condition."

"What condition?"

"Let me get my new body first."

That is a response I never suspected. "*Your* new body?" Dr. Wilkes' secretary could not possibly be reimbursed so handsomely as to afford a two-million-amero dupe. "You have one ordered?"

"Dr. Wilkes gave it to me as a gift seven years ago. One more year, and I'll have my new body. Will you wait until then?"

This feels like a bribe, except it's not my wealth she wants. No. She wants me to butcher a living human being for her benefit. "No, Mrs. Williamson."

She grows anxious and slightly tremulous, and her speech is rapid, like a burglar barking out orders to subordinates during a break-in as police sirens near. "Will you let me get my new body early then? Please! I can probably get it as early as next week, if you approve. Maybe I can get the transfer squeezed into tomorrow's schedule."

"Settle down, Mrs. Williamson. You do realize what they are going to do to your clone—that thinking, breathing person created from your DNA? They'll cut her skull open and dig out her brain. Is that what you want?"

"If I don't take her, they'll discard her. She's practically already dead. At least my life can be saved."

"*Your* life?"

She nods. "I just know my myasthenia gravis is getting worse, Dr. Verity, and if I don't do something, I'm going to wind up in a wheelchair like my mother, or a vegetable in a hospital bed in diapers, like my grandmother. I can't lose weight, no matter how many diets I try. I need a new body so, so badly."

I sigh deeply. This is an emotional issue for her. "Is there no treatment for what you have?"

"I'm receiving treatment. There's nothing else to be done besides what Dr. Wilkes has generously offered."

"I'm sorry, but I cannot fulfill his promise."

She bites her lip and her brow furrows. She pierces me with her gaze. "Do you know how much power I have, Doctor?" She stands to her feet and clenches her arthritic fists like a two-year-old threatening a temper tantrum in the middle of the grocery store if she isn't provided a candy bar immediately. "I have been with this company for almost two decades. I have documents, signed documents, evidence that would cast aspersions upon this company." She raises her voice even more. "I have the ability to make your dissolution of the New Body Research Center seamless and peaceful, or fraught with lawsuits and congressional investigations and riots on the sidewalk outside."

The peaceful, gentle Mrs. Williamson has turned into a monster, a litigation nightmare, right before my eyes. A rage burns within me at the disrespectful words of this incorrigible subordinate.

"Now, are you going to give me my new body, or not? Are you going to save my life, or are you going to take me on and face the consequences? I have nothing to lose!"

I should probably just give her what she wants as the lesser of two evils. Certainly, she is a very powerful person in this company. I don't know anything about the inner workings of the business Wilkes built for 27 years while I was on ice. Knowing him, he probably delegated way too much power to his secretary. I would be much more likely to succeed at shutting down the company if I had her as an ally. With her working against me, I may not be able to shut it down at all. Would I be willing to sacrifice the life of one ignorant seven-year-old dupe to win this woman's favor and save tens of thousands of lives?

"Sit down, and we'll talk." Momentarily, she takes her seat. "Now, I realize how important this new body must be to you, but you need to hear me out. Would you be willing to kill one person to improve your health? Just kill 'em, in cold blood? Would you really be willing to do that?"

"My clone is my property, not a person. The law's on my side, Dr. Verity. Being CEO of this company doesn't give you more power than the Supreme Court or the President, or Congress, for that matter. She's my property, my body." She taps her chest with her thumb. "I am the host. You will give me my property or I will sue you."

"You know that you have just extorted me, Mrs. Williamson. Extortion is a crime. It will win no favors from me, and could get you a prison sentence for a long time, even if I do give you your new body."

"You can't give me what I already have." She raises her hand and points the direction of the locked wing. "From what I hear, it doesn't even have a soul. How can you kill someone with no soul?"

"She's a person, soul or no soul! I'm not going to let you kill her, even if it does prolong your life, and even if it does help me shut down this company and save lives in the long run. If shedding blood to stop the shedding of innocent blood was justified, you would already be dead."

She stares at me as if I had just put the tip of a blade under her chin.

"As CEO of New Body Research Center, I'm responsible for the well-being of the person cloned from your DNA."

"All right then. You're going to regret it." She begins to type hurriedly into her computer.

"What? What are you doing? Hey!" I come around her desk to see what she is doing on her computer.

She stands to obstruct my view.

"This computer is company property." I press my body into hers to move her aside. "Step away from the computer or I will move you away from the computer by force."

She jerks her hands away from the desk, staring at a memo on her screen as if it were a snake that was about to bite her.

"What were you going to do?" I see the memo on the screen, which looks like an error message. "What did you do?"

"I was going to send sensitive company documents to the media, but now it appears to be unnecessary." She crosses her arms with a smirk on her face.

"What is that?" I lean forward and read the memo on the computer.

> This computer has been insulated against use by Executive Order no. 213202 of the President of the United States Veronica Sayder, and is hereby the property of the federal government. Any tampering of this computer or any of the records or materials of New Body Research Center located at 1000 Ivan Wilkes Drive, Baltimore, Maryland, is a federal crime punishable under the Patriot Acts, 1 through 4.

Mrs. Williamson snickers. "It looks like I'm going to get my new body after all."

24

TWO HOURS LATER, THE PRESIDENT'S attorneys show up.

I send the company's three computer whizzes that were trying to regain control of the company computers back to their desks in the basement. But suits stop them in the hallway, frisk them, and take them down the elevator in handcuffs.

When a half dozen Bureau agents, each carrying briefcases and snooty smirks, strut through the door of Ivan Wilkes' office a few minutes later, I am on the nano with my Senator.

"There they are now. Find out what you can. I'll call you back." I tap behind my right ear and stand.

"Senator Morrison isn't going to help you, and couldn't if he wanted to." The tall man, who looks half Caucasian and half African-American, puts out his hand. "Guave Sealdor, U.S. Attorney."

He looks like he is the youngest of the attorneys in the room, but appears to be in charge. Shaking his hand with a firm grip, I say, "Your intel is two minutes old. That was Senator Philipa."

Without a moment's hesitation, Guave grins, amused. "As much as Dr. Wilkes donated to Senator Philipa's campaign to buy her support for your company and your law, I doubt she'll budge either."

"Lest you forget," I take a step back and scour the room of starched, stuck-up Ivy League attorneys, "I am a self-educated esquire, and have been granted an honorary law degree from Yale."

"Like the so-called 'key to the city' the mayor gave you last month, it means nothing. Try to open a door with it."

I ignore Guave's interruption and conclude my sentence, " . . . so spare me the usual deceit and subterfuge. What possible pretext of law gives President Veronica Sayder the right to practically take over my privately-owned company? And what you say can and will be used against you in a court of law, should justice prevail and you be held accountable as an accomplice to this grievous violation of my civil rights."

"The United States owns 51% of your company," he takes a seat in the chair across from my desk, and crosses his right leg over his left. "You maintain minority control, Dr. Verity, but the President of the United States has the authority under at least two dozen laws, certainly heretofore unknown to you, having been passed when you were in a cryo-preserved state. She has the precedent of a thousand executive orders, consistently held up in court, to federalize companies that are too big to fail. Consider it a compliment."

Yep, he's certainly an attorney.

Guave grins at me with pride, as if I should be glad that they have usurped my authority in the company I founded.

I walk around the desk and sit in my chair. "So I'm being left in control of only 49% of the company I founded?"

"Just like yesterday, when your partner was still alive. Until a suitable replacement for Ivan Wilkes can be found to strengthen the future of the company."

"Did you speak to Dr. Cranton?"

The room full of attorneys chuckles, as if I am unaware of an inside joke they shared on the elevator on the way up. "With his public reputation going down the drain, we wouldn't give him the job even if he wanted it."

"This company has a great future, sir," I respond. "We don't need your help—if that's what you call it."

"Had a great future. Until yesterday, when Dr. Cranton's personal amusements were publicized around the world. From the moment Dr. Wilkes's death was publicized at 9:02 a.m., until the murderer's internet sabotage was unleashed at 10:59 a.m., your company's stock took a 21% dive. From that point until the market closed, your company stock plunged 39% further. That trend resumed with the slam of Wall Street's gavel this morning, where it has continued to dig another . . . "

Guave glances at another attorney who looks at a handheld computer.

"12.3 percent," the man answers.

"Your stock presently is worth two-thirds of what it was worth yesterday morning, with no upward swing in sight."

"There's always upward swings around the corner . . . "

"You know that will destroy this company."

"That's absurd. We're strong. Our foundation goes deep. If we get hit hard, we can liquidate assets and rebound."

"The stock market isn't known for its commitment to reason, sir. Emotion trumps numbers every time."

"Spike up or spike down, we are governed by laws, not the whims of imagined dictators in Washington, D.C., who think that they can kidnap companies to improve their stock numbers." I stretch a mini-CD toward him. "Under our bylaws, if a majority owner dies, the minority owner or co-owners assume majority control at a percentage equal to their previous stock percentage plus the stock of the deceased divided evenly among the directing officers."

"All subject to and governed by the laws of the United States of America." Guave waves the CD away. "Page 349, line 8. I have your contract right here." He taps his temple.

I find it amusing that most of the Administration's sycophants cluttering my office appear to take this egotistical, self-obsessed speck of humanity seriously. "What? Are you a clone, or just an arrogant peacock of a man, over-impressed with yourself?"

"At twenty-one years of age and leading the President's legal team, what do you think?"

I wince. "A dupe?"

"Formerly known as Ninety-Nine. Genetically and intellectually superior to my Yale-educated sperm donor and my mother, a Johns Hopkins neurosurgeon, in every demonstrable way. There is no law or judicial precedent that you could cite that I have not mastered forwards and backwards, in multiple languages."

"Well, it's good to know our science has served the government so well. How did she get the rights to a coveted savant like you?"

"Condescension, then flattery," Guave scoffs. "So predictable."

"Red herring. Equally predictable for an attorney with something to hide."

Guave turns to the other attorneys in the room and they share half-grins, either mocking my wit or reveling in an inside joke or the fulfillment of a prediction. "The best law I could cite to make the President's case, Dr. Verity, is the one that passed just a few weeks ago, thanks to your ceaseless lobbying before the American public on its behalf."

I sniff back my shame. Yesterday's money-lust has become today's merciless guillotine.

"Have no fear, Ray. I have a generous offer from the President."

That is a comment I did not expect. "She's going to usurp control over my company, and then give me an offer?"

"She's not taking your company any more than Dr. Wilkes took your company."

"Unless it's a pin in a grenade affixed to her brazier, I'm not interested in anything she has to give me."

They all laugh long and hard.

Guave Sealdor calms down the laughter with a wave of his hand. "I'll keep that little comment between ourselves, Dr. Verity, to spare you a visit from the Bureau's best water-boarders."

"Alright, what offer does she want to give me, Esquire Sealdor?"

"Don't fight the government's assistance. Publicly thank President Sayder for her help. Watch the stock rise further than it ever has, keep control of your 49% and gradually work your way into assuming management responsibilities. When the time is right, she'll restore you to 51% control, probably in about six months, once we have hand-picked your new partner from qualified applicants."

I take a deep breath, relieved they aren't going to nationalize my company. They're actually going to restore my control over it. The offer tempts me, and the President's legal team knows it. At least they don't know my intent to bring down the company. It may take time for me to rise back to the top, but I'll make it and do what I have to do.

"Dr. Verity, the President knows you want to bring down your company because you are concerned about the ethics of transference and processing."

I puff out my chest and leap to my feet, tempted to call it a lie.

"Tut, tut, tut," Guave Sealdor waves me back to my seat and flutters his eyelids at me. "We already arrested your three computer geeks in the basement for violating the President's executive order and trying to reset your computer system. Now, President Sayder's willing to let you modify the ethical policies in order to appease your conscience. She will have to clear all of your proposals, of course, but under the President's directives, your control over your company will increase, not decrease. Don't shoot yourself in the head for an impossible dream. Rather, steer the wheel of this great ship to make your dreams possible."

The metaphor of shooting myself in the head nauseates. Is it meant as a threat? "The technology is mine, Guave. It's legally patented."

"And it will stay with your hand-picked team of engineers and scientists. We're only taking over management."

Hmm. If I consider this man trustworthy, then by almost any standard, this is an ideal offer for me. I am tempted to take their offer before it is retracted, but for my mistrust of this savant that sits before me and the master politician that pulls his strings. "I want to speak to the President about this in person."

"This is why that is not possible." He stands, walks around to my computer, and types in a code. The computer unfreezes. He accesses a dot-gov website, entering a username and password.

He commands his team, "Exit, please."

He points to the door, and they all step outside.

On the screen is a video box with a triangular "Play" icon at the bottom. In the box is an image of the surgical suite where Dr. Wilkes and those nurses lost their lives yesterday morning. I am in the bottom left corner of the image, and Jeremy Porter appears as if he's about to push the button to make the transfer.

What can he possibly show me that I don't already know? Guave points behind me into the corner of the room. "Your security camera has been disabled, and so has the recording device Dr. Wilkes installed in the desk."

How did he know about Ivan Wilkes' recording device? I didn't even know about it.

He clicks "Play" on the video. It begins with Jeremy Porter unveiling a handgun and shooting the anesthesiologist in the head. As he turns on the nurses, Dr. Wilkes lifts his shirt and reaches into a holster in the small of his back, removing a handgun. In the video, I reach for his weapon, and wrest it from his hands.

My jaw drops. "That did not happen!"

"Shh, just watch." From the look of satisfaction on Guave's face, he is entertained by my reaction.

When Jeremy Porter has shot the nurses, he turns the weapon on Dr. Wilkes as I hold him by the scruff of his shirt with one hand and press his pistol into his abdomen with the other.

"Raymond, why are you betraying me?" Ivan squirms.

Blam!

Ivan Wilkes goes limp when Jeremy Porter's bullet pierces his forehead.

"Thank you, Dr. Verity," Dr. Porter is heard saying in the video.

"He never said that!"

In the video, I place Wilkes' weapon under my belt as the security guards begin to frisk Dr. Porter.

I turn to the attorney, shocked, frozen in disbelief. "That's an absolute lie! That's doctored footage. That did not happen!" I search his light brown eyes, and find no sympathy or vestige of conscience therein. "But you know that, don't you?"

He smiles warmly, as if I'd just offered him a compliment.

"You know it'll never hold up in a court of law . . . "

Guave crosses his arms over his chest. "With this footage, we don't need it to hold up under court of law. The President could hold you as a terrorist. No trial, no charges, no rights. You'd never see the light of day again."

I sneer at his threat, but my mind goes blank of sensible words to rebut him.

He takes a step away. "President Sayder has not seen this footage. If and when she does, do you think her friendship with you and her previous political alliance with you is going to mitigate the executive fury that she will level at you, just to save her political future?"

He knows about our secret political alliance to pass the law that bears my name. I shake my head, as if I misunderstood him. "What?"

He grins condescendingly. "Like all good Presidents, she surrounds herself with people who protect her from information that could be damaging to her. People like me, delegated to act in the best interests of the country, insulating her from the political and emotional consequences of difficult, heart-wrenching, yet absolutely necessary decisions."

Guave logs out of the website, and walks around to take a seat in the chair across from my desk. "Now, have I just sweetened the deal for you, or what?"

Friendless, without direction, without hope of ever accomplishing that which my conscience appears to demand, I find myself in a mental purgatory. How can I ever get out of this dilemma? With the stakes so high, the President's offer is the equivalent of a presidential pardon for a capital crime of which she accuses me, simultaneously merciful and cruel. How can I not consent? Who would not raise an arm to block the striking fist of a powerful assailant? Am I not expected to preserve my own life? I tried to do the right thing, but now it appears I must accept the inevitable. Forced to choose between being 49% responsible for the bloodguilt of the New Body Research Center—and a recipient of 49% of the immense wealth—or to be locked away in a maximum-security facility like a despised terrorist for the rest of my life for a crime I did not commit, what can I do?

"I accept the President's offer."

Guave Sealdor nods and clasps his hands. "Of course you do."

"Upon one condition."

He snarls at me bitterly, as if I do not have the right to amend the President's deal. "I'll have to take it up with the President, and I can make no promises."

"Drop all charges against my sister, and I'll consent." I cannot tell you how good it makes me feel to make a demand, however inconsequential, of this demon in human skin.

Guave Sealdor presses his lips together and nods. I know they must do it. With Ivan Wilkes dead and Redd Cranton publicly disgraced, they'll need my help to manage the transition and the predictable backlash of the public.

"I'll discuss it with the President."

25

MY BROTHER, THOMAS, IS KIND enough to come to Dr. Wilkes' funeral to offer me comfort. I wish I could tell him—anybody—about the doctored video footage. In the several days since the threat to extort me, I stayed up most nights, pacing the floor, looking for a way out of this trap. With Morgan's abandonment, I feel deserted, isolated, confined to a sequestered pit of self-loathing and self-pity. But Thomas would think me mad and the President's attorney insisted that strict secrecy was essential to keep me out of the Bureau's interrogation cells.

Thomas hugs me warmly. "Brother, I'm sorry."

The backslapping that characterizes the conclusion of his greeting embrace usually irritates me, but today I appreciate it. It's surprising he is kind to me, given the verbal thrashing I gave him the last time we spoke.

"I'm fine, Thomas." By his raised eyebrows, he knows I'm not. "I hope you can forgive me for speaking to you so cruelly."

He smiles at me and rests a hand on my shoulder. "Almost everyone who gets involved in politics for the right reason has an idealistic vision that is admirable, though impractical. It's time and patience that tempers the ideals and accomplishes long-term success."

I nod.

"Do you have a counselor you can trust? Maybe a grief counselor?"

I swallow hard. The last thing I want to do is cry in a room full of friends and family. I have to be strong.

"Ray, can we spend a few minutes together before I head home?"

"Maybe after the funeral."

Morgan stands in the back of the funeral home, holding Savannah's hand.

I walk several steps toward them and then pause in a cloud of perfume and flaunted tanned skin. It's been a long eight days since I laid eyes on Morgan, and I drink in her beauty. She drives me crazy, but beneath all that vanity and indiscretion is a woman I committed to love forever.

She and Savannah dab tissues in the corners of their eyes to absorb their tears. Their manufactured grief distracts me from more pleasurable thoughts. Their sadness—it's all manufactured. Savannah was not close enough to Ivan Wilkes to mourn his loss so. But was Morgan close to Ivan Wilkes? She might have partied with him and slept with him when I was a withered old man on ice, but in the days since my resurrection she obviously was not so close to Wilkes to grieve his passing so pitifully. They're probably faking their tears to elicit the sympathy of friends and neighbors—and mine. They are so much alike, always craving to be the center of attention.

I am so emotionally isolated right now, going to an empty home seems more excruciating than a home with my nag of a wife. With our distance, maybe she'll be warm up to me.

I make my way to Morgan. She turns away, but I pick up my pace and wrap my arms around her. "Morgan," I whisper into her ear, "please forgive me for being such a, such a . . . "

"Jerk!" Her tone is loud and harsh. She pulls away and, surprisingly, smiles broadly at me. By the glint in her eyes, that's all the punishment I've got coming. At least she forgives me.

I hug her again, giving her what she craves, groveling in her arms, letting her be the center of attention and the envy of the party. It's

better than being alone. "I'm sorry, Morgan. I do care about your opinion. I'm sorry for shutting you out."

"Just promise me you'll meet with Dr. Devonaire."

I groan my disapproval.

"Please?" She kisses me on the cheek. "I'll go with you."

Savannah lays a comforting arm over my shoulder.

I almost ask her how Mary Nell is doing, but that will provoke some
unresolved, ill feelings, and I don't want to do anything to upset either
of them. I need to strengthen Morgan's and Savannah's trust before I
dare to assert anything to them again.

A vaguely familiar effeminate man standing before a microphone
on a stand offers me the opportunity to say some words about my
departed colleague, Ivan Wilkes. I cannot bring myself to do it. In my
stead, Dr. Cranton heads to the microphone. He is not treated with the
respect I'm sure he feels like he has earned with the company, not after
the slander Jeremy Porter publicized about him. Morgan and Savannah
whisper their suspicion to one another as he begins to reminisce.

"It would be easy to speak of Dr. Wilkes' awards and Nobel prizes,
his degrees, both earned and honorary, his breakthroughs and the
unparalleled wealth that his hard work and visionary determination
amassed, but that is not the Dr. Wilkes that impacted me most. That is
not the Dr. Wilkes that elevated him to angelic heights in my mind. No.
I think of the time," Cranton thrusts out his chest with pride, "that Dr.
Wilkes and I presided over the passing of Raymond Verity." He motions
to me, and all eyes turn to me. Cranton's eyes glisten with nostalgia,
while my gut twists with some vague disapproval of all the attention.

"Did you know that Dr. Verity changed his mind at the last minute,
deciding that he didn't want to be preserved?" The room gasps, surprised

at my heretofore undisclosed weakness of mind. "It's true," he assures them in his charismatic fashion. "In the dimness of his final moments, he wanted to live, even if it was just a few moments longer, and even if it made his cryo-preservation and future resurrection impossible.

"Dr. Ivan Wilkes had the courage, and the love to make the tough call to honor Dr. Verity's original wishes. Dr. Verity had signed a contract that made the decision to cryo-preserve his body practically irreversible, even by him. A feebler friend would have given in to the unreasonable wishes of a cancer-ridden, delirious old friend in misery in a hospital bed, but not Ivan Wilkes. He knew what was best for his friend and colleague, he knew what needed to be done to bring him back, and he braved the criticism of lesser mortals and made the right call, as time has proven over and over again. Now, look what he has resurrected!" He points to me, and all eyes fasten on me again. "Look at the path he forged and the company he founded!"

There is a flurry of applause, but Redd calms it with a wave of his hand. He turns to look upon the stiff, makeup-dyed cheeks of Ivan Wilkes, spread out in his coffin, his bangs covering the hole in his forehead, and Redd raises his voice like a preacher, "As a famous man once said, 'Wisdom is justified of its children.' Dr. Ivan Wilkes, we who are your children, your friends, and your admirers, we applaud you."

He begins to clap, slowly and softly at first, and the whole room full of friends and family imitates his praise until there is a rigorous clamor of applause and hoots of praise.

I, however, cannot. I remain as stiff as a stone statue. Cranton's speech affected me, but not as it did the others in the room. The memory Cranton shared made me despise myself, even my own flesh. I am growing to hate myself.

Thomas' firm hand on my shoulder turns me toward the door. "Let's get outta here."

26

IN MY HOVER-LIMO ON THE way to the restaurant where we have made reservations, I begin to open up. "Guilt, Thomas. I feel guilt."

My eyes roam the streets of Baltimore's inner city outside the reflective window, but my brother keeps his eyes fixed on me. "We all feel guilt, Ray. It's in the nature of things."

"Not me. Not since I was a kid."

He reflects for a moment. "When did you stop feeling the guilt you felt as a kid?"

I lean my head back and look up at the raindrop-speckled window in the roof of the hover-limo. "When I was in high school. When I stopped going to church and started sleeping around."

Thomas nods. "When did you start feeling it again?"

"Acutely? On my deathbed."

Thomas nods sympathetically. "That would have been hard, yes, I can see that."

"Then I saw Tamara get arrested. Then my daughter's dupe in the Verity Wing was liquidated because of a head laceration." A lump wells up in my throat, but I swallow it away. "They were rolling her into a Medical Waste room, Thomas. They put her down over a cut ten stitches would have cured."

He squinted, a shroud of disbelief about him. "Because of a cut on her head?"

I nod. "That and a violation of a stupid policy against dupe emotions. All of this has very personal implications for my family. My daughter has a Down Syndrome daughter—"

"Mary Nell. I know her."

"Savannah's planning to replace Mary Nell with a cloned, genetically perfected replica."

"Replace her? What's going to happen to Mary Nell?"

"The highest bidder."

His face contorts in utter disapproval, but he keeps his criticism to himself.

"Pure gold for a research company. I tried to dissuade Savannah, but to no avail."

"Well, there's no reason to feel guilt for that. You tried."

I glance at him like he's an idiot. "She'll be dissected and divvied out to research contractors in my company, with the technology I pioneered." I tap my chest with my thumb. "I profit off it."

"But what can you do about it? Donate the profit to charity, or something."

I roll my eyes at his proposal. "Please tell me you're joking."

"Ray, why beat yourself up about something you can't change? Did you speak to Tamara?"

"I visited her in jail."

"She has a liking for that girl. Did you tell her what's going to happen to her?"

"I couldn't lie to her when she asked."

"I suppose your guilt trip got worse after that, didn't it?"

I chuckle. "You know it did."

He crosses his arms over his protuberant belly. "Just like those Personhood purists. They are good at preaching law and prophesying doom and judgment. They may go to jail and even die for the cause, but it's the pragmatists that actually accomplish something for the good. The abolitionists would rather die than get only 99% of what they want. Our sister has put you on a head-trip. I don't even read her letters anymore."

"She's got a good heart."

He harrumphs as if he disagrees. "She slams God's gavel harder than He does. If she was God, she'd have destroyed us all by now."

"I suppose you're right."

"Ray, you're the head of this company now. You can do something short of jail to right some wrongs, to improve the ethics of your company."

"You heard the news reports this morning, right?" He nods. "I'm not the head of this company. Not anymore. The President is taking control by executive order, until the stock price levels out in the proximity of last week's peak. Apparently, we're considered too big to fail."

"Even so, you are in a unique position to use your power to do some good for the clones, to help them, to protect them as much as the law allows. To affect the culture in a positive way."

I take a deep breath. "The Administration's attorney did give me the freedom to propose some modifications to the ethics rules and policies." I wince at Thomas' hopeful grin. "Aren't you against cloning, Thomas?"

He nods. "For religious reasons. But we have a separation of church and state. I'm glad we do. History shows that religious governments tend to be more godless than secular ones."

I squint my eyes at his apparent ignorance of history. "You cannot be that ignorant of the hundred million killed in communist massacres during the last century."

"I'm not a purist, Ray," he continues, changing the topic. "Ideals are like the Ten Commandments. We aim for it, but nobody reaches it. That's why we all need grace. Ideals like the right to life and liberty are the target for which we are aiming, but what society reaches it perfectly? We're all sinners, Ray. Just do the best you can, accept grace for your failures, and stop feeling guilty about what you can't do. Jesus bore my guilt, so I don't have to. It is inevitable that circumstances transpire requiring a pragmatic approach to bring about improvements for the better. My actions may violate the letter of the law, but not the spirit, because my motive, my end game, is always the ideal, knowing we may never reach it until heaven."

Impressive rhetoric. He's definitely matured since the days when Dad used to severely scold him in front of us just because he couldn't talk fast enough.

"What's your organization's position on New Body science?"

"You mean Iowans Supporting Life?" I nod. "Compassionate care for all parties involved. We don't judge, but we don't want to see clones terminated for cuts on their forehead either. We supported your law because it regulated clone termination compassionately, requiring multiple physicians to confirm that it was necessary, kept it privately funded and not funded by the taxpayers, and ensured that processing and transference was painless. We would like to see the donor notified that their clone meets the scientific criteria for life before obtaining their consent for transference or processing. But that's a battle for another day."

I'm aghast at the crumbs that appear to please them. "So, let the donor know that they're killing someone, and then they can kill them? That's pro-life?"

His lips turn down at my underhanded mockery. "Let's not do this again, Ray . . . "

My limo driver keeps looking back into the rearview mirror. Curious, I turn my head to see what has piqued his interest behind us. "See something, Jim?"

"Possibly."

"What?"

He doesn't answer. "We may have a tail."

Thomas looks through the rear window. "A tail?"

"Glass is bulletproof." I turn to Thomas. "You were saying?"

"Legislation like this saves lives, Ray. Clones are people and all people deserve the right to life. But we accept that it will never happen, so we try to regulate the inevitable for the better. We're mechanics, not philosophers, and we've got to get our head out of the clouds and get our hands dirty to fix this. The culture's not ready for a ban on terminating clones. It would bankrupt the politically and culturally popular industry. The culture, like a big ship, turns slowly. Sometimes we simply must accept that the best we can do is just slow down the unavoidable slide of moral degeneracy."

"Slow it down, by being an accomplice?"

"No. Not an accomplice. Go no further than the left's well-publicized hatred of us to see whose side we're on."

I smile at his ability to calmly articulate his beliefs. I even feel a hint of pride on how my brother has risen to leadership in the pro-life community. "I'm sorry I've been so critical. I'm just sorting things out in my own head."

"Brother, if you expect perfection of yourself, you have a bloated view of your own abilities. We all sin. Jesus obeyed so you don't have to. Do penance and be at peace with the good you can accomplish."

His counsel fills me with a renewed determination to intervene in the treatment of clones. I'm expecting too much of myself.

"Tell you what," he continues. "I'm allocated some time as director of Iowans Supporting Life that allows me to meet with policy makers to make changes for the better. Can I come and help you for a month?"

"You mean, help with my ethics policy recommendations?"

"Yes."

A burden begins to lift off my shoulders. "Ah, I would love that."

My driver drops us off at the front entrance of a classy Italian restaurant downtown. Jim opens the limo door and, when I step out, he murmurs, "Sir, may I have a moment?"

"Sure, Jim."

Jim rests his arms against the top of the open door, leans close, and whispers, "The past couple of days, we've had a black town car following us."

I look back. A car parks by the road behind us. The windows are reflective, and I cannot see how many people are inside. "Are you sure?"

"I spent my last two years in the Corps as a personal bodyguard to a high-ranking intel officer. I'm pretty confident in my ability to discern these things. Do you want me to do anything about it?"

I sigh. It must be government agents assigned to watch me. Just a few days ago I, one of the most influential and powerful men in the nation, was trying to bring down one of the most profitable companies in the nation, a company personally favored by the President. They don't trust me.

"Come with me." I start walking away from the restaurant toward the black sedan, with my burly limo driver right behind me. He unbuttons his jacket in case he has to reach for his concealed handgun.

I motion to the occupants of the town car to roll down their window so I can speak to them. "Hey! Come on in and eat with us!"

When I get within two feet, they drive off.

"I got it." Jim turns to me.

"Got what?"

"The tag number."

When we walk back toward the restaurant, Thomas gestures, "Do you have some enemies?"

I chuckle at his choice of words. "You have no idea."

He rests a hand on my shoulder. "You're in good company."

Jim opens the driver-side door. "I'll check it out and pick you up in an hour and a half."

"Perfect." He turns to leave. "Wait, on second thought, feel free to not be on time. I'm sick of perfect."

27

MY WIFE'S NEURO-PSYCHIATRIST, DR. DEVONAIRE, has more degrees than a compass. The wall of her luxurious waiting room is covered with the frames. Morgan has stacked the deck against me, conspiring to have Thomas present to help the graceful and intelligent Harvard-trained neuro-psych try to flatten the scruples that punctuate our strained discourse. Although Thomas has changed and doesn't appear to be the pushover he used to be, I doubt he has the courage to take my side in any contention with Morgan and her ivory tower psych-quack. Morgan may have buttered him up to her view of things already, recruiting him to induce change in me.

My first five minutes with Dr. Devonaire tells me a lot about her. First, I'm not even sure it's a *her*. She has a well-crafted balance of both masculine and feminine features, flaunting a pompous pink-and-black metrosexual fashion that fudges the ordinarily broad line between gothic and gala. I can't describe her as handsome or lovely—she's an unnatural mixture of both. When I catch a glimpse of her pointy elf-like ears through the tufts of her golden curls, my heart sinks. This is going to be a difficult hour, I fear.

The love seat in which she comfortably reclines across from me is crisscrossed with cursive splatters of every hue of pastel seen throughout the meticulously designed office. The pastels suggest innocence and openness, more like a nursery than a psychiatrist's office. A thin wisp of smoke on a corner table is the source of the scent of some kind of calming incense.

She has a naturally seductive tone, like a highly compensated European-accented voice at an upper-end Las Vegas strip club. The accent is invitingly surreal and as pleasant as her vocabulary is broad. Is her voice natural, or has she modified it in some way through vocal training or surgery? By the way her voice dances like gently flowing water over rocks, I imagine her teaching a Yoga class in her spare time.

The chatting abruptly ends when Dr. Devonaire implies that if I appreciate my new body, then it is hypocritical for me to criticize others for what I do. That's similar to what Thomas said to me during our contentious phone conversation, and he nods with her counsel, concurring. The psychiatrist has engaged my conscience, and tilted the majority in her favor right at the onset. Yep, she and Morgan have definitely prepped for this encounter.

Unable to refute her point, I appeal to a metaphor that they will find offensive, but is accurate nonetheless. "I appreciate my new body," I alternate flexing and extending my fingers, "as much as a Nazi would appreciate a lampshade made from Jew hide."

Morgan gasps, and Dr. Devonaire sighs heavily, appearing to accept that this conversation will be inescapably volatile.

"I appreciate all of the wealth and perks I have legally accumulated over the decades, like Dr. Cranton, like our body-marketing counterparts in Germany's National Socialist Party, but that doesn't mean I have to continue to perpetuate the gross inhumane injustice associated with it."

Thomas' countenance exudes disappointment, as if I dared to articulate something he boasted that he had successfully convinced me not to believe anymore. At the mention of Redd Cranton, Morgan looks confused, like she cannot comprehend the comparison.

"Is this you talking, or your sister?" Dr. Devonaire sits upright in her love seat, wrapping her hands around her knees. Morgan affirms the question with an aggressive nod, as if she knew that Devonaire's attempt to set me at odds with who she suspects to be a moral authority in my life is the next strategy to disarm me and leave me malleable like putty, like a rudderless yacht susceptible to their hot air in my sails.

Morgan leans forward to make eye contact with me. "You know her organization almost killed you when they bombed the television studio. How can you defend her?"

"Tamara provided evidence that the suspect had long been kicked out of her organization for encouraging violence."

"And you believe her?" Devonaire sneers. She fixes her gaze on Morgan. "Does he believe her?"

Morgan puffs out her cheeks and her limbs grow restless. My pulse pounds in my temples as my suspicion of their conspiracy to gang up on me increases.

"Dr. Devonaire, do you know the President released her from custody just this morning? Isn't that sufficient proof for you that she is innocent of any crimes?"

"It was a technicality, as I understand it," Dr. Devonaire leans back in her plush seat and puts an arm over the side. "I'm not denying she's a good person deep down inside, and I think your disposition to respect your sister and believe the best is admirable. But I would withhold from vigorously defending her, especially publicly, for fear that you may be wrong and it may mar your reputation if it turns out she was conning you all along. She has said some very radical things, I'm sure you will agree."

The psychological effect of Dr. Devonaire's demeanor and seamless fluctuating gestures is fascinating, always calculated to condescend to me, yet intermittently settle my frustrated tone and relax my naturally defensive response to her interrogation.

"You said you have been trying to sort out the science and ethics on your own ever since you came out of cryo-preservation."

"That's true," Thomas affirms.

Dr. Devonaire gestures to Thomas. "Why don't you solicit the help of those pro-life and pro-family leaders you respect, like your brother?"

So that's why they conspired to have him present. They want to distance me from my sister and link me more tightly to my brother.

"I am soliciting his help." I nod at Thomas.

"Why don't you trust him to help you navigate the ethical landscape? And your wife?" She winks at Morgan, who casts a seductive smile back at her. "She knows you better than anybody. Plus,"—Dr. Devonaire grins mischievously—"she's hot."

"Why thank you, Dr. Devvy." Morgan bashes her eyelashes at her.

"Being Morgan's partner makes you the envy of the known world. Don't you trust her as your confidante and partner in life, Raymond?"

I can't believe it. She's hitting on Morgan right in front of me, and Morgan's loving it. They both turn to me, awaiting my answer. Morgan sees that if I answer, I will answer honestly and embarrass her with an emphatic *No*, so she speaks up before I can respond.

"We only want what's best for you, sweetheart."

"And Mary Nell?" I lean forward.

Dr. Devonaire sighs and looks away. Thomas shrugs and glances at Morgan.

"Do you want what's best for Mary Nell?"

Morgan clears her throat, licks her lips, and turns to face Dr. Devonaire, as if she is either unwilling or unable to handle this issue I've raised and is punting this topic to her.

I am disinclined to allow Morgan to squirm out from under this burden. "The researchers with whom we contract are going to experiment on her, put needles in her veins and arteries, extract her bone marrow, put tubes in her orifices—"

"Please!" Morgan objects.

"And then market her body parts out to the highest bidders, making Auschwitz's butcher Dr. Mengele look gentle and loving by comparison."

"Raymond!" Thomas' piercing voice snatches my breath away. "Such hyper-emotional words do not produce meaningful conversation."

"Butcher is an accurate term," I respond calmly, "with one exception. They kill the cows and pigs before they butcher them for the market. Mary Nell will be afforded no such luxury, lest the sedation minimize the profitability of the tissue. She will be experimented upon, exploited, Cranton-ized—and all of it's legal."

Morgan opens her mouth to upbraid me, but Devonaire speaks up first.

"Thanks to *your* law." Devonaire keeps her voice steady. "Don't you think it's hypocritical to oppose what people do when they are in compliance with a law you so adamantly defended just a month ago?"

"I was wrong." I shrug. "Dead wrong."

"It's Savannah's choice," Morgan blurts out, "being Mary Nell's lawful mother and legal caregiver. You used to respect personal choice."

"Caregivers have no right to consent to the exploitation and killing of those people under their care, Morgan! No right! What about Mary Nell's choice?"

"Unfortunately, it's legal." Thomas speaks as if his conclusion is irrefutable. "We've got to work within our system of laws."

"You mean lawlessness," I respond.

"What?" Thomas furrows his brow.

"Throughout history, many evils have been legalized, from slavery to genocide to sexism. But that doesn't make those evils less wrong."

"Brother, we've been through this. You have to work within the system to make positive change."

Thomas is interrupted with a wave of Dr. Devonaire's hand, as if she were the puppet master and they her obedient wooden toys. "We have been conversing for just sixteen minutes, and we've only briefly touched on at least a half a dozen topics that we could never conclude in our hour together. So out of respect for your valuable time, may I request that we focus on one very critical presupposition you unconsciously make?"

I take a deep breath and nod.

"You are a scientist, Dr. Raymond Verity—one of the best."

"That's true," Morgan responds for me, stretching a hand onto my thigh and patting me lovingly.

"Celebrated," Thomas adds.

Normally, such flattery would calm my racing heart and dry my sweaty palms but, in anticipation that they are simply holding me steady for a knock-out punch, I stay on the edge of my seat, apprehensive and irritated.

"As such, you are committed to the scientific method as a means of obtaining facts, of discriminating between truth and error in nature." Dr. Devonaire's tone is as graceful as it is conniving.

I nod. Where is she going with this line of reasoning?

"Throughout our discourse, you have continually referred to metaphysical myths such as evil, right and wrong."

I clear my throat. "Is love a myth, Dr. Devonaire?"

She smiles and leans closer to me. "A wonderful, amazing, profoundly enjoyable myth. A story, a feeling, an opinion—not a fact and certainly not objective evidence. Let us help you distinguish between what is factual and what is whimsical and fleeting, and you will be the better scientist for it."

I find myself unable to instinctively object to this line of reasoning, so I listen intently.

"How would you even perform an experiment to determine right from wrong, Dr. Verity? Would your conclusion be dependent upon your feelings, or the feelings of the consensus, or an archaic book of Scripture? Would that be a good experiment?"

I look down at my hands. "No."

"Why not?"

"Science looks at facts. Verifiable, documentable facts to support or refute a hypothesis."

"Facts are verifiable through our senses, our five senses with which evolution has equipped us. Feelings are not facts. Facts are reliable, but feelings about love and morality and justice are notoriously unreliable. Feelings fluctuate with our upbringing and culture, and sprout from humanity's desire for purpose and belonging. Subjective feelings may prompt us to hunger for understanding of the mysteries of nature before reliance on the scientific method can produce more accurate data. Myths and unfalsifiable beliefs are useful, but like children's stories are useful—to teach important lessons about life and help us discover our personal preferences about what makes us happy. You can believe the universe is a dream of the Hindu god Brahma, or that Jehovah created the universe in six days. Equally implausible scientifi- cally, but your personal choice nonetheless . . . "

Thomas chuckles condescendingly. I fully expect him to be disin- clined to appreciate Dr. Devonaire's shrewd refutation of the reliability of spiritual truths, because he claims to believe the Bible, but I remem- ber he is a theistic evolutionist. He mocks the literal interpretation of the Genesis record. "Do not mistake unverifiable, unscientific myths to be facts, Ray."

"Morality is more like your favorite flavor of ice cream than it is like a measurable law of gravity," Devonaire continues, "so let us not be so quick to judge those who prefer a different flavor. If you would personally prefer to care for a genetically defective child than to ex- change her for a genetically perfected, mentally superior clone, that's your preference, but don't you dare put that yoke on anybody else as is the custom with bigots, homophobes, jihadists, and sign-wielding Personhood fanatics."

She smiles contentedly, giving me a moment to process her brilliant argument. Her false dilemma between science and morality is designed to set me squarely on the side opposite of those she has demeaned with her straw man argument.

My silence has her basking in the admiring gazes of Thomas and Morgan. Morgan sighs lustfully, as if she was experiencing sensual plea- sure out of seeing her psycho-quack in action, intellectually spanking her incorrigible husband. Thomas bites his fingernails nervously, as if he doubts the doctor's presuppositions but hopes it is useful nonetheless in calming my deleterious scruples.

Her mention of Personhood fanatics makes me think about my sister. How would she answer this challenge? I smirk, recalling a similar conversation I had with her in my younger years. "Is the scientific method reliable, Dr. Devonaire?"

Dr. Devonaire nods and responds in a smooth, seductive tone. "Of course, Dr. Verity. You know my answer to that."

"Can the scientific method prove the scientific method reliable?"

She opens her mouth to speak, but halts. "Well, uh . . . "

She stops again, appearing to be holding her breath.

Now, I'm the one smiling contentedly. "If the scientific method is necessary to prove something reliable, then the scientific method is itself unreliable. For to use the scientific method to prove the scientific method would be circular reasoning and, therefore, a logical fallacy. See, even the scientific method relies on presuppositions that the scientific method cannot prove, like the immorality of falsifying data. Can the scientific method prove that falsifying data is wrong?"

Dr. Devonaire stands up and makes her way behind her desk.

"You say only what is sensed with the five senses is a verifiable fact, but which of your five senses told you that?" Again, silence. "If your theory that only what is sensed with the five senses is factual and reliable, then it does not meet its own criteria for reliability, for your theory cannot be sensed with any of the five senses."

"So now you're a believer in God?" Morgan throws her hands up.

So predictable. An *ad hominem* logical fallacy to detract from the bankruptcy of their circular claims. It's not Morgan's fault. I taught her how to do that. I'm the expert at smoke and mirrors to keep from facing the truth.

I close my eyes and lower my head. "I don't know what I believe, Morgan, but I certainly don't believe that random chance multiplied by time can result in all, all"—I wave my hands over my head—"all this!" I grab my chest with both hands. "Or this. That's the greatest leap of faith of all, and contradictory to everything we see in the realm of science." I turn to Dr. Devonaire, who is typing on her computer. "Science is observation. Has any man in the history of the world ever recorded the observation of life coming into existence from non-life?"

She purses her lips, continuing to type what I suspect is her summary of our meeting. I have a feeling she's going to simply relegate me to her heap of non-compliant egomaniacs. "All right, Dr. Verity. You can have your magic genie, but don't expect me to call it normal or healthy."

I smirk at her condescension, and decide to turn the tables on her. "You're the one with the magic genie."

"Oh, really?" She leans back in her wicker chair, her jaw agape, as if she is aghast at my arrogance.

"You believe all of life came into existence from unintelligent non-life, something neither you nor anyone else has ever observed. And science is observation, remember? Now, Dr. Devonaire, what's the greater miracle? Life coming from life—something observable every day? Or life coming from non-life? You make a much greater leap of faith than six-day creationists—blind faith at that."

"So, you're just going to throw everything away to try to save your precious clones? All for your newfound love of the Creator?" Morgan's tone is shrill, louder than necessary, almost painful to my ear. The rising wave of her unpredictable emotional tsunami threatens to transform this enjoyable clash of intellects into a cause for personal offense.

"I didn't say that, Morgan. But morality is not like a graying, wrinkled body that you can just throw away when another one suits you better. Objective morality is a presupposition we all make,"—I glance at Dr. Devonaire—"*before* we perform an experiment,"—I look at Thomas—"before we make ethics suggestions to a presidential panel on the New Body science,"—then my eyes fasten on Morgan's—"before we decide whether we should butcher our grandchild so as not to be inconvenienced with her handicap. It's hypocritical not to acknowledge that even the scientific method is only as reliable as it is objectively and inescapably religious."

An eerie stillness descends upon us. With Dr. Devonaire's intellect disarmed, everyone is inclined more to listen than to offer advice. As she turns her eyes and her fingers to her computer, I fetch her attention with a direct personal question. "Do you fear death, Dr. Devonaire?"

She lifts her eyes from her computer screen with an uncomfortable flinch, as if I'd just poked her in the forehead with a toothpick. "Well, no. I don't want to die. That would not be a psychologically healthy emotion."

She glances at Morgan, and I think I see a glint of anxiety in her eyes, like she's worried that the conclusion of the conversation would disappoint the one paying the bill. My question was not in their script.

Perhaps Dr. Devonaire is fearful of me, wondering if my words are intended to preface the unholstering of a weapon or some other threatening act. I should calm her nerves, but decide to let the fear remain, as it is useful to drive my point home.

"Three times, Dr. Devonaire,"—I raise three fingers—"I have looked death in the eye. I had wealth beyond my wildest dreams, fame and power, the most beautiful wife a man could ever hope for. But when faced with what I thought were my last breaths, my last thoughts, I would have traded it all for one thing. You cannot put it in a test tube and compare it to a placebo in a double-blinded study, but I would have sacrificed everything for just one thing."

I let those words hang out there for a moment.

"What?" she finally asks.

"Forgiveness."

At those words, she concludes the appointment prematurely, hardly directing another word at me, but speaking to Morgan instead, like I'm not even in the room.

Dr. Devonaire kindly gives me a book by an atheist professor, *Finding Godlessness at Harvard*, with the request that I read it before next month's appointment. I insist on knowing what diagnosis she is inscribing into my medical record, and she reluctantly consents. My stubborn scruples and delusions of guilt were relegated to a phenomenon associated with my microvascular ischemic brain disease and a serotonin deficiency, as well as post-traumatic stress disorder related to my brushes with death.

Her diagnosis is laughable. "I don't have a serotonin deficiency," I insist, "and I'm not post-traumatic."

"Being in denial of it does not bode well for your therapy, Dr. Verity. Remember, your brain is 96 years old." She stares at me as if I'm a stubborn psychotic patient who thinks his pills are space saucers from Mars.

"Can you prove that my serotonin is deficient?"

She smirks at me. "If you'll take the SSRI, you'll feel better."

"Not a chance. Not risking the E.D."

"Not with these fourth generation SSRIs, Raymond. Morgan will be more appreciative of the improvement in your sense of happiness and well-being than anybody. That'll be proof enough that you need the med."

"Then we all need placebos, because they improve our sense of well-being better than anything."

"But—"

"If you give it to anyone they'll get a boost in their sense of well-being. That proves nothing." I pause and absorb her critical glare—and Morgan's. I lean toward Thomas and quip out of the corner of my mouth, "No category of western medicine is more like voodoo than psychiatry."

Dr. Devonaire snarls at my witty insult.

"If you don't do what she says, I promise you, you will regret it." There is utter disgust in Morgan's tone as she upbraids me.

"I'll double my L-methyl folate, which as you know, Dr. Devonaire, is a readily absorbable serotonin precursor, but there's no way I'm following any of your unscientific medical advice unless you can prove to me that my serotonin or norepi levels are low."

My intentionally rude words appear to offend my wife more than they do the neuro-psychiatrist.

"I can schedule a brain biopsy to prove it," Devonaire sneers.

"Very funny," Morgan snarls. "You wouldn't." It's her first favorable disposition toward me during the meeting, and I'm flattered.

"She's trying to intimidate me, Morgan. She knows a biopsy wouldn't discover what the physiological serotonin would be intra-synapse."

"All right, Dr. Verity," Devonaire snaps, as if it is anything but. "You know I can't prove it in a way that you will accept. Let's try your remedy first, as it is an acceptable first line option." She also recommends increasing some of my daily supplements for cerebral health. The notion that a chemical imbalance and the hardened capillaries in my brain have somehow negatively affected my reasoning faculties is downright laughable. Nevertheless, on the ride home I can clearly tell that Thomas and Morgan have a heretofore undiscovered respect for my opinion.

Inwardly, I'm more distraught by my statements than they are, because if I'm right, then I'm in big trouble with God.

28

THE ADMINISTRATION'S CHIEF ATTORNEY, THE brilliant clone
Guave Sealdor, informs me that the President has given me the authority to create my own panel to develop ethics recommendations
for submission to her for consideration. Since I know no one on the
front lines of the pro-life battle and do not consider myself an expert
on the matter at all, I happily delegate this duty to my brother Thomas.

My first committee meeting with him and his hand-picked team of
religious conservatives and pro-family leaders is refreshing. Everybody
seems excited to be in the same room with me, savoring my opinions
and my experiences, enthusiastic about the opportunity to positively
affect the ethics of New Body science and save lives. For the first time
since my resurrection, I feel like I'm in charge of something positive.
Thanks to Thomas' personal counseling and spiritual guidance, my
insatiable feelings of guilt and regret have been replaced with a sense
of divinely orchestrated purpose.

I uphold no false pretenses with these political and religious leaders,
freely telling them of my experiences facing the impending recycling
of Savannah's clone, the difficulties working with Dr. Cranton after
the publicizing of his sexual exploitation of dupes, and the realization that my loving, Down Syndrome granddaughter was going to
be killed for the benefit and convenience of her loved ones. For the
first hour of our two-hour meeting, I do most of the talking, gaining
the empathy and respect from everyone in the room. They hail me

as a William Wilberforce, a Norma McCorvey, a Bernard Nathanson, an Abby Johnson—a leader akin to the converted Saul of Tarsus, a God-ordained spearhead to win hearts, change minds, and ultimately transform the culture toward respect for life.

The meeting continues with a unanimous insistence that they issue a formal condemnation of the Personhood movement, which has been the predominant force behind Alabama's and Mississippi's defiance of the federal judiciary in their arrest and attempted prosecution of those accused of terminating clones. What Alabama and Mississippi are doing, everyone agrees, will ultimately hurt the pro-life movement and cripple our ability to save lives. Those fringe fanatics are more like the John Browns of the abolitionist movement who do more harm than good, and we are the heroic pragmatists like Wilberforce who actually accomplish something meaningful.

During the rest of the meeting, the leaders banter back and forth on what should be the primary focus of our committee. To me, a newcomer to this side of the line in the sand, it's simple: protect the unprotected. However, these men and women have spilled sweat and blood in these trenches, and their comments make me feel naïve.

After much discussion, it becomes clear that the judiciary is the highest hurdle for this movement. Almost all of the meaningful legislation that has curtailed the exploitation of some by others—whether dealing with abortion, physician-assisted suicide, or the abuse and exploitation of clones—a federal judge has, with the stroke of a pen, overcome their meticulously-developed democratic consensus, nullified their protective laws, and sent them, discouraged, back to the starting line.

A consensus develops that the only kind of recommendation that is likely to pass the muster of the President and her team of attorneys is the same kind of restriction that has survived the judicial gauntlet in the past. Everyone settles on informed consent as a recommendation that should carefully be developed to submit to the President.

Informed consent. That's the battle line upon which they want to fight.

I don't want to act like an idiot asking a question of which everyone in the room appears to already know the answer, but I refuse to raise my hand for a vote, and Thomas notices.

Thomas is apologetic. "I'm sorry, Ray, uh, I'm sorry, Dr. Verity . . . "

"Just call me Ray."

"I'm sorry. We've probably been talking over your head . . . "

"No, you haven't," I interrupt with a wave of my hand. "I do understand the issues better, and I thank you, but I want you to define what you mean by informed consent. Typically, in medicine, we define informed consent as the patient having sufficient understanding of the risk and benefits of a medicine or procedure in order to responsibly agree to the prescribed therapy."

Thomas shakes his head back and forth. "This is a modification of that kind of informed consent. Our aim would be to get owners of the genome to have sufficient understanding of the humanity and viability of their clone. They should know that the clone's heart is beating and their brain waves are measurable before they consent to, to—"

"To what?" I interrupt. "To suck the brains out of their skulls? To rape them? To cut them up and exploit their cells and body parts for profit? Are you kidding me?"

The room erupts with murmuring and frantic fidgeting. I have hit a nerve.

"Help me out here," I look around the room. "Please, explain how consenting to a violent evil against an innocent person is mitigated at all by being adequately informed? My daughter has given fully informed consent to the death and exploitation of my granddaughter, and the policies you are proposing would permit it. How can we ever consent to such a, such a, such a horrible crime?"

The attendees begin to talk over each other.

"We've got to work within the law . . . "

"We can save lives with this recommendation . . . "

"At least this may actually be implemented. Better to succeed in a lesser battle than to lose in promoting a dreamy ideal."

"We *do* want to protect every clone!" Thomas transcends the dozen comments thrown at me all at once with his sheer volume. "We do, Raymond! But we have to be strategic and incremental, or we're just going to be a John the Baptist in the wilderness, and then ultimately in the dungeon. Or a Maurice Whetley, fighting a battle that can only result in a token defeat, wasting immense opportunities on behalf of a sincere but hopeless ideal. If you want to sit at the table with the President and make meaningful recommendations that save lives, you have to be realistic and work within the system."

This is my introduction to pro-life political action. If I want to sit at the table of power, I have to sacrifice ideals and promote policies and legislation that I consider immoral. Principle, be damned—for the sake of principle, of course. Facilitate the killing, because that is the cost of successfully introducing more compassionate means of killing.

This is how we promote the respect for life in the culture? By staining our hands with bloodguilt?

29

ON MY WAY INTO WORK after a sleepless night, I'm perusing the emails Mrs. Williamson, my new personal secretary, has thought worth my attention. It's her memo, however, that has captivated me:

"As always, I'm removing all the messages that include threats against your life and property. But you should be aware you are now receiving dozens a day, half of them from leftists furious about your attempt to restrict the New Body science, but half from anti-cloning extremists. I have forwarded them to the FBI as you requested."

I don't recall making such a request, but I'm glad she forwarded them nonetheless.

I shouldn't be surprised at threats to my life, but kept relatively insulated from my gigabytes of email, I am usually comfortably unaware of these threats. It's hard to believe there are those who hate me so much that they consider it worth the risk to send me a message threatening to kill me—or worse. Reminders like Mrs. Williamson's memo reinvigorate the familiar fear that so horrified me when I was dying in that hospital bed, or looking down the barrel of Jeremy Porter's pistol, or seeing Dr. Cranton's mouth move but hearing no words when I was stroking out. It's in moments like this that I wish I was not alone. I wish Thomas was here to comfort me with the promise of forgiveness and the hope of heaven.

Jim, my limo driver, keeps looking in his rearview mirror. I set my coffee mug down in the cup holder and look back through the rear window to see what keeps drawing his attention away from the road.

I tap the button to speak to him. "Jim, is that the same black town car that was following us last week?"

"Yes, sir, it is. Two occupants."

I squint to try to make out the two figures in the vehicle, but I cannot see through the mirrored windows. "How can you see them?"

Jim taps his sunglasses. "They block UV light. Nice for fishing, too."

"Did you figure out who they were from the tag?"

He shrugs. "It was a dead end. As far as I could tell, the tag doesn't exist. It's not a government-issued tag and it's not a civilian tag."

"Criminals? Or government?"

"Both, probably. I'm actually quite mystified by it. It's against state law to create a tag that doesn't exist. It's also against FBI policy to use a false vehicle tag in the line of business."

"There are many government agencies besides the FBI."

"But why would they be following you? They can legally put GPS tracking and listening devices in this hover-limo, in your home, in the very jacket you're wearing. They can see your heat image through the roof of this limo from a satellite in orbit. Why would they waste time and resources having two agents follow you around?"

"The capacity of the federal government to waste the taxpayers' funds is certainly not new."

He nods. "I haven't put all the pieces of this puzzle together, but something unusual is definitely afoot."

"My secretary just notified me that the threats against my life are at an all-time high."

He snickers. "Congratulations."

"Thank you."

"You're as safe as you can be, Dr. Verity."

"For a man who's been so adamantly opposed to firearms his whole life, I never thought I'd be so appreciative of being protected by one."

"My greatest concern right now is that my weapons may not be able to give you the help you need the most."

"What do you mean?"

"A trained federal agent could have you killed and leave no trace of evidence that you died of anything but natural causes. They could poison you and make it look like a heart attack. They could gas you to unconsciousness and then slit your wrists to make it look like suicide, complete with a suicide note in your handwriting. A radiated noodle in your lunch or biological-warfare-agent-embedded multi-vitamin tablet could kill you within a few days, and no civilian physician would ever be able to figure out what happened to you."

After a pause, I say, "Well, that's unnerving."

He sighs noisily. "Yes, it is. Maybe they just want you to know that you're being followed."

I roll down the window, stick my half-filled mug of coffee out and give the liquid a toss into the air. I look back. "Bull's-eye."

Jim laughs. "You did not do what I think you just did."

"Ah, Jim, sometimes you've just got to grow down."

I turn around to watch the black Lincoln's windshield wipers try to clean off the coffee. The driver increases his distance behind us.

When I arrive at my office, I feel like a hypocrite logging in my hours, powerless to do anything because the federal government's team of bureaucrats is managing the business. I feel worthless going through the slow, tedious process of arguing legalese at weekly meetings with pro-life leaders exalting informed consent measures as the best recommendation worthy of our historic effort. But every time I see an unfamiliar employee roaming the halls, and feel my pulse quicken in my temples, I realize my fear of persecution for my hypocritical, worthless measures almost adequately compensates me for the stab of my hard-to-please conscience. Almost.

At the end of the day, Jim and I are speculating once again about the black town car that follows us. Jim turns off the interstate and the sedan follows closer around the off-ramp.

"Man," Jim complains, glancing in the rearview. "Back off, already."

"Got any soda or coffee in your cup up there?" I ask, looking back. "Something sticky?"

Before Jim can answer, a flash shines through the grate in the radiator of the sedan, coinciding with an audible "pop" in the rear of my limo. One of the four hover-engines has blown and the limo swerves to the right side of the road.

"Hold on!" Although Jim is driving a safe speed, losing an engine on the sharp turn causes him to lose control and take the limo over the small shoulder of dirt beside the road. I am buckled in, but the base of the hover-limo colliding with the dirt at 25 miles per hour causes me to lurch toward the roof. My head bumps the ceiling. I wrap my arms around my head to try to protect myself from injury. Jim manages to keep the vehicle from flipping down the steep embankment, and he brings the limo to a halt before it drifts over the drainage pond.

Jim unbuckles and tries to exit, but his door has jammed. He reaches across the front seat to try to open the front passenger door as I look back to see two men with ski-masks crest the hill and come running toward us, holding handguns with long barrels, which I assume are silencers.

"Jim!" I point. He opens the passenger door but before he crawls out, he reaches behind his back and brings his handgun up to aim at the oncoming assailants through the rear window.

"Duck!" he shouts.

"It's bulletproof."

"Not from the inside."

A sharp, raspy gunshot—Blam!—precedes the shattering of what I thought was bulletproof glass. Jim never got to pull the trigger.

"Jim!" He has taken one bullet in the chest and falls out of the open passenger door onto the wet ground, his body shaking.

I scramble to open the door, and step out to face my attackers. We are in a recess in the landscape. This location has obviously been carefully chosen to conceal this event from the eyes of passers-by. With the limo to my right, the muddy retention pond to my back, and a steep hill to my left, there's nowhere to run and nothing I can do but die bravely.

I straighten my back and stretch out my hands toward the two masked men. They wear black clothes and wool facemasks, so I fix my gaze on the white of the eyes of the nearest assailant. "You won't get away with this."

My lips speak the words, but in my mind I hear my sister Tamara speaking those words across the bulletproof glass of her prison.

The first man to reach me chuckles at my admonishment, raises his handgun to me, and my heart squeezes painfully. I can't believe this is happening again. The same nauseating fear seems to possess every cell of my body and consume every nerve cell in my brain. I close my eyes and try to imagine what will happen to me in the next few moments.

I swallow hard, and hear two gun blasts, but feel no projectile penetrate my body. The sound of the blasts knocks me on my heels, and I stumble two steps backward. I am ankle-deep in muddy brown water when my two masked assailants fall to the ground, face first. The mud in which I stand is speckled with maroon-colored drops of warm blood.

Stunned, I look up the hill to see silhouettes of four men crest the orange-yellow sunset back-dropped horizon, rushing toward me. "Dr. Verity!"

My mouth is dry, but my palms are as wet with sweat as my feet are with rainwater runoff. They reach me and a man wearing a black cap with bold "FBI" white letters on it steps into the water beside me. He puts his arm under my shoulders to guide me out of the mud. "Dr. Verity? Have you been shot?"

"No, no. I'm fine, I, I think." They set me down beside the two corpses, who bleed out on the dirt beside me. I fix my eyes on Jim's pale lips and gaping mouth. His eyes are open slightly. "Is he dead?"

A second agent checks Jim's carotid artery. "Yes. It was quick."

The agent who helped me out of the mud takes a knee beside me. "You're in shock. Everything's going to be fine."

"Who are you? Who were these men?"

"We're agents assigned to protect you from the flood of threats aimed at you. I don't know who these men were, but we will soon."

With night falling fast, two agents help me up the hill and offer to give me a ride home, while the others commence an investigation beside the limo. I stand in front of the black sedan by the road, the one my attackers drove, as a pretty female agent interviews me, holding a recorder. I duck to look through the radiator grate where I saw the flash, and see two thick black barrels aiming forward.

"We saw that. Please, give me your undivided attention for just a few minutes, Doctor."

I walk to the rear of the town car to examine the license plate. It's an Alabama license tag. "Alabama?"

"So?" She follows me with her hand-held recorder.

"This is not the same vehicle with the tag Jim searched for me."

I walk toward the rear of the vehicle the federal agents drove, which is also a black sedan. Something's not right. I see the sticky coffee stains on the hood of the vehicle.

My interviewer follows, asking questions I continue to ignore.

A police officer with flashing blue lights drives up and parks behind the train of black cars on the side of the road. An agent steps out of the rear vehicle, speaks to the officer and, momentarily, the officer turns off his lights and leaves.

"Dr. Verity?" the interviewer tries to call my attention back to her. "Just a few more questions, please, sir, and then we'll get you home to the best cold dinner with your wife you've ever had."

I spurn her attractive smile and continue to walk back to get a look at the tag on the second black sedan.

She calls after me. "Dr. Verity? Where are you going?"

I turn and look at the tag. Here is the license tag Jim had searched for me.

The interviewer reaches me. "Dr. Verity? Are you all right?"

I study the white FBI letters on her wind-breaker. "May I see your ID, ma'am?"

"Why?"

"I'm curious." I take out my handheld computer to get a picture of her ID.

The agent sitting in the last car, as well as one of the agents down the hill, where they collect evidence by flashlight, approach me. "Is there a problem, Agent Penny?"

"I want to see her ID—and yours." I point at the agent coming up the hill. The agent from the last car draws near and stands behind me. I turn 90 degrees, to keep my back to the car. I give the third agent a careful stare. "And yours."

"Why?"

"Yeah, why do you want to see our IDs?" Agent Penny asks.

"My curiosity is stimulated by your reluctance to show me your ID. Now, please, show me your identification. I'd like to confirm you are who you say you are."

The man from down the hill flashes his badge toward me. I get it on my video app. I look at the woman. "And yours?" She shows me hers, and immediately they both try to put away their badges. "Not so fast."

I adjust the light-gathering capacity of the camera to better visualize their facial features in the low light. Agent Penny stiff-arms my handheld and knocks it away.

"Why did you do that?"

I bend down to grab my handheld at the same time as the agent behind me, and we bump heads. I pocket the handheld, and the agent threatens to forcibly take my device. I tap my nanophone to call a cab. Soon, I'm surrounded by three men and one woman claiming to be federal agents but who refuse to let me leave and refuse to let me document the details of their badges. Even the investigators at the bottom of the hill have abandoned the crime scene and come to the top of the hill to try to persuade me that I'm being paranoid and unreasonable, and I should be thankful that they have saved my life.

The cab arrives and I hop in and leave, much to their dismay. Thankfully, they do not try to prevent me.

"Where to, Dr. Verity?"

I am surprised by his lack of inquiry into why I appear to be leaving the scene of an accident, and I am puzzled as to how he could possibly address me as Dr. Verity. "How did you know I was a doctor?"

"You're Raymond Verity." He twists and swings his arm over the back of the front seat, thrusting a ballpoint pen toward me.

"Whoa!"

"Sorry. Do you mind giving me a signature?"

"What?" I cautiously take his pen.

"When you called for a cab, headquarters told me your name was Raymond Verity." He then hands me a business card. "You're famous."

"Oh."

Maybe I am being paranoid.

30

I WAKE UP TO THE sound of our cleaning lady rapping her knuckles on the door of our bedroom. "Dr. Verity? Morgan?"

I sit up in bed, but Morgan remains motionless beside me. The half-drunk bottle of wine on the nightstand enlightens me to the fact that her drinking continued long after I dozed off. "Yes?"

"There are media personnel gathering outside your gate. I thought you'd want to know."

I grab the remote and turn on the security feeds to confirm her observations. I flip to several news stations, but cannot discover what has drawn these talking heads to the sidewalk in front of my property.

When I filed the police report late last night, I was assured that this attack would not be publicized, at least until the investigators could confirm the identity of the four people posing as federal agents at the crime scene. Fortunately, I did have sufficient video footage on my handheld for them to commence an investigation. So how could the media have possibly heard about the attack on me and the killing of my bodyguard last night? I hoped to learn at the edge of my driveway exactly what had attracted these parasites.

I'm a little nervous about driving the hover-sedan, as I rarely have an opportunity to drive it. But it'll take me a few days to find a new driver/bodyguard.

The media personnel obstruct the passage of my vehicle with shouting, bright lights shining into my car, and extended microphones. "Dr. Verity! Dr. Verity!"

I roll down my window. "Yes?"

Three or four questions are thrown at me all at once, but I catch the words of a thin woman with long, straight black hair, and wearing a short black miniskirt. "How do you feel after the attempt on your life last night?"

I raise my eyebrows. "How do you know about that?"

"What do you think about the findings that agents of the vigilante Alabama government are responsible for the attempt on your life, and the murder of your bodyguard?"

That news surprises me indeed. "Who told you that?"

"The FBI just gave a press conference on the steps of your Research Center."

"Oh? I didn't see any press conference on television."

My nano buzzes and informs me Redd Cranton has left a message for me. I tap it twice, and the message plays. "Did you know that the government is giving a press conference in the foyer of NBRC?"

The media personnel and cameramen press into my car on every side, vying for the better image.

"Do you think," the black-haired woman asks, "the President should issue sanctions against the radical Alabama government if it is proven that they knowingly attempted to assassinate you?"

I am immediately suspicious. I feel like I am being scammed—and the public—in some elaborate government campaign to malign those resisting the New Body science. These media puppets clogging my driveway must have obtained this information before it was actually given at the press conference. Like an expert in chess, the puppet-masters make a move predicting what I will do next, all the while planning on me to be predictable and move my piece as they have foreseen. They count on me being distracted about what's going to happen in the immediate future, but they are several moves ahead.

I should be unpredictable and throw them off.

"The Alabama agent tried to *save* my life," I assert with confidence.

"What? Excuse me?" A tall, stately man pushes back against the mob of media personnel that press against him. "Did you say that the agents from the state of Alabama were actually trying to *save* your life last night?" The surprised look on their faces gives me a twisted sense of entertaining satisfaction.

"Yes, the Alabama agents are heroes. The ones that threatened me were falsely posing as FBI agents. They were actually impostors trying to cover up the crime. The Alabama agents saved my life. I wish they could have intervened to protect my driver and bodyguard, Jim Keppler, a war veteran and my friend. He's the one that deserves your honor and respect, not the FBI, and certainly not me." I rev my engines and the reporters and cameramen in front of me move aside and let me pass.

The thrill I experience in playing with their heads soon dissipates, and I begin to doubt the wisdom of what I have done. Yes, it was immensely pleasurable to contradict the government's official story, knowing that they are unlikely to offer evidence to confirm their version of events, but I do not want to hurt anyone who is innocent any more than I want to praise someone who is guilty. Those two masked agents clearly are responsible for the death of my limo driver, and they were driving a car with an Alabama tag.

I find it difficult to wrap my mind around everything that has happened. I detour and drive back home the way I came the previous night. I pull over to the side of the off-ramp where we went off the road. Besides several tire tracks in the soft shoulder, and huge divots in the softer mud down by the retention pond, there is little evidence that what happened last night ever took place.

Down by the pond, it appears some sort of rake has been applied to try to obscure the location of the spilled blood. From the spot where my feet sunk into the soft mud, I am able to pinpoint right where Jim fell down dead with a bullet in his chest. There is an elusive, pillow-sized area of darker soil, where his blood poured out on the ground through his wounds. The edge of the blood puddle appears to have crusted and has turned maroonish-brown in the morning sun.

I carefully investigate where the two masked attackers were shot down, supposedly by federal agents cresting the hill. I again find evidence of a rake application to obscure the evidence. However, there's one unmolested spot where what looks like their blood spilled. It does not look the same. It has not turned maroonish-brown like Jim's blood, but is still bright red.

What's going on?

The masked agents clearly killed Jim, but I begin to wonder if they were ever truly shot by the men and the woman posing as my FBI rescuers. Perhaps I am a deluded victim of some kind of Hollywood trickery, some kind of Copperfield stunt.

The sound of an approaching helicopter raises my eyes toward the blue sky overhead. I can hear it faintly in the distance, but cannot see it. Jim had commented that the government has the ability to see me and eavesdrop on me any time they wish. I make my way to my hover-sedan, and leave before I ever see the approaching copter.

Fear grips my heart as I drive home. These are powerful people toying with me. I seriously consider simply disappearing, driving straight to the airport and purchasing a one-way ticket to Nassau with nothing but the clothes on my back.

Then I remember Mary Nell. I open a file on my handheld to view a clip of my three-year-old granddaughter in her frilly swimming suit on the white, sandy beach. She has two more months of life. That's it. Who will defend her if I give up? In her smiling face and squinty eyes, I find the courage to keep fighting, to keep hoping for some miracle that will save her.

I change directions, heading back for the office. I do not have ready access to my granddaughter, and can't see how that could make much difference anyway, given my daughter Savannah's commitment to have her replaced. Every attempt I make to change her mind seems to cause her to dig her trenches deeper—with Morgan's help—and become even more determined to resist my counsel.

However, I'm the CEO of the business where Mary Nell's scheduled to be butchered. That tilts the outcome slightly in my favor.

31

WHEREAS BEFORE I WAS ONLY casually interested in the wording of the ethics recommendations we were planning to submit to the President, now I wholly devote myself to it. I accept the limitations of my ability to immediately criminalize the termination and exploitation of cloned people, and begin to work diligently within the law to undermine my company's successes. Although I can never consent in my heart to the killing of one innocent person, I accept that an informed consent policy may be useful to save some lives and to awaken the culture to the crisis of the American holocaust.

In my position as New Body CEO, although I am subject to federal control, I have access to information that would otherwise be kept under lock and key. Having shut me out of my own company's computer system, the feds appear to care little about what I do in my office, as long as I stay out of the forbidden wing that bears my name. So I spend most of my time on my personal laptop compiling information to hurt the industry. Any time there is a death or injury of a scientist or nurse from a clone's outburst of violence somewhere in the world, any time there is an industrial accident in a cloning facility, or whenever an employee of a cloning facility is accused of a crime, I compile the information in an encrypted file online. I leak the hyperlink from an off-site computer to a pro-life contact, one who has a history of working closely with activists on the front line. Within a few days, the information is widely published on the web and in print, citing me only as "an anonymous source from inside the industry." I take up the role of corporate spy, doing everything in my power to exploit the power of my position to undermine my own company's success.

I constantly worry that one of the many federal agents embedded in the company will discover me, but surprisingly, using off-site computers at coffee shops, employing anonymous servers overseas, and working through underground contacts, it seems I am able to get away with everything.

Morgan keeps our weekends scheduled with parties and trips. I can't believe one person can spend so much money for entertainment, clothes, shoes, and every conceivable form of pleasure. I tolerate her addictions and excesses as amiably as possible, careful to give her the attention she craves. Our next scheduled engagement, however, is one to which I have looked forward with eager anticipation.

It is only 8 p.m. and already the Country Club house wine is having its inebriating effect. My wife's left arm is intertwined with my right, more to keep her on her feet than any sincere expression of affection. We are celebrating the conclusion of our ethics panel's mission. We reached unanimity in our approval of our ethics recommendations, submitted it to the President, and just this very day, just an hour before the party was to begin, the President approved our recommendation without amendment! Everyone is ecstatic, celebrating the providence that clearly is on our side! The room is filled with tuxedo-clad men, their wives in colorful evening gowns, and alcohol-drenched mirth.

The conservative governors of Georgia, South Carolina, and Virginia are present. Dozens of representatives and Senators, including the Speaker of the Republican-dominated House, and several conservative judges are present. The room of pro-life and pro-family leaders herald the presence of these government leaders as if they were badges of honor. They especially savor the presence of the Senator who many predicted to be the next Republican candidate for President of the United States, a staunch advocate of limited federal control of cloning, who boasts that he is "personally" against the termination of clones but, with the separation of church and state, would not employ the power of government to enforce his religious views on the rest of the country. It's amazing how the right will tolerate the leftward lean of their electable Republicans as long as they don't lean as far to the left as their Democrats counterparts.

"Who cares if he's personally pro-life," I hold court with a group of pro-life leaders who cluster together in the corner of the room, "if he's not going to act pro-life in his position of leadership?"

"At least," a pro-life leader from Ohio boasts, "he would appoint strict constructionists to the Supreme Court." He raises his eyebrows hopefully.

I cast a contemptuous smirk in his direction. "The same kind of Republican-appointed strict constructionists that have perpetuated legal abortion and physician-assisted suicide over and over again, and buried traditional marriage in our country?"

"Huh?" All three pro-life leaders exclaim with blank-faces.

"Come on, fellas. Those who don't learn from history are bound to repeat it."

These hypocrites are pathetic. For conservative leaders to so mindlessly echo the sentiment that Republicans appoint pro-life judges is gross incompetence at best, or being an accomplice to mass murder if you view their incompetence in the worst light.

Thomas overhears our conversation and steps into our circle. "Even Jesus left the ninety-nine for the one, brother."

Now it was me giving him the blank stare. "Huh?"

The Right to Life leader from Ohio glances at Thomas and nods. "The parable of the shepherd and the lost sheep."

"That's correct." Thomas rests a hand on my shoulder, and gently turns me until I am facing him. "The point of the parable is that sometimes Jesus leaves the majority to save the one that is save-able. If we can't save all the children, we try to save the one lost sheep we can save. And when we do so, we're in good company."

Good point. Except the 99 left behind weren't lost and didn't need saving.

Most of the conversation in the room lacks spirituality and depth. I'm floating on a sea of sugar cubes and Champaign bubbles, all smiles and small talk, but no truly gratifying substance. Just listening to all of the insincere adulations soon becomes laborious. Every conversation seems to be teeming with futile vanity. Every person who utters a word of praise to anybody is simultaneously spreading a net before his feet. I would have left after half an hour if it were not for my wife's manic determination to share cheek kisses with every politician in the room. Their gawking stares at her low-cut silk blouse and her tight, skin-colored miniskirt are growing less obscure with every emptied wine bottle.

A spoon clinks against a half-filled wine glass. All eyes turn to my brother. "I raise a toast." He pauses, as everyone hushes and turns to him. "A toast to my big brother and bigger friend."

Thomas will be the first of many to raise a toast to honor the exploits of our historic panel, filling me with a nauseating dread.

"With Dr. Raymond Verity at the helm of this ship, we have done something heroic, something historic, something that has never been done before. For a panel of pro-life and pro-family leaders to agree on a formal recommendation of ethics policies for the largest cloning research facility in the world and the newest Fortune 500 company to break the trillion-amero mark . . . " His words are punctuated with cheers and slurred 'Here-here's'! " . . . And to put that recommendation on the desk of a Democratic President and have her approve it with such speed—that, my friends, has never been done before!"

The place practically explodes with the jingling of spoons tapping against wine glasses, vigorous applause, and exuberant ovation.

Thomas clears his throat, and raises his Merlot solemnly into the air. "To my brother."

"Cheers!"

We all share a drink, but I have reached my limit of both alcohol and homage. Especially given that the President approved our recommendations without amendment. You would think that would be a strong hint that our recommendations were pathetic and toothless, but these leaders didn't get it. We should have asked for more. We were so scared of rejection that we signed off on an ethics recommendation that possibly would not save a single life—not even the "one lost sheep" in my brother's parable.

Another beckons everyone to listen to his belched tribute to me and our historic panel. I set down my wine glass, pry my arm free of Morgan's grasp, and weave my way through the admiring eyes, ignoring the amiable words and outstretched hands, making my way into the men's room. Even there, I cannot escape their backslapping

congratulations of narcissistic, self-promoting fund-raisers and perpetual campaigners.

Risking the charge of rudeness, I bypass several commendations
and slither my way into a stall. I lean against the locked, gray metal
door. Why have I become so sickened of the commendations in this
circle of powerful leaders whose whims sway the world?

It is quiet for several moments, and I think the men's room is empty
when a gentle rap of knuckles on my door startles me. "Dr. Verity? May
I have a word with you?"

"No, you may not," I blurt out more rudely than I should have.

"I bring thanks from Alabama Governor Maurice Whetley, and
from your sister." Those unexpected, whispered words have the aura
of one of those silk-tongued word masters who are recorded reading
popular novels for people to listen to when they don't have the time or
the inclination to read. Those words snatch the breath out of my chest.

I throw open the stall door and am taken aback by the ordinary appearance of this thinly gray-headed, short man sporting an overgrown,
pepper-gray mustache. "Where is my sister?"

He smiles, and in an artful tone, declares, "In the sovereign state
of Alabama."

I'm not surprised. "How does someone who naively thinks Alabama
is a sovereign state, someone close to Maurice Whetley and my felon
of a sister, find his way into this elite gathering?"

"She's not a felon. She was released on a technicality."

Here I am reminded that my secrecy as to the true cause of her
release is a condition of her continued freedom.

"How did I get here, you ask?" He shrugs his shoulders, with caution in his demeanor, as if to remember he should craft his sentences

carefully in my presence. I suspect another self-adulating fund-raising pitch. I cast an optimistic glance toward the door, hoping for an interruption to save me from this unwanted smooth talker. "Let's just say that the Alabama and Mississippi state governments think *you* are worth the expense."

Something doesn't smell right. "Me? Why would Governor Whetley want to thank me? The federal law legalizing the terminating of clones bears my name. This very celebration commemorates a pro-life panel that formerly condemns Maurice Whetley by name for defying federal law and disobeying a federal judge in his state government's prosecution of clone industry leaders."

"He thanks you for not taking the President's bait after the murder of Jim Keppler. It would have been easier for you to simply join her in blaming Alabama leaders for attempting to assassinate you. Although, praising us for saving your life when we clearly did not was unnecessary, and still has you in hot water with President Sayder. You've yet to endure the peak of her wrath for that bit of sophistry."

I laugh at his comment. "Please tell me that you are kidding me! This has got to be some sort of sick joke."

He doesn't flinch at my mocking chortle. "One of the President's many secret black-op agencies was probably setting everything up to garner your condemnation of our leadership, and to take out your limo driver, who we suspect was compiling evidence of the President's personal conspiracy to extort you." He flashes me a wide smile, beaming with enthusiasm. "If she hasn't already. But you didn't fall in line like she expected you to. That's admirable, though it doesn't . . . "

"Admirable?" More accolades, yet not as nauseating as those previous, as it comes from the unlikeliest of sources.

He bulldozes over my interruption, " . . . It doesn't quite make up for all the stupid things you've done trying to regulate the killing with this panel of slave traders and flesh peddlers."

Admirable and stupid—now those are two words I certainly never expected to hear directed toward me in the same sentence. I straighten my posture. "Slave traders and flesh peddlers? Who do you think you are?"

He keeps calm. "No need to put on a show, Dr. Verity. I know about your corporate espionage to help disparage the New Body science, and I thank you."

What? How could he possibly know about that?

"You are probably more disturbed about selling out to the butchers as anybody in this gathering."

"What are you talking about?"

"Isn't that what you squabble about in your panel discussions? What category of innocent people should you permit to perish in your pro-life laws, all for the hope of some speck of success at the table of blood-letters?"

I can't figure out if he's a fan or a critic, but I know for sure he's a stranger and I'm in no mood to bend my ear to his reproofs. I aim a stiff finger toward the door of the restroom. "These people sincerely want to save lives, sir. I agree that our ethics recommendations do not go far enough, but it's a foot in the door, and there are more to come. You have no right to indict our motives."

"Oh, yes I do. God said, 'Do no murder'—none! God forbids extending leniency to murderers. You either agree or disagree—there is no middle ground. He that is not for Him is against Him. You unwittingly worship the author of the standard by which you live, whereas you

234 BODY BY BLOOD

should worship the Lord your God, and Him only should you serve. In your counterfeit laws and your"—here he flashes two fingers with each hand as makeshift quotation marks—"ethics recommendations, you permit the murder of some innocent people. That is a clear violation of divine law, all your sincerity notwithstanding."

"People are dying anyway. At least we are saving those who can be saved."

"It remains to be seen whether you will save anybody, Dr. Verity. You certainly won't save your granddaughter."

It's as if he has plunged a hot knife into my gut, and holds it there to sadistically observe my response to his cruel experiment. I try to hold my countenance firm, to conceal from him just how his intrusive reminder of my granddaughter's fate has pained me. I take several deep, cleansing breaths. "I assume Tamara told you about Mary Nell."

"Do you have a plan to save her, besides your worthless ethics recommendations to the President?"

Worthless?

That did nothing to prop up my dwindling self-esteem. I judge it less painful than what I deserve, and simply respond to the question without criticizing the demeaning choice of terms. "I tried to save her. My daughter Savannah would not be dissuaded. It's an impossible situation. I've managed to postpone the transfer, but besides that there's nothing I can do."

"Unbelief is not a good platform from which to save lives. You cannot rise above your faith, Dr. Verity."

I poke my chest with both of my thumbs. "I work within the system. Unlike Alabama's and Mississippi's leaders, we believe in the system."

"We believe in God."

"And your God, has He stopped the Holocaust?"

"He shows us how to. He shows *you* how to. But you can only conquer that Promised Land through faith, my friend. Faith is the victory that overcomes the world. You may build a grand castle on any other foundation, but it won't quench bloodguilt any more than it will withstand the fast approaching storm on the horizon. Unbelief leads to fatal compromises, Doctor Verity, and compromising God's principles is not the path to success, no matter what your brother tells you. Spurning God's Word for alternative standards, however promising and seductive, lets you continue to gain wealth in the largest corporation in the world that kills people for profit. Blood money—that's what it is."

"I do a lot of good in that position!" I raise my voice.

"Yes, you and Dr. Redd Cranton, your partner in virtue."

"Innocent until proven guilty," I remind him.

He nods. "Of course, and in a court of American law where people are property, he probably won't even be charged."

I hold my peace. My words are just giving this fanatic more wood to throw on the fire of my guilt.

"You'd fare better on Judgment Day if you would shed Saul's armor and trust God. Quit being the President's puppet—and your brother's. God will show Himself strong on behalf of him whose heart is perfect toward Him." He assumes a humble posture, shoving his hands in his pockets and waiting patiently for my response.

Shed Saul's armor? What's that supposed to mean?

For a long moment, I just stare at this strange messenger. How could so much time possibly pass without the hordes of wine guzzlers with enlarged prostates entering the restroom to interrupt us? There's no avoiding this moment of painful self-reflection. This messenger's poignant words resonate eerily with my conscience, though I am loath to admit it to him.

I have to appreciate him for his edgy, but honest assessment of our pathetic panel of wet-finger-raisers. They—no, we—abandoned every single proposal that would have clearly been more protective, in favor of the weakest possible proposal that was more likely to win the President's approval. Why? Because we didn't *believe* that more protective laws were possible. Unbelief—that was our chief motivating factor to determine where we were going to draw our battle line. But we have drawn it so far to the left that even many of the scientists and physicians on the New Body killing squad were on our side of the battle line!

What good is informed consent, after all, when it's the killers doing the informing? If they butcher innocent people for a living, how can we expect them to be honest in informing genome donors of the humanity and viability of their victims? And even if the killers refuse to give informed consent, our ethics recommendation doesn't even pretend to give teeth to the policy. We proposed no enforcement whatsoever, fearful that it would sink the whole effort. What kind of punishment for non-compliance should we expect from those who manage teams of butchers and Mengeles? Who's going to impose punishment on themselves, simply because we asked nicely? In truth, this panel of pro-life leaders has done nothing but empower President Sayder to perpetuate the shedding of innocent blood, making her look more moderate than she is. She wears us like a rainbow-colored sweater over her blood-stained filth. She needs us, and we have bowed before her altar, linking ourselves inescapably to her appalling agenda.

"I have a clip of two of the four who were posing as federal agents." I change the topic and, in offering personal information, extend an olive leaf to the man. I open my handheld to the file, and finger through the images to try to find the clip I took of the agents after the shooting. "There were several of them, but I got a few seconds of a man and a woman. They refused to let me take a close look at their ID badges."

"And, surprise, surprise, your images are missing."

I furrow my brow. He's right. They're gone. This phone hasn't been out of my possession. How could the file be missing? "I shared it with the police, but I know I didn't delete it."

I begin to search the trash file.

"You won't find it there either. And I suspect the P.D. either lost their copy as well, or won't return a copy to you."

I look up at him and see him in a brand new light.

"Expect only defeat and disappointment wielding carnal weapons on a foundation of sand."

I have no idea what he's talking about, but clearly, this messenger is much more than an ordinary mailman.

"Your sister sends word that she could use your help in several southern states. There's a groundswell of resistance that would break through into enforceable state laws protecting the innocent, but the bravest of leaders are hindered by a blanket of fear the federal government has dropped on them. She said you could help the cause tremendously."

"My sister said that?"

He nods.

One corner of my mouth turns up at the thought of Tamara's obsessive-compulsive nature, her self-imposed standards of moral perfection strangely annexed to a judgmental attitude toward every other form of perfection, whether intellectual or physical. She treats the perfection for which most craves as a shackle that hinders our true potential. She's the oddest mix of self-loathing and liberating joy, of convicting quips and sacrificial service. "Sounds like her."

He nods. "Things may get worse before they get better, Doc. Don't be discouraged about that. God's going to test your faith. Be true to God and you'll discover that His ways are always best."

Two snickering men enter the restroom, and I glance at them hoping they do not interrupt.

"Well, I've delivered my mail, Dr. Verity. Thank you for your time." He pushes his hands deeper into his pockets and heads toward the exit.

For five minutes, I've been waiting with baited breath to get out of this conversation, and now, for some reason, I'm disappointed he's leaving. "Wait, wait, sir. Can I get your name?"

"You can reach us through Phil Stephens." He exits without looking back.

32

THAT CONVERSATION SEEMS TO TRIGGER a change in me, but not for the better. Things began to transpire in my life that I never thought possible.

That night, thumbing through my handheld computer, I cannot find a novel I was reading. I ask Morgan, "Where is my novel?"

She's painting her nails in the bathroom, complaining about her personal masseuse abandoning her post due to pregnancy leave.

"Hey," I call out to her. "Where's my novel? It's not on my handheld."

"You need to make up your mind."

"What?"

She pokes her head out of the bathroom to make eye contact with me. "You were right here two minutes ago complaining that the plot was sagging in the middle. You deleted it."

I check the trash can of deleted files, and sure enough, it's there. I stomp into the restroom. "Are you pulling some kind of prank on me? Did I really say that?"

"You're starting to forget things."

I restore my novel to the desktop and head into the bedroom. After a few minutes of reading the sagging middle of my novel, I remember. I had deleted the file. It's like five minutes of my life had been excised as if it never happened.

My mood begins to cloud alongside my intellect. It is as if my conversation with the stranger from Alabama withdrew fifty years of life out of my body. Maybe it is my general lack of purpose after the conclusion of our pathetic political panel, or my relatively meaning-less existence in the office of my burgeoning company—whatever it is, something significant is missing from my life.

My fit, muscular body begins to sag over the next several weeks, as my exercise wanes from an increasing feeling of general malaise. I keep reading the same twenty opening pages of my novel before bedtime, as I keep forgetting what I read the previous night. For the longest time, I cannot even recall the name of the man the strange messenger gave me as a way to contact my sister. I have always thought that there was nothing worse than being old in a wrinkled, shrinking, graying body, but feeling old in a young man's body is no better—there's actually more shame annexed to the mental handicaps if you look brighter than you are.

After a long night of ten restless hours, Morgan wakes to find me sleeping in the bathtub with my handheld computer in the trash can.

"I need help, Morgan," I admit over a 10:30 a.m. breakfast. "Something's wrong."

She accepts my acknowledgement of weakness with pride. She never quips, "I told you so," but her facial features seem to scream it at me.

"You were right, babe," I finally admit.

You'd have thought I had given her a million-amero diamond ring; she was so happy at my heretofore undisclosed humility. She has not seen me so needy since my deathbed experience almost three decades ago. It almost offends me how she appears to thrive in my vulnerability. I have always had a paralyzing fear of mental and physical frailty, but cannot deny that an occasional virus that lands me on my back for a couple days is a sweet thing indeed when my wife dotes on me like this. I wonder about her motive, given her history of approving of my euthanization after I clearly ordered it halted. In that light, her more attentive care could be compared to getting a lollipop from a physician who's planning to amputate my arm without anesthesia. Nevertheless, her desire to serve her mentally-weakening husband is a positive outcome of my increasing confusion, erratic irritability, and worsening depression, even if her motive isn't entirely selfless.

Once Morgan's neuropsychiatrist learns of my confession of mental frailty, she jumps at the opportunity to intervene in my care. It must be a trophy for Dr. Devonaire that her most famous, previously non-compliant patient finally admits he needs her help. She adds me on to the end of her schedule on the very day Morgan calls her.

This time, I listen more than I talk, and assent to her diagnoses and her prescriptions. Although Dr. Devonaire doesn't exactly gloat in my newfound mental-cognitive deficiencies, she suspects it is further evidence of my worsening microvascular brain disease, and she indicts my stubbornness to receive her SSRI script at the last visit as part of the problem. "You need to know when you need help. Evolution can give us new bodies, but not new brains, not yet."

By the way she's glaring at me, she's challenging me to counter her reference to atheistic evolution. But I am silent, fearful of stumbling over my words and embarrassing myself even further.

The MRI confirms it—my cerebral capillary plaques are getting thicker, my arteries growing harder, despite the best supplements available.

In addition to three prescriptions and a predictable bi-weekly appointment with her staff psychologist for counseling, I receive a lengthy lecture on the need for strict compliance if she is to continue to offer me care. At first it seems belittling to be addressed with such sneering condescension, but as I accept my frailty and submit to the need for counseling, I find it astonishingly refreshing.

33

I SIT AT THE KITCHEN island, playing a word game on my handheld computer. It was one of the activities Dr. Devonaire said may improve or, at the least, stabilize my diminishing communication skills.

Morgan pauses her dinner preparation to respond to a text message on a computer screen embedded into the wall in the kitchen.

"Good," she mumbles.

"What?" I used to be able to shut out the world when I was working, but my attention span is about as long as my average sentences nowadays.

"Oh," she glances at me over her shoulder as if she was surprised to see me there. "Savannah's flying down in her boyfriend's private jet to spend a weekend with us."

"Is she bringing, uh, Mary Nell?"

The teapot begins to whistle on the stove and she drops a tea bag into a porcelain cup. "No, she isn't, Ray."

She pours the hot water into her cup, acting like she's offended that I even asked.

"Why not?"

At first I think she is not going to answer. Then finally she mumbles a belated response. "I think it's quite obvious why not."

"Not to me."

She responds with her right hand planted firmly on her right hip, exaggerating the slit in her silk nightgown. Her left hand grasps the handle of her teacup like she is tempted to toss the hot liquid at me.

"What, Morgan? Why are you upset? She's in the last weeks of her life. Don't you have any natural affection for, uh, um . . . " My mind goes blank. Ugh! I could thrash my skull against the wall when this happens!

"You've grown rather attached to that defective girl . . . "

"Mary Nell!" I snap my fingers, recalling her name.

"I think it would be in the best interest of all that you grow unattached to her."

"Why do you keep talking about what's best for all without, without, uh, without thinking about what's best for her?"

She huffs at me, drops a sugar cube in her chamomile and, without even bothering to stir it, stomps from the room with an exaggerated hip wag, as if she is letting me know what I am *not* going to enjoy with my inappropriate inquiry.

I pick up the hardline phone and speed-dial Savannah's mobile number. My hippy of a daughter refuses to upgrade to a nanophone. She doesn't answer. I hang up and dial her home. Again, she doesn't answer. Surprisingly, there's another voice on the answering machine. I leave a message. "Savannah, call me immediately. It concerns your inheritance."

Within thirty seconds, she calls me back, but not before Morgan stomps into the room, having overheard my voicemail.

"Shh!" I order her. "She's calling me back . . . "

Morgan snatches the phone out of my hand.

"Hey!" I reach for my phone.

She holds it out of reach. "Don't you dare make this more difficult for everybody than it already is!"

Then she presses the button to hang up the phone and slams it down on the marble countertop.

"There you go again, Morgan!"

She stomps from the room.

"Shouldn't everybody include Mary Nell?"

"I'm telling Dr. Devonaire about this outburst." She disappears down the hall toward the bedroom.

"*My* outburst?"

The phone, thankfully, rings again. I answer. "Hello, Savannah. How are . . . "

She doesn't even wait for me to finish my introduction. "What about my inheritance?"

I take a deep breath. I am treading on tenuous ground.

"Has your mother told you what's been happening to me the past few weeks?"

Her tone relaxes when she realizes that I'm not mad at her. "No. What?"

"I'm developing some strange form of dementia."

"What?"

"Yes. I'm more confused and forgetful, and the doctors don't know why. They say it won't get worse as long as I don't have any more strokes. My bloodwork is normal, and all the brain scan shows is that some diseased small arteries in my brain are getting more clogged, putting me at high risk for more strokes."

"I'm sorry, Daddy." There's a hint of satisfying sadness in her tone.

"If this progresses, I think it's a good idea to be surrounded by those I love. My business has always come first in my life, but I'm changing a bit, for the better, I believe."

"We're coming this weekend. I want to introduce you to Argentino, my new beau."

"You've got a new man? What's the matter with the old one? Uh, what was his name?"

"He was, well, too much like you. All work, no play. This fellow will make for a better long term relationship, and he has the credit to keep us comfortable in spite of his short work weeks."

I try not to be offended at her comment that her ex-boyfriend was too much like me. "I look forward to meeting him. But the one I am looking forward to meeting more than anybody is Mary Nell." There is silence on the other end of the line. "I love her. I think about her all the time, Savannah."

"But what does this have to do with my inheritance?"

I sigh heavily. "To be blunt, Morgan gets half, Louie gets a fourth, and you a fourth. I'm willing to take the portion devoted to my children—you and Louie—and divide it by three, and set one-third of that aside for Mary Nell. So you'd be responsible for twice Louie's portion."

"For my daughter?"

"Yes."

"That would be nice, Daddy. We have already begun an account to save for her college."

She's talking about the dupe scheduled to replace Mary Nell in three months. Mary Nell would never be admitted to any college. "No, Savannah. I'm not referring to Mary Nell's clone. Different brain, different person. I don't love her, not yet. I will, I'm sure, but I'm talking about your daughter."

She growls. "Oh, Daddy, why are you doing this?"

"I love her, Savannah." The thought of Mary Nell's affectionate hugs moistens my eyes. "Can you blame me?"

"This is a difficult decision, Father." She sobs for a few seconds.

"I'm sorry, Savannah. I don't want to make you cry." I'm stroking a spoiled brat who needs a thrashing more than anything, but with my granddaughter's life hanging in the balance, I don't want to upset Savannah more than I have. "She reminds me of you when you were a little squirt. Do you remember being that age?"

"Not a lot of fond memories, Daddy."

"And that's my fault, I know. But they could have been worse. Imagine being in your daughter's shoes, with your momma planning to trade you in—"

"Father!"

"Please, please don't hang up on me, Savannah."

"Well, quit, then! You make me not even wanna come anymore."

"Because I tell you I want her here in my final days? Savannah, I tell you what. You bring her this weekend and we'll talk some more about the amendments to my will. I'm open to your advice."

"I'd rather not."

Mary Nell may not even have a mother figure anymore. Savannah is not just withholding love from her daughter—she's probably actively spurning her affection. I hope Mary Nell's not suffering emotionally or physically.

"Mary Nell's spirit will live on, Daddy. Trust me. I feel right about it."

My heart pounds with a mixture of fear and rage. She is going to kill my granddaughter because she "feels right about it."

"You tell yourself that if you want, but I'm a scientist. There are two people right now—one residing in the Verity wing of the New Body Research Center and one with you, perfect only in her demented Gwampa's eyes." Here, Savannah giggles nervously. "One's a genetically perfect dupe and one's not. But make no mistake—there are two of them. Sisters."

A moment of silence. My daughter's respiratory rate has increased slightly, making me suspect that I have kindled a discomfort deep in her heart. Good. I've been there, and without this inward pain, there can be no genuine change.

"Perhaps we could trade, Savannah. You let me see Mary Nell, I'll let you see her perfected dupe."

Savannah's voice bursts with renewed enthusiasm. "You can do that?"

"I can."

"I'd love that!"

"Is it a deal?"

She sighs. "We were planning on leaving her with a sitter, but I suppose we could bring her."

34

WE MEET THEM AT A small, private airport. The "green" jet in which they arrive speaks volumes about my daughter's new man. So committed is he to protecting the environment that he owns a jet designed to run off of hydro-processed algae biofuel, costing fifty times as much per gallon as archaic fossil fuels.

When they finally disembark, Savannah introduces her new man as Argentino Sarsparelli. His name is fittingly affluent, perfectly compatible with his aloof demeanor and his cologne-and-coconut-scented aura of a billionaire playboy. He's the son of the son of a duke in some withering European enclave—I catch only bits and pieces of Savannah's elaborate explanation of this spectacle of toned and envied handsomeness.

Savannah has covered the stroller with a blanket. Mary Nell must be sleeping. I kiss Savannah on the cheek and bend down to take a peek at Mary Nell.

"Don't wake her, Daddy," Savannah pleads. "Later."

"Of course."

"Argentino!" Morgan gives him a peck on the cheek, which he leans in to relish with more pleasure than I would expect him to, at least in my company.

He stretches a hand toward me. "Mr. Verity."

"Dr. Verity," Morgan corrects him.

He laughs like a bad actor. "Doctor it is."

I belatedly shake his outstretched hand.

Morgan doesn't stop praising Argentino for his handsome features, his diamond ear-studs, his waxed eyebrows, his classy clothes, his highlighted hair, his shiny beige shoes, his diamond-studded gold watch—all things vain and superficial. His teeth are equally flawless, though he would never smile broadly enough to let you admire them. He looks like a self-obsessed underwear model who must consume a thousand credits of cocaine and spend an hour and a half in front of the mirror before he can go out in public. That makes him and Morgan two peas in the same pod, with him the less manic of the two.

If anyone in the terminal wasn't already staring at my wife, as immodest as she is with her long brown legs under her black leather miniskirt and her low-cut, see-through, silky white blouse, certainly everyone was turning her direction with her shrill voice recklessly extolling a man she has never even met.

We men are so predictable, so superficial, and such pathetic let-downs, more or less. A woman like my wife can draw you in like the smell of a candy factory would attract a starving man, the general lack of nourishment notwithstanding. But the pleasure dissipates with increasing familiarity and one day you're left with a façade of a real woman who cannot satisfy herself, much less your deep-down hunger for love, any more than a breath-mint could strengthen a famished, withered body. Once the honeymoon wears off, a vain woman like my wife cannot keep you warm any more than a painting of the sun. She cannot gratify your insatiable addictions sufficiently to maintain your interest for the long haul. The very appetite that leads you to her leads you away from her. How I pity the shameless gawkers who are endlessly fascinated with my wife's body! How I pity Morgan for her dependence on their worship and flirtations to maintain her self-esteem. Flesh-obsessed men who lack all love created this monster, and now she lives to feed off her makers. Could something truly great ever come out of the ornate treasure chest of marshmallows that is Morgan Verity?

My mind retreats from this gavel. I don't belong behind that bench. How can I give her what I don't have? And how can I lavish judgment on her and hope for mercy for me? Isn't her sin the fruit of my own? If anything, her transgressions are just one more burden on my own sinking ship.

Morgan completely lacks all discretion with her ambitious hugs and relentless praise of Savannah's hair and attire, and her intensifying admiration of Savannah's boyfriend. He appears aloof to our presence with his constant attention to his handheld. Only occasionally is he distracted from whatever he's reading to look at my wife's bosom. He's not even pretending to look at her face. He's turning his handheld toward her, aiming it at her chest. Is he taking a picture of her? Pathetic.

The blanket falls off the stroller and I see only a diaper bag in the stroller. "Wait." I point. "Where's Mary Nell?"

"She's, um, she's coming." She stops and looks back toward the jet. "She's sleeping, like I said, but her nanny's got her."

"Oh! I'm so glad you got a helper," Morgan squeals. "Mine does everything for me . . ."

They start going ahead, but I hesitate.

Morgan glances over her shoulder. "Ray?"

"You go get the luggage. I'm waiting for Mary Nell."

At the end of a long line of disembarking passengers, I see a thin blond teenage girl with a diaper bag over one shoulder. Mary Nell clutches her nanny vigorously until she gets a glimpse of me and stretches her arms toward me.

"Gwampa!"

I run to her and she practically leaps out of the nanny's arms into my own. I embrace her fully. Her innocence is refreshing, yet her detachment from her mother is grievous. She nudges her chin into the crook of my neck. "Wuv you, Gwampa."

"Ah, now that's a hug. I wuv you too." I turn to face my wife and daughter, hoping that they are enjoying our affectionate moment as much as I am, but they are nowhere to be seen. I carry Mary Nell into the terminal and find them leaving me behind, rolling their luggage to the car. It's unlike them to not even wait for someone to carry their luggage.

I ask her nanny, "Does Savannah spend any time with Mary Nell at all?"

She shakes her head. "No. She insisted on sitting far apart from her on the plane. I do everything for Mary Nell now. I look forward to my week away."

"You've got a vacation?"

She nods, appearing tired. Relieved. "Yes, a much needed one. Mary Nell requires a lot of attention."

I kiss my granddaughter on the cheek. "And worth every minute of it."

Mary Nell turns toward the exit to see Morgan leaving. "Mama?"

"You'll see your Mama soon." Her nanny tries to comfort her, but it's all in vain.

"Mama? Mama weaving? Mama!"

Savannah's detaching, and Mary Nell is resisting. I embrace her tightly. "I'm not leaving, baby. I'll take care of you."

The nanny's eyelids rise. She smirks. "You'll take care of her?"

When the girl gets her luggage, we go our separate ways.

In the hover-limo, Savannah sets Mary Nell in her lap, but only briefly. Mary Nell keeps trying to pull her close, and Savannah acts irritated. Finally, I distract Mary Nell from her mother with a gift of a new doll. Savannah is disinterested in Mary Nell's new doll, appearing curt, tight-lipped, and as aloof as I've ever seen her. She crosses her arms over her bosom, even appearing unmoved by her mother's giddy rambling. Her eyes intermittently fixate on me, as Mary Nell is perched enthusiastically on my lap, holding her doll tightly, expressing her childish admiration of even the most mundane of passing buildings, trees, and people on the sidewalk.

Savannah's boyfriend rudely shuts out even Morgan's relentless prattle as he thumbs through his handheld computer.

"When can we see my new girl?" Savannah finally speaks. "Today?"

"Who's dat?" Mary Nell perches up higher on my lap so she can touch the window in the roof.

I'm amazed by how aware the little girl is.

Morgan clears her throat loudly. "Oh, Mary Nell, look at that."

Morgan points out the window at some artful structure made of brass and colored glass on a street corner. "Look at that pretty thing, Mary Nell."

She's trying to distract her, but it doesn't work.

"Who's dat? Mama?" Mary Nell's eyes are hopeful, as if she's expecting a potential playmate or a pet. With her mother's reluctance to answer the question, Mary Nell grows stiff, as if she suspects something uncomfortable is afoot.

"No shot, Mommy. No shot . . ."

"You're not getting a shot."

"She hates shots, huh?" Morgan comments with a feminine giggle.

"What's her name?" Mary Nell asks.

Savannah sighs deeply. "Nellie. Nellie's her name."

I try to comfort Mary Nell with a pat on her back. "You're going to meet Nellie and be good friends."

"Raymond!" Morgan blurts out.

"Oh, don't make a big deal about it."

"They'll let you do that?" Savannah asks. "Let them meet?"

"It's still my business."

"I thought it was the government's business," Morgan retorts. I think she means it as an insult to me, but her reassuring smile toward Savannah indicates that she's motivated more by a desire to comfort my daughter. Savannah looks worried. She knows I object to the transfer and, it being my company, she fears I will put my foot down and intervene to protect Mary Nell.

"Ray's just the face of New Body now," Morgan assures her. "He doesn't really do much of the work."

Morgan turns to me. "Did you get permission to see the dupe early?"

"She's still my company's asset until the transfer is made. I can take my granddaughter to my office if I want to," I insist. "Mary Nell? Would you like to see Grandpa's office?"

She may not understand what I'm offering, but hearing the tone in my voice and seeing the smile on my face, she begins to bounce and squeal as if a cartoon character had just handed her tickets to an amusement park. She rambles incoherent, child-like exclamations as if she was prattling away in a foreign language, oblivious to our lack of understanding.

"Stop squealin' gibberish!" Savannah scolds her.

Mary Nell withdraws back into her shell, growing sullen and quiet.

I call Mrs. Williamson on my nanophone and order her to set up the tour. "I'll have Savannah, Mary Nell, and Morgan with me. And Savannah's boyfriend Argentina."

"Argentino," he corrects me.

"I'm mistaken, it's Argentino Sarsparello . . . " Hopefully showing off that I've got the pronunciation of the last name right will make up that I missed the first name.

"Sarsparelli," he corrects me.

"Mrs. Williamson," I ask her over my nano, "will you get VIP IDs made up?"

"Yes, sir."

35

"HAVE YOU GOTTEN TO KNOW little Mary Nell, Argentino?" I am careful to pronounce his name properly.

He lowers his handheld computer and makes eye contact with me. "Excuse me?"

"Mary Nell. Have you gotten to know her?"

"Yes. Sweet girl. For all her deficiencies, quite extraordinary." He talks to me as if she isn't even present. We are walking into the private entrance at the New Body Research Center. I look down to admire her as she sits comfortably in her stroller, unrestrained in her playful gibberish as she points at the elevator entrance, appearing entertained by the mirror on the other side of the elevator and the reflection of the lit button panel.

Savannah backhands Argentino's hip. He clears his throat. "Nevertheless, I agree with the transfer."

He raises his tablet again, as if he's hoping I'll take the hint and stop interrupting his endless surfing. Savannah has co-opted him already.

When we step into the elevator, a dozen scientists with lab coats enter the building, strangers I do not recognize. I prevent the elevator door from shutting in order to study the badges on their lapels. They are medical personnel from the World Health Organization. The ones in the rear are pushing wheeled computer systems and boxes of reagents and equipment into the building. Since the government took over management, medical specialists from all over the country have free reign of the place for all kinds of consultant opportunities, but this is atypical. There's even a FEMA insignia on the lab coat of one of the strangers as she walks past, talking in quiet whispers on her nano as she looks at something on her handheld computer.

I exit the elevator, telling Morgan, "Hold on."

I walk up to the nearest WHO personnel. "What's this about?"

The woman tries to ignore me but then recognizes me. "Just a precaution."

The pretty, young woman pushes a long machine on wheels into the building.

I show her my badge. "What kind of precaution?"

My ID is inadvertently upside down, but she brushes it aside. "I know who you are."

"It's my building, my business. What kind of precaution?"

"You'll have to go through the proper chain of authority for information that I am forbidden to share." She glances into the elevator. When her gaze settles on Mary Nell's characteristic facial features, she scrunches up her nose in disgust. Thanks to the prenatal standard of care and "wrongful birth" lawsuits in which physicians have been sued for not providing prenatal diagnoses to allow the woman an opportunity to abort handicapped children, most Down Syndrome children are killed via abortion. They're as rare as conjoined twins. But this WHO scientist studies my granddaughter not like a scientist fortunate to observe a rare genetic disease, but as a pest-controller would look at a termite—with disdain and contempt. Without another word, she turns and begins to wheel her cargo down the hall.

"The New Body Research Center is my property. I want to know why you and your colleagues are here."

"Then it won't be a problem for you to gain clearance," she responds without looking.

"Clearance from whom?"

"Whomever answers to the President." She banks toward the elevator that is dedicated solely to the Verity Wing.

It's hard to put your finger on who really is at the top of the totem pole in my company. All the federal agents who act like their authority transcends me are just nameless bureaucrats in acronyms of government agencies—the FBI, NIH, CDC, WHO, and the Department of HHS, as well as several others less familiar to me. They don't even know the bounds of their own jurisdiction, and so of course cannot explain it to me. Maybe it is the President at the very top of this pyramid, throwing nosy and domineering agents from three dozen agencies around these four floors just to torment my managers and supervisors with a thousand irritating pecks.

As we take the elevator to my penthouse office, Morgan jabbers about the success of our business and the perfection of our new bodies. This interests Argentino to no end. His personal computer is finally resting in his pocket, and he is asking her question after question. You'd think he would ask me questions, since I'm the one that pioneered the science and the first successful regeneration after cryo-sleep, but he appears much more interested with my wife's answers, and she has no problem with rewarding him by drawing inside his personal space and showing off everything from her scalp scar to her freckle-free, tanned skin, to her lean abdominal muscles, to her cleavage when she bends down to act like she's situating a poorly fitting sandal.

He runs his fingers across the skin on her neck and shoulders as Morgan describes how she was covered with freckles from her original, un-doctored genome. Their mutual infatuation is nothing new between Morgan and her flesh-obsessed friends, but I'm still taken aback with their audacity to do this right in front of me. Even Savannah appears uncomfortable with their exchange. Morgan even has the courage to turn toward me and wink, as if she fancies a threesome, like the old days.

We were so pathetic—at least I was, she is. *No, thank you,* I do not say. We were the rare couple back then, on the cutting edge of sexual liberation in an open marriage, but now it appears to be the cultural norm. Now, everyone is as pathetic as us. Argentino leans close to Morgan's neck to enjoy some scent Morgan is tempting him with. I am tempted to intervene to break up their obsession with each other, but I am distracted when the elevator doors slide open and right in front of us is the new Mary Nell, grasping onto the hand of a staff member that works in the Verity Wing.

"I'm sorry, Dr. Verity." The staff member, an atypically thin woman with a short haircut, displays a nervous grimace. "I intended to have her in your office on time, per Dr. Cranton's orders, but you're a few minutes—"

"No," I interrupt her. "Don't trouble yourself, Sharon"—I read the name on her badge. "All is fine."

Dr. Cranton would have no problem checking a dupe out of the Verity Wing, whereas I would have. Thankfully, he honored my request, delivered through my secretary.

I drop to one knee to introduce myself to the girl, who appears timid in the unchartered territory of the unlocked floors. Savannah steps up on one side of me, and Morgan the other. Mary Nell's dupe—her genetically perfected, cloned replacement—is instantly recognizable. Morgan squats and begins to squeal about how she is such a pretty girl, but Savannah remains speechlessly amazed.

"I am Dr. Verity," I say to her. "We're going to call you Nellie. Is that okay?"

She looks up at Sharon, whose hand she still holds. The worker nods. "Yes, sir."

At hearing her first words, Savannah and Morgan both put their hands over their mouths, astounded.

I motion to Morgan. "This is Morgan, my wife, and this is Savannah, my daughter." I see little Mary Nell stretching her neck around Savannah to try to see the strange girl who has so enraptured us.

Nellie freezes for a moment, glancing worriedly up at the staff member.

"Go ahead, shake hands," Sharon tells her. "Be nice." She motions toward us with a flick of her wrist, and Nellie shakes our hands.

I glance at Savannah. She has tears in her eyes.

"Amazing." Argentino has broken out of the sophisticated playboy aura that characterizes him, appearing genuinely interested. His gaze darts back and forth between Mary Nell and her dupe Nellie. "Just amazing."

"Hey," Mary Nell calls out to Nellie.

I move aside so Mary Nell can see her more clearly.

"Hey." Nellie waves and gives her an embarrassed smile.

I grab the bottom of Mary Nell's stroller and pull her closer, hoping that they will interact.

"No, no, uh, quit, Dad," Savannah reaches for the stroller handles.

"No, dear." Morgan grabs Savannah by the arm.

"We just got here." Argentino draws closer to the two little girls.

Argentino and Morgan apparently cannot comprehend why Savannah wants to leave, but I understand it fully. Seeing Mary Nell and Nellie interact like two normal children is like a bright light through the fog of sophistry Savannah has built up around her to justify the transfer and abate her natural affection for her own flesh and bone.

I help Mary Nell out of her stroller and the two girls stand toe to toe. Nellie is several inches taller. "Say hi to Nellie, Mary Nell."

Instead of greeting her with words, Mary Nell leaps toward her and throws her arms around Nellie's neck, giving her a hug.

Nellie is reluctant to reciprocate at first, but eventually she lets go of Sharon's hand and hugs her back.

"Hi, Mary Nell," Nellie mumbles.

"Speak up," the worker barks.

"Hi, Mary Nell," Nellie says with more robust enthusiasm, even as she tries to pull away from Mary Nell's ambitious embrace.

Mary Nell doesn't answer, but looks to me. I wink at her.

"You be my friend?"

I look back at Savannah. Hopefully some motherly affection is resurrecting within her.

Our gaze connects. She wags her head, and her lips mouth the words, "This is not a good idea."

"Oh, everything's fine," Morgan coos. Morgan's conscience appears further out of reach and seeing the two girls together does not stimulate any love in her for her soon-to-be-euthanized granddaughter, and so she does not urge me to separate the girls. She glances at Savannah, appearing to not have any understanding as to what is troubling her so.

I lead the crowd to my office. Nellie insists on pushing the stroller and Mary Nell squeals with glee as her new friend begins to playfully push it in a zig-zag pattern down the hall. Nellie appears to relax and be more playful as she distances herself from Sharon, who follows behind us.

"Be careful," Morgan grabs a stroller handle to steady it around a corner.

"It's nice to see your protective maternal instincts kick in," I say to her. She nods and grins, apparently not catching my meaning. "You're gonna be a great mom."

When we walk past Mrs. Williamson's open door, she pulls away from her desk and comes to the opening into the hallway to watch us pass. "That's something you don't see every day," she comments.

We walk down the hall and into my office. Morgan and Argentino begin to admire the view, but Savannah and I are fascinated by the communication between Mary Nell and her genetically perfected twin. They sit on the ground and pull toys out of the diaper bag.

Mary Nell speaks a long string of gibberish words as she holds her new doll up for Nellie to see.

"Your grandpa certainly has a nice taste in dolls, though I much prefer a colorful dress than the white."

Mary Nell again speaks many unintelligible words.

"Really?" Nellie cocks her head to the side. "Well, Mary Nell, I don't get a chance to get my white pants dirty, so I wouldn't know . . . "

It appears Nellie understands Mary Nell's gibberish.

"Do you understand her?" Savannah asks.

Nellie nods.

The worker from the Verity Wing stands by the door, acting as Nellie's manner policeman. When Nellie doesn't speak, she looks down at her with a frown. "Yes ma'am?"

Nellie nods again. "Yes ma'am."

I glance at Savannah. "You know, this has never happened before."

"What?"

"A donor and a dupe actually treating each other like people before the transfer." I point at the girls and smile. "They're friends."

Savannah sighs. She's troubled. I love it.

"What am I going to do now, Daddy?" Tears well up in her eyes.

I must proceed with caution. If I plunge the sword in too deep, she may harden her heart against my counsel. But love for my granddaughter constrains me to speak up in her defense.

I motion to Sharon. "I'll bring her back. You go."

"I was told not to leave her." Her countenance is stiff and unfriendly.

"By whom?"

"Dr. Cranton."

"Let me see your ID." She unclips it and shows it to me. "Sharon Molla." I look into her eyes. "Do you know who I am?"

"Of course."

"Do you know Dr. Redd Cranton works for me?"

"Yes, sir."

"Just wait outside the door. Please. We need some private family time. I'll speak well of you to Dr. Cranton, so you have nothing to worry about."

She reluctantly steps out of the room.

For several minutes, we all just watch the two girls play. Nellie looks happier than Mary Nell, embracing her fully, even with her quirky habits of wanting to touch her face and hug her excessively.

"Look how that, Savannah. They're like, like, like sisters."

"Maybe I'll give Nellie a sister one day." Savannah's eyes are cold again. This girl constantly fluctuates between contradictory emotions.

"Savannah, look, look, uh, look at me." Our eyes meet. She softens at the tears in my eyes. "Nellie already . . . already . . . already has a sister."

My stuttering prompts Mary Nell to point at me and try to explain to Nellie in broken gibberish how my halting speech makes us alike.

"I love your eyes." Nellie reaches for Mary Nell's cheeks and pinches them teasingly. "And I love your funny voice." She releases a girlish cackle. "Though I don't think the grown-ups can understand you."

Mary Nell responds unintelligibly, at least to me.

"I don't know," Nellie answers. "I wish I did know." She glances at the door. "Probably the same age as you, Mary Nell."

Savannah flinches. She leans forward with her elbows on her knees. "Nellie? What did Mary Nell just ask you?"

"She asked if we were the same age."

"I don't know how she can understand her. I can't understand her half the time." Savannah turns to her mother. "It's so frustrating."

"I know." My wife pats Savannah's shoulder. "And it would be so even for the best mother."

I stretch my hands toward them as if they were my final argument in defense of my granddaughter's life. "It's a match made in heaven."

Savannah turns to Nellie and stretches her arms toward her. "Come here, Nellie. Let me hug you."

While grasping Mary Nell's hand, Nellie walks toward Savannah and brings both of them into her embrace.

There is tenderness in Savannah's eyes as she embraces the two girls. Mary Nell grunts with pleasure, as she does when she's eating a delicious snack or having a pleasant dream on the edge of a meal, as she did when she napped on the beach and I gently caressed her back with the tips of my fingers. Savannah has distanced herself from Mary Nell to protect her own heart from being torn apart when the transfer takes place. To see her embrace these two three-year-old girls gives me hope.

"Sissie!" Mary Nell blurts out. She reaches and touches Nellie on her full pink lips. "Sissie."

Nellie smiles. "I don't have a sister, but I would love to pretend to be your sister if your mommy permits me."

They both look up at Savannah, wide-eyed, hopeful, as if expecting her to grant them permission.

With tears running down her cheeks, Savannah glances at Argentino, who shrugs.

Morgan speaks up. "I just want you to be happy."

"True happiness is to love, without condition or exception." I lean forward. "Savannah, will you let them be happy?"

36

"WHO? WHO TOLD YOU THAT?"

Sharon Molla, the short-haired, board-thin female Verity Wing worker, is adamant. "I'm sorry, Dr. Verity, but . . . "

"Because if it's someone I hired, I'm going to fire them right now."

Mrs. Williamson has come to the door of her office, listening in to our contentious conversation with great interest.

"She's from HHS. Dr. Brie Mallory," Sharon finally blurts out. "She's in charge of the care of the dupes. She didn't want to let Dr. Cranton find a way to check Mary Nell out, so she made the rule unconditionally applicable to all."

"Nellie. We're calling Mary Nell's dupe Nellie."

"Dr. Mallory insisted, in no uncertain terms, that she cannot leave the premises."

I turn to Mrs. Williamson. "This dupe is the product of Mary Nell's genome, which legally makes her Mary Nell's property, and Mary Nell, being a minor, is under the authority of her mother, which makes her legally the property of Savannah Verity, my daughter. I'm sure Dr. Mallory doesn't want legal trouble. Get her on the phone."

"Yes, sir." She disappears back into her office for a moment.

"I'm sorry, Doctor, but Dr. Mallory was insistent that the dupe cannot—"

"Nellie!" I shout, turning to point at her. "Her name is Nellie!"

Sharon Molla and Mrs. Williamson share a cold stare. Sharon calmly responds, "You can call her what you want after the transfer."

"The mother of the donor"—I point to Savannah—"is right here! My wife, who ordered the transfer, is right here!" I point to Morgan.

"Do you really want to mother them both?" Sharon turns to Savannah, her hands planted firmly on her lips. "I find it very hard to believe."

"Yes. I think so." Savannah glances at Argentino, and stutters, "I, I think so."

Sharon blows noisily through her cheeks, appearing to doubt Savannah's sincerity.

"I do," Savannah asserts more confidently.

"Perhaps an exception to our handicapped transfer protocol can be made for you then. But you have to understand, there are channels for that kind of request, and Dr. Mallory personally insisted that I am not to let her out of my sight. She is the lawful property of the New Body Research Center until the transfer."

"Of which I am the top dog—the toppin-est dog that's not a government agent anyway."

Sharon Molla develops a fine tremor to her lower lip. "Yes, sir, you are, but with all due respect, you are not the top dog in the Verity Wing. As a matter of fact, you are not even allowed to step foot in the Verity Wing."

"Five more months! That's how much time until the government gives up their dictatorial powers over my business, the company I founded. Then you know who's going to be the top dog again?"

Sharon swallows hard. "You, sir."

"Do you want to keep your job here in five months, or are you counting on a transfer to Dr. Mallory's federal agency? Because I think the Department of Health and Human Services was forced to make cuts recently, and I don't suspect they're hiring terminated dupe baby-sitters from research centers."

She stares at me with fear in her eyes.

Mrs. Williamson sticks her head out of the door. "Dr. Mallory is now out of reach until tomorrow morning."

"Doesn't she have a nanophone stuck in her skull like everyone else?"

"They wouldn't give me her number."

I turn to Sharon Molla. The initial stone-faced countenance she wore has dissolved in fear over her contention with the founder of the New Body Research Center. If she makes one call to a government agent, I will be in so much trouble for defying the rules that they may ban me from my own facility but, at this point, I'm confident that she's seriously considering letting me have my way.

"When does Dr. Mallory usually arrive in the morning, Sharon?"

"About 9 a.m."

"Be in my office at 8:30 tomorrow morning, and everything will be fine." I raise a finger to halt her protest. "One more word of resistance from you and not only will you lose your job, but I will make sure you never get a job anywhere else either. I promise you."

I guide Savannah and Morgan into roomy office and slam the door in Sharon's face. The whole room erupts in a cheer. I swell with pride, but shush them quiet. I listen intently through the door, hoping Sharon will submit and just leave. I hear her quietly tiptoe away and out the door. I hear the ding of the elevator and the swish of the closing of its doors.

Yes! I have stood up to the tyranny and won. I sigh with relief.

Nellie is the only one who appears confused.

"What's happening?" she asks Savannah.

"You're going home with us." Savannah grabs Argentino's hand affectionately. "You're going to be our new daughter, Nellie." Nellie and Mary Nell squeal with glee, squeezing each other's hands and then clapping playfully.

Morgan's eyes dart to me. "But you said you're bringing her back by 8:30."

"I told Sharon to be here at 8:30," I whisper, "and all would be well, and it will."

"Why do I feel like a great burden has just been lifted from off my shoulders?" Savannah bends down to hug the girls, tears in her eyes.

Oh, those words are such music to my ears!

"Savannah, I will do everything in my power to let you keep your daughters."

I open the door and peek into the hallway to confirm that Sharon is gone and the opening and closing of the elevator doors wasn't a ruse. "Let's get out of here."

As we are leaving, I say goodbye to Mrs. Williamson, and she responds, "Be safe."

Be safe? That's not something she would normally say. "What do you mean? Why that look in your eye?"

She steps closer and whispers, "Oh, I'm referring to this morning's threat."

I stare at her, puzzled.

"I have all the emails forwarded to our contact in the FBI and that attorney, oh, what's his name, the smart aleck . . ."

"Guave Sealdor."

"Yes. Him. Don't they update you?"

I shake my head side to side. "What?"

"The right-wingers are after you, too. Some crazy militia fanatics. I think all the new government activity on the Verity Wing has made the right-wingers upset and suspicious."

"What's that international team of medical investigators doing on the Verity Wing anyway? They won't tell me."

"I don't know. I just know that a team was sent by HHS to investigate some of our transfer procedures."

"What? It was agreed that they wouldn't pry into our transfer protocol. That's outside their jurisdiction, by patent, by contract."

"Well, the President said it was a security issue, and the President's men carrying her message had guns when they delivered it to Dr. Cranton. At least, that's what I've heard."

The President is clearly bucking against our agreement that the science stays with my team and the management with the government. I am helpless, like a paralyzed man watching mosquitoes swarm all over his body and is unable to swat them away. "Mrs. Williamson, will you see what you can dig up and let me in on it tomorrow?"

"I will."

I stare at her for a moment. I wonder if seeing these two girls together impacts her at all, prompting her to rethink her decision to go through with her own scheduled transfer.

I ask Morgan and the others to wait by the elevator. I step into the room. "Mrs. Williamson, will you do me a favor?"

"Yes, sir."

"Remember the love you have seen here today."

She smiles. "It's hard to believe that Nellie is half the age of Mary Nell. The dupe is so mature. They're like sisters who've been together their whole lives . . . "

"You have a sister on the Verity Wing, too. Remember that."

Her grin dissipates. She now looks like a toddler grasping onto a piece of candy an angry parent has threatened to take away.

"One more favor," I say.

"That depends on what it is. If you get in trouble, you know I cannot risk my job."

"I just need you to keep a secret for me if you're asked about something. The lives and the happiness of those girls are at stake."

37

WHILE IN THE HOVER-LIMO HEADING home, it gradually dawns on me what I have done. Everyone else celebrates the potential for a new life with Mary Nell and Nellie as sisters. Everyone except Argentino, whose attention has returned to Morgan's boisterous mania. But as I pass a "Do Not Enter" sign on an elevated intersection above downtown, at Main and Broad, a paralyzing fear begins to grip me. How in the world can I possibly get away with this?

As my driver Jim told me before he was killed, the federal government has no limitations on its ability to spy on us, and no one has given them better reasons to do so than I have. Perhaps they know I'm the insider responsible for releasing information harmful to my business to the right-wing press. If the anti-cloners were to co-opt me to go on the record, I could become a considerable threat to the government's hold on the burgeoning New Body industry. The feds may have been enthusiastically anticipating my attempt to take Mary Nell and Nellie off the premises, in defiance of the inflexible policy of the managing bureaucrats, knowing that this would give them the justification to ruin my reputation and to revoke what little power I have in my own company. Or worse—they could even prosecute me for kidnapping.

"What is it?" Savannah rests a hand on my shoulder from the back seat. "What's bothering you?"

I turn to look into her eyes. "We're going to have to take her back."

"Who? Nellie?"

Careful to be certain Nellie appears oblivious to our conversation, I nod, and speak softly. "Like it or not, she's government property."

Savannah turns to gaze at the girls, who play on the floor of the limo. "What? Why?"

"Sharon Molla was right. There are proper channels for this, for, um, for getting exceptions to the protocol. The feds have every alternative covered. They protect their investments. The bureaucrats are not just going to let me walk away with her." I glance at Mary Nell in the rearview. "Not unless they have Mary Nell as contractually agreed upon. I worry that, uh . . . "

"What?"

"How can we hide from, from"—I look toward the sky—"from the feds? You know the power they have, to snoop, to spy? I worry that they know what I've done and they've let me do it to, uh, you know. To justify getting rid of me."

Morgan glances at the dash. "But your cloak's on."

I see the white light on the dash, letting me know my vehicle's digital cloak (identification blocker) is functioning to conceal the identification of those with electronic devices inside the car. It's true, this is the best technology in the world for remaining digitally *in cognito.* "But we are talking about the federal government, Morgan. No technology like this can be sold without a license, and that license is granted by who? The feds. They wouldn't allow the public to access it if they didn't have the means to bypass it."

Nellie rises and comes to stand in the front of the cabin beside me. "But I belong to you now." Her pleasant features are now strained and gloomy. Her pink cheeks appear to fade to gray right before my eyes. "They can't take me back, right? I belong to you."

"Nellie, do you really know what I'm talking about?"

"I can play with Mary Nell and listen at the same time. I'm a very good listener."

I've hardly heard Nellie speak a word. This little one-and-a-half-year-old is five pounds larger and several inches taller than her three-year-old genetic donor. She speaks as fluently as most adults. With a perfectly engineered genome, there's no telling what magnificent gifts this little girl has trapped inside her, waiting for just the right stimulus to manifest.

"What is your understanding of what's going on?" Savannah asks.

"Based on what I've overheard you saying, I know that legally you can only take me or Mary Nell. Not both of us. I know that you're worried about what will happen to me if I stay there, just a number without a number. And I know that if you go through with the trade . . ." She pauses and the biggest tears I have ever seen in my life come instantly dripping down her cheeks. She turns to Mary Nell, who plays with her doll on the ground. "I don't understand everything, but I know we've got to take good care of my new sister."

I reach over my shoulder to grab her hand warmly. "Nellie, you listen to me. We love you and we're not going to let them keep you, but we probably are going to have to take you back there, at least for a while."

Nellie begins to sob and beg, "Why? I want to stay with you. I don't want to be a number without a number anymore. A dupe."

Savannah also bursts into tears.

"Don't worry. We'll get permission to get you back."

"You're going to be safe," Savannah encourages Nellie as Mary Nell affirms her mother's affection with unintelligible gibberish. "Both of you."

"What if they don't give you permission?" Nellie tries to control her crying.

"They have to," Morgan opines. "Your Grandpa is second-in-command of the company. Your mother, who's in charge of you and Mary Nell, will not sign either of you over to them."

"Tell me the truth. What will they do to everyone there? To my friends? Why do they teach me math and reading and so many wonderful things, and they do not teach the others? Why is everyone a number except a few of us who are given names? We are told that when we are ready, we get to move on to a better life. Every once in a while, someone disappears. But tell me, what really happens?"

Savannah and I trade glances in the rearview mirror. How can I lie to her? And if I do tell her the truth, how can I ever take her back there? How would she ever trust me again, knowing that just minutes ago, for fear of my own well-being, I insisted that we had to take her back?

"We're not going to worry about that right now," Savannah interrupts my troubling thoughts. I bring the limo slowly to a stop at the hotel at which Savannah and Argentino have a room.

"Do you all want to swim?" Argentino inquires.

The girls suddenly cheer and clap.

"No," I respond. "You can't."

The girls settle down as Savannah leans close to protest my usurpation. "What do you mean? Why not?"

"Savannah, I need you to trust me." I turn to make eye contact with Argentino and Morgan. "Will you both trust me?"

38

GUAVE SEALDOR NORMALLY WOULD NEVER desire to be present at such an interrogation. His job is to manage the government's takeover of the New Body Research Center, not to coerce truth out of liars. But so much was at stake. President Sayder personally ordered him to "Make this legal! The law is a means to an end, Guave, and our end justifies any means. If we must modify the law to legitimize the means, so be it."

If he were to fail her, he may, as a dupe with intimate knowledge of the President's lies and abuses of power, be too great a threat to simply demote. A massive investment of federal ameros has already been allocated for the construction of three more medical centers integrating the New Body science into ordinary, every-day healthcare: one in Jacksonville, one in Sacramento, and one in Chicago.

"There's too much power in the New Body Research Center," the President told him. "We need to send in every medical expert at our disposal to master the science and force those we cannot co-opt into accepting our control."

"Too big to fail" was what the President had told Raymond Verity, the board, the platinum investors of the New Body Research Center, and the press. But in the President's words to Guave, "It's too big *not* to fail."

"We're not going to sabotage the company," she informed him, "we're just introducing some fair competition. The needs of the public transcend the greed of the New Body patent holders. The law is irrelevant. If the public sector cannot compete because of New Body's patents, then the government's going to level the playing field. To respect the validity of those patents would be to sentence millions of Americans to their deaths every single year and risk the dwindling of national resources due to the overpopulation of 'useless eaters'—to borrow a phrase from Sanger. For the greater good, we need to harness this technology and mass replicate it all over the nation, and if that puts the enigmatic Dr. Verity in bankruptcy, well, that's a small price to pay."

With the disappearance of Dr. Verity and his family with the dupe known as Mary Nell illegally in their possession, the federal investigation team had launched into high gear to find them, co-opting every agency's resources and every security feed in the whole country. Turns out, Raymond Verity's cloak device did conceal their hand-held computers because those computers also employed stealth technology that was very expensive. Both are traceable separately, but not in combination. The cloak device in the vehicle did not, however, secure their nanophones. Fortunately, the super-wealthy frequently purchased their nanophones from the Asian black market, since they did not have the GPS tracking capability of American-licensed nanos, and Dr. Verity and company all had the expensive foreign implants, a luxury politically tenuous for Congress to regulate. The feds easily confirmed that all their vehicles were stationary and unoccupied, and there was no trace of their presence in the vicinity of their homes or their properties. Thus, the investigative team had to resort to aggressive interrogations and relentless threats of those close to them.

Guave sensed his blood pressure rise as the beefy FBI agent with the big ears leaned in close to the sweating face of the aging secretary of Dr. Verity, the sly Mrs. Williamson.

"You already told me that!" the agent shouts. "We picked Sharon Molla up even before you! You're not giving us any new information."

The FBI had grabbed Mrs. Williamson and Ms. Molla soon after their arrival at work after the dupe was discovered missing. For the sake of time, these agents are interrogating the secretary in the back of a black, windowless van as we cruise the beltway around Baltimore.

"It's the truth!" she insists. "It's all I know!"

"Are you listening to what I'm saying?" The beefy agent pounds the car's wall, frustrated at their lack of progress. "We sent agents to his Caribbean island to scope out his home. He's not there! His jet has never even left the airport."

"He asked for a favor," she calmly states. "He told me not to tell anybody that he was taking his family to his island. He asked me to call his pilot and have him meet him at the airport."

"So you knew he was kidnapping the dupe and leaving the country, and you didn't report it?"

"I told you. I, I was going to. I tried to talk him out of it."

The agent leans back and crosses his thick arms over his wide chest, sighing wearily.

"Please," Mrs. Williamson begs. "I was due to get my new body next week."

"You're not getting anything until you can help me find Raymond Verity and his family. If I find out you are withholding anything from me, I will personally dispose of your dupe myself."

"I am telling you everything I know."

From the corner of the van, Guave glances at the laptop that shows the live feed of the interrogation of Sharon Molla, who was ordered not to let the dupe out of her sight. Guave is one of the few aware that his superiors had intentionally chosen Ms. Molla for this task because they deemed her most likely to be amenable to any potential persuasion or threats from Dr. Verity. They *wanted* Dr. Verity to take the dupe. It was part of the plan to push him out of leadership and justify perpetual federal control of the New Body science, and to simultaneously disarm him from ever being a threat to the industry again. Even so, Ms. Molla violated protocol and must pay the price for it.

Guave reaches for the earpiece and puts it in his ear to listen to the questions they are asking her between applications of violent coercion. But hearing the zaps of their electric batons, followed by her terrified shrieks of denial and fits of sobbing, he changes his mind and sets down the earpiece. They must believe she is withholding something from them, or they would not treat her so.

What is happening has already been hashed out in Congress and a consensus solidified, though the fact brings him little comfort. For fear of terrorism, the people gladly surrendered many freedoms. The people want this. Somehow, however, it doesn't quite set his mind at ease. It could just as easily be him sitting in that chair if he had bumped into Dr. Verity on the day of his crime. Except he is not a legal person. He is a dupe. He is property. He has no human rights, unlike Mrs. Williamson and Ms. Molla, and thus has no expectation that he would be treated as humanely as they.

A text flashes on the top of his laptop screen. It is from the FBI's Virginia office, addressed to all of the agents doing the interrogating. "We've found eyewitnesses that saw them at a pharmacy in Richmond, VA. More intel forthcoming."

39

AFTER LEAVING SAVANNAH'S HOTEL, I direct the limo driver outside the city limits to a home where I remember seeing an "RV Hover for Sale" sign out front. Fortunately, the RV owner recognizes me and accepts my 55,000 amero bank transfer via his computer. It's a great deal, given he lets us drive off his lot in a first class luxury recreational hovercraft, in spite of incomplete paperwork.

We pack into the RV and head south, with no particular destination in mind. I inform everyone we are going for a week of celebration at a park. Amidst the cheers of the girls, everyone settles into the RV's cots to get some sleep.

Nellie and Mary Nell insist on sleeping together on the same pull-out bed. I glance at them through the night in the rearview mirror. They embrace each other so lovingly, as if they had known each other their whole lives. Before they drift off to sleep, they whisper back and forth for several minutes. I think I hear the humming of a tune—"Jesus, Loves Me." It's what I sang to Mary Nell as she dozed off on the beach the first day I met her. Now Mary Nell's teaching the song to Nellie—at least the tune.

I turn off the A/C, hoping I can better discern their whispered discourse, and I overhear Nellie tell my granddaughter, "No, Mary Nell, you're perfect."

That's the last thing I hear before Mary Nell's gentle snoring informs me that she has fallen asleep with Nellie's right arm draped over Mary Nell's smaller frame.

To think that we were going to kill the weak for the strong, trade the imperfect for the perfect—the thought fills me with disgust. It seems as if the most defective of the two has been the missing piece of the other's life. What a paradox! The defective one has perfected the flawless one. I study them for a brief moment in the rearview mirror. Mary Nell rests her palm against Nellie's cheek. They have perfected each other.

"We should have flown to our island," Morgan mumbles from the passenger seat as she has done through the night. She's finally beginning to nod off, but continues to rouse herself intermittently to nag me about something. I wish she would be quiet before she wakens the girls. Her condescending and self-absorbed prattle has managed to help me more easily stay alert for the late night drive.

With as much adrenaline—and coffee—as I have coursing through my bloodstream, I think I may just continue all the way to Orlando. However, as dawn breaks just outside the city limits of Atlanta, an alarm on the dash informs me that I must re-energize the batteries in the next dozen miles. Hopefully, I have enough cash in my wallet—or Morgan does in her purse—so that I can refill without having to mooch off Savannah or Argentino or risk using my credit.

Unfortunately, most stores do not take cash anymore, but in poorer areas of a larger town I may find one. I check the pocket in my leather handheld cover, where I keep my credit cards and ID, and I discover eighteen 100-credit ameros. I predict it's sufficient to energize the batteries at least twice more. I plug my handheld into the computer on the dash of the RV, ensure the stealth technology is active, and then begin a search for fuel stations nearby that will accept cash. I find one in downtown Atlanta. It's not a good idea to refuel in a big city, given there are security cameras everywhere, but cash has become a rare commodity in our credit-saturated economy.

"Why don't we just go to our airport and take our jet to our island," Morgan mumbles. "Or just"—she yawns and points to the GPS on the dash—"just GPS the nearest port and buy a plane . . . "

This woman will continue to nag me until she gets her way. She doesn't quite understand the danger of using our credit and showing up on the grid, and I really don't want her to. Since she's even more impervious to reason when she's half asleep as when she's awake, I don't have the inclination to try to explain myself.

It is exactly, after all, what I told Mrs. Williamson when we left my office: I am going to my island with my family. She promised to respect my privacy and keep my secret, but, upon reflection, I realized it would be unwise to trust her. If she is willing to go through with her own transfer, exploiting the killing of her dupe for her own health benefits, then she would have no ethical problem with ratting out my destination the first time she was questioned about where I might have gone with Nellie. You can never trust a murderer to be honest, especially when they have something to gain from the dishonesty, or discomfort to avoid.

I log into my security website to view the various camera angles of my two homes—the one in Baltimore and the one on my Caribbean island. I have been doing this every hour of our nine-hour drive thus far.

What I see now, however, makes me shudder and swerve off the road, lighting up the angry red warning light on the dash. The electricity has suddenly been shut off at my island mansion. With dawn just breaking in the east and the night sky still hovering overhead, the landscape lights should still be on. My battery-operated security cameras have switched into night-vision mode and there are black-clothed SWAT agents making their way down my long driveway. They creep toward my home, assault weapons at the ready. One of them taps the concealed camera with an object, and now I see only static.

I click the link of my Baltimore residence and witness the innards of that home being raided by FBI investigators. Normally, my handheld computer would buzz me if the alarm went off, but there was no warning. They are breaking into my safes, dumping out all of my drawers and cabinets, uncovering all of my secret compartments.

I try not to overreact, not wanting to startle my wife out of her uneasy sleep. She would be more troubled at the sight than I could possibly imagine.

Dawn begins to break on my left. The cloud of greenish-brown smog on the horizon ahead of me reminds me that Atlanta looms like a great big trap ready to clamp down on us. I am risking running out of power, but I am desperate to find a way around Atlanta. I take the exit before the beltway and park at the far end of the parking lot of a dilapidated truck stop, careful to keep out of the view of any security cameras that may be watching. It's just a matter of time before federal investigators find out that I purchased this RV and begin to hunt us. Is it possible to stay off the grid on back roads and campgrounds? Maybe, if I drive the speed limit. I can probably convince some unsuspecting storeowners of small chains to let me pay cash for food and energy for the RV's batteries, but how can I withdraw from my accounts without using my ID and pin-pointing my location for federal investigators?

Have they tapped into my accounts already and confiscated my massive wealth and savings? Or maybe they will leave it like bait, hoping that I will be drawn to it like a hungry fish to an irresistible lure. I haven't driven a vehicle since ten years before my retirement in my previous life, so reliant I have become on my chauffeurs and pilots. What do I know about living off the grid? As I think of it, my driver's license probably expired forty years ago . . .

Argentino stirs. "We need a pit stop." I see him turn on his hand-held in my review mirror.

Hiding may not be as easy as I initially thought.

40

I LEAVE THE CREW AT Tofu Palace, a fast food restaurant that boasts an indoor playground for children, complete with colorful slides and mazes. I assure Morgan, "I'm just going to get some work done on the RV. Stay here."

I urge her, Savannah, and Argentino to stay off their nanophones, and handhelds, even if they are in stealth mode. "I don't want this much-deserved vacation ruined by having to consult my team of lawyers to stave off the company's bureaucratic regulators. Let's allow my secretary to stall and we'll postpone that battle for next week."

Thankfully, this explanation satisfies Argentino and Savannah. Morgan, however, remains resistant to my counsel and suspicious of my motives. She mindlessly believes that we have nothing at all to worry about and that everything will be fine if we continue life as usual.

"Oh, just call Vlad," she mumbles. "He'll handle it."

Yeah, right.

I study the two girls on the playground. Savannah watches them from a distance, a thin smile on her face. Argentino holds his handheld with one hand, and his coffee in the other. I fear he's going to start surfing again as soon as I leave.

"Please, Morgan. Please. For me. Stay off your devices." Without another word, I dart out of the store and toward the RV. I don't know how this is going to end, but if I am able to save Mary Nell and Nellie, I suspect things will get worse before they get better.

Inside the RV, concealed by the digital cloak, a quick search on my handheld informs me that there's an auto repair shop across the street. Perhaps they have a mechanic who can disable any uncloakable tracking mechanism inside of our RV. Once my bank transfer to the RV owner's account is investigated or my limo driver is questioned, I'm certain the investigators will discover that we are in this vehicle. It's just a matter of time. Disabling a vehicle's tracking mechanism is probably illegal, so I find a fellow in the bathroom, young, pierced, and tattooed, the kind of fellow who looks just like the person who'd take me up on my offer. As he's washing his oily hands, I flash four of my 100-credit ameros in front of him. His eyebrows rise and the corner of one side of his mouth turns up. Now I have his attention.

"I need a favor," I say. "It's not a stolen vehicle and I've committed no crime. I just don't want to be found. No questions asked, no receipt or ID requested."

He appears pleased with the transaction, especially when I pay him three of the four bills up front. He asks me to park out back, which I do. He comes out with a red toolbox. "I've got only a ten minute break. If I can't finish, it'll have to wait until noon."

I glance at my watch. It's 8:15 a.m. I cannot afford to wait till noon.

Not ten seconds after I flip the hood for him, I hear an approaching roar from the sky, appearing to come from every direction at once. At first, I think we are near an airport, but soon the unmistakable thumping of a helicopter's rotors begins to blow our hair around like we are in a tornado. I cover my eyes from the dust thrown up at me from the stiff downward draft's collision with the concrete, hoping that this is an emergency helicopter for a customer in the store who is having a heart attack, or something like that. The mechanic abandons his tools and runs for the shop. As the helicopter lowers to the ground directly in front of me, I see the unmistakable black metal of a weapon protruding from the open side door of the copter. I jump in the RV and slam it in reverse. However, in the rearview mirror I see another copter landing behind me, blocking my exit.

A loudspeaker announces, "Raymond Verity! Step out of the vehicle with your hands in the air! Now!"

Behind the helicopters are several black vans and trucks. They break with a squeal and dozens of SWAT agents descend upon me, shouting orders to get out of the vehicle and fall to my knees with my hands behind my head.

I pray a prayer for Mary Nell and Nellie. Even now, even with all the risk I have taken to protect those girls, I still feel like an impenetrable wall separates me from my Maker.

I get out of the car, and following their orders, fall to my knees and place my hands behind my head. The first agent to reach me aims a weapon at me and fires. It feels like lightning strikes my right shoulder. I hear the zapping of his Taser as he holds down the trigger. I fall to the ground. After ten seconds of immense pain, he ceases.

Another agent bends down near to me. "Where's your family?"

"My family?" I repeat through gasps of pain.

"The dupe, Mary Nell. Where is she?"

I hesitate to answer and the agent pulls the trigger again. Finally, after I think I can take no more of the pain, he releases the trigger. I am surrounded on all sides by a wall of black-clothed federal agents, concealing my suffering from the eyes of any passers-by. There is no way out of this.

The agent bends close to my ear and calmly asks again. "Where is the dupe? I will ask one time, and then we will give you ten to sixty seconds of electricity."

"Across the street!" I spit out the words, trembling for fear of the pain. "At the chicken place."

They give me erratically-timed moments of electricity every twenty seconds or so. I guess they don't want to give me any relief in case I am lying, so they keep torturing me. They are merciless and my screams in between bursts of spasm appear to have no effect on my tormenters. This period of suffering feels all the more sadistic because of its purposelessness. They ask me no questions and give me no answers.

"Why are you hurting me?" I inquire between gasps of air. Then more pain. Over and over.

Finally, after what seems like an hour but probably isn't over three or four minutes, the agent who addressed me earlier raises a hand to stop the voltage. Several feet run toward me from the direction of the store. Then I overhear some dialogue I cannot understand due to the ringing in my ears. The agents dissipate, getting back in their vans and helicopters. I am hoisted up by two men, who support my weight with their arms under my arms.

I suspect they have caught my family. At least, my suffering is over.

Then the agent who has been speaking to me announces, "You're lying. They aren't there."

This is simultaneously encouraging and horrifying. Encouraging, for my misdirection must have worked. My family must have fled when they saw federal agents charge the restaurant adjacent to them. Horrifying, because the federal agents are probably just changing my

location so they can be more creative and intentional in their inflic-
tion of suffering.

I am seated in the back of a windowless van. My hands are shackled
behind my back and my feet to a stainless steel U-shaped bar on the
floor beneath my bolted seat. Then they pull a black cloth bag over
my head.

"What are you going to do to me?"

Silence.

"Hello?" The door behind me slams shut. "Anybody there?"

Nobody is in the back of the van with me. I am alone with
my thoughts.

The van lurches forward and then, suddenly, its hover-engines
brake hard, throwing me forward. The jerk of my chains against my
wrists and ankles pulls at my flesh, testing the limits of my joints and
stretching my tendons. I scream—for fear more than for pain—and
try to perch myself precariously back up on my seat.

I suspect that there has been a collision. "Is everything okay?"

There is some shouting in the front of the van and behind me.
Then gunshots. From all directions.

A bullet pierces the van, and I lower my head.

A gunfight commences outside the van. After a pop, the van drops
behind me. An engine has gone out.

After a few minutes, the back door opens and someone jumps
inside. Then the van begins to move again, scraping the bottom right
of the van intermittently against the concrete.

"Ha ha! We got him!" The man in the back of the van apparently
shouts to someone through a communication device. The van acceler-
ates over a speed bump, knocking me out of my chair again.

"Ow!"

The man pulls me back into my seat.

"Who are you?"

"You are now the people's property. Let's go! Quickly."

I overhear a voice on the man's radio. "We've lost the other vehicles, but—"

"You haven't lost them! There's a beacon on this vehicle. Removing it is a priority—"

"No, listen—"

"Remove the beacon, then move to position two, like we planned . . . "

Another helicopter is rapidly approaching, and then several high caliber rounds fire from overhead.

The vehicle lurches to the left, and I hear the rear bumper scrape against the ground and then, with a loud bump, it falls off, scraping against the cement. We lurch to the left again. Only my chains keep me in the seat.

"What the . . . !" The man in the back of the van with me is thrown against the wall and falls hard to the floor. He taps his communication device. I hear the metallic smack of his rifle against the metal floor of the van. "What are you doing?"

"That's what I've been trying to tell you! We have two rapidly approaching helicopters. Our men on the ground have engaged with one of— "

Several rounds of the helicopter's guns shatter glass and silence the van's driver. He lets out a bloody gurgle as he heaves several noisy breaths.

"Bear One!" The man in the back with me calls out, "Bear One!"

The hovering helicopter fires several more rounds. Given the sound of shattering glass, piercing metal, and billowing flame, it has struck vehicles nearby.

The man behind me curses, then pulls on my chains. He curses again then fires at the chain between my legs. Shards of metal strike my leg, startling me with searing pain. "Ahhh!"

He grabs me by my collar and flings me to the floor. My leg bonds have been loosened and are no longer binding me to the floor.

"Stay down!"

The pain in my left shin makes me wonder if he has shot me in the leg. I wiggle my foot and it still functions.

He begins to search my body with a beeping device.

"What are you doing?"

He does not respond. He removes the bag over my head and runs his hand through my hair. I jerk my head away from his probing fingers. "What are you—"

He smacks me in the face. "Shut up!" My cheek stings.

The gunfire grows in the distance. He taps his communication device. "Bear Two! Wolf One! Elk One! I need a driver, now! Bear One has been shot!"

Rapid gunfire echoes through his communication device, and a fretful voice responds, "We are forced to retreat. We have a copter in pursuit . . . overpass . . . fourth street and . . . "

"Engage! Do not retreat!"

"Ground forces are converging on the other side of the overpass! Half my men are down! Abandon . . . !"

"Do not abandon your post!"

There is silence on the communication device. "Elk One! Come in, Elk One!"

The man curses when there is no response. It sounds like the gunfight has moved about a block away. The man unzips something, and removes something metallic. After several clicks, the man stands in front of me and turns his back to me. "Camera, check. Mic, um, check." I hear him flip some switches. "Wireless connection, check."

A helicopter whizzes past, firing its machine guns at a distant target. "What are you doing?"

"Broadcasting your execution to the world." He turns to me and flips on a blinding light that forces me to close my eyes and turn my head away. He grasps my jaw and pulls my head back around to face him. "No, no. Keep your head this direction and say hello, Dr. Raymond Verity."

I squint against a battery-powered light he has aimed at me.

The man turns to face the camera and ensures his assault rifle is off safety. "This is Raymond Verity, the man who has been most responsible for the Holocaust of cloned people, handicapped children, butcher extraordinaire of aborted babies . . . Yada yada yada. You know him . . . "

My eyes begin to adjust to the bright light as he aims his weapon at my head. I hear the whistle of a rocket—either a surface-to-air or air-to-air, I cannot tell. Then, a massive explosion overhead, which rocks the van slightly with the percussion, causing the man to lose his footing. I am confused and disoriented from the extreme volume of the nearby blast. Either the percussion of the blast or a piece of shrapnel has ripped some of the bag that covers my face, allowing me to see through my left eye. Shrapnel has punctured the side of the van, and sunlight comes through the angular holes in the black metal. The man's camera, propped up on his book bag, has fallen. He curses and then repositions it. I hear high caliber automatic machine gun fire from overhead, and then a copter speeding past.

There are screams in the distance. More heavy-caliber machine gun fire comes from a copter hovering above me.

My anxious captor aims his weapon at me.

I squint and try to make out his facial features. I see a black hood, and a black hole where the face would be. It reminds me of the black beast of bones that sat upon my chest as I breathed my last in my previous life. Here I am again. Facing Death. It appears there is no escape. I have tried to make amends. Why do I yet fear it?

"I have changed!" I wheeze through raspy breaths. "I was wrong, and I'm trying to fix it."

"What? You want mercy from me?" I look, and now see a man's face where the black hole was before. "Only the merciful get mercy. How many dupes has your organization de-brained? How many others will die in the name of that vile law that bears your name?" He presses his finger against the trigger.

"If only the merciful get mercy, then what are you going to get?"

"The satisfaction of justice," he responds coldly.

I close my eyes. What will happen to me in the next few seconds? Will I even hear the sound of the gun blast? I have really tried to do right. I have tried to prepare for this moment so that I would be at peace. But, here at my end, I still fear what will happen to me. "Oh God," I mumble. "Help me."

In the blink of an eye, a massive gunshot tears a hole the size of a softball in the side of the van. The sound is so loud that my rapid, anxious respiratory rate doubles, inebriating my senses. The man's brains ooze on the side of the van beside me. His headless body seizes on the floor, causing his trigger finger to pull in secession.

Blam! Blam! Blam! Blam!

I cower from his gunshots, throwing my body away from the trajectory of his bullets, screaming. The chains that have bound me to the chair are loose, broken by some chunk of shrapnel or a bullet.

There is a gun blast at the back door and it thrashes open. Someone shoots the seizing guard several times, causing the headless man's firing to cease.

"Raymond Verity?"

Though I can only barely hear the man's voice due to the ringing in my ears, I can still recognize it. I cannot place it, but somehow it brings me relief.

"I'm here. Who are you?"

"Are you injured?"

"I think so." I examine my painful leg through the rip in the bag that covers my face. The wound has bled my shoe wet.

"Where?"

"My ankle."

The person opening the back door turns away from me and yells, "I have the target!"

I look at him. It is the stranger that spoke to me at the party celebrating our pro-life ethics panel.

"Are you going to tell me who you are now?"

"Alabama State Guard Intelligence officer." He kneels to tend to my wound. "Let's relocate you and then we'll doctor that."

"Alabama? They have intelligence in Alabama?"

He chuckles at my choice of words.

"No, I didn't mean it to sound like that. I mean, um . . . "

He slings his rifle over his shoulder and helps me to my feet. "Tod Farrell. Your attackers were from the Free America Militia."

He helps me out of the van and moves me into another windowless van. My ankles function better than I suspected, probably from the adrenaline.

Bodies sprawl on the ground around me, lifeless in red pools reflecting the scattered clouds of the sunny day. Many are in suits and ties, others in black SWAT outfits with black helmets. Others are dressed in camouflaged outfits who, by their long hair, facial hair, and the diversity of their weapons, I assume to be civilian militia. On the other side of the auto shop, a large fire billows smoke into the sky, apparently from where one of the copters went down.

"My family? They were in that fast food restaurant with the indoor playground."

"They're safe." He removes the hood off my head.

"There were three adults and two girls . . . "

"All of them are safe," he assures me.

"How, how do you know?"

"We were tailing you."

I glance at him cockeyed.

"When we saw what was happening, we intervened. Fortunately, the Free American Militia took out most of the feds . . . "

"The feds?"

"We took two casualties from a sniper on top of the building. We still don't know if that was the feds or the militia."

"How did you find me?"

"We have insiders in the Bureau helping us."

He sits me into a metal chair by a black van with rubber tires . . .
Only in Alabama.

"I don't understand. Were you trying to capture me, prevent the
feds from capturing me, prevent the militia from . . . ?"

"No." He grins and shakes his head as a medic begins to clean and
bind my superficial ankle wound. "No. You're valuable to us."

He looks at his handheld computer and reads a message. He looks
up at me and grins broadly, his eyebrows raised with surprise.

"What?"

"Congratulations."

"For what?"

"For breaking the world record on the most hits in ten minutes."

"Hits? You mean hits on my life? I only got hit once, in the ankle."

"No. That was probably a world record too, but the man that was
about to execute you was live-streaming wirelessly through multiple
servers simultaneously. It was still streaming when we left the van.
Looks like the feds only just now turned it off, but not before it was
shared tens of millions of times. Looks like your courage with his
rifle in your face, as well as my team's rescue has made the both of
us famous."

"I didn't feel that courageous. That's for sure. How did you shoot
that fellow through the wall of the van anyway? You know, you
could've shot me."

"I assumed that he wasn't the one chained to a seat and you weren't
the one shouldering a rifle."

"You saw us? Through the wall of the van?"

He taps the square-shaped scope on top of his fancy black rifle.
"Thermal image scope on a Tracking Point PGR."

I wince from the pain of the bandage application. "PGR?"

He chuckles. "We'll keep you safe. But all of it's not for nothing. We need you to do something for us."

"For Alabama?"

"And Mississippi. And some other states at the table."

I assume he means at the table of states resisting or planning to resist the federal government in some way. His friendly countenance and the words of wisdom he shared with me the first time we met has instilled in me a deep trust for this stranger. I feel like I trust him more than I even trust myself. He fixes his eyes on me, expecting me to accept his offer.

"Yee haw," I say with a grin. "Alabama it is," I bellow in my best cowboy accent.

"I think you're confusing Alabama and Texas." He does not reciprocate my light-hearted smile.

What dire straits have he and his superiors conspired for me?

41

IN TWENTY MINUTES, I AM enclosed in the trunk of a brand new luxury hover-sedan, chained onto the upper deck of a semi carrying a dozen of them, and told not to worry. I am assured that a dozen Alabama intel agents will be monitoring me constantly. They give me a small portable temperature regulator to keep the air in the trunk tolerably cool, and a handheld computer with some articles and videos on its desktop which I am told to watch to pass the time.

They give me several bottles of water, anti-motion sickness medicine, and instructions on some exercises to keep me from getting stiff. Before they lock the trunk, I ask, "Can't they see me through satellite?"

"No." One of them pats the trunk. "Lead paint. And on this sunny day, the surface will be too hot to allow them to evaluate any heat signature inside."

When they shut me in, I tap on a video entitled, *Watch first*. It is a video of Savannah, telling me about their rescue and safety in a location she assures me is secure. It brings me so much comfort to see her smiling face. I see the girls behind her sitting on the ground against a couch. Nellie is reading Mary Nell a children's storybook.

"Mom wouldn't stay. Neither would Argentino. They were encouraged by those who rescued us to write down their story about everything and send it to the media as soon as possible through electronic and snail mail, and then approach the government and tell their side of the story as soon as possible. So that way they wouldn't be suspects, and having told the media, they were less likely to be mistreated."

There's also a video of an Alabama executive cabinet meeting. Maurice Whetley, the Alabama Governor, sits at the head of the table. I think this is the first time I have ever laid eyes on him, and I'm taken aback that he's African-American. By his immense size, I suspect he is a retired professional athlete. He would have the handsome face of a Hollywood actor if it were not for the three-inch horizontal scar above his left eye. Why hasn't a plastic surgeon repaired that?

Whetley begins with a prayer, which is unusual for a political meeting. He then tells the staff that the meeting will be recorded "for the sake of Dr. Raymond Verity, whom we suspect will be rescued soon and will take us up on our offer to help him stop the killing."

The camera pans out as he introduces those on his trusted council, including his Attorney General Shane Mease, a red-haired, weirdly-shaped youngster who looks like he'd have the physique of a long-distance runner if it weren't for the twenty pounds of flab that conceals his belt buckle.

Whetley introduces Phil Stephens, the face of Personhood Now in Alabama. Like his small voice, his head and chest appear too small for his tall body and long limbs. He appears to be all joints and sinews. I immediately suspect a severe case of Marfans Syndrome, a connective tissue disease causing long limbs and flexible joints.

Then, to my surprise, Whetley introduces my sister, Tamara.

My sister! Sitting with the Alabama Governor's council? How did that happen? I can see only the back of her head. She is looking down at something. Knowing her, she's probably searching her Bible for a verse with which to rebuke me.

"Doubtless, all you've heard about Alabama leadership is what the media has reported." Governor Whetley speaks into the camera on the far side of his long, oblong table. "As you have learned by now, Dr. Verity, the media is practically an arm of the federal government, and is proof of the old adage that the power to license is the power to control and censor." His voice has a rich, raspy quality to it, like a coach who has screamed himself hoarse on the sidelines for twenty years. "Nevertheless, there are some things you must know about those who have surrounded and empowered you since you were brought out of cryo-preservation. Vlad Riddell, your attorney, has been recruited by President Sayder. She coopted him when you were in suspended animation, persuading him to include clauses in that big stack of papers you signed your first day in the office giving her full uncontestable rights to the dupes she persuaded Redd Cranton to design for her personal use . . . "

That must be how she obtained Guave Sealdor, her savant attorney. I wonder what other super-soldiers she has under her control.

"For a decade, as a Washington insider and then V.P., Veronica Sayder had direct licensing access to the New Body Research Center, requiring special treatment off the record to gain approval for federal funding and licensure. Given that not all of his victims are clones, Cranton would have been convicted of child sex charges and child prostitution years ago if he hadn't been guaranteed immunity by President Sayder, and President Wimble before her. We have on tape President Wimble's wife admitting that immunity for Cranton was the price for her husband to be moved to the front of the line for a new body . . . "

Unbelievable!

"Thus, President Sayder is presently aiding and abetting a child sex ring that runs from New York City to Richmond and all the way to Charlotte. We would never have learned this if it were not for an FBI insider who prosecutes child sex crimes objecting to the backroom immunity deal for Cranton by, in essence, defecting to Alabama.

"Even Quaid Sandman was in on the conspiracy. For several years, he received insider information from someone in the Securities and Exchange Commission—likely a presidential appointee—allowing him to increase the value of all of his investors' portfolios far beyond his peers. Either to ensure his complicity with the government offering licenses and taxpayer-funding in exchange for dupe-slaves for government leaders, or they suspected that the wealthier you and your wife were, the more likely you were to play nice within the corrupt system. Few are willing to break the shackles that enrich them."

I shake my head. This is all too surreal to fully embrace. My sister's words from three decades ago flood back to my mind, a memory as fresh as if it happened yesterday: *Hardly will a rich man enter the kingdom of God.*

"Your brother offered his services to you to help you craft your company's ethics policies as a direct result of President Sayder's prodding for him to do so," the Alabama governor continues. "His devotion to you was purchased with hundreds of thousands of taxpayer ameros. I have bank records of the transfers, and proof of ownership of the otherwise anonymous accounts." He clasps his hands tightly together and takes a deep breath. "We confronted your brother and he confessed that President Sayder, knowing that you had some strong objections to the exploitation of your clones, persuaded him to be Karl Marx's opium to you, if you will. She was hoping some good deeds would appease your guilty conscience, help you be at peace with your impenitence. Doubtless, you will learn what I have learned the hard way: there is no appeasing a guilty conscience without repentance, nor without the cross."

He turns to look at the far end of the table, and nods at someone. Phil Stephens stands. His thin face is drawn and sad, as if he is not accustomed to smiling. "Dr. Verity, we wanted to bring you here to help.

Very soon, there will be a gathering of governors and their executive cabinets. Seven states altogether, two of whom are already committed to resisting federal tyranny in defense of the innocent. The other five are undecided, but troubled sufficiently by the federal usurpations that they have agreed to come to the table to discuss our strategy. We are convinced that your presence and your testimony would turn the tide and at least double the number of states committed to prosecuting the killers and exploiters of human clones. We pray that you will help us."

Phil Stephens sits back down and nudges my sister beside him. "Tamara, didn't you want to say something?"

She rises and turns to look at the camera. Sure enough, there is a worn out Bible in her hands. "Hello Ray, I pray you are well. It says in Hebrews, chapter 12 to be exact, that Jesus' blood speaks better things than that of Abel . . . "

Finally, she's going to tell me what that means.

"Cain and Abel were two sons of the first couple, Adam and Eve. When Cain killed Abel, God told Cain that the blood of his brother cried up out of the ground, crying out for justice. God then judged Cain, putting a mark upon him. Numbers 35 and Deuteronomy 21 confirm that innocent blood shed in the land brings God's curse upon the people, a horrible doom, a curse that only justice can can abate . . . "

The politicians around her shift uneasily. From their strained countenances, I suspect they are wishing she would be more winsome in her remarks. No doubt, her sword has dripped with their blood.

"In the book of Revelation, the souls of those slain unjustly cry out, 'How long, Oh Lord!'" She thrusts both hands heavenward, one holding her Bible and one clenched into a tight fist. "How long until you avenge our blood!" She lowers her hands and lets her arms dangle by her sides. "Imagine for a moment, brother, the chorus of the slain that are crying out against you."

Her words impale me, exposing the guilt I have vainly tried to suppress for so many years through constant pleasure-seeking, wealth and fame, and recently, through good works and the deceptive comfort of my brother's assurances. However, I hear in my mind and in my heart the cry of a thousand aborted children, euthanized elderly and handicapped patients, and brain-evacuated clones like Savannah's liquidated clone, like the beautiful girl Forty, and little Nellie, all crying out for justice. Crying out to God with *my* name on their lips, crying out for vindication. It is a formidable shriek that drives fear into my heart and breaks me out in a sweat. I turn down the gauge on the portable temperature regulator.

"The sting of death is sin, and the strength of sin is the law. You may despise the guilt and conviction that deprives sin of its luster, but your guilt is God's mercy to you, showing you your need for a Savior. God's commandments are aimed at you like ten massive cannons. You have violated the sixth, 'Do not murder,' innumerable times. You violated 'Thou shalt not steal' by stealing another's body, and 'Thou shalt not covet another's wife', through enjoying women to whom you aren't married. Your meager attempts to collapse your company and save your granddaughter are like trying to block that cannon with a pillow. No good works can ever wash away the guilt of a murderer in the court of man, neither in the court of heaven. Only at the end of a noose would your conscience be at peace, brother, if it were not for the blood of Jesus shed for you.

"Jesus became a curse for you, Ray, suffering the penalty for your sin. You cannot earn His grace. Put your trust in God, not in yourself. Call upon Jesus' name, and you will be saved. Abel's blood cries out for justice, but the blood of Jesus speaks better things. It speaks of your redemption."

She's done. She turns and sits down. My hair stands on end. The screen blackens.

My redemption?

I do not quickly reject her counsel as I have always done. It is not so much a bitter pill to swallow as it is an attempt to take my bitter pills away. My misery is undeniable. My fear of death is inescapable, all of my attempts to reform myself notwithstanding.

I meditate on her words and, before long, I am weeping tears of repentance heavenward, calling on Jesus to save me.

God's love has always been a distant island in my mind, admirable, but unapproachable. Not an island like my Caribbean get-away, my little paradise on earth, where my every whim and need is met yet peace remains elusive. But paradise on the inside, an island of inward ecstasy that I, one of the richest men in the world, would give everything I have to inhabit, yet it has always been so far out of my reach. But here in the trunk of this hover-sedan on the back of a semi headed south, a fugitive and an outcast, I feel like the ocean has overflowed the island. Like the waves breaking forth repeatedly upon the shore, billows of refreshment seem to flow back and forth across my mind and body, breaking up my hard callouses, sweeping away my filth, restoring my tenderness and innocence.

I don't ever remember enjoying crying so much. I could just stay here forever.

Before long, there's a beep on my communication device that connects to the semi's driver, "We have a checkpoint ahead."

The semi slows to a crawl, and jumps a couple of speed bumps—an uncomfortable lurch toward the roof of the trunk, to say the least.

I grunt with disgust. "Rubber tires."

When it finally slows to a stop, the soft beep precedes the message, "The feds are here."

I tap the receiver to speak. "What, what does that mean?"

"Just stay calm."

Momentarily, the driver warns me, "They're going to search the lead-paint coated vehicle."

"But I'm in here!"

"I know. Don't worry. We have a plan for this."

"What plan?"

"Listen, doc, you're going to have to stay calm. You're going to have company in about a minute."

"Company?"

"Radio silence."

The suspense of the next five minutes tempts me with doubt and fear, but I can't seem to wipe the giddy smile off my face. I am too captivated with a mysterious joy, knowing that God no longer holds my past against me. I commit my future, and the well-being of my family, including Mary Nell and Nellie, to Him, and experience a peace that surpasses all understanding.

Finally, I hear at least two voices outside the trunk. The trunk cracks open, and I see the torsos of two men.

"What's that?" One of the inspectors, dressed in black, looks over his shoulder at some commotion toward the left.

The other man, who looks familiar, raises the trunk's lid, extends a handheld stun gun toward the neck of the inspector, shocks him for several seconds, and then pushes him toward me. The stranger plops in beside me, and the other man, whom I presume is the Alabama agent driving this semi, picks up and tosses his legs over beside me. "Hurry! Take off his shirt!"

"What? Why?"

Gunshots ring outside the trunk as I unbutton the unconscious man's shirt. The crack in the hood of the sedan shows me we are parked at what looks like a semi-truck weigh station beside the busy interstate. "Who's shooting who?"

"It's a diversion, a staged robbery with blanks. Take off his shirt! Faster!" The semi driver puts on the man's black cap and, when I hand him the shirt, he puts it on with his back toward the station, buttoning it up.

I hear a buzz from the earpiece of the man lying beside me.

"Hand the earpiece to me." The agent stretches his hand to me, and I give him the unfortunate fellow's communication device.

He puts the earpiece over his ear and, while rubbing it with his index finger, speaks in a gruff voice. "I can barely make you out. What's that shootin'?"

"Hendrix was robbed at gunpoint while eating lunch out back."

"What?"

"Yeah. We're in pursuit."

"Trunk's empty."

"Well, get back here and get some new batteries in that earpiece. Say, where'd the driver go?"

The semi driver turns and gives a thumbs-up toward the weigh station with one hand, and tosses the stun gun in the trunk with the other. "He climbed down when he heard the gunshots."

He slams the trunk on us and begins to climb down.

Now what am I supposed to do?

I stretch the self-defense stun gun toward the stranger. By the light of the handheld computer, he appears to be coming out of unconsciousness. "Don't move, or I'll zap you again!"

The man just moans, holding his neck in pain.

Finally, the semi-truck begins to move forward. My communication device beeps and relays the driver's voice. "We have a contingency plan for this, so keep calm."

"He's waking up!"

"Well zap him then."

"I'm not going to zap him if I don't have to!"

"If he wrestles that device out of your hands and zaps you . . . "

"That won't happen. I'll watch him."

I search for the button of the stun gun. I give it a push just to test it, and I end up zapping myself. "Ahh!" My wrist and numb fingers throb with electrical pain!

The device falls and I fumble for it with the hand that still has feeling. I stretch it toward the stranger. He turns toward me, his eyes widening.

"What happened?" He stares at the darkened ceiling for a moment, his full consciousness returning. "Where am I?"

I push the button, unleashing a small voltage between the metal bars at the end of the device. His head jerks toward me. "Ah!"

I stop.

He gasps in pain. "Who are you?"

"I'm Raymond Verity. Who are you?"

He studies me in the dim light for a moment.

"Why are the feds looking for me?"

"You kidnapped a dupe."

The beep informs me that a message is coming through from my driver. "Alright, Raymond. You're going to pull the emergency release handle to pop the hood, and you're going to jump into the bed of a large pick-up coming up beside us."

"What?"

"And do it quickly!"

The stranger besides me inquires, "Who's that?"

"The driver." I still hold the stun gun with both hands, keeping it between me and the stranger.

The driver similarly asks, "Who's that? The inspector?"

Before I can answer, the inspector lunges for my arms and grabs my wrists. I push the Taser's button and zap the ceiling of the trunk. We wrestle while the driver urges me, "Oh no. We've got to get you off this semi and onto this other vehicle ASAP. The feds are in pursuit . . . "

"I can't!" I grit my teeth, alternatively pushing and pulling the handle of the stun gun to try to loosen it from the inspector's grasp. "Let go!"

"You let go! You're breaking the law!" He knees me under our twisted arms, knocking the breath out of me. I push the device downward to try to zap his leg, and deliver a voltage.

"Ow!"

Then I head-butt him, busting his nose and loosening his grip. I give him another zap for good measure.

"Dr. Verity!"

"I'm getting out now." I reach over the unconscious inspector and pull the emergency release handle to open the trunk. We are racing along the highway, and the wind is blowing furiously.

"You've got to jump into the bed of the pick-up beside us! Hurry!"

I look over the edge of the trunk. Six-feet below me is a pick-up truck with big wheels—the sort that rednecks drive down south. It actually has a confederate flag tinting on the back window, believe it or not. It has several stacks of hay around the walls of the truck bed, with loose hay along the bottom of the bed. I duck back into the trunk. "No way! You're crazy! Pull over."

"We don't have the time and we don't want to raise suspicion of a transfer."

A transfer. The thought of a transfer invokes a sense of obligation. The body I am inclined to protect—it's not mine. I stole it.

"They're watching us," the driver continues. "Do it now, or you will be captured and you will be tortured until they find your family. Do you understand? You must jump!"

Finally, I manage to bring one leg over the trunk and stand on the edge of tracks upon which the four luxury sedans are chained down on the upper level of the long semi-trailer. The wind is gusty and unpredictable. I don't think I can do it, but the stranger in the trunk awakens. He reaches for my wrist. I try to pull away from him and lose my balance. If he were not holding onto me, I would have fallen to the highway. He extends the stun gun toward me with his free hand. He yells something at me, but I cannot hear him from the fury of the wind blowing past us. I reach for the trunk's lid, which is snapping up and down in the stiff wind. I raise it as high as I can and slam it down on him, hitting him in the head and slamming his wrist between the trunk's lid and the frame with a bone-thumping thud. He releases a voltage from the stun gun when I do, striking me in the elbow.

It knocks me backward, and I fall head over heels off the semi.

I do not remember landing.

42

I WAKE UP ON A hospital gurney, but I'm definitely not in a hospital room. The room is dimly lit by a projected 3D image of a news reporter on the wall beside a pile of beige charts on top of a file cabinet across from me. Beside me, it looks like chairs are stacked on top of each other. Looks like a storage closet. There's an IV in my arm, but the bag of fluid hanging on the wall behind me is empty. A man to my right is reading a book by the light of a cracked door.

"Where am I?"

"You're safe." It's Tod Farrell's voice. There's a gentle click and he says, "He's awake."

"Where, um?" My whole body aches. Everything is a blur.

Farrell stands to his feet and comes to the side of my bed. "You're in an unused back room office of an Emergency Department in Montgomery."

I try to sit up, but am pressed back down into the bed by the sheer weight of my throbbing head.

"You landed on your head in the back of the truck."

"He, he shocked me. I fell."

"We thought you may have broken your neck, but the doctor said it's just a concussion. You've been out for hours, but your vitals have been stable." He takes a closer look at me and then flips on a lamp beside the bed. "Uh, smile for me?"

I try to smile at him, but the left side of my face feels numb and weak.

"You have some facial asymmetry there. Not, not too bad."

"Not again." I touch the left side of my face, but it feels like I'm feeling someone else's face. My cheek and brow have no sensation. I move my hands and feet. At least I still have strength in my extremities.

"This happened before?"

"I had a stroke a few months back. It went away with the exception of some occasional stut-stut-stuttering."

He chuckles at my humor, and pats me on the shoulder amiably. "When you were out cold in the back of that pick-up truck, we couldn't risk stopping on the side of the road or going to a hospital, and we had hours more to drive. Thank God you made it."

I turn my eyes to the projected 3D image on the wall. My vision is unaffected. On the television is the very same semi-tractor trailer carrying the hover-sedans in which I rode. There are dozens of police lights reflecting off the windows.

Farrell turns toward the projection. "The driver of the semi you were in is about to give himself up. Tom Studdards is his name. Good man. Three kids, lovely wife. Fortunately, his sacrifice saves your life. The feds didn't see you jump. Their satellite wasn't quite pin-pointed on your location yet. The copters forced Tom over about five minutes later, and the pick-up truck had already exited the interstate, continuing on back roads south."

The driver's side door of the semi opens and Studdards steps out and falls to his knees, placing his hands behind his head.

"He's been stonewalling for hours with a handgun in the cabin."

"What?"

I watch as Federal agents approach him cautiously, and then the driver falls to his face. Dozens of agents rush the semi, climb to the second level, and force open the trunk of the lead-paint-coated sedan, only to find a semi-conscious truck inspector with a bump on his head and a fractured hand.

"We have to change everything now that Tom has been captured."

"Tom? The driver?" Several federal agents frisk the semi driver roughly. I experience a brief, painful flashback to my pitiful condition in the back of that black van that seems like it was weeks ago, but in reality was only half a day ago.

"Help me up." I grab the rails of the bed and try to pull myself to a sitting position. Farrell tries to convince me to lie still but it feels selfish to just lie there while I watch a man getting dragged away in cuffs, probably to be tortured.

"The doc'll be here in a minute. Lie still."

My head begins to spin as I raise my head in bed, and I lay back down. "What's he gonna do? The driver?"

"He'll hold off as long as possible, and then spill his guts. It's protocol under these situations. That's why we have to modify things. Don't look so surprised, Doc. When people are property, and all property belongs to and is under the absolute control of the state, torturing an innocent person for information is like flipping a switch or muting the television." He mutes the projected news story and our eyes fasten. "If people aren't souls, but are just matter in motion, then killing a dupe or torturing a dissident is like sweeping the floor with a broom and dustpan."

A familiar woman's voice sounds behind me, "It's *the* Dr. Raymond Verity, back from the dead again."

I turn. My sister has entered the room.

"Tamara." I stretch out a hand to greet her as the tears burst from my eyes. "I'm so sorry. I've been so, so wrong."

She inches toward me, hobbling more from her arthritis than she did the last time I saw her. "Before we go another second, please, tell me, a man that's brushed up against death as many times as you certainly must realize that you've got to be ready to meet your Maker at any minute."

She grabs my hand with both of hers.

I smile broadly at her. "Any minute." Half my face feels weak, but I hold the smile firm regardless, feeling somewhat proud of my new-found deformity. "I'm ready. I did what you said. I'm trusting in God."

She smiles warmly, but doesn't seem as excited about my profession of faith as I suspected she would be. "It's not those that begin the race, but those that finish that get the prize."

I sigh, nodding as I meditate on that truth. "True, but I am so, so excited about starting this race. I'm sorry about Tom, Tamara."

Grief wells in my heart over the suffering he may have to endure for my sake.

A gray-haired man in green scrubs rushes into the room. "Don't mean to interrupt, but I'm swamped out there and need to move quickly before the nurses get suspicious."

I am somewhat taken aback at his southern drawl.

"I have a left-sided facial neurological deficit from a hemorrhagic stroke of the right cerebral hemisphere," I tell him.

He nods and prepares to place his stethoscope on my chest. "You a doctor?"

He must not recognize me. "Several times over."

After listening to my heart and lungs, he looks carefully at my face. "Wrinkle your brow like this."

"No, it's not Bell's palsy." I imitate his brow raising. "It's cerebral. My vision and my extremities are mostly unaffected, unlike last time. I had a TIA once before and had similar symptoms. It'll pass."

The physician asks several more questions. He shines a penlight in my eyes to check my pupillary reflexes, and asks me to follow some simple commands. Besides a reversible ischemic neurologic deficit, contingent of course upon it reversing, an improving headache, a sore neck and back, and bruised ribs from the knee in the gut I took from the inspector in the trunk of the sedan, I'm fine.

"I need to know if you get any neurologic symptoms, any general weakness. All right?" His gaze darts to Tod Farrell. "I'm not putting him in the system, just like you asked, but I still need to follow up with him. It's just good medicine."

"I understand." Farrell nods.

"If his stroke doesn't clear up—"

"If it doesn't clear up," I interrupt, "it'll be permanent, and there's nothing you can do about it here." With all that has happened to me, I am not as concerned about my visible defect as I was last time. "Only at my facility could they fix this."

"Your facility? What facility?" The doc glances at Farrell, who clears his throat with his eyes fixed on Tamara.

From the look on Farrell's face, it appears he doesn't want the doctor to know who I am.

The doc's tone changes. "Tod, you told me he was critical to Alabama's resistance to the fed's takeover of healthcare."

"He is."

"I am?"

"You are." Farrell turns back to the Emergency Department physician. "That should be enough."

The physician shrugs and turns back to me. "Just let me know if you get new symptoms."

"My body's good, doc." I glance at Tamara. "At least whoever-had-this-body's body's good. It's my brain that's weak, I suppose, which is all that's left of me."

The doc looks at me like I just declared I was an alien from outer space.

Farrell grunts uncomfortably.

Whoops. I am risking the discovery of my identity with dumb comments like that.

Tamara hobbles around to the other side of the bed. "It's Jacob's limp. Jacob got it when he got right with God and it forever changed the way he walked. In our weakness, God is made strong."

She's not referring to her handicap, but mine. I don't know quite what she means by Jacob's limp, but I realize that Jacob was a famous biblical figure—the father of Israel—and a limp is a defect in appearance, so the metaphor fits.

The doc gasps, and turns to Farrell, wide-eyed with wonder. "Is this Dr. Raymond Verity?"

I can't tell if he's looking at me like I'm a poisonous snake poised to strike, or a famous celebrity from whom he wants an autograph and a selfie.

Farrell puts his index finger over his lips and whispers, "Shhh."

I spend the night in the back room of this ER, kept away from the nurses and patients to protect my identity. To the physician's dismay, my facial weakness and numbness do not resolve with my headache. I convince him to spare me the scan, which would just increase the likelihood of being discovered. The neurologic deficit really doesn't bother me that much. When you're thankful for the half you don't deserve and still can enjoy, you are less distraught about the half you don't deserve that's lost.

I can't describe how beautiful the night sky was as I walked with Tamara out of the ER toward her car at the far edge of the parking lot. The whole galaxy took on a new aura of beauty and meaning. I couldn't wipe the smile off my face—at least until I saw Tamara's car.

I don't ever remember being driven in a car that looked so decrepit, much less by a driver that doesn't appear fit to be on the road.

"Buckle up." Tamara dons her bifocals in her three-decade-old two-door rust-bucket economy car. As if having rubber tires wasn't bad enough, they were tread-less and hubcap-less. To make matters worse, she informs me that exhaust fumes come in through the A/C vents, so I had to roll down the window if I wanted some fresh air.

I comply without argument, still euphorically fuzzy from either my head injury or the medicine they administered to me. This is a perfect metaphor for my life, going from a half-million amero hover-limousine, driven by a professional armed bodyguard, enveloped by a perfectly toned and tanned body, accompanied by a magazine-cover-of-a-wife that was the envy of every whoremonger within gawking distance, finally ending up in a miniature, rust-covered economy car designed for impoverished old folks driven by a skinny gray-haired prophetess with a fat rear and deforming rheumatoid arthritis in every joint of her body—and me without an amero to my name and with only half a working face!

I've gone from the most elite, careless playboy with blood on his hands, to a guilt-ridden, miserable scientist futilely working to clean them off, finally to a humble, defective fugitive thrilled out of his wits by simple grace.

She cranks the car, and it sputters briefly but quickly falls silent with a "bang" that sounds like a gunshot from the back end of the car.

I look over my shoulder. What in the world caused that violent noise?

She answers my unspoken question, "This old thing still has a muffler."

"A muffler? Are those still legal?" Talk about old school.

She attempts to crank it again. "The Lord tests my faith every day with this car." She finally gets the thing started. For a tiny car, it sure does create ruckus under the hood. She raises a trembling hand. "Thank ya, Jesus."

The formalities do come crashing down when it comes from the heart.

"Where are we going?"

She drives us out of the hospital parking lot. "A meeting."

"With Governor Whetley?"

"He will meet us there, yes. We have a two-and-a-half-hour drive to Atlanta, and much to discuss on the way."

I begin by telling Tamara about what happened to me in the trunk of that sedan, there at the end of myself. We both cry, rejoicing in what God has brought me through.

"Once Thomas conned you into sitting on that panel, I wondered if you would ever get born again."

"Born again?"

"It's what happens when you turn from your sin and trust in Jesus." She places her hand over her heart. "You become a new creature."

"A new creature, huh?" I've been a new creature, in a sense, ever since they brought me out of cryo, but the same miserable person in my soul. "Thomas didn't con me, Tamara."

"Oh, he didn't?"

"He believes in Jesus," I say, trying to defend him.

"Thomas believes in working for his salvation, atoning for his own sin, which, by the way, he will not forsake. Jesus' blood hasn't cleansed him of sin because he doesn't believe it can, and we cannot rise above our faith. He believes in God like the devil believes in God and trembles, yet remains in rebellion."

I love my sister, but her judgment of our brother just doesn't settle well with me. Of course, I've got my problems with Thomas, but he tries. "He means well."

"Brother, nothing short of our eternal damnation can satisfy the claims of God's law if we have ever violated it. All the good works of religion will never make up for sin, and it's an insult to the sufferings of Christ to cling to sin and a false hope of salvation. Like that panel Thomas got you on, hypocrites do more harm than good when they appeal to godless remedies to improve the quagmires of godlessness."

I take a deep breath. "Most of the members were pro-family and pro-life leaders who claim to believe in Jesus. Where did we go wrong?"

"The Bible says that we do not war against flesh and blood, but against principalities and spiritual wickedness in high places, against evil spirits. The Word of God is our offensive weapon in this battle. If we try to fight it through carnal means, without the spiritual armor—"

"Whoa. Milk, not meat. You're talking over my head. Bring it down to your baby brother's level."

She smiles at my childish, enthusiastic desire to understand. "Your panel concluded that people can be murdered as long as certain conditions were met first, right?"

I nod. "Correct, but it's the best we could do."

"Says who?"

"Says the conservative, Christian trench warriors, the leaders of the political right."

"That's unbelief when God says otherwise."

"Unbelief?"

"Yes, unbelief."

"Given the present law, given our President, and given the admittedly pagan culture in which we live, we've got to save who we can save. It's like, uh, Christians in the German Holocaust saving the Jews they can save. It's like Jesus leaving the 99 sheep to save the one lost sheep."

"Just because Christians couldn't save all the Jews, that doesn't mean that they intentionally sacrificed some in their law proposals to save the ones they did save. And Jesus left the 99 in a safe place. The pro-life movement leaves the 99 to die while trying to save the one—big difference. But even in trying to save the one, you resort to a plan that defies God's authority, violating His law." She pauses to give me a chance to assimilate.

"You mean, because our recommendations allowed legal murder to continue?"

"No, you did more than allow it. God allows sin in the sense that He doesn't forcefully prevent our evil choices. But He doesn't grant permission to sin. You and your panel gave permission to shed innocent blood. When you give permission for someone to do what God forbids them to do, you have usurped God's law for a devilish alternative, a counterfeit standard. You've tried to supplant Him and put yourself on His throne. He's the King of kings and Lord of lords—it's up to us to submit. To break His law because we think that breaking it can help us accomplish His will better—that is unbelief. That is rebellion."

"So, if you were on that panel, would you have insisted that if we can't protect all the clones, then we shouldn't protect any?"

"Not necessarily, but I would never grant permission for one to die in order to save another, for permitting murder is to sin against God. The Apostle Paul asks in the book of Romans, 'Should we do evil that good may come?' Then he answers his own question: 'God forbid!' See, God is holy, and cannot bless evil. When you try to regulate the evil for compassion's sake, hoping to save one, yet permitting the murder of some in your regulations, you become an accomplice in the very crime you hope to prevent. If you get your hands stained with innocent blood, you sacrifice God's blessing and come under God's wrath, your motive to 'save the one' notwithstanding."

After a moment's reflection, I respond, "With that purist ideology, how could you ever succeed in any political aim? Without compromise, how can you get anything done?"

She smiles. "Compromising the inessentials in deference to others—that's just loving your neighbor as you love yourself. But to compromise God's law is to abandon faith in Him. Faith in God—that's the victory that overcomes the world, Ray, not disbelief. Not abandoning the Word of God, sheathing the sword of the Spirit. Ray, if God be for us, who can be against us? Thanks be to God who *always* causes us to triumph in Christ. Through God we shall do valiantly, for it is *He* that shall tread down our enemies."

She studies me briefly, and then turns back to the road. "You see, Ray, God always tests our faith to see if we will obey Him when it is inconvenient, when the odds are stacked against us. Will we be faithful when it looks like God's ways are *not* best, that His will is an utter impossibility? Or will we resort to carnal, godless remedies when it looks like they are more plausible alternatives than compliance to God's will and ways? 'Cursed is the man whose strength is in the arm of the flesh.'" She glances at me. "That's another Bible verse. God commands obedience, not success. In His eyes, obedience *is* success, even if we die martyrs never seeing our dreams fulfilled. If His will looks like it leads to a cross with your name on it, will you give in to the temptation to circumvent the cross in hopes of an easier, alternative route to the resurrection? Or will you take up your cross and follow Jesus?"

43

THE WALK FROM THE PARKING lot into the Georgia statehouse in downtown Atlanta is surreal. The sky is blue, as usual, but it is as if I have never seen the color before. The firmament is clear of clouds, the breeze is cool and light and perfectly balances the sting of the hot Georgia sun just peeking over the horizon. I don't think there has ever been a more beautiful day in the history of the world! I feel so refreshed, so light and clean. Even my aches and my facial weakness are perfect in light of how much worse it could be, especially given that I'm living on borrowed time. Following my sister on the busy sidewalk, I don't ever remember being so happy. I whisper thanksgiving to God for not giving up on me, and for the safety of my family. I don't know what the future holds, but I have full confidence that if it includes suffering to right the wrongs for which I am responsible, God will give me the strength to endure it with cheerfulness.

As soon as I walk into the Statehouse for the 8 a.m. meeting, even before I line up behind Tamara to go through the security detector, two tall, lean, plain-clothed men just inside the door grab me by my shirt and thrust me forcefully against the wall. They inadvertently bump into my sister and knock her down in the process.

So much for my usefulness to the resistance.

I expect to be told that I am under arrest for some federal crime, but I am given no explanation for their rough treatment of me, making me wonder if these men are private citizens. As soon as Tamara rises to protest, one of them stiff-arms her and she falls again to the ground again with a painful grunt.

"Be careful!" I object. "You hurt my—"

Before I can get "sister" out of my mouth, one of them pressed my face against the wall, putting his thumb deep into my cheek until it is jammed between my jaws, forcing me silent.

A Statehouse security guard sees the commotion and intervenes, notifying superiors through a nano communication device. "I have a violent unprovoked assault of two men against one at the east entrance." He quickly approaches. "Get your hands off him!"

The two agents handcuffing me look at the security guard, whose hand rests on his holstered handgun.

"We are federal agents arresting a fugitive."

Three more security guards surround me and the two plain-clothed federal agents. One of the security guards taps his nanophone. "They claim they are two federal agents, arresting Dr. Raymond Verity." He apparently recognizes me. "We're not going to let them take you, Dr. Verity."

Two of the security guards get between me and the door, trying to block the exit.

The federal agents keep glancing anxiously through the glass door, as if expecting back-up to assist them at any moment. One of the security guards hits a code on the panel by the sliding glass doors to prevent them from opening from the outside. The two agents push me along the wall toward the exit, their hands resting on what I suppose are their weapons in the small of their back.

One of the agents unfolds a badge toward the nearest security guard. "Federal law, federal jurisdiction. Back off!"

The agent nearest the glass doors points at the security guard by the doors. "Open that door, now!"

"Don't let them take him!" Tamara squeals. "Raymond Verity is under an invitation from Governor Jeffries, and has been promised safe passage, along with the rest of Alabama Governor Maurice Whetley's entourage. Those federal agents aren't following the law!"

Someone must have given an order to all of the security guards simultaneously through their communication devices. All four immediately unholster their Tasers and shoot the two federal agents. They both seize under the voltage. One of the federal agents manages to unholster his weapon before he loses control of his body from the electricity, and his black handgun slides across the floor until a security guard stops it with his foot. The agents fall hard to the ground, grunting.

Outside, two black-clothed agents bang against the sliding glass doors, shouting threats for them to be opened. They attempt to breach the locked glass doors through a panel on the wall outside. Tod Farrell steps around the security guards and walks toward me, twitching his pepper gray mustache to the left with tic-like constancy. "I'll take him."

The chief of security gives him an affirming nod as two other security guards begin to frisk the stunned federal agents and bind their hands. Several security guards come and stand between the glass doors and me, facing the frantic federal agents fiddling with the panel outside.

A black SUV parks on the curb behind them and several more agents step out, decked out in SWAT gear, carrying what appear to be short-barreled automatic weapons with long ammo clips. As one agent hooks a laptop up to the panel outside the door, others alternatively bang the glass and try to pry it open.

Farrell fidgets in the pockets of the guards for the keys to my cuffs. "You"—he turns to the nearest guard—"keep these agents locked away and out of sight. Do not let them speak to a lawyer or anybody else. Got that?"

"Get him out of here," Tamara urges Farrell.

"I can't believe I just zapped a federal agent!" a security guard exclaims.

"Are we gonna get in trouble if we do this?" one of them inquired of Farrell.

"In this Statehouse, with this Governor and this Speaker of the House, I suspect you're gonna get in trouble if you don't." Farrell uncuffs me.

Tamara is halfway down the hall toward the elevator. She waves Farrell toward her as he whisks me out of the foyer. "Come on!"

Farrell puts his hand on my shoulder and leads me to the elevator. Over his shoulder, he hollers at the chief of security, "Full alert at all entrances and exits. Resist them with force."

"Yes, sir." He glances at the glass. "Backup's a minute out . . ."

"Why don't you stop and get a coffee on your way?" Tamara goads Farrell.

Farrell rolls his eyes to her sarcasm, but picks up his pace nonetheless.

"The feds are giving up, it looks like," the chief of security shouts down the hall. "Driving off."

"Good." Farrell leads me into the elevator.

"They are not giving up!" Tamara sticks her head out of the elevator and shouts down the hall. "They have contingency plans and they will stop at nothing to shut up Raymond Verity and shut down state opposition."

As we head up to the seventh floor, I put a hand on Farrell's shoulder until we make eye contact.

"You can't save me from them. Let them take me, and save yourself the hassle of a federal warrant, or a deadly raid—"

Tamara steps forward and taps her index finger right in the middle of my forehead. "Don't you know you're going to walk on water, Raymond Verity? Stop believing the ten false spies!"

Walk on water? Ten spies? What in the world is that supposed to mean? Her biblical metaphors are so frequent and fluent, I've got to start reading the Bible just so I can understand what she's saying.

"Okay?" I respond, shirking from her pointy fingernail.

She grins and steps back. "Keep your eyes fixed on the water-walker, little brother." She turns to Farrell. "You too, Tod. No fingers in the wind. Don't fear what man shall do to you."

He reluctantly gives her a short nod and bites his lip.

What has my sister become? Some kind of spiritual chaplain for Jesus freaks accused of treason? I rub the spot on my forehead, which I imagine has her fingernail's indentation in it.

"I wasn't fearing anything," Farrell finally responds.

"I saw that look on your face. Your little mustache was just a jitterin'." The elevator dings and she takes a step toward the door. "It was fear. Our faith puts God on the spot, and gives Him a chance to show Himself strong."

Tamara leads us out of the elevator and stops, as if she cannot make up her mind which way to turn. Farrell and I come to a halt behind her.

"You lead." Her aged voice is unbending.

Farrell grunts approvingly, glad to be back in the driver's seat. "Sure. But my mustache wasn't jitterin'."

She grins and keeps silent, content to let him have the last word.

That's Tamara—always leading the charge through the storm of fiery arrows, and when all is safe, pausing to follow the man she lets get in front of her. She's always trying to prod on the men around her to greatness, with a sharp dagger poking them in the rear if they begin to reek of cowardice. Yet she is always careful to give the man the credit for the mission accomplished. No wonder she never married—too few men rose sufficiently above mediocrity to be a good candidate for her.

We're five minutes late for the meeting that is taking place around a long oval table. The Alabama, Mississippi, and Georgia representatives are very generous in welcoming me, but the leaders of the other four states appear nervous about the morning's violence, and act like they are about to abandon ship before it even leaves the dock.

Governor Whetley gives me a crushing hug. "Can't wait to hear about your change of heart." His exaggerated features have all the caricature of the African race: skin as black as night, wide nose, strong jaw, full, wide lips, and the frame of a professional athlete. He holds onto the hug longer than is customary, and afterwards looks me in the eyeballs, way inside my personal space. There's something I really love about his wide, unashamed smile.

The Alabama A.G., Shane Mease, is behind him with a firm handshake. "Good to finally see you."

His red hair is even more fiery in person. His strong handshake strangely doesn't seem compatible with his whiny voice and protuberant belly on his otherwise thin frame.

Phil Stephens, Tamara's lanky right-hand-man and fellow Personhood leader, goes out of his way to greet me kindly, but he keeps silent as Tod Farrell briefly informs those gathered of the details of the feds' attempt to extract me from the premises.

Farrell expresses firm confidence in the competence of Governor Jeffries' security team covering the roof, and all entrances and exits, but that does not appear to put the most anxious of them at ease.

Whetley leans toward me and quietly asks if my facial asymmetry is from an injury sustained during their arrest. "No," I whisper. "It's unrelated."

The Georgia Governor, a full-featured retired farmer named Vince Jeffries, loudly orders a subordinate to contact the Sheriff's office and the police department, and have them keep squads around the building in case any federal forces arrive to retrieve their men or try to apprehend me. His southern drawl is so thick I initially suspect he is mocking the accent.

"Any retaliation for our justified resistance," Governor Jeffries confidently announces, "will be met with vigorous defensive force."

He orders a man in military garb beside him to position Georgia Guard forces in four fully-armed hovercrafts around the block. The hovercrafts are an immense improvement over the antique Humvees, as they are not susceptible to IEDs, can travel over ditches and even water as easily as land, have stealth technology and can sneak up on enemies. He orders two armed, stealth Guard copters to their position, one to monitor the scans of the vicinity from the roof and the other to maintain flight between them and the nearest military base. Four Guard jets were also ordered to fly the capital in a grid pattern.

"And Farrell, notify me immediately if the feds try anything."

"Yes, sir." Farrell taps his nano and walks to stand beside the door, whispering quietly to his security team leaders.

Governor Jeffries faces those surrounding the table, pointing north. *"They* are the lawless criminals in this confrontation." He points at the Florida governor, a short Hispanic man with a goatee who appears to be packing up his briefcase. "Put that down, Felipe! Dr. Verity did nothing but save a little girl from a gruesome death, and the feds want to arrest him for it? Not on my watch! Georgia will be governed by law, not the federal government's godless tyranny."

"That's exactly the kind of leadership the moment requires," Tamara mumbles, adding a vigorous "Amen" from where she sits behind Phil Stephens, her colleague in the Alabama Personhood organization.

It's beginning to sink in just how much is at stake, and how much these leaders are risking to meet with me here.

Soon, a refreshing calm settles upon the room. Even the Florida governor appears at ease. I take my seat between the Alabama Attorney General Shane Mease, and the ageless Alabama Supreme Court Justice Ron Moore, a brilliant man who once got kicked off the bench for refusing to cease acknowledging God in the course of his judicial duties, but who ran again for office years later and amazingly re-took his seat.

I am thrilled to be able to tell them of my conversion in the trunk of that sedan. They are all very warm and welcoming toward me.

"Has the dementia affected you at all?" Governor Jeffries asks.

Presuming him to be referring to a stroke-related loss of neurologic function associated with my facial droop, I point to the left side of my face. "My stroke hasn't affected my intellectual capacity at all."

"Was it caused by the same thing that's causing the dementia?" he asks.

"Excuse me?"

They all just stare at me for a moment. "Is what caused your facial droop the same thing that is causing dementia in the New Body clients?"

"What dementia? What are you talking about?"

"You haven't heard?"

I shrug, having no idea what he's talking about.

Phil Stephens turns to Governor Whetley. "He doesn't know."

Governor Jeffries taps a button on his laptop and his desktop is projected onto the white wall behind him. It is a news story. The top headline reads, "New Bodies, Disabled Minds: Viral Vectors Causing Dementia."

"In everyone who's undergone a cerebral-ocular transfer?"

Phil Stephens responds, "According to the CDC and WHO officials quoted in this widely published news report, about half of those who had their brain transplanted into a murdered cloned person are coming down with rapid-onset dementia."

By the look on Tamara's face, this must be the first time she has heard about this as well. "Oh, Ray," she utters under her breath, "I pray you aren't affected."

"It must be the viral vectors." I recall the increasing number of WHO, FDA, and CDC scientists entering the private entrance of the Center the last time I was there, and how they were unwilling to tell me the reason for their increased presence. This must have been the reason. "We use viruses to modify the donor's genome, to remove deleterious genes and mutations, like cancer genes, and to improve strength and intelligence and coveted physical characteristics. We thought we eliminated their pathogenicity. Apparently the trace viral elements must have an effect on the unaltered brains of the clients."

Governor Whetley responds, "It sounds like you understand it better than even the author of the article does."

"Of course." My eyes are still transfixed on the article. "I received a Nobel Prize for the technology."

"It also sounds like you have not come down with the rapid-onset dementia," Mease adds, provoking a nervous laugh among the others.

"This is the Tower of Babel all over again," Tamara comments, grief evident in her tone.

"Excuse me?" An Alabama cabinet member with a confused look on her face, asks, "Say again?"

"When mankind had one language and one government," Tamara explains, "they were building a tower they intended to reach to heaven. Perhaps they wanted to protect themselves if there ever was another flood, like what happened when God judged the world in Noah's lifetime. When the tower was under construction, God said that if He did not intervene, then nothing would be impossible for them. So He confused their language. They naturally separated into language groups and the project came screeching to a halt."

Everybody in the room had already read the article apparently, but they had not yet made the connection between this setback for the New Body science and the solemn mission that brought the leaders of seven states together in this room. A gasp of awe sounded around the room as they begin to realize the perfect timing of the publication of these findings.

"God is again confusing the language of those who aspire to heaven without God," Tamara comments.

Whetley's thin grin beams with determination and confidence. "God is fighting for us."

"Doesn't this resolve our dilemma?" the Florida governor asks. "Doesn't this make the purpose of the meeting null and void?" Everyone is silent as they consider the question. "After all, the industry is done, for now. The New Body science cannot survive this."

Georgia Governor Jeffries adds, "Felipe has a point. This politically risky venture may be completely unnecessary at this juncture."

Whetley raises his eyebrows, as if the governors have made an undeniably good point.

"Why would the federal government release these findings to the public?" I ask aloud. "It certainly may help justify increasing federal control, but it can only hurt the New Body industry, in which the federal government has invested much. Why didn't they vigorously conceal their findings?"

"This very meeting may be the reason the findings were released when they were," Jeffries opines. "Perhaps they wanted to snatch the motivation out of the uncommitted state leaders, turn us back to apathy." He makes eye contact with the Florida governor, who turns away. "Perhaps they wanted to give us all a false hope that the killing industry would falter without any state having to make hard, costly choices to resist the feds."

"Regardless, we cannot let these findings dissuade us," Tamara answers. All eyes turn to her as she stands to her feet. "Did the Confederacy's banning of the import of slaves at the commencement of the Civil War protect the ones that were already here?" She pauses to let the others think about that for a moment. "Did it protect the ones the North were still importing?"

"No," Shane Mease concedes.

"Neither did it abate the wrath of God, or mitigate the judgment they had coming to them," Tamara continues. "There are thousands, if not tens of thousands, of people whose lives are at risk, people who will be exploited and experimented upon if we don't protect them, even if the New Body scientists have to go back to the drawing board for better ways to modify the human genome."

"Expect more federal government intervention." Stephens taps his pen—a truly rare sight in today's technologically advanced world—against the desk. "Expect more control over the industry, and in the name of the public good, more bloodshed."

"I'll tell you exactly what the New Body Research Center will do in response to this." All eyes turn to me. "For a handsome price, they'll market out the existing clones to research companies for exploitation, and probably start growing clones from unmodified donor DNA, or modify it only with non-viral vectors. They won't stop killing, be sure of that—especially with unaccountable federal bureaucrats at the helm of the company."

No one can argue with that.

"You have to protect them," I insist. "These clones are real people with genuine emotions, with souls. We do them a terrible wrong—*you* do them a terrible wrong every single day you hesitate to come to their defense."

"This," Stephens adds, his gaze drifting from governor to governor, "does make your job significantly easier. You all have a sworn duty to protect the innocent within your states. Your obligation is not assuaged by the fact the federal government is the one you need to protect the innocent *from*. Yet you each are democratically-elected politicians who want to stay in office. With this news," he motions at the news report still projected on the wall, "the public opinion will turn against the New Body science."

"Dr. Verity, can you help us?" Whetley asks me. "You wrote the law that gave us this problem."

"You had this problem before the law was written," I respond, "and you didn't prosecute murderers then. And I didn't write the law. The President's people wrote it. I just defended it."

"The President wrote it? What? I'm confused." Governor Whetley's eyes drift from person to person around the table. "I thought President Sayder opposed your law just as vehemently as you opposed hers."

"The President recruited me to oppose her initial proposals, predicting I would be launched into hero status on the right. From the beginning, she admitted that my counter-proposal to her attempt to legalize cloning and clone termination was all she really wanted all along." I clear my throat to let those words sink in. "Her first bill was a ruse. She tricked the Republicans into thinking my proposal to compassionately regulate the technology was the best way to protect the nation from her radical proposals. It was all a farce. The President's debate team instructed me on how to defend the law she penned, and her media managers scheduled my appearances around the nation."

The state leaders are aghast. My face burns with shame. "I'm sorry."

Several moments pass as the leaders begin to comprehend the gravity of the conspiracy they are up against.

"If God has tilted the battlefield in our favor, thanks to this new devastating side-effect to cerebral-ocular transfers, then you need to move quickly before the federal-government-controlled media begins its spin campaign to fix the public image or appeal to the crisis to justify more government control."

"It's already begun." Someone at the far end of the table has their gaze fixed on their handheld computer. "They're putting the blame on you, claiming that you sabotaged the CMV and Epstein-Barr viral vectors to cause the rapid-onset dementia. They claim they have documentation of several attempts on your part to destroy your own company."

"What?" several simultaneously exclaim.

"Yep. Quoting Dr. Redd Cranton and several CDC and WHO leaders at a press conference that concluded just a few minutes ago."

"It's true." Another briefly raises his handheld.

I take a deep, raspy breath. I came here to help, but it seems I have only become a liability. The CDC leaks the story about dementia-related side effects to strike up fear and rouse anger, to justify federal intervention and further regulation of private industry involvement into New Body science, and to throw frigid water on these conservative governors' determination to unite in resistance to the feds. Then government-employed medical leaders step in to put the target for all this fear and rage right on my back.

"Did you?" Governor Whetley leans forward. "Did you sabotage the technology?"

I shake my head. "No. If customers who underwent transfers before six months ago are experiencing rapid-onset dementia induced by a pathologic viral vector in the modification of the dupe's DNA, how could I have been responsible for that? I was on ice. It was not until at least a couple of months after my resurrection that I got so fed up with the killing that I tried to dismantle the company."

"How did you try to dismantle your company?" someone asks.

"When Ivan Wilkes was killed and I was at the helm, I tried to simply dissolve it before the government took over and prevented me. Then I exploited my access to company records and concealed studies to disseminate dirt on the industry to negatively affect its public image. Finally, I kidnapped a dupe slated for destruction."

"Your granddaughter?" Whetley asks.

I nod. "Yes, sir. My Down Syndrome granddaughter, Mary Nell."

Means turns toward me, his elbows on the table. "With this publicized indictment of you. I suppose that our chances of leveraging your influence with the public to help us protect cloned humans in our states have shifted from good to extremely slight. That you were willing to risk your life to save your Down Syndrome granddaughter worked in our favor, as you earned the respect of the common man with a functioning conscience. But with the accusation that you sabotaged the viral vectors to cause rapid onset dementia, this drastically hurts your influence with the public."

As the disappointment in the room rises, my sister sighs noisily.

"Not necessarily." I turn to Mease. "You have arrested David Starr, but do you have a good case against him?"

"Unfortunately not." His tone is gloomy. "Those who stepped forward to testify of his order to kill cloned humans have since retracted their story. Right before being whisked off to the Bahamas or the Swiss Alps for a six-month paid vacation, landing back in D.C. soon after for a cushy job, of course. A federal judge has blocked my ability to go after the company records, saying that it violates constitutionally-protected policy. The front door of Starr's office is protected by armed federal Marshals. We're still working on the case," Mease assures us. "We're not giving up."

"Has any one of you prosecuted a single murderer of a clone yet?" There is silence.

"Then, I can help you." I extend my wrists to Mease. "Prosecute me."

Several simultaneously object and I raise my hand to halt them. "Starr's company, Mirror Mirror, operates under the direct supervision of my company as a kind of subsidiary, cloning and recycling clones—that means killing them."

"Then testify against him," Mease suggests.

"It'd be my word against his."

"I'll take it."

"No. You need a case to turn public opinion quickly, and discovery would be dramatically shortened if I gave you a full confession." Everyone seems to hold their breath as I lay my neck on their chopping block, offering myself up as an opportunity for them to prosecute a murderer of clones under state law.

"I need to prosecute a crime in Alabama. By law, I need a body and a weapon—or a means."

"Dr. David Starr murdered human beings in Alabama with my permission and under my authority. I can tell you exactly which research companies in Alabama receive his dissected organs and tissue, and there you will find evidence that they are shipped from his facility. That is a body, a genetically verifiable human body. David Starr admits to the means. It's a clean case. I'm probably the greatest mass murderer in Alabama history, even though I have never stepped foot in Alabama."

A long silence follows, as everyone just stares at me wide-eyed in wonder, like flames had just burst out of my ears as I spoke.

"What more do you need, Mr. Mease?"

"I'm sorry, I can't prosecute you. Not you. Not now that you've done a 180."

His confidence in me alleviates my fears. I don't have a death wish.

Tamara speaks up, "Doesn't the same God that insists you protect the innocent people in your state also forbid you to extend leniency to murderers? Is that all a murderer has to do in Alabama? Convert to Christianity, and then the Attorney General foregoes prosecution?"

Wow. That's a surprising twist, my sister urging the A.G. to prosecute me.

Mease takes a deep breath, fixing his eyes on Tamara. "When a murderer like Saul of Tarsus becomes Paul the Apostle, the rules change, Tamara."

"The rules do *not* change," she insists. "It was not illegal when and where Saul of Tarsus was arresting and persecuting Christians, and even aiding and abetting the murder of Stephen. Should it have been, Mr. Mease?"

Momentarily, he answers, "Of course."

"If you protect the innocent in Alabama, as you are obligated to do, you must not pervert justice in the cases in which our brothers and sisters are the accused. Someone on death row may be forgiven their sin, yet it is still your duty to do justice."

Mease is speechless. My sister may have just single-handedly spear-headed the line of reasoning that could lead to my prosecution, conviction, and even my execution. I, too, am speechless.

The Alabama Supreme Court Justice nods at Mease. "His prosecution would add teeth to your heretofore untested law, Mr. Mease. You want a law that holds, maintains public opinion in your favor, and impacts the other states to follow your lead? Prosecute him, convict him, and have him approve of your defiance of the predictable federal judicial attempt to negate your law."

From the looks on people's faces, they pity me, and I don't like it. "Stop acting like women," I say. I turn to the corner of the room where several women sit. "No offense." My gaze darts back to the men. "Little girls. My sister is right. The New Body science is my technology. Mine!" I raise my voice. "All the blood-letting for profit"—I slam my fists against the table and leap to my feet—"it was my idea! I made billions off it. I have cut open premature babies who survived abortions to simply observe or harvest their organs for profit. I've counted the body parts after elective abortions, as all abortionists do. I don't deserve your pity. At least now, I know where I'm going when I close my eyes for the last time."

All eyes fix on Mease. "Did you sabotage those vectors?"

"No. But you can bet that they've invented evidence that they will surely expose to the public any day. If you want to turn my presence here into an asset instead of a liability, prosecute me. Please!" I smile warmly. "If my sister's right—and she usually is—God is a much greater threat to your people than President Sayder, because of the shedding of innocent blood of those you are obligated to protect. It would be my greatest honor to take the fall I deserve to help you protect them. Can there be a better case, Mr. Mease? I'll even surrender my right to an attorney to keep costs down."

I glance over my shoulder at Tamara. Tears drift down her wrinkled cheeks. It wasn't as easy for her as it sounded.

"Isn't that what our Lord did for us?" I smile warmly, fully embracing my inevitable prosecution, and feeling a great peace flood over my body. "Aren't we called to take up His cross and follow His example?

He became a curse that His children might be saved, right? His blood, it, it speaks better things than that of Abel."

I hear Tamara sniff, and I look back to see her wipe her tears and nod at me, affirming my decision, accepting my fate.

"Mr. Mease,"—I extend my wrists toward him—"so will mine."

44

IN LIGHT OF MY SACRIFICE, the resistance of the reluctant states fades and they come to a unanimous consensus. They rally around my sacrifice. The governors and their respective Statehouse leaders will assert before their legislatures that they must proactively protect all the innocent within their state, and not wait for that elusive Supreme Court majority to give them permission. Duty is not diminished by the negative consequences at the hands of tyranny. In response to the forthcoming long list of federal charges against me, Mease planned to both pull jurisdiction and to cite my constitutional right to a trial; he will claim his duty to prosecute for murder under Alabama law takes precedent over the accusation that I intentionally manipulated viral vectors to induce dementia in clients of the New Body science—especially since I would not be granted my constitutional right to a speedy trial under federal policy.

Mease orders me to be taken into custody, kindly sparing me the cuffs. Tamara smiles warmly at me as I am led from the room, tears still streaming down her withered cheeks, but I do not feel the emotional heaviness that I expect to feel. I am elated! The leaders stand and applaud.

I try to spurn their praise. "Quit. I'm only doing my duty, which is the least . . . "

The applause increases and drowns me out, resonating throughout the room as I am led out the side door, down the long marble hall into the elevator.

The elevator doors shut. I take a deep breath. Everything is changing now.

I step out a side door into the bright sun directly overhead under a cloudless, baby blue sky. I am surrounded by a half-dozen Statehouse security guards donning black masks, I suppose, to conceal their identity to protect them from federal charges. News station vans with satellites affixed to the roofs line the streets. Like the chaotic roar of an approaching fighter jet, the sound of a hundred fast-talking media personnel rush around the corner of the building toward me, carrying microphones and cameras and shouting out my name. More security guards sprint in front of them and try to corral them onto the sidewalk. Several cameramen and journalists quickly carve out their square footage of the sidewalk in anticipation of the best view of my departure, whereas the more ambitious journalists push against the guards, shrieking my name and screaming out questions as if their life depended upon my answering. I am forced to a standstill in the middle of the lawn, as security tries to control the mob and one of Mease's guards uses a specialized weapon to zap an approaching camera drone.

Upon my insistence, Mease finally consents to let a Georgia deputy in the foyer put the cuffs on me. The bald deputy does not take Mease's reluctance to do so under consideration, and is rough as he binds my hands tightly behind my back.

Mease's plan is to let the Atlanta police take me into custody now and transfer me to Alabama's custody at the jail.

An officer leads me and Shane Mease through the thick haze of cameras, frantic journalists, and extended microphones. Another police officer follows close behind me.

"What would you say to your wife," a female journalist shouts, "who was quoted this morning saying you have betrayed your family?"

The question is unexpected and painful.

"I adore my wife—and my family," I shout back over my shoulder. I hope they play that on the news. That'd make Morgan's day! "And my two grandbabies," I add.

The question instantly troubles my heart. Even if Morgan did say that, I do not condemn her. She may have been under duress. Who knows what threats she endured before they coerced her into making such comments to the press? I keep my eyes fixed on the flashing lights on top of the Georgia squad car beyond the throng of people, reminding myself not to be deterred by questions designed more to provoke an emotional outburst than to pursue any actual truth.

Our pace slows as the maze thickens near the sidewalk. The shouted inquiries are unrelenting. "What happened to your face, Dr. Verity?"

"How are you going to plead in court?"

"Why did you want to bring down your own company?"

"Did you help Jeremy Porter?"

I turn at the mention of his name. "Help Jeremy Porter?"

The journalist elaborates on the question. "Did you help Jeremy Porter escape from federal custody this morning?"

One reporter actually obstructs my path with her microphone, which hits me in the neck. "What do you say to your brother, Thomas Verity, and the Pro-Life Legislative League president, Jim Cobb, who publicly condemn you for breaking the law in kidnapping your company's property?"

"My granddaughter is a person, not property," I reply.

Several loaded questions amount to nothing more than insults. I keep my countenance firm against the rest of their inquiries and their baseless charges.

Shane Mease and I are briefly separated. He turns, reaches for me, grabs my shoulder and pulls me through the merciless gauntlet of bodies, wires, and bright lights affixed atop camera lenses.

At the squad car, I look over my shoulder, hoping to see one last smile from my sister, but she is nowhere to be found.

When we arrive at the unmarked car, the police officer puts his hand on top of my head and helps me into the back. Mease hurriedly motions for my driver to hit the road as the officer affixes my seatbelt. "I'll see you at the station." My eyes follow him as he turns and heads toward a black hover-mobile idling behind the squad car. I wish I could stay with him. I trust him.

Before the door is shut, a muscular male journalist inserts a microphone into the open door to prevent it from closing, and asks, "Have you heard they found your daughter? They've taken custody of your granddaughter's dupe and are planning to go through with the replacement Monday?"

The news is like a bolt of lightning right to my heart. The officer slams the mic into the door just to spite the journalist. He then pushes the journalist and his busted microphone away and tries to shut the door, but I unfasten my seatbelt and stick my leg out to stop it from shutting. "Hold on. They have my granddaughter?"

The bald police officer appears irate that I have obstructed his attempt to shut the door. "Put your leg back in the car or I'm going to break it!"

I comply, and he slams it shut.

I keep looking back to see if Mease's hover-mobile is following. He is, closely. From the silhouettes visible through his windshield, there are others in the vehicle with him. There are two officers in the front seats of my car. The bald officer in the driver's seat is speaking in soft tones via his nano.

"Officer?" I seek his eyes in the rearview mirror. "Do you know who I am?"

He ignores me.

The dark-skinned officer in the passenger seat keeps turning and looking back at me, appearing to be unsure of himself.

"Raymond Verity?"

I nod. "*En route* to this squad car, a reporter claimed my granddaughter Mary Nell Verity has been taken into custody and returned to the New Body Research Center. Do you know if that is true?"

He shakes his head. "No. But I want you know that I think you're getting a raw deal. You risked your life to save your granddaughter, and that is an honorable thing."

"Stop talking to him!" the bald driver orders.

"Please, officer," I beg. "I just want to find out if it's true. Can you check for me?"

They refuse to answer. The younger officer dons mirrored sunglasses and ignores me.

I am surprised by the speed with which we are moving on the interstate, passing cars and hover-mobiles like we're an ambulance racing to get a dying patient to the E.R. I look back to see Mease's driver struggling to keep up. Behind him are several television vehicles also bypassing cars, attempting to keep us in view.

"Excuse me, sir?" I search the driver's eyes in the rearview mirror. "Why is it necessary to drive so fast?"

"Yeah, Will, don't let your Nascar obsession go to your head," the officer in the passenger seat mumbles.

The driver taps behind his ear, disconnecting his nanophone. His gaze is darting from the rearview mirror to the road, back and forth. He gradually slows until Mease's hover-vehicle is right behind me. Without warning, he swerves from the far left lane of a four-lane highway between two vehicles all the way to the right exit ramp. The momentum of the sharp turn throws me against the wall. With my cuffs, I am unable to brace my collision.

I don't know how long I am out, but when I awake it is to the sound of a gun blast. My ears are ringing. I open my eyes. My vision is blurry and my head throbs. I look up. The dark-skinned officer in the passenger seat is seizing from a bullet hole in the side of his head. His blood has splattered between the seats. I feel its wetness on my knees. The driver is breathing heavily. Still grasping his weapon, he looks back over his seat at me. I close my eyes, feigning as if I'm still unconscious.

He unbuckles his seatbelt and steps out of his car, leaving his door open.

"Why did you shoot Jake?" someone outside the car asks.

"He wasn't with us."

The second man—who I presume is an accomplice—is furious. "You idiot!" he screams. I get a glimpse of the side of his face. He's young with black hair, with a thin 5 o'clock shadow. "We are not the bad guys here, man. Raymond Verity is a terrorist and we're going to get him to the FBI for a fair trial."

"And if Jake wouldn't help us, he's helping him! Jake was threatening to turn us in."

"Why didn't you talk to me about it first?"

"Because I didn't want you to talk me out of it! If we want the reward, at least one of us has to be willing to do the hard things."

"Why the police car?"

"It's unmarked!"

"It's still traceable. Why in the world didn't you change to a civilian vehicle like we planned?"

"I didn't have a choice. I was being followed closely."

"What happened to him?"

"He hit his head. I've checked him. He's fine."

I hear the accomplice angrily smack the car.

"They can track these cars!"

"I disabled the tracker." The driver reaches in and pulls a handle to pop the hood. "See for yourself . . . "

When they are on the other side of the raised hood, I raise my head and take a look around me. My blurry vision has resolved, but my head still throbs severely. I am under what looks like a wide overpass beside a narrow stream. Trees obstruct my view of the skyline. From the infrequent sound of passing automobiles overhead on the bridge, we are in a more desolate place than downtown Atlanta, for sure.

I listen carefully to the conversation.

"If he's a terrorist, he goes down either way," the driver argues. "It's the feds for five or FAM for seven and a half. That's two and a half mil more, man. That makes it a no-brainer."

FAM? They must be referring to the Free America Militia, the same group of thugs who tried to execute me on the internet before Farrell and his team rescued me.

The hood slams shut and they come back around to the side of the vehicle. One of them opens the door and reaches in to check my carotid pulse.

"As soon as he comes to, we're handin' him over to FAM."

"That was not our agreement!" The accomplice is insistent. "This is more about justice than it is about money."

"Georgia's leaders are joining the alliance Alabama is building. Whether we go with the feds or FAM, either way, we're jobless, and probably indictable. But with FAM we can afford to get out of dodge."

"If you hadn't killed Jake, we wouldn't need to flee! The feds were going to scratch our records clean outside of Georgia for returning Raymond Verity, but for killing your partner?"

"Why do you talk like you are in charge of this thing?" The driver curses. "This was my plan! My plan! And we're going with FAM."

The accomplice's protest dwindles. I hear some digital numbers pushed in a phone beside the door.

What should I do? With my hands cuffed behind my back and car doors that cannot be opened from the inside, all I can do is pray. I pray for the leaders of the resistance to be brave and do right. For their people to support them. For the life of my granddaughter. For the soul of my wife. For my captivity or death to mean something.

"Alpha–Tuna–4–3–6–Alpha." The driver pauses and listens to the person on the other end of his phone. "Seven and a half, and he's yours. You've got to come to us. We are at 33.313997 north, -83.436919 west. We're under the bridge where it crosses Badger Creek, in Oconee National."

With FAM on their way, my death is near but I feel no fear of it. As a matter of fact, I feel like a coward for not rebuking the betrayal of these officers.

"What you're doing is wrong!" I sit up, and fix my eyes on them through the window.

The accomplice is shorter, with a thin, deeply furrowed face. He pokes his head through the open driver's door and aims a black hand-gun at my head.

"I'm not scared of you," I say. "Those militia fanatics are going to execute me on the internet. What can you do? You're going to stand before God with my blood on your hands."

"You have the audacity to preach to me?"

I turn my gaze to the bald officer on the phone outside, and overhear, "He's a feisty fellow, Jase. Just heard him say that he's not scared of you."

He pauses, and then laughs a long gravelly cackle.

"My granddaughter is going to be killed if you don't let me go. If you want profit, I can double it."

The officer snarls at me and brings his handgun to my upper lip. "I thought I told you to shut your trap!"

"You can listen to money talking, I think." I grin at him and wink.

He cocks his gun. I see hate in his eyes.

The two men are obviously not very kind to each other, so perhaps I can use that to my advantage. "If you shoot me, you'll lose your por-tion and your partner here will probably give you the same treatment he gave Jake."

The snarl dissipates and the man glances at the bald officer outside the door, who continues trading belly laughs with the FAM leader on the phone.

"Do you really think he wants to split his profit with you? He did all the hard work. He's already shown he has no strain of conscience in killing a fellow officer."

"Eavesdrop on two minutes of a conversation and you have already become an expert? Please. There are things you don't know. I'm indispensable. I'm a pilot, and I have a friend in the TSA who owes me a couple favors. I can get us to the coast and to the Dominican Republican on one tank."

Well, so much for Plan A.

"Are you a father or a husband?" I ask him. "Don't you care about them? If you hand me over to them, you're going to be a hunted man."

"Not outside of Georgia. Besides, my wife has spent more time in the psych ward than in my bed since my only daughter died a year ago. I won't miss much."

"I can respect you handing me over to the feds, given what the government's saying about me. But the Free America Militia? Do you think you can hand me over to a bunch of militia terrorists and the government won't know? They have insiders in all those groups."

The man coldly turns his gaze away from me, appearing resistant to my reasoning.

I overhear the bald guy on the phone. "The coordinates are right. The Oconee National Forest . . . "

Maybe there are bow-hunters nearby. The shooting may not have alerted nearby hunters, but my screaming might.

I lay down, raise my legs, and kick the window with all my might, cracking it.

"Hey!" The officer reaches over the seat and tries to restrain me. He grabs me by the laces of my right shoe. With my left foot, I kick the window again, and with the right I kick the officer in the face. My left foot impales the window, and the officer falls back from my right kick, striking the horn.

The door I smashed is thrown open and the bald officer begins to beat me in the legs with his baton. They are designed to cause pain without fracturing bones, but I cannot imagine the pain being any less severe if they had run me over with a semi. I scream and shirk away from his repeated blows, trying to pull myself across the seat away from him. With my hands cuffed behind my back, my movement is limited. I do manage to kick the officer in the front seat in the face again—accidentally this time. As the officer outside leans in and continues to strike my knees and ankles, the officer in the front seat wipes his bloody nose and unsheathes his Taser.

The electricity seizes my body. I scream a teeth-clenched, gurgling cry against the uncontrollable spasm, not even feeling the continuous violent blows on my legs.

Suddenly and surprisingly, I am covered with blood. Is it mine?

The voltage finally ceases, though I continue to cramp in my chest and shoulder. The man with the Taser frantically turns toward the window.

A loud blast precedes the splattering of blood all over the windows on the driver's side of the vehicle, casting an eerie red hue on me from the sun's rays through the glass. The officer yells loudly. I cannot hear the words projected from his lips, as the Taser has caused a persistent high-pitched squeal in my ears.

Whatever he sees strikes fear in him—I see it on his face. His lips move, "Don't shoot! Don't shoot!"

He places his hands on the back of his head and falls out of the car, landing on his face.

Gradually, my senses return and I am able to sit up. The blood on my legs and the driver's-side windows is not mine. The bald officer who was beating me with his baton took a shot in the head. The Taser barbs are still stuck in my chest and shoulder. Their spring-shaped wires go over the front seat, down to wherever the Taser landed when the officer dropped it.

I turn to the window and see a face I never thought I'd see again—Tod Farrell, with his odd-looking assault weapon, rushing toward me. This time he is wearing camouflage.

"Dr. Verity!" I see his lips move, but his voice sounds distant, like an echo across a great canyon. He helps me out of the back seat of the squad car and, with a pair of special pliers from his backpack, removes the Taser probes from my chest. He unlocks my cuffs and begins to lead me up the hill toward the road as a dozen camouflage-clad Alabama agents surround us in a diamond-shaped pattern. One of them drags the surviving police officer in cuffs behind me. I can barely walk from my leg pain, but the attempt to walk up the hill helps restore my bearings.

"How did you find, find me?"

Farrell reaches down by the back of my belt and slowly pulls a paperclip-shaped device from it. "I put it on you in the elevator in the Georgia Statehouse, when you were preoccupied." I furrow my brow as I study his illegal contraption in between his thumb and index finger. "Sue me."

"They're coming," I say.

He stops and grabs me by both shoulders. "Who?"

"The feds?" a soldier besides him inquires.

I shake my head. "The Free America Militia."

Farrell's brow furrows, and his mustache begins twitching to the left again. He glances at the surviving police officer. "You were going to turn him over to FAM?"

"I was planning on turning him into an FBI contact in Roswell, just north of Atlanta. My partner had other plans. He shot that other officer in the squad car, Jake Camma. I wasn't in on that! Dr. Verity is my witness. My intent all along was to help the government."

Farrell gives some unintelligible orders to his team, and they scatter into shadows under the bridge and into the tree line.

"He's right," I say between deep gasps of air from the climb. "It was the bald guy that took charge and called FAM."

"They offered more," the young police officer added. "Seven and a half mil compared to the feds' five mil."

Farrell scowls, which surprises me. He always seems so light-hearted under pressure, an easy smiler, in spite of his involuntary lip tic.

"What is it?" I ask.

"The feds control the Free America Militia!"

"What? That's crazy," the bound police officer objects.

This doesn't compute. "How can that be, Tod? The militia killed several feds when they captured me north of Atlanta and tried to kill me."

"That was a splinter group in defiance of FAM's leadership. The feds have been using FAM to create crisis in order to set the stage for further erosion of constitutional liberties. Whenever they do capture one or more of them, they protect them. They release them from custody and even provide new IDs for them. The princes and the pirates are holding hands, I'm afraid."

"What does this mean?" I ask. "Could it be another splinter group?"

"Don't think so. I have an insider in D.C. who keeps me up-to-date. If FAM's coming, we could expect either FAM with the feds' permission, or the feds. But either way, they are certain to have their eyes in the sky on us any minute, if they don't already."

"Why are we sitting around here waiting?" the bound officer asks, an anxious tremor in his voice. "Let's just leave!"

"I didn't want our vehicles attracting attention on the side of the road, so I sent them down a bit and told them to turn around and come back. Should be here in about"—he looks at his watch—"a couple of minutes. What's your name?"

"Pete Kragg," he answers. "Why would FAM offer us more money than the FBI, if FAM works for the FBI?"

"I didn't say they work for the FBI, Pete, I said they work for the feds. The FBI is only one of many tentacles on this monster. The feds were probably testing your loyalty. Now that you've defied them, they've probably set their crosshairs on you, too."

The officer's face contorts. "I have a daughter; she's sick. I just needed the credit, and I thought that . . . " He turns to me. "I thought you kidnapped those kids."

"How can you kidnap your own grandkids when their mother—my daughter—voluntarily goes with us?"

"How's I supposed to know it was voluntary? The news said you kidnapped all of them, and caused the dementia in all those patients." Pete Kragg turns frantically to Farrell. "I ain't waiting around. We've got to get outta here." He begins to walk up the hill into the open and the agent holding his cuffs pulls him to the ground.

"I don't think you're in the position to be giving orders!" the agent shouts in his face.

I lean close to Farrell. "The Georgia governor seemed sympathetic to Alabama and Mississippi's cause. Do you think he would help us?"

"And resist the feds? Ha!" Farrell smirks. "No, I think Alabama and Mississippi are alone in this battle. And we are far behind enemy lines."

"The border between Georgia and Alabama is not an enemy line, Tod."

"This side of it is." He taps behind his ear and speaks a number. Leaning away, he chats in whispered tones.

The bound police officer sits nearby, his eyes downcast with shame.

"I was a mass murderer just, just yesterday, it seems," I say to him. "I can't blame you, Pete, for wanting to turn me in, with what the media is saying about me. But I assure you, the media and the government bureaucracies feeding them have hands that are just as dirty as mine used to be."

"Used to be?"

"By God's grace, I've changed. People can change."

He turns his eyes away. "From freedom to prison, that's how I'm changing."

"Prison, if you're lucky," the agent holding the young officer's cuffs responds. "You've put all our lives at risk with your betrayal."

"Freedom's a state of heart." I lean close to Pete Kragg, who is beginning to tremble with fear. "If my heart can change, anybody can change. And not just outwardly." I tap my chest. "I'm talking about a deep down, new-reason-to-live change."

Farrell gets off the phone and turns back toward me.

"When are your vehicles coming?" I ask.

"They're not."

"Why?"

"We won't escape by road. It's too vast a stretch between exits." His eyes search the woods, and he mumbles to the agent holding the officer. "Brendan, do you think we can escape into the safety of the forest without detection?"

The lean and muscular Alabama agent removes a handheld computer from a pouch on his hip. "If the feds are coming, it's only gonna buy a few of us some time."

Brendan glances at a radar showing, I assume, approaching aircraft. "Incoming?" Farrell asks him.

Brendan shakes his head. "No, sir, not yet. But they'd probably employ stealth with such a high-value target."

"They're going to kill us all," the police officer warns us. "Whether it's the Free America Militia or the feds, our best chance of living is getting out of here, quick!"

Farrell reaches for his nano. "Hold on. He's calling me back."

"Who?" I ask. Farrell doesn't answer, but turns to converse in whispered tones.

Glancing at the radar on his handheld computer, Brendan utters under his breath. "Escaping now would require the elusiveness of Jeremy Porter."

"What do you mean, the elusiveness of Jeremy Porter?" the police officers wonders.

"Jeremy Porter escaped last night. From an impossible-to-escape facility . . . "

"Here they come." The agent monitoring the radar on his handheld turns his screen to Farrell. "Blinking on and off because of their stealth technology. We can see a little bit of 'em from their sound."

Farrell's eyes widen as he watches the screen, still communicating through his nano. "We don't have one minute, much less one hour. Two V-22 Ospreys, by the looks of their signatures. 270 knots northeast. Less than a minute out. No, three Ospreys." He pauses for a brief second. "Make up your mind. Gotta go. Farrell out."

He taps his nano and communicates orders to his troops.

The Ospreys are tilt rotor aircraft that can take-off and land like a jet or a helicopter, and carry massive loads. A tad noisy, and that's why we can see them. Farrell starts scattering his dozen troopers to various places of cover, instructing them to replace their rifle's hollow point-filled magazines with armor-piercing.

"Randy!" A huge man at the edge of the woods holding what appears to be a very heavy, long-barreled rifle, turns to us. "We'll cover for you after you make your first shot, but you've got to hit rotors to take one out. Then take aim at the others, but be quick."

Farrell leads me and Pete Kragg underneath the bridge.

In the shadow of the bridge, Farrell pushes our heads down until we are sitting on the ground. "They're going to use small arms fire, I think, not rockets, because they need Verity alive."

"No." Brendan, still holding the officer's cuffs, disagrees. "Percussive munitions. Those bombs will knock unconscious anybody within 30 feet, and bust the eardrums of anybody within 50."

Pete Kragg tries to stand to better see the screen of Farrell's pocket computer and he actually strikes Brendan on the face.

"Ow!" Brendan brings his hands to his bleeding lower lip.

"Sorry," Pete says, squatting back down, fearful of the rage behind Brendan's eyes.

"Why do they want me alive, Tod?" I ask.

"You're more dangerous as a martyr," Farrell responds.

"Well, thanks," I say sarcastically. "Good to know my existence is so meaningful."

"At least you being with us gives us a chance to survive this."

"God's the one with us that gives us a chance to survive this."

"Shoot smart!" Farrell shouts to his men. "You're only going to get a couple off before their smart-guns will pinpoint your location." Smart guns have the capacity to shoot at muzzle blasts and heat signatures in combat situations without the risk of having a human eye behind the gun sights. "Shoot and duck, shoot and duck! Keep radio silence, as their weaponry can hone in on radio signals."

All is quiet for a half a minute until we hear the whistling sound of speeding rotors rushing toward us. I try to stand and look over the edge of the bridge to see what is approaching, but Farrell grabs my shirt and prevents me, telling me to stay low.

The relative quiet is interrupted by what sounds like a cannon on the other side of the bridge. Farrell stands and peeks over to see Randy's large caliber, explosive-tip bullet hit its mark. Keeping his eyes on the damaged Osprey, which banks away and careens over some trees, he mumbles, "Fighters are only as strong as their weakest link."

An explosion shakes the ground and flames reflect off of Farrell's eyes. Farrell grins as his men cheer.

Randy, the sniper, takes an immediate, direct hit from a thick hailstorm of high-caliber bullets from several guns on an Osprey that speeds overhead. The other flying monsters change course, turning away from the barrage of small arms fire unleashed by Farrell's men.

When the pitch of Osprey's motors changes from low to high, Farrell announces, "They won't make the same mistake again. They'll both come full speed, weapons ablaze. Stay under the bridge, behind the piling."

Rock and cement seem to explode into dust as the low-flying Ospreys race over our heads so fast you can barely see them, leaving in their wake dozens of groaning and bleeding bodies.

I press my hands over my ears just in time to avoid the massive concussion detonation about 50 feet away. I see Pete Kragg scream in pain, unable to cover his ears due to his hands being bound behind his back. His ears begin to drip blood. He lowers his forehead to the ground in misery.

The screaming Ospreys seem to disappear quietly among the obscurity of the forest's trees, with only the moaning of the injured breaking the pulse-pounding stillness. But the repose is brief. They return as quickly as they left, flying fast and low, at a different angle, seeming to target even those who are taking cover behind boulders, trees, and bridge pilings.

This time there is much less return fire from Farrell's men, and when the fighting copters have passed, there are more screams and groans.

I see but can't hear Farrell's lips speak to Brendan, "We cannot win this."

I reach for Farrell's shoulder. "Tell your men to drop their arms and let me ascend the bridge." I shout to be heard over the incessant buzzing in our ears. Farrell's eyes search mine. I discern both admiration and fear behind those eyes, as if I am provoking him past the edges of his comfort zone. "They'll let you go, Tod. They just want me."

The police officer who kidnapped me raises his eyebrows, stunned at my offer. With the blood pouring from his ears, I'm surprised he can hear me. "You're going to give yourself up?"

The whistling sound of the Osprey rotors changes pitch and Farrell shouts, "Take cover!"

Just as the two Ospreys begin to spray their bullets and percussion rounds down around us, two massive explosions sound off above our heads, sending fiery debris down on both sides of the bridge.

At first, I suspect the Ospreys unleashed their heavy artillery at us. I doubted Farrell's suspicion that they wanted me alive. Even if they did, the destruction of one of their Ospreys surely resulted in an appropriate modification of their rules of engagement. I hold my hands over my ears and duck lower, but Farrell's eyes widen enthusiastically, as if the explosion brought good news. He rushes out from under the bridge into the open to watch one of the Ospreys flip and strike the tail of the other. Both of them descend into the forest, spinning wildly, crashing about a hundred yards away in a massive explosion of billowing flames. The blast is so bright, it hurts my eyes. The heat of the explosion seems to singe the skin of my face and the exposed part of my arms. A large area of the forest around the wreckage is instantly aflame.

Farrell stands, his mouth agape, as two fighter jets zoom past, their engines screaming a high-pitched growl. Farrell holds his rifle high above his head, cheering, joined by his surviving men who are able.

"Who are they?" I ask.

"Georgia Guard. F-35, Lightening 4s." His countenance shines with pride. "I guess Alabama and Mississippi are not alone in this fight after all."

45

THE INJURED AMONG FARRELL'S MEN are field dressed and treated with
IV fluids and pain medication as quickly as their medics could manage it.
Those who were hemorrhaging most severely were given IV drips of novaglo-
bin; the substance has oxygen-carrying capacity like blood but is not rejected
by the host, and thus requires no timely "type and screen" procedure to
ensure blood compatibility—a spectacular breakthrough of medical science
new to me. The injured are reclined on the floors of Farrell's vehicles and
sent west via different routes toward Alabama, so as not to arouse suspicion.

Once Farrell is on the road with the sickest of his men and two medics
in a long, 12-seat hovercraft, he calls a number to update surgeons who
are heading their direction in surgical suites installed in windowless vans.

Farrell has directed me to sit on the floor between the two front
seats as we obey the speed limit westward on two-lane back roads. I
turn my back to the dashboard.

He is not happy about my repeated insistence, "I can't go to Alabama."

"Stop saying that." He slaps the steering wheel with his right palm
for emphasis. "You've got to come with us. You agreed to be prosecuted."

"I will, but not now."

Farrell looks down, disappointment etched in his face.

Facing me, with his back to the first row of seats, is the handcuffed
police officer who kidnapped me, Pete Kragg. In the front passenger
seat is the Alabama agent Brendan, who has assumed responsibility
for the Georgia police officer.

"I'm sorry, but I must go home. My granddaughter—"

"This is bigger than you!" Farrell interrupts me. "This is bigger than me! This is bigger than your family, and even bigger than just one state! This is about stopping the American Holocaust, Dr. Verity! This is about saving freedom for another generation."

"Even so, my family comes first to me, just as your family comes first to you."

Farrell throws his hands up in the air. "I can't believe this! After all we have done for you, getting you before the governors and their cabinets, even saving your life. Don't you feel some obligation to keep your word?"

"I will, but not now."

"What's going to happen to me?" the Georgia police officer, who sits beside the Alabama agent Brendan, asks.

Brendan turns to angrily shout his response, "Duct tape over your face is what's going to happen to you if you don't exercise your right to remain silent!" He stretches a gloved index finger at him out of a tightly clenched fist. "Ya got me?"

"Hey, take it easy," I tell Brendan. "He's not a monster. His motives were not malicious."

"Least till he busted my lip."

An argument ensues, and Farrell shouts to be heard above the raised voices, "Doctor, you played a pivotal role in the success of this killing industry. Don't you feel some obligation to stop it?"

"Obviously, or I wouldn't have turned myself in."

Pete Kragg interjects, "Wait. You turned yourself in?"

Ignoring him, I tell Farrell, "But I just learned that my little Down Syndrome granddaughter has a date with death in three days at the killing center I founded. That, sir, is my priority."

"You're under arrest," Farrell reminds me. "I am duty-bound to—"

"What would you do?" I ask him.

"I am duty-bound," he repeats, "to keep you safe until we get to Alabama, and then you are in the custody of the Alabama criminal justice system."

"Criminal justice system?" Pete Kragg appears excruciatingly confused. The agent in the front turns to scold the officer again but the officer will not be silent. "Wait, wait for a sec, why the criminal justice system? You turned yourself in to them and they arrested you?"

I nod, and then turn back to Farrell. "And I will turn myself back in with a full confession to everything I have done that resulted in the deaths of clones in Alabama, but only after I retrieve my granddaughter. Without my confession, you can't do anything to me, and my confession is contingent, sir. So if you want a successful act of defiance of federal tyranny, if you want to defend Alabama citizens, then your best and only option is to let me go so I can fetch my Mary Nell!"

"And how are you going to do that, Doc?" Farrell condescends to me like I'm a child insisting on visiting Santa's workshop at the North Pole by flapping my arms and jumping off a cliff. "You are not being realistic. You're a wanted man. The feds can tap into any security camera in the whole country. They will pin-point your location before you get within one hundred miles of Baltimore."

"Not with my facial palsy and some hair dye. It's like, like camouflage."

"Camouflage on half your face is not very good camouflage. How would you get there, Dr. Verity?"

"I'm one of the richest men in the nation—"

"One of the stupidest men in the nation," Farrell adds.

I ignore his interruption, "I can buy a space shuttle and tour to the moon on the way if I want."

"With what credit card, Doctor? Think about it! You don't have any credit, any car, or any insurance! You're a fugitive. You're broke! If you so much as use a card to put fuel in this vehicle, they'll have their satellite imagery on us before the receipt's even printed."

I am silent as I consider his valid point. I know he's right. I'm broke.

"Let me fly him there," Pete suggests.

"What?" Farrell exclaims.

"I'll fly him to Baltimore."

"Before or after you fly out this window onto the side of the road?" Brendan mocks from the passenger seat.

I try to measure the sincerity of the Georgia policeman. He is serious. Dead serious. "Thank you, Pete."

Farrell's mouth drops open. "You can't be that foolish, Dr. Verity. He tried to kill you an hour ago."

"My partner did, not me," Pete assures us.

"You are under arrest!" Brendan shouts at the police officer. "Don't you get it?"

"I was only trying to get Raymond Verity to the feds, believing the press' report on him, that he kidnapped his daughter and grand-daughter and was trying to sabotage the American economy by trying to bring down his massive company. Obviously," he turns to me, "I was wrong."

"I was trying to protect my family, Pete. I was trying to protect the people my company kills for profit."

"I understand that now." Pete nods and licks his lips. "I'm deeply sorry, Dr. Verity. I'll make it up to you. I have a friend in the TSA who can get me access to any airport in the nation off the books."

Farrell slams the steering wheel. "I can't believe you! You guys are going to give me a heart attack."

I smile. "You fly me, Tod Farrell. That way you can fly me back when I've secured her safety."

"Are you listening to a thing I'm saying? There's no way I can get a flight into Baltimore without getting us both caught and shipped to CIA Waterboarding School."

Pete Kragg clears his throat. "I can get him in."

"Shut up!" Farrell and Brendan shout simultaneously.

"Do you know how to pray, Tod?" We make eye contact in the review mirror.

He sighs heavily. "Of course."

"Then you have nothing to worry about. I'm stepping out of this boat with my eyes to the miracle-maker, just like Tamara said. Stay in the boat if you want, but I'm walking on water."

When Pete Kragg sees that my comment was not intended as a joke, his eyes widen. "Come on, Mr. Farrell. You gotta let me take him now."

"You aren't going anywhere without my fist around your throat." Brendan aims an index finger at the Georgia officer.

"Lighten up, Brendan," Farrell interjects. "Your busted lip was an accident."

"Fine," Officer Pete responds. "That way you can throw me out the window if I try to escape."

"I'll do much worse than that," Brendan sneers.

"Would you stop being such a jerk, Brendan?" I say.

I turn to Farrell. "What about you, Tod?" I say. "You staying in the boat, or are you coming with me?"

46

FOUR HOURS OF FLYING AND driving gets us to the doorstep of Savannah's new home she shares with Argentino in Columbia, Maryland. Officer Pete did more than just fly me, Farrell, and Brendan to Baltimore incognito, he rented the car for us and pointed out the locations of security cameras so that I could better avoid exposing the good side of my face to the facial recognition software of the federal government's supercomputers. Pete also dyed my brown hair and eyebrows blond, bought me a pair of tennis shoes, Baltimore Ravens sweats and hoodie and, of all things, a poodle from a pet shop, hoping to further mask my identity. Thanks to the painful bruises in my legs and ankles, my limp adds another dimension to my disguise.

Farrell and Brendan were impressed with Pete's work, but wouldn't cooperate with his suggestions or my pleadings. Farrell would go no further than shaving his mustache, and Brendan would do no more than buy some second-hand store clothes and a cap.

When we discover Savannah's home appears to be abandoned, I am tempted to despair. Not knowing where she has taken up residence, I don't know what else to do beside head toward the New Body Research Center and pray for a miracle.

I sit at a roadside café one and a half miles from my company parking lot in downtown Baltimore, mulling over my options.

After twenty minutes of sipping cappuccinos on the outdoor patio, feeding stale pretzels to the poodle under our table, and watching the hovercars float by, my desperate brainstorming hasn't come up with a single remedy. How can I get inside the New Body Research Center? Once inside, how can I intervene to protect my granddaughter and her clone before tomorrow morning?

"Why didn't we figure out that we couldn't figure this out before we flew into the lion's den and before I shaved my mustache?" Farrell wipes his mouth with a napkin as he watches traffic pass by.

"Shh," I plead. "Keep your voice down."

"Maybe we'll see your daughter's car on the way," Brendan proposes. "What's she drive?"

"Uh, she's got a convertible red hover-supercar, I think."

Farrell straightens up. "Well, that can't be too difficult to pick out of the crowd."

"Plus a couple other cars." Now, his shoulders droop. "Besides, this will not be a transfer, but a trade, Mary Nell for Nellie. Even if I can find Savannah and save Mary Nell, Nellie would then be sacrificed. I cannot think of any way to save them both."

"Are there any other options?" Officer Pete leans in. "Let's think."

I sigh. "I'm completely in the dark. I just know God can do it, and He wants to do it. All we can do is show up and ask God to do His will. In refuting all of my medical justifications for abortion, my sister used to say that it was not God's will that one of His children would perish."

Pete chuckles at my choice of words.

"What?" I turn to him. "It's in the Bible."

"If it were God's will, He'd do it. I was raised in church and I'm familiar enough with the Bible that I know God's in control, right?"

Pete's assertion piques my interest. "Oh, you think He's got all this sin and murder under control?"

"I do, or He wouldn't be God."

"If evil was under God's control," I respond, "we'd be fighting God to fight evil."

Pete and Brendan both jolt. "Huh?"

"If, if, a driver is under control of his car that runs over innocent people, or if an officer is under control of his weapon that kills innocent people, how aren't they responsible? How aren't they to blame for doing something God forbids—intentionally killing innocent people?"

Pete and Brendan both object simultaneously, but it's Farrell who takes the floor.

"Pete, hold up, don't you think God's loving?" Farrell asks.

Pete takes a deep breath. "He is loving, but He is also all-powerful."

"I agree." Farrell nods. "Unless you define all-powerful in a way that contradicts the Bible's description of God's love and goodness."

"Wouldn't it be hypocritical to forbid murder and simultaneously permit it, Pete? Brandon?" They turn to me, Pete twiddling his thumbs and Brendan keeping his hand wrapped around a pistol in the pocket of his red windbreaker. "What would you think if Tod helped prosecute those who were killing dupes while all along he was having a clone created and primed for him to murder and assume his body? Wouldn't that be hypocritical? Shouldn't Farrell also be arrested?"

Pete purses his lips and looks down at his twiddling thumbs.

"If something happened that wasn't God's will," Officer Pete speculates, "then God wouldn't be sovereign."

"Better that than sinful," I respond.

"That's heresy!" Pete objects.

"It is?" I turn to Farrell. "I don't know the Bible very well, I'm just thinking through it."

"Oh, they're just being protective of their orthodoxy," Farrell says. "You're not a heretic."

Pete acts offended and looks away down the road.

"Pete, hey, Pete," Farrell calls his name until Pete's eyes fix on Farrell's. "Better His power be restrained by His love than He violate His own law mandating love, setting a poor moral example for angels and men. Tell me, what does the Bible say the angels cry as they worship around His throne?"

He shrugs.

"Holy, holy, holy," Brendan answers.

Farrell nods. "Yes. Not power, power, power."

"Really?" I say. Farrell nods.

"Murder is not God's will." Farrell taps his index finger against the table with each syllable. "Why doesn't He stop it? I don't know, but I am confident there's a reason consistent with His love and His law. And I know that just because it looks like murderers get away with it today, there will be a day of reckoning. The first will be last, and the last first. We shouldn't mistake God's long-suffering for tolerance. He will punish all unforsaken sin."

I point in the direction of the New Body Research Center. "I know right from wrong, and I know God is good. What more do you need to know to realize that what they conspire to do to my granddaughter tomorrow morning is not God's will? Do I need the Bible to know that any more than I need the Bible to know two plus equals four?"

I head toward the bathroom and Brendan gets up to follow.

As soon as I'm inside and see the bathroom empty, my heart begins to be weighed down with grief over what is happening to my family, my grandchildren. I begin to pray fervently for Mary Nell to be saved.

I'm aware that Brendan is behind me watching my outburst, but I don't care. I'm desperate.

"So you want God's will, huh?"

I think it's Brendan's voice behind me, but then I hear a thump, and I turn to see Brendan has slumped to the floor. A hooded person is standing there with a spray can in his hand. He stretches it to me, and I back up and open my mouth to scream, but before I can, he has sprayed the white substance into my face.

Instantly, a darkness overcomes me.

47

I OPEN MY EYES TO a blinding light shining in my face. All around me is blackness. My hands are tied behind my back. The first words that come out of my mouth are, "Oh no, not again."

A figure steps between me and the light. "What are you doing here?"

I squint to try to see the facial features of the man whose voice I vaguely recognize. "I suppose you kidnapped me and carried me here."

"When you're hanging by a thread over a hellish death, you don't mock the hand that holds the thread. What are you doing in Baltimore?"

"Where's the man I was with?"

"Brendan Carpenter's fine."

"How did I . . . ?"

He sighs and interrupts, "Oh, the wasted space of lesser mortals' minds. Please, spare me your dozen questions. Tell me why you're here, or I will draw it out of you quickly with pain."

I wince at the man's threat of violence. Is there any reason to withhold the truth? "My granddaughter, Mary Nell, is due to be traded in for her clone tomorrow morning."

"The one you kidnapped . . . "

"Kidnapped? No." I shake my head side to side. "No."

"Why are the two Alabama intelligence agents, Tod Farrell and Brendan Carpenter, and the Georgia police officer Pete Kragg with you?"

I'm stumped. He knows their identities. How?

"Do you work for the government?"

He sighs anxiously. "Please, answer my questions simply and quickly."

"You're wrong about that."

"About what? Causing you pain?"

"No, about me fearing it. I'm not scared to die."

"Death can be a wave of pleasurable euphoria compared to more severe forms of suffering. If you think that little intramuscular paralytic injected into your facial nerve to disguise your appearance was a painful injection, it is nothing compared to what I can do to you."

What is he talking about? Ah, he's referring to the weakness in the left side of my face. He thinks I injected medicine into my jaw to intentionally disfigure my face. I turn my gaze from the shadow of this clearly cruel creature and look down at the floor. It appears as if I will not be able to save my girls. "I'm in God's hands," I mumble gloomily. "Do what you will."

My comment has his quick tongue momentarily paralyzed. He stands still with his arms crossed over his chest. Finally, he asks in a softer tone, "Tell me, why are those men with you?"

"To help me."

"Help you do what?"

"Help me save Mary Nell." I clear my throat. "And Nellie, her, uh, clone."

"Do you know how many defective people like your precious little Mary Nell and how many clones like Nellie you and your company have butchered?"

"All too well. I live with the guilt. The pain of knowing it's all my fault."

"Oh, you're being too hard on yourself. It's not just your fault. Some people pay for the killing. Then there are the doctors who do the killing and the cutting, the scientists who do the experimenting, the lawyers and bureaucrats who justify it. All of them deserve to suffer."

I gaze to where his eyes would be if I could see into the blackness of his shadowy face. "They are suffering."

The man leans in to me and screams in my face. "If they all breathe one more breath that isn't a scream of utter terror, it's more than they deserve!"

The hot steam of his words pains my ears and makes me gasp. This man certainly has a personal stake in the suffering of those associated with this industry. His unnatural outrage makes my heart speed up and a cold sweat break out on my brow. I attempt to subjugate my involuntary autonomic outburst through intentionally turning my thoughts and my prayers to God. I close my eyes and pray for Mary Nell and her new best friend Nellie. *God, protect them. Save them. I am willing to even die for their sakes.*

"They should all suffer!" he shouts. "And they will suffer. That's my will! My will be done!"

"Yes, they will suffer. You know about the rapid-onset dementia? It's going to bankrupt the company probably. Everybody that's received a new body . . . "

"I know all about it. I know they're blaming you for it."

"I didn't do it."

"And I know it won't bankrupt the company. You'll modify your protocol, amend your contracts to obtain informed consent, and the killing will continue. See, if you tell a crack addict that 90% of crack needles on the street are contaminated with some horrible pathogen, they still abuse. The addiction blinds him to the statistical realities of his actions. He convinces himself that he will be that lucky person who will have all the pleasure and none of the pain. Just like you Americans, drunk with pleasure and Hollywood waste, to risk your sanity and two million ameros for just the rare chance that you'll get immortality without the downside."

"I can stop it. If you want to stop the killing, then help me."

He takes a step back, and laughs a hard cackle. "Help you do what? Save your own skin and blood, your family? What about all the other innocent people condemned to die in the course of your human farming, your slave-trading?"

"Help me save them all, if you can. If you can't, just help me save . . . " I hesitate. I will not rely upon limited man to do what only an unlimited God can do. And I will not rest content with saving only those close to me. No, Tamara was right. We need to love "the least of these"—all of God's children, especially those least likely to be rescued. "I may not be able to save them all today, but I know I need to save Mary Nell—and her clone. Once they are safe, I have offered to turn myself in to the Alabama authorities who are with me today. They're going to prosecute me under their new state law, defy the predictable judicial nullification of it, and if they succeed, then several other states are going to join them."

As I say this, he back-peddles until he is behind the light. I squint from its brightness. "I am doing what I can do. What about you? What are you doing? Why don't you help us save them?"

"Us? You mean you and those three men that are with you?"

"And the leadership of seven states. And God."

"God? Why doesn't the big shot just do it then?"

"He wants to! What we're doing is not His will! It's not. Our duty is to believe and obey, and let Him work His miracle and do what a loving God loves to do. Save people. Help people. Alleviate suffering. Do justice."

"You and God, huh? And your little 'Star Chamber' of justice." He heaves a belly laugh.

I furrow my brow. "God won't be mocked."

"Well, for a God who won't allow Himself to be mocked, there's a whole lot of people doing it."

"He won't let them get away with it."

"The old, wait-and-you'll-see-I'm-right proof. Yet God continues to tarry as the suffering continues with no end in sight. Is this horrible injustice one more thing your God won't prevent because of His commitment to let our wills remain free? Or can't do, because He's impotent? Or maybe He doesn't require Himself to be as loving as He requires us to be?"

"Hey!"

"Oh, don't get so offended. If God allows it, so should you. So, tell me about this great plan your God has given you to save every clone from dying?"

I take a deep breath. I don't have a plan, but it's probably not wise to tell him that.

I hear his breathing rate pick up. He steps closer, casting a shadow across my face. "You don't have a plan, do you?"

"Not yet," I finally admit. "You obviously want to save them. Tell me your plan, and I'll help you."

He crosses his arms over his chest and steps to the side of the light. I listen for an answer. I begin to search the shadows for his figure, but the light is too intensely bright to see anything except his right leg and arm.

"Oh, I see," I sneer, "that's the kind of person you are. Curse the darkness, damn the blood-guilty, and do nothing to help the helpless. For a man with so little mercy, you sure are going to need it on Judgment Day, for God will show no mercy for those who show no mercy." I pause, expecting a witty come-back, but I hear nothing. I plunge the sword deeper. "You swing your gavel against others to your own peril, for as you judge, you will be judged."

I hear the faint clapping of his footsteps retreating across the carpeted floor.

The overhead light comes on. I'm in what looks like a hotel bedroom, facing a twin bed. I fix my eyes upon the face of a man I never thought I would see.

"Jeremy Porter?" I try to not act surprised.

He pulls the hoodie down around his neck and sits on the bed in front of me. The last time I saw him, he pulled a trigger of a gun that was aimed at my face.

"I think you have to have a soul to stand before God on Judgment Day, Dr. Verity, so I might not be invited."

Briefly, he has given me a glimpse of what lies behind his veneer of lawless brutality. Behind those words is a man despairing, hopeless. Those words are his excuse for his own evil.

"If you don't have a soul, then you're not a person, are you?" He raises his eyes to meet mine. "If you're not a person, then neither are your brothers and sisters, and what then is wrong with killing your brothers and sisters locked up in the New Body Research Center? Hmm? Why's it any more wrong to do it to you than it is to do it to a bug or a rock?"

He leans forward with his elbows on his knees, and clenches his fists. "God—if there is one—is *not* good."

What are the chances that my last thirty minutes of conversation with the Farrell, Brendan, and Pete helped equip me, a biblically-illiterate newborn Christian, on how to defend my faith under such scrutiny?

"What do you find so humorous?" he barks with rage in his eyes.

"I'm chuckling because I've been where you're at, and almost envy you because of the euphoria of the revelation you're about to experience."

"Really?"

"If there's no good God, Jeremy, then there's nothing wrong with killing people, is there?" I smirk at the doubt in his eyes. "You know it's wrong to intentionally kill an innocent person, for Redd Cranton to hurt a scared and lonely little boy, as evidenced by your righteous fury over it. Thus, you know there's a good God."

"Well, if there is a God, then He's not as strong as you make Him out to be."

"And He's worthy of your love for precisely that reason."

He jolts, surprised at my response.

"Jeremy, God is not so powerful as to be unable to genuinely love. Love makes Him vulnerable . . . "

"Vulnerable?"

"Yes, vulnerable! He's freely susceptible to grief and sadness. My sister told me several times that God was grieved over my sin. She quoted from Exodus that He was actually sorry that He made man, and regretted doing it."

"Genesis."

"Oh. My point is that God allows others to spurn Him and His love, and break His heart . . . "

"God is vulnerable?" He squints at me in disbelief. "Come on."

"Just look at his whip-mutilated back, Jeremy! His love led His Son to a cross to suffer. His power could have prevented it, even at the last moment, but for love He suffered. For us. For you. Have you ever read the Bible?"

"Memorized every word of it with my first reading." He raises an index finger. "In the time it took for you to fall asleep one night and wake up the next morning. I read the whole thing in English. Had the Greek, Hebrew, and Aramaic passages memorized in a few days. Do you realize that I have mastered every scientific and mathematical fact and theory obtainable online or in a library? I can hack into any computer in the world right from this room."

I'm aghast at his arrogance, but cannot deny the child-like way in which he boasts in himself. He longs for recognition. "You must be proud of yourself, Jeremy."

"I embrace an honest, objective assessment of myself in the scale of being."

"Doesn't it say something in that Bible you read about pride coming before a fall?"

He shakes his head side-to-side. "Nope."

I turn my gaze to the ceiling, trying to recall the passage.

"It's a myth. Not in the Bible."

"Doesn't it say something in there about being a hearer, and not a doer? And to whom much is given, much will be, uh, how's it go?" I snap my fingers trying to remember. "My sister quoted it to me recently. Oh, you know."

He grins mischievously. "I forget."

"With all your learning, you haven't wrapped your mind around the one thing that is the most important thing to learn."

"You're going to tell me what I need to learn?" He snarls at me.

"Love, Jeremy Porter. Love."

He leaps to his feet. "I don't need you or your God's love."

His whole countenance reeks of self-adulation. His extraordinary gifts—coupled with the horrific abuse he must have suffered—have turned him into a monster, apparently without a functioning conscience.

He walks toward the desk and moves his finger across a laptop, which appears to bring several hard-drives to life with their characteristic hum. Something beeps and he lifts what looks like a metallic cup affixed to a flexible base toward the window. He carefully angles it toward the sky until there is another beep from his laptop. Then he begins to type.

"What are you going to do?"

"I am," he pauses to type a few words into a laptop, "going to kill them all." He punches the last key harder than the others, and then crosses his arms over his chest and gives me a subtle wink. "It is mathematically impossible to save all of the innocent cloned humans. I can, however, avenge them."

"What? Who? Who are you going to kill?"

He puts an index finger one inch over one of his keys. "You have a great privilege, Dr. Verity. You're an eyewitness to my first act of nation-shattering cyber-terrorism in what will doubtless turn out to be a long and illustrious career. Once I hit 'Enter', the first to go will be the murderers who do the splicing and the cutting and the raping and the killing. At least, the ones in Baltimore. Then when the dust settles and the feds realize that they can't figure out what I did and expend billions fishing in shallow swimming pools for killer whales, then"—he gives me a wide boyish grin—"when they least expect it, I'll set my sights on the CEOs and the business leaders with blood on their hands. I will be what you pray God will be. The father to the fatherless, the avenger of the innocent. Then, when the prosecutors are despairing for a lead, the lawyers and bureaucrats who justify and perpetuate the slaughter will sup with the Reaper."

This man plans to go on a massive killing spree.

"I've got a better plan."

He laughs, pulling his finger back from the keyboard. "And what is that, genius?"

"Love."

"Oh, really?"

"Don't kill people, Jeremy. Treat 'em as you'd want to be treated. It's the golden commandment."

"Rule."

"Huh?"

"That's interesting coming from the man that has single-handedly built an industry that has probably killed more people in the history of the world than anyone, who naively professes a faith in a loving—"

"It's more than interesting, it's revolutionary!" I can tell he's not accustomed to being interrupted, and he looks like he's going to explode again. "I'm a new man, Jeremy Porter. God's love has changed my heart. Let me help you stop the killing without killing people—especially innocent people! How is your weapon of mass destruction going to kill the butchers without killing the innocent?"

The lines in his forehead deepen yet his voice is calm. "It's unavoidable. Every avenue I've considered that spares the innocent lets the killing industry continue to thrive. That is not an option. The innocent die by any route. At least now, the killing business will die with the innocent."

"Oh, what a weak mind indeed." He shrinks back from me as if I've crossed an invisible line he didn't know existed. As I sit bound before one of the most brilliant human beings that probably ever existed, the confidence of my charge surprises even me. "If anybody's blood should be shed to save the innocent, it should be mine. Not the innocent. That is an avenue you have not considered, am I right? Self-sacrifice?"

He stands, amused. "Self-sacrifice? Really?" He removes a knife attached to an unseen holster under his black sweatshirt and begins to walk threateningly toward me. I do not tremble at his intimidating posture, but for a moment I think he intends to test my theory about shedding my blood to save the innocent. He puts the blade to my neck. "Your blood for theirs?"

"That's not a meaningful sacrifice. I have no death wish, Jeremy."

He comes around in front of me with a carefree chortle. He crosses his arms over his chest, his knife still clenched in his right hand. "Tell me, Dr. Verity, how can your sacrifice save anybody?"

"You want to sacrifice the weak and helpless as necessary collateral damage in a war against tyranny. What is that but tyranny fighting tyranny? There's no liberty at the end of that bloody rainbow. But when we sacrifice ourselves to protect the weak and helpless in a war against tyranny, that, my friend, makes us like Jesus. That is greatness. That unleashes His power. He's the only hope—"

"What fantastic fiction you preach."

"You can't convince a man who's been to the moon that no moon exists, Jeremy. I've tasted and seen the Lord is good. Won't you join me?"

"Oh, Dr. Verity." His tone reveals his disappointment.

Maybe he doesn't have a soul. Maybe he is just a demon set on vengeance and chaos. But he wasn't born so. It was Redd Cranton who molded this monster through years of abuse. If hate mutilated his spirit, then maybe love can redeem him. What Jeremy Porter needs is what I received in the trunk of that lead-covered sedan.

"The offenses against you do not justify your own offenses. You have offended your Creator, and stand in need of forgiveness."

"My creator's a scientist with the New Body Research Center."

"No, you're wrong. We can't create a grain of sand from nothing, Jeremy. We only take what God has made and build things with it. God made you, and He loves you. He wants to heal you and save you from what that pervert did to you. From your own sins . . . "

By the way he steps closer to me with that knife in his grasp, his respiratory rate increasing, his laser-like blue eyes fixed on mine, I cannot tell if he's going to kill me or cry.

"Do you thank God for your new life in your new body?"

I shrug. "I do thank God for my health, but I regret the death of my clone."

"Do you believe your health is evidence of God's goodness to you?"

"Yes, but it's because He's made the best of a bad situation and—"

"Even as you sit there with half a working face?"

"My facial paralysis saved my life, Jeremy. It kept me from being identified through the hundreds of security cameras I passed from Atlanta to here. You see, if you trust in God, even our weaknesses are evidence of God's love."

"That's an interesting theory." He takes a step back and massages his chin with the hand that holds the knife. "Did you also know that the stroke saved you from the rapid-onset dementia that 98.5% of those with new bodies are experiencing?"

My jaw drops. "What?"

"Turns out that those who had complications during their transfer, resulting in at least some brain death, are protected for some reason. Apparently, two fully functioning cerebral hemispheres are necessary for the dementia to progress."

"Wow. My stroke saved my life." I wag my head back and forth. "What you perceived as a handicap is one of my greatest blessings. God is good."

He steps closer. "Tell me this, Dr. Verity. Is the love you experience from others evidence of God's love to you? The love of your mother? Your father? Your wife, your children, and your granddaughter?"

"Of course. All good things come from His hand."

"Do you believe God loves me just as much as He loves you?"

"He loves everybody, Jeremy."

"Then why was the young woman I loved killed and butchered for that fat old European princess? Where's the love of my mother? Where's the love of my father? Why was I abused and exploited for so many years, over and over again, with no hope of ever being free? Where's God's love for me, Dr. Verity?"

I search for the right words, but I don't even know how to begin to answer those questions. How can I justify the undeserved and unjustified suffering of a little child? "But you are free now, Jeremy. You are free now. Can't you see that as evidence of God's love for you?"

"If the love of others is evidence of God's love for us, then what does that pervert Redd Cranton tell you about God and His love?"

"Redd Cranton was possessed by Satan. But God loves you. *I* love you."

He raises his eyebrows and licks his lips. "*You* love me?" He pauses and pokes his thumb in his chest. "Me?"

"I would die for you, Jeremy."

He stands and begins to pace, mumbling incoherently to himself.

"My granddaughter Mary Nell—she would love you like her own flesh and blood. Have you given God thanks for the little bit of love you have experienced, for the love you shared with Forty? For the food you enjoy and the bed in which you sleep? Or are you so bitter for what you don't have and haven't enjoyed in life that you can't be grateful for all the good things you have been given, all of which are sufficient evidence that your Creator loves you?"

With a frustrated grimace, he turns his eyes heavenward and raises his voice. "Why does God give Redd Cranton health? Hmm? Why does he enjoy pleasure, food, sleep, wealth and fame?"

"God's going to judge him soon enough, Jeremy. But He's patient. He's long-suffering and merciful, even to the people who don't deserve it. I'm glad He is, Jeremy. Otherwise there would be no hope for the worst of sinners like me and Dr. Cranton, only an unbearable guilt and, and a fear of the Day of Judgment."

Jeremy Porter breaks out in a full laugh. "You are quite the phenomenon, Dr. Verity. I think you would extend a hand of mercy to Redd Cranton himself."

"As my sister told me once, those who are forgiven much love much. When you realize how bad you need forgiveness, you find the strength to give it away to those who wronged you. Even to Redd Cranton."

That comment wipes the smile off his face and he brings his knife inches from my face. He grips it so firmly his knuckles whiten. Right now, it appears difficult for him to *not* kill me. I stare into his eyes. "Just yesterday, a police officer kidnapped me and conspired to turn me over to the Free America Militia for seven and a half million ameros. FAM wanted to execute me and broadcast it on the internet. That police officer, when I forgave him, became an invaluable asset for me getting here in time to try and save my granddaughter. See, Jeremy? God loves to take the devil's best weapons and turn them into heaven's greatest trophies. You can be one, too."

The fury in Porter's eyes intensifies further. Was mentioning God's willingness to have mercy on Cranton a strategic error? It appears so. Why then did it feel so perfectly appropriate to bring up?

He blurts out a phrase in Latin, turns on his heels, and marches toward the computer.

"What does that mean?"

He doesn't answer me. He rams the tip of his knife into the table, leaving it upright next to his keyboard, and he begins to type.

"Please, don't, Jeremy!"

He types a few keys and then walks to the door without saying a word.

"What did you do, Jeremy?"

With his hand on the doorknob, he turns to me and speaks calmly. "You have ten minutes until the blast. If you scream, you will be discovered, the authorities will come and call the FBI, and their best may be able to stop it. With their skill sets at the nearest office, I give them a

20% chance. But you will get captured, and you will endure much pain and suffering at their hands. The President has a personal vendetta against you because of your betrayal, and there will be no bargaining. Are you really willing to sacrifice yourself to save those innocent dupes?" He points in the direction of what I presume to be the New Body Research Center. "Are you willing to let that killing business continue at the cost of saving those dupes and your granddaughter?"

"They're people, not dupes." I struggle against my wrist ties. "Mary Nell—she's a precious child, Jeremy!"

He smirks at me with raised eyebrows before he exits, appearing amused by my dilemma. As the door slowly shuts behind him, he speaks without looking back, "It's your choice."

"Jeremy!" I pull as hard as I can against my wrist ties, but they hold fast to the back of the wooden chair to which I am bound. My feet also are tied to the legs of this chair. "My granddaughter's there, Jeremy! So is Nellie! Stop! If you would murder her, Jeremy, you are no better than the monster who abused you!"

His footsteps walk away down the hall.

"Jeremy!"

48

HE LEFT ME WITH A hard choice indeed. Scream for help, and people will arrive who will notify federal agents, who will tap into Jeremy Porter's computers and hopefully dismantle his elaborate plan to destroy the New Body Research Center and everyone in it, including Mary Nell and Nellie. Savannah and Morgan are most certainly on site. But if I scream for the authorities, I will be taken captive. What will happen to my girls then?

I would be pushed to despair in this lose-lose dilemma, if it weren't for God. Maybe, just maybe this is all just a test of my resolve to trust God. Tamara said God would test my newfound faith. Maybe this is just a test. Can this be what God has planned? Is He putting my willingness to sacrifice my life to save my granddaughter to the test? Perhaps this is the trial I must pass for Him to do His miracle. Stepping out of the boat is scary. Walking on water is impossible! Trying to feels insane. But unless I do step out of the boat, how can I experience God's power in my life?

Time is running out. No time for an inward metaphysical debate on the exercise of faith.

Maybe I can break loose and find someone to alert the authorities, allowing me to leave before the police arrive. I begin to rock my chair. I might be able to loosen the joints and free myself.

"But what if I do nothing?"

The words come through my lips, uninvited and unwelcomed, but I cannot resist the gravity of their logic. It's not *my* destructive weapon of war that somehow has been planted within the New Body Research Center. How can I be responsible for it? Is it possible that the New Body science and the associated killing industry can be brought to a screeching halt in one single moment of billowing fire, torn flesh, and scattered debris? Maybe this is my sacrifice. Give up the lives of my family for a greater good. Let hundreds or maybe thousands of people die by another's hand in order to save hundreds of thousands of lives in the long run—maybe millions. Then—the thought comes to me like a cup of water to a man about to die of thirst—then I can avoid capture.

This is my Gethsemane. Indecision cripples my resolve. The temptation pulls at this cursed body, lulling my conscience numb with its delicious alternatives to sacrifice. I am torn betwixt two impossible choices.

But how can I sit still and do nothing while so many lives hang in the balance this very moment? All future contingencies are based not only upon reason, but also upon faith. The future is uncertain. There is a God in heaven who answers prayer. I must act based upon present circumstances, and I must act in love toward those people that are in that building right now. How can I not have compassion on all those innocent people *and* all the guilty ones who've yet come to the light? They walk unknowingly toward the precipice of their eternity. Can I sit still and let another's devilish plan transpire?

I take a deep breath. I know what I must do.

"Help! Help me!"

I continue to scream for help until a woman knocks on the door. "Hello?"

"Help! Call the FBI immediately! I'm tied up in here and there's a bomb at the New Body Research Center down the street!"

She wiggles the doorknob. "I'll get the manager—"

"No! The police or the FBI! The FBI office is nearby. Now! Hurry!"

In a moment, an elderly man who I presume is a manager opens the door. He is startled when he finds me bound and sees computers and wires all around the room. "Mr. West?"

"No, I am Dr. Raymond Verity. I have been kidnapped! Did you call the FBI?"

The woman behind the manager nods anxiously.

"*The* Dr. Verity?" The manager has wonder in his eyes.

"Yes, hurry . . . "

"What happened to your face?"

"Hurry, untie me . . . "

"You said something about a bomb?" The manager hurriedly bends down and tugs at my wrist ties.

"Not here, somewhere else. You're safe. But here is the computer that detonates it." I motion with my head to the laptop on the table. "Hurry!"

He cuts my ankle and wrist ties and I begin to bolt for the door. "Tell the police to evacuate the New Body Research Center immediately! Tell them everything I told you. I need to go!"

"Wait!"

I rush from the room without another word, but before I can push the button for the elevator, it opens and eight black-clothed, federal SWAT agents and two police officers begin to rush past me.

I turn from them to show them the sagging left side of my face, and point down the hall toward the room. "That way!"

They fly past me and I breathe a sigh of relief as I enter the elevator. I press the button to close it as several more police officers come rushing out of the stairwell down the hall. One of them has a glimpse of me through the closing elevator door and inserts his hand to re-open it.

"Raymond Verity?" He speaks the words in disbelief. I should've turned the weak side of my face toward the open elevator door. "You are Raymond Verity!" He unholsters his Taser and aims it at my torso.

"Please, don't." I raise my hands. "Man, those things hurt."

The officer reaches in and hits the button on the elevator to stop the doors from closing. He presses the Taser against my back. "Get down on your knees and lock your fingers behind your head . . . "

49

I AM WHISKED AWAY BEFORE I learn whether the FBI is able to deactivate the bomb, or that they've successfully evacuated the New Body Research Center. They blindfold me and push me out of the building and into a vehicle. After a ten minute ride, I am led into a building and down several halls.

My feet are bound to a cold metal chair in a chilly room, and my arms are strapped to a table in front of me. I am left blind-folded, ear-muffed, and left all alone as far as I know in what I presume is an interrogation room. Someone places something to my nose and I am forced to inhale this sweet scent for several seconds.

I can't believe that Jeremy Porter gave up his computers and his software in order to test me. It doesn't make sense. My mind buzzes with a thousand tragic scenarios. Certainly if the bomb detonated, and it was powerful enough to kill everyone in the building, I would have sensed the percussion. We didn't drive that far away. Maybe it was a biological warfare agent or toxic gas bomb. Certainly, if it detonated, they intend to blame me for it. Maybe there is no bomb, and I gave myself up for nothing. Maybe none of it happened and all of it is some elaborate nightmare. Maybe I'm still in cryo, and all of this is in my head. Maybe I'm dead and suffering in some sort of purgatory for the evil deeds of my life.

The more my mind drifts from one crazy scenario to the next, the more I realize that either my stroke is progressing to affect my psychological state, or the sensory deprivation of this blindfold, these earmuffs, and these tight wristlocks and ankle-locks are pushing the limits of my sense of reality. Or they gave me a psychedelic medicine to break down my resistance.

After what seems like hours, my blindfold is snatched from my face. Before me stands a tall, thin man with a reddish complexion. He pushes a button on the table, and my wristlocks are loosened. I look around the room, trying to gain my bearings. I move my feet and discover I am no longer fastened to this chair. He looks strange, imbalanced, like his features are fluctuating right before my eyes. Everything looks sharpened, like the contrast is too high on the photo-doctor app. Something is definitely wrong with my sensory capabilities.

"Did, did they stop the bomb?"

He peels several sensors off my chest and arms. "Come with me."

He pulls two wires from off my temples and then walks toward the open door.

Confused, I follow him. I'm a little uneasy on my feet for a second, and nausea swells up inside my stomach. Fortunately, it lasts only a second. "Did you evacuate the building?"

We exit into the hallway and quickly enter the next room. "If you want to be free, stay on my heels."

He unholsters a weapon and approaches a side door.

Two agents appear to be unconscious on the floor in a room filled with computers and large panels of buttons and knobs and holograph screens. One large screen has my name at the top and several of my vitals, including pulse, respiratory rate, and blood pressure. They are all blank. The EKG line is flat. A security camera hangs from the corner of the room, but the wires leading to the back of it have been severed. I do not follow him across the room.

"Who are you?"

"Do you want to see your granddaughter again?"

"Yes. Is she— "

"Then do not ask one more question until I give you permission. Do you understand? Not one word! Stay right on my heels."

I come and stand behind him as he crouches next to the door, presumably to stay out of view of anyone who might pass by and see him through the small window in the door.

He glances at his watch and opens the door. "Stay close."

He darts down the hall to the right and stops at a large glass door. Seeing someone inside, he ducks low and crawls past the door to avoid being seen. I imitate him, staying low to the ground. There seem to be security cameras at every corner we pass. How can they not see us? What in the world is going on? Is this the work of Farrell, or Porter, or have the remnants of FAM paid someone off to break me out so they can get their hands on me? If I follow this strange thin man, am I voluntarily walking headlong into a fate worse than what the feds have in mind?

I have no choice. The man is armed. I am compelled to follow. He leads me down a stairwell into a lower floor without windows. He stops and glances at his watch. I am tempted to ask a dozen questions that torment me, but I keep quiet. The man is obviously under tremendous stress—maybe even duress. I pray as I watch his lips count down from eleven to zero. He opens the door and I follow. With his weapon at the ready, he sprints toward an exit sign. He looks up at the security camera, waiting. The light on the panel beside the door turns from red to green, and the thin man nods. He opens the door and points out into what looks like an underground parking lot. "Turn right twice, and you'll find a red hover sedan parallel-parked, idling, with the keys in it."

"Wait, who are you?"

"No questions! No time."

"No, you listen to me. I have no idea what you are doing, but I am not going one more step until you tell me—"

"I received a message!" His face breaks out in a fresh sweat. "Someone's got evidence of something I've done. They promised to destroy the evidence if I will break you free."

My gratitude for this man's help in freeing me suddenly goes out the window, now that I'm aware he only did this because he was being blackmailed. "What did you do?"

"It doesn't matter. You're free."

"It *does* matter! You need to make it right, whatever you did wrong."

"Leave or we both go to prison!"

"Prison is the least of your concerns. You're going to give an account to God."

"There's no time!" He frantically tries to shut the door, but I insert my hand to keep it open.

"Well, make time! Your sin will never leave your shadow till you come to terms with your guilt and make it right."

The man sighs heavily, glancing over his shoulder. "I can't make this right."

"Don't flatter yourself. You insult God to think you are beyond redemption. God's grace is greater."

The man gives me a half grin and wipes the sweat off his brow. "If God can redeem someone as depraved as you were, He can probably redeem the devil himself."

I smile at the compliment—or was it an insult? At least something good came out of the pit of my depravity.

"Who was it that put you up to this?"

"I have no idea, but whoever it was handled security for us, so they are either high up in government or they are the government's worst nightmare. Now, go!"

He shuts the door and I begin to trot along the parking lot. After the second right, the light of the setting sun glows through the exit ramp out of the basement. Two security guards are in a small room beside the exit that leads up to the street. It appears that they are sleeping. As I pass them, a faint white mist exits the A/C vent above them.

My quick pace turns to a run once I hit the sidewalk. Adrenaline has helped my bruised legs recover their strength. This new body is truly amazing. The idling car is right there, waiting for me. The windows are tinted, so I cannot see inside. I open the driver's side door. There is a note on the seat with hurriedly printed words in all caps: "FOLLOW GPS IF YOU WANNA KEEP EM." I wince. What does that mean? I duck in to take a look at the old GPS device on the dash.

"Gwanpaw!"

I look back. Mary Nell and Nellie are side-by-side, holding hands, buckled into twin child seats! I blink hard. My senses must be playing tricks on me. I can't believe it! I squint my eyes hard, shake my head, and look again.

"Gwanpaw!" she repeats.

"Hello, Dr. Verity."

"Ah, my girls! It's so good to see you!" I come around to the side door but it is locked. I reach in to the driver's side to unlock the door when suddenly, I hear an alarm so loud that it hurts my ears. It seems like the whole city block turns into one big siren. The celebration of our reunion is going to have to wait. I jump into the driver's seat so fast that I bump my head on the top of the car. I buckle up and say, "Hold on, girls! Gwanpaw's movin' fast . . . "

Mary Nell's "Yee-haw!" brings a smile to my face. I can't believe it! They're here! Both of them.

The GPS points straight with an instruction to turn right 0.4 miles ahead. It looks like it has been modified. An old-fashioned beeper—the kind I wore in med school before smart phones really took off—has been affixed to the back of the device. A blinking cursor is at the bottom of the screen. As I'm looking at it, words appear. *Slow down! 25 mph!*

I glance down at the speedometer. I'm going 35. I am reluctant to slow. I will soon be pursued.

The next message on the GPS reads, *You are not being pursued.*

I look back briefly at the girls. "How did you get here?"

"They kicked everybody out of the building," Nellie announces without emotion.

"You mean the New Body Research Center?"

She looks at me with an inquisitive grimace. She may not even know the name of the building in which she has been born and raised.

"When they evacuated us, a man named Thirty-One got me away, promising to take me to you."

What a relief! It sounds like they evacuated everybody. "Never go with a stranger."

"That's what he said. But he was like me. Except a number for a name."

Mary Nell's happy, nasal voice adds, "We be together! Yay!" She raises three of her fingers on her left hand to Nellie, careful to hold the pinkie down with her other hand. "F-wee. No, four." She extends the pinkie. "Four of us, together."

"Mary Nell," I glance at her in the rearview mirror, "where's your mother?"

"Mommy meets us d'air."

"Where?"

"D'air." She points at the GPS.

I turn right as the GPS instructs. My next turn is in 0.3 miles. Jeremy must be watching me, because his message on the GPS reads, *Slower. Your next right turn has no road sign, and comes quick.*

"Mommy d'air, but not Gwammaw."

What does she mean? As if reading my mind, Nellie interprets with her little adult-like voice. "Thirty-One said that if you follow the GPS, we'll meet our mother, not Grandma. He took us both during the evacuation." She glances at Mary Nell. "Give him the letter."

"Oh!" Mary Nell reaches into her pants pocket and extends a letter toward me. "Can't w-each . . ."

"Who's it from?" I ask.

Nellie answers. "From Grandma. She gave it to Mary Nell with instructions to give it to you if you ever take her away again."

"Will you read it for me, Nellie?"

"Mary Nell says that she can only give it to you. She won't let me read it."

"For you, Gwanpaw!" Mary Nell reaches as far as she can forward to try to give me the letter.

I reach back for it and then see Nellie's frightful grimace. "Turn right, Grandpa!" She points ahead. "Right!"

I brake hard, almost missing the turn.

"I'll get it from you later, Mary Nell. Just put it away for now."

The GPS is leading me down an ally, a back road between two buildings not one mile from the FBI office building. Why is he taking me here?

"Don't deviate."

"What? Why?" I find Nellie's eyes in the rearview mirror.

"Thirty-One said not to deviate."

The GPS reads that my destination is on this narrow one-lane road, 0.1 mile ahead. I pull around some trash and large potholes until something slaps the passenger side of the vehicle.

"Ah!" Mary Nell cries out.

"It's okay," Nellie reassures her.

I push the button to roll down the window. It's the Georgia police officer who flew me to Baltimore. "Pete Kragg! What are you doing here?"

"Quick! No time!" He hops in and points at the GPS.

It reads, *Pull to the right side of this ally under the awning! NOW!*

I obey and pull into a two-car parking lot under an awning just as a fleet of helicopters speeds past us overhead.

"He told me to make sure you read and obey everything he writes on that contraption. Even if it doesn't make sense."

"Who?"

"Some really smart guy who wants to help you."

"It's Jeremy Porter."

Pete blinks hard. "The one that escaped that maximum security federal prison?"

I nod.

"How can that be possible? I thought it was a government insider trying to help you. How can a civilian . . . ?"

"Jeremy Porter has mastered every branch of science and math possible. He's got a photographic memory, speed-reads faster than you can dream, and can get by on an hour of sleep a night. He speaks and writes every language accessible online. He's a digital Jedi."

Pete looks over his shoulders to the two girls. They hold hands happily. Mary Nell waves, and Nellie follows suit. He waves back. "Your granddaughters?"

I turn to enjoy them for a moment. "That," I say, my heart bursting for joy at the sight of them, "is perfection. Not this"—I pinch my forearm—"artificial vanity at another's expense, but that." I study them for a moment. Strength holding hands with weakness. Tears for pain, laughter for joy. Love. Perfection."

I turn to him. "I'm glad you're okay, Pete. When I saw you on the floor of that bathroom . . . "

"No small talk." He points at the GPS. "I need to take Nellie."

"Take Nellie? Why?"

"Satellites can gather heat signatures inside of automobiles, I guess." He points at the GPS. "Read."

It reads, *They are looking for one adult driver and two children, so Pete take Nellie.*

"Do you really think you can trust this guy?" Pete asks the question I was at that moment asking myself. "What's his agenda, Doc?"

"I don't think we have the luxury of another choice."

I turn back to Nellie. "You need to go with this man, Mr. Pete, for just a little while."

She nods confidently. "I know. Thirty-One told me."

She leans over and kisses Mary Nell on the cheek, and Mary Nell throws her arms around her neck.

"Wuv you."

Nellie kisses her again and imitates her lisp, "I wuv you, too."

She and Pete Kragg exit the car.

"When will I see you again?" I ask him through the open window. "Where's Tod Farrell?"

Pete points at the GPS. "Drive."

I glance at it. *Drive.* As I'm watching it, the words change to *Drive now.*

The GPS flashes black, and then a new destination suddenly shows up on it. Twenty-one miles away.

"I know, he's irritating. The hover-mobile this guy apparently is giving me to get out of here is on the next road over." He turns to the open door of the dilapidated apartment building. "It's a sweet speedster, he said. Paid for. Hope he lets me keep it."

"Don't covet what doesn't belong to you. It's poisonous candy."

I glance at the GPS, and read it aloud. "Tell Pete to shut up and leave."

Jeremy Porter must have a camera or a listening device inside the vehicle.

One last wave goodbye, and then I accelerate down the alley, following Porter's instructions. It takes 45 minutes to drive the 21 miles. He has me stop every few miles in an underground parking lot or under an overhead bridge, probably hiding from the government's ubiquitous eyes in the sky, or simply to confuse those chasing the sat images and documenting the trajectories of similarly colored sedans.

I pull into a parking lot just as the last of the sun's rays are transforming the thin layer of clouds on the horizon into a diverse spectrum of colors I wish I had the time to enjoy. My apparent destination: a hover-train station in view of the Chesapeake Bay.

The GPS reads, *Go inside, sit on right of waiting room, keep gaze rightward, away from security camera opposite corner. Take GPS with you.*

What? That doesn't make sense. I say out loud, "But they'll see Mary Nell."

Momentarily, the cursor goes blank and then reads, *Put MN in blue duffel bag.*

"Blue duffel bag? What?"

In trunk.

He can't possibly want me to put Mary Nell in a duffel bag. I must have misunderstood him.

That was not a typo, he texts.

Before I even open the car door to fetch the duffel bag, my imagination is hard at work figuring out how I'm going to explain this to Mary Nell.

Jeremy texts again. *Remember what you said about pride b4 a fall?*

"Yes?"

My pride, your fall. Found me. Goin dark.

"What? What am I supposed to do, Jeremy?" At this point I'm about to pull out my hair in utter frustration. I feel like I'm at the open door of a high-flying plane, waiting for my parachute, and being told to jump and I'll be given a parachute on the way down. I don't know how I can venture down this road blindly with half a map. But what alternative do I have besides walking this tenuous plank?

I wait several minutes. No more texts.

I turn my eyes to heaven. "I need You now, Lord."

50

HOW CAN I TURN THIS into a game for the sake of my Mary Nell? My mind draws a blank. Time is quickly running out, so I look into her eyes and tell her the truth. "Baby, I need you to listen to me very carefully."

"Uh huh?"

I unbuckle her from her child seat.

"There's some bad people that want to take me away from you. And I need you to help me trick them so we can be together. I can get you back to your Mom and your sister Nellie, but I need your help. Will you help me so we can be together again?"

I expect to see fear in her eyes, but instead I see courage.

She bites her bottom lip. "O-tay."

My own quivering steadies with the confident way she squeezes my hands. "We're gonna be toge-ver."

I smile at her and kiss her cheek. "Yes, Mary Nell, we will. I need you to sit in this blue bag here." It has a spine and a handle, so I set it upright and move it from side to side on its wheels. "It'll be a bit bumpy."

"O-tay."

When I take her out of her seat, I see the letter that she had stuck under her leg. I pick it up. She reaches for it. "Ooh, ooh, ooh," she squeals until I give it back to her. She holds it to her chest for a second and then hands it back to me. "For you, Gwanpaw."

"Thank you." I put it in my shirt pocket and zip her up in the duffel bag. As I wheel her inside, she begins to giggle. "Shh. You have to be very quiet."

"It tickles."

"Please," I lean down to whisper, "try to be quiet."

"O-tay."

I begin to wheel her toward the building and she says, "O-tay?"

"Yes, Mary Nell."

"Am I being quiet?"

"Good job. No more talking, o-tay?"

"O-tay."

I sit on the right side of the waiting room, careful to keep my gaze rightward. Thankfully, there is a holographic screen on the wall to justify my rightward gaze. Unfortunately, I have once again become the lead story. I am being labeled an accessory to Jeremy Porter's foiled terrorist attack on the New Body Research Center. They show the footage of me bypassing officers after leaving the hotel room where Jeremy kept me captive. They show me jumping into the elevator, being recognized by the police officer, and him drawing his Taser on me.

I take stock of who is in the waiting room. One of them may be there to help me board this train. After all, I cannot use my credit cards and a cash transaction in an upscale business like this hover-train station is unheard of; even proposing to exchange cash for a service or a ticket would arouse suspicion.

Fortunately, most people in the waiting room are so hopelessly addicted to physical perfection, they turn their gaze from me as soon as they see my asymmetric countenance. This deformity of my facial features is saving my life. Again.

I look down at the GPS I have laid in my lap. For all Jeremy Porter's brilliance, you'd think he'd get a GPS with longer battery life when unplugged from the vehicle. It has only one of four bars of power remaining.

Come on, Lord, help Jeremy get away so he can tell me what I need to do.

Careful to keep my hand on the blue duffel bag, I retrieve the letter from my pocket, open it and begin to read it.

Would you sacrifice yourself for that worthless, defective child?

That's it. One cold sentence.

The message does not have the effect the author intended. Instead of provoking me to waver on my commitment to protect this helpless defective girl, my affection for her deepens. Every tragic rejection my Mary Nell receives because of her Down Syndrome creates in me an even stronger love for her and a heightened awareness of the depths of the cruel betrayals we have endured, and the beastly malice of the powers who hunt us.

With my own defects in my facial features, which frequently prompt others to turn away from me in disgust, how does Morgan not think I will take her implications personally?

Something else is written on the back of the paper. The handwriting is barely legible, hastily written. Once I decipher the scribble, my lips mumble the words.

Would you, if you knew your sacrifice would not save her?

Good question.

Would I give up my freedom to save Mary Nell if I knew failure was inevitable? Would I give up my life for her if I knew she was still going to die?

As I think on it, doubt begins to inebriate me. My confidence is being shaken. I struggle against the sluggish pull toward apathy by ceasing to think about me and instead focusing my thoughts on my granddaughter. Her innocent smile. Her slobbery kisses. Her sincere affection, even for those who spurn her love. I remember that day on the beach when Savannah pushed Mary Nell away, repulsed by her affectionate touch and words. Yet Mary Nell persisted. She wouldn't take "no" for an answer. She tried to press inside her mother's arms, and didn't give up though she never succeeded until that day in my office when we met Nellie. Who is more worthy of my love than my little Mary Nell?

Very quickly, the poison of my doubt is conquered by the power of love. How weak this flesh is! I am resolved to subjugate it through love. Even when my faith is weak, even when the consequences of doing right appear unbearable, even when my sincere prayers go unanswered and God seems elusive and distant, I will do right for love's sake.

I shove my wife's note back into my shirt pocket. It is a grievous insult, a defiant jab from the one whose betrayal I find most excruciating. Morgan's audacious malevolence horrifies me. She must have known all along I would try to intervene to save Mary Nell, and conspired to have her give me this letter to try to change my mind. Mary Nell probably cherished the note, proud of her being trusted with this solemn responsibility by her beloved grandmother. How dare Morgan try to tear away from Mary Nell the last person on earth to care for her? My wife has become the serpent in my Garden, tempting me with forbidden fruit, trying to dissuade me from loving my Mary Nell.

Why didn't Morgan sign the letter? Hopefully, for the shame she feels in asking the spiteful questions, void of any vestige of warmth or pity. Or, perhaps, she is beyond the point of shame. Adrenaline rises up within me like a volcano threatening to erupt—I am so furious at what we have become.

The word *if* in her second question invites more meditation. Would I still sacrifice myself for Mary Nell *if* I knew my sacrifice would not save her? I cannot deny that hope is a powerful motivating factor. I hope to save Mary Nell, to love her and enjoy her, to see her happy. Without hope, would I even be here in this train station right now? If I had no hope for her at all, would I still pay this price and walk this path?

Isn't a similar *if* at the very heart of the Gospel? A threat annexed to a hope, grounded in the reality of Jesus' sufferings and resurrection, contingent upon our response—that is the Gospel. If we believe, we will be saved. If not, we will be condemned. Jesus tasted death for all, knowing that only those who trust Him will receive the benefits of His sacrifice. If someone foolishly disbelieves, did Jesus suffer for them in vain? Even if so, what did Jesus do but suffer for them anyway, and pay the full price for their redemption? Jesus' sacrifice proves love is worth the cost, even if it is love unrequited. Even if the hope of mutual love never materializes. Considering His example, should we not love one another—even the least of His children—as He loves us? Greater than faith, greater than hope—that is love.

At the thought of Jesus' sufferings for me, I close my eyes to shut out the world, and I worship Him deep in my heart.

We are the defective, undeserving ones, hunted by devils, hounded by doubts, yet recipients of His pity and love. I am Mary Nell, and He, my Savior.

I sense a slight tremor in the duffel bag, and I think I hear Mary Nell's melodic hum. Someone nearby may see the duffel bag move or hear her unintelligible clamor, so I begin to quietly sing the song that lulled her to sleep on the beach. The song that I remember from my youth, which means more to me now than it ever did.

> *Jesus loves me this I know.*
> *For the Bible tells me so.*
> *Little ones to Him belong.*
> *They are weak but He is strong.*
> *Yes, Jesus loves me.*
> *Yes, Jesus loves me.*
> *Yes, Jesus loves me.*
> *The Bible tells . . .*

There is a commotion in the corner of the room. An elderly woman is speaking to a security guard. She points at me. He turns toward me, his brow furrowed.

If they are not the ones Jeremy Porter has assigned to help me, then I have been caught.

I look down at the GPS. Still no message from Jeremy. I gaze around the room for a place to exit, hopefully with a door that locks. Is escape even possible?

Emergency Exit Only, a sign on a door reads. *Alarm Will Sound*. It is a door that leads to the tracks over which the hover train glides. I hear the approaching whoosh of its quiet engine. It would be a dangerous place to exit, but the lesser of two threats if the officer approaches me. I glance back at the woman and the officer. He is speaking to someone through his nano, even as he keeps his eyes fixed on me.

I feel a subtle motion of the duffel bag, and hear a whispered, "Gwanpaw?"

"Shhh," I whisper back.

A man across from me jerks his gaze toward the bag. He must have heard her, or seen the duffel bag move of its own accord.

I stand, shove the GPS into my pants pocket, and begin to pull the blue duffel bag on its wheels toward the door.

"Stop!" The security guard points at me. "Stop now!"

"Move!" I urge others to move their legs out of the aisle.

"Is that a bomb?" someone asks.

"A terrorist!" someone else screams, pointing at me.

"Gwanpaw?" Mary Nell gets louder, the fear evident in her voice.

I stop at the emergency exit, unzip the duffel bag, and lift her out. I hold her closely. She wraps her legs and arms about me, trembling. I push the door handle and immediately the alarm sounds, but the door does not open. I look closely at the small print on the door. "Door handle must be held down for ten seconds to open."

The guard stops a dozen feet away. We are separated by several layers of people frightened by the commotion and the deafening alarm. The guard's hand rests on a handgun in its unsnapped holster.

I glance at the anxious passers-by rushing for other exits, tempted to try to duck into their throng.

"Don't run or I'll shoot! Are you Raymond Verity?"

"Gwanpaw? Is he da' bad man?" She is trembling.

"They are going to kill my granddaughter, sir. I just want to keep her safe."

"Who is going to kill your granddaughter?" He fixes his eyes on her, his hand still resting on his holstered weapon. "What's wrong with her?"

"She has Down Syndrome. The government wants to kill her. Please, just leave us alone and let me leave." I press against the door, but it holds fast.

"I've called my manager, and I just want to ask you to stay until he comes."

The heavy metal door finally opens behind me. I push it and enter a tunnel as the hover-train passes, the rushing wind of its speedy passing blowing my hair and causing Mary Nell to bury her head in my chest.

The guard barrels through several people and reaches for me, grasping my sleeve. I pull away, ripping my shirt. I slam the door shut and the guard jerks his arm back just in time.

There are dim lights on the walls in the tunnel. A shovel rests on the ground beside the two stairs that descend into the tunnel. I set Mary Nell down, jump over the handrail to grab the shovel and push it through the handle and between the metal handrail and the wall, effectively barring the door shut. The security guard tries to kick the door ajar, but it does not budge. Mary Nell begins to cry as we are temporarily parted, especially when she sees the rage of this officer banging against the door. I see him through the small window notifying his superiors via his radio.

Now what?

I pick up Mary Nell, look to my left, the direction of the train, and then back in the direction from which it came.

I turn left, toward the bay. If I am to be captured, it seems to be fitting that it be at the edge of the ocean. If she is to die, let it be in my arms as we try to swim away from the monsters who try to separate us.

I run about twenty yards when another train begins to speed past me. I see two security guards burst through the next emergency door ahead and swing their flashlights back and forth, trying to locate us.

I duck behind a narrow piling. I cannot exit ahead, and I cannot go back toward the station. It is a long train. I must go under the hover-train and search for another way out.

"This'll be fun, Mary Nell. We're going under the train."

"O-tay?" The anxiety in her tremulous voice makes her statement sound like a question.

I peek around the piling. The guards have split up and are going different directions, one toward me and one the other way. I close the distance to the train. The officer heading toward me screams an order for me to stop. I get on my knees and begin to roll under the train, its high-pitched hum causing my eardrums to vibrate. Mary Nell clutches me tightly with her arms and legs, even as we roll. I barely miss a low-hanging metal hook that almost impales me. We come up on the other side and Mary Nell celebrates.

"O-tay!"

"Yay. Was that fun?"

She shakes her head side to side, a frown on her dirty face. "No."

Ahead is a double door that is chained shut, but the opening appears sufficiently wide that we might be able to squeeze through, and get out of this dusty dark tunnel. The probing flashlights and shouts of the guards and policemen searching for me on the other side of the speeding train give the tunnel an eerie glow. The door leads to a room with restrooms, drink and snack machines, and beyond that, a passageway that looks like it leads to a poorly-lit boardwalk on a canal that seems to run perpendicular to the bay. I start to set Mary Nell through the opening first. She resists me.

"I tay wiff you. I tay wiff you." She clutches my arm.

"I'm coming next."

"No!"

"Shh. Mary Nell. Look at me." She trembles as she looks into my face. The shouts of our searchers draw nearer, and the arc of this concrete tunnel appears to brighten with the illumination of a dozen flashlights. I look back and realize the end of the train nears. "I'll be right behind you. You must go. Trust me."

She finally lets me push her through the narrow opening. I stretch the padlocked chain in order to get her to fit.

I put my leg in first, but it appears that the opening is too narrow.

"I tay wiff you!" She squeals and begins to pull on my leg.

I cannot get through. I abandon the narrow passageway to find another opening ahead, but when Mary Nell begins to frantically scream, I return. Officers are coming toward me from both directions now, their weapons drawn, shouting orders for me to freeze. The officer on the other side of the train daringly tries to follow us under the train. He's our greatest threat, as he is nearest to us.

Again, I try again to squeeze through the narrow opening. "Lord, help . . . "

No sooner than that prayer exits my mouth does the guard under the hover-train get impaled by one of the low-hanging metal hooks that almost hit me. His scream and the thumping of his body against the rails and the bottom of the train are obscured by the screeching of the air-break that has been automatically engaged from the collision.

I insert my leg and shoulder through the opening again, pushing against the loose door, stretching its hinges, tightening the loops of chain.

I clench my teeth and grunt with the strain. "Pull me, Mary Nell! Pull!"

With Mary Nell's vigilant pulling of my leg and then my arm, I inch through the opening as the guards and officers rush ever nearer. Finally, I pop through just as they arrive, cursing and shouting threats. One of them aims a weapon through the doors toward me, and seeing it aimed briefly toward Mary Nell, I violently knock it away and the officer screams in pain, withdrawing his arm.

Mary Nell wraps her arms around my leg. "I tay wiff you!"

I pick her up and another officer extends his handgun through the narrow opening in the double doors, as we run from the room.

Blam! Blam!

Mary Nell screams and I dive into the hallway, out of his line of sight.

With the death of the guard under the hover-train, their rules of engagement have changed. It's shoot to kill now.

Holding Mary Nell, I run to the boardwalk with all my might until it finally comes to a T at the edge of the beach. I look back just as several security officers come running onto the boardwalk, screaming incoherent threats at me. Gasping for air, I look left and right. Couples and groups of people are strolling, enjoying the clear sky and the crashing of the waves on the sandy beach below. At the shouting of the officers and the loud sound of their running footsteps on the boards, people around me are alerted to the chase and glare at us frightfully.

A steep sand dune comes close to the boardwalk about thirty yards away, so I run to it and forewarn Mary Nell that we have to jump.

"O-tay?" She clutches me tightly. I climb up on the handrail, hoping to reach the dune before the officers see me jump. It is dark and I cannot make the distance well, but with no other alternative, I leap off and land softly in the sand. But she has fallen out of my grasp.

"Mary Nell?" I grope for her in the dark.

"Ow." She begins to cry. "Owwie . . ."

"Shhh. It's okay." I feel for her in the darkness of the moonless night. "There you are, baby."

"Owwie," she whines, grasping her forearm.

I look back. The officers have apparently not seen me jump.

"Shh." I hold her close, feeling her arm carefully. There does not appear to be any break in the skin. Now it's her shoulder she's holding. "Dear Jesus, help my dear little Mary Nell's arm feel better. Keep us safe. Keep us together."

She whimpers pitifully as I climb over the edge of the dune, out of the view of the officers who are now shining their bright flashlights on the sand below the boardwalk. Fortunately, the gentle crashing of the waves is sufficient to drown out Mary Nell's whimpering.

Several small boats are anchored in what looks to be just a few feet of water offshore, dimly lit by propane lanterns. They must be fishing or gigging. Maybe one of them will be sympathetic and help. At this point, I am desperate.

Seeing no other alternative, I run through the shallow dunes and cattails toward the sandy beach of the Chesapeake Bay. Hoping one of the boaters will help, I run toward them along the sandy bar, holding Mary Nell. Their faces are dimly lit from their lanterns.

"Help me!" I cry out, softly lest I startle them. "Can you help?"

A bearded man in the middle turns toward me, a frown on his face. He raises a high-powered flashlight toward me. Others in the nearby two boats do the same, shining their flashlights at us for the guards behind us on the boardwalk to see. Mary Nell squints and turns away from the bright lights. I stretch a hand toward them. "Please, turn your lights off. "

"Who are you?" the bearded man inquires. He has a beer in one hand as he sits before a fishing pole that is affixed to the bow of his boat. By the light of the flashlight, I can see their fishing lines taut, angled toward the ocean. Two younger men come walking on the sand bar toward us, one with a cast net and one carrying a bucket of baitfish, curious as to who we are. I walk closer to the boat.

"I'm Ray. This is my granddaughter Mary Nell. I need your help."

"How are you dry? You had to walk through six feet of water to get to this sandbar."

"I need your help." I look back. A dozen flashlights are coming through the cattails towards me. "Those men want to take my granddaughter back to a place where they will kill her."

"Why?"

"She's got Down Syndrome." I turn to Mary Nell. "Look at them and say 'Hi.'"

She does so, and they appear surprised at her unusual facial features. The middle boat, with the bearded man, has thick black letters on its side—"Lucy."

The boat to my left has been given the name "Little Mag" in an elaborate font on its hull. The third boat drifts around Little Mag, thankfully obstructing my view of the officers that chase us. It has the name "Laodicea" on its hull.

"What's wrong with your face?" A man on Laodicea holding a beer has a snorkel mask around his neck.

"Please, I don't have time. Will you take us away from the shore?"

The sound of the waves barely obscures the shouts of those who pursue us. Two vehicles are speeding down the beach toward us.

"Where ya think we can take ya?" The woman in the driver's seat of Little Mag is wearing a halter-top and has a beach towel around her waist.

"Anywhere. Please. It's a matter of life and death."

"I know you!" The bearded man announces. "You were on the news. You're wanted for something." He snaps his fingers, looking around at the others.

"That doctor that kidnapped his granddaughter," the woman in the halter top reminds him.

The others moan their disapproval.

"He's a terrorist," the woman behind the steering wheel of Little Mag adds.

"There's a reward for catching this guy," says an obese man on the Lucy.

The bearded man twists his flashlight until the beam is tightly focused on our faces. Mary Nell shuts her eyes and presses her head into my neck. The two youth, who are about ten feet away in ankle deep water, set down their cast net and bait bucket and walk closer toward me.

"Come on in," the bearded man smiles, nearing the edge of the boat and extending a hand toward me. "I'll get you to safety."

His invitation is about as sincere as cheese on a mousetrap.

My heart throbs with a mixture of adrenaline and grief. What can I do now? I feel like I need to say goodbye to Mary Nell, but that seems like giving up. But what else can I do? The armed pursuers are rushing through what sounds like thigh-deep water toward me.

I walk toward the bearded man in the boat until I am in waist deep water beside his outstretched hand, but I do not reach for him. I keep walking, toward the blackness of the open ocean. They shout for me to come back, but I ignore them and continue away from them until my feet can no longer touch the bottom.

Mary Nell clings to me tightly, her teeth beginning to chatter. "Cold."

I glance back. The guards and officers have reached the boats. Several officers board the larger boat Laodicea, start the engine, and turn it toward me.

Exhausted and shivering, I begin to tread water, fighting a fearful dread of what they are going to do to my Mary Nell.

I do not say the words, but in my heart I begin to pray for the Lord to take us. *Let us die here in this cold ocean, together. That is so much better than our endless suffering apart. This world is so dark and evil. Take us, Lord.*

The boat slows and their flashlights focus on me. As the boat circles me, I am so tempted to get mad at God. Why won't He help? I'm doing everything I can.

The engine idles as the boat nears. The other boats have raised anchor and they near us slowly.

"Get in the boat!" a gravelly voice orders. The man's handgun stretches past his light, so I can see it. Another person lowers a ladder into the water.

I turn and begin to swim away.

"Just shoot him," someone on the boat urges.

"The sharks'll get him," the woman with the halter top complains.

"Get in the car or your girl will drown," one of the younger people respond.

"Who cares?" the young man behind him exclaims. "She's a defect."

"Get in the boat, Dr. Verity!" the man carrying the beer urges me. "They just want the girl. Trust the system. With a good attorney and a sympathetic jury . . ."

"Gwanpaw," she whimpers in my ear. "Don't weave me."

"Get on my back, Mary Nell." I begin to swim as fast as I can with Mary Nell clinging to my neck. "I'm never going to leave you, baby. Never."

An engine revs, but the sound is eclipsed by the rotors of an approaching helicopter.

An explosion makes the night sky as bright as day.

I turn towards the source. Flames leap from the boat's engine. Several officers exchange gunfire with the helicopter.

"Gwanpaw! Gwanpaw!"

An officer on the boat, apparently realizing that they cannot win this exchange with a fighter copter, turns his weapon on me. Bullets strike the water around us. Mary Nell squeals, clinging tightly to me.

"Hold your breath!" I sink under the waves. She struggles against me, and I am forced to the surface, worried that she will drown. No sooner do we get a breath of air than I am hit in the chest with what feels like a bolt of lightning. My mouth fills with hot liquid. I gasp from the excruciating chest pain and a sudden breathlessness. I feel weighted down as if by an anchor. I sink under the waves, with Mary Nell clinging frantically to me. I struggle to return to the surface.

Her hands claw my hair and face. I try to keep afloat, but my arms feel heavy. Exhausted. I cannot catch my breath. I cannot hold onto her. My consciousness wanes. I kick with my legs as hard as I can, trying to keep her above the waves. A man jumps out of the helicopter and, from the sound of his splash, lands nearby. Mary Nell grasps tightly to my neck and hair, and will not let go.

My vision dims as I sink again below the waves. I kick with my legs, but I cannot feel them.

She claws at me for another moment, and then she's gone. I open my eyes beneath the surface, searching the green salty water, dimly illuminated by the bright lights aimed at us from the hovering helicopter. I cannot see her. I see a stream of blood pulsating into the water from the right side of my chest, and I catch the glimpse of a pale shape of a man-sized shark just a few feet below me. Where is Mary Nell? I am sinking down to the depths. I have not the energy to kick to the surface. I feel an extreme urge to cough, and can hold my breath no longer. I breathe in the salty water, inviting my end.

God, save her.

51

"WE COULD HAVE CAPTURED HIM alive in the Chesapeake Bay," the FBI director informs President Sayder through her encrypted video-call connection. She's alone in her Oval Office, getting an update on the conclusion of the manhunt. "It was probably an Alabama Guard stealth copter, but we cannot be sure."

"Are you sure he is dead?"

"There was a pool of blood as big as your desk, Madame President. The place was crawling with sharks."

"And his granddaughter?"

The agent shrugs. "The Alabama authorities could have her in their custody, or she could have drowned. It matters not. She's no threat to us."

"I want her dead anyway, if only to spit on her rescuer's grave."

The FBI director, even with his long history of callous disregard for human rights for the sake of a superior's order, flinches at the President's spite.

"Find her, Bill. And I have decided that we should go ahead and commence Operation Red Tide."

The FBI director's eyeballs bulge momentarily. "What? Red Tide?"

"Wipe Alabama's leadership off the map. Black ops."

"I know what it is, Madame President. They have stacked up their defenses. I beg you to reconsider."

"This isn't up for discussion!" It's as if she predicted the FBI director's objections, and decided beforehand that his opinion was irrelevant and she was going to cut him off every time. "Pinning it on a power struggle between FAM and Personhood radicals will help win the minds of the religious right, especially down south. Hurry up, because Mississippi's next."

"But we have no evidence whatsoever of any attempt to resist us violently, nor have they ever justified violent resistance against us."

The President leans into the camera, frustrated. "Bill! I can't believe what I'm hearing. When do the facts have anything to do with what we do? We create the facts we need, Bill, to get the job done."

"And we aren't even sure that the helicopter was controlled by the Alabama authorities. Raymond Verity was a billionaire with multiple international connections with some very powerful people. He could have ordered a stealth fighter copter created from scratch with the cost of his wife's jewelry. Even if we do succeed with Red Tide, we may not be able to sell our version of events, especially to the citizens of Alabama. They have an alternative press with a deep-rooted distrust of our version of any event, and predictably will be fighting mad after an aggressive invasion of their soil to kill or capture their democratically elected leaders."

"We can justify Red Tide based on the explosion that took out Aaron Little, pinned firmly on the Personhood contingent that's entrenched in Montgomery and ever-present in Governor Whetley's inner circle." She smiles. "You're getting worked up over nothing."

"But Madame President." The FBI director pauses, hesitant. "You personally ordered that bombing yourself to take out Aaron Little—"

The President explodes in a rage and leans toward her laptop camera. "Don't you think I know that, you moron? This isn't about truth; this is about winning! It's about putting these religious fanatics in their place, and putting their God under our feet once and for all." She takes a deep breath and leans back into her chair. "When the nation's at war, presidents can bomb and murder anyone they want to. It's unpatriotic to challenge the wartime decisions of commanders-in-chief."

"But Congress will doubtless—"

"Would you quit! This is not up for discussion. What's the matter with you?"

The FBI Director grimaces at constantly being interrupted. "Yes, ma'am."

"At least Raymond Verity's dead." The Presidents puts her hands behind her head and lets out a long sigh. "What a relief."

"It appears so."

"Oh, I wish I could have seen the horror on his face when he dropped below the water the last time, knowing that cursed genetic mutant of his was probably going to the grave with him." She laughs sadistically. "The greatest threat to the federal government's intervention into the New Body science has finally been eliminated. It's smooth sailing to paradise from here on out . . . "

* * *

Lips crack a mischievous smile from a penthouse on the other side of the Potomac River. Jeremy Porter sits in front of a digital camera at a table of computers running a program that has altered his voice and facial appearance to imitate the FBI leader conversing with the President.

"Perfect." Porter flashes a toothy grin.

"Tell me when it's done."

Jeremy Porter meditates for a moment upon one of his favorite passages of Scripture from Psalm 37, and utters it aloud.

> *The wicked plotteth against the just*
> *and gnasheth upon him with his teeth.*
> *The Lord shall laugh at him:*
> *for He seeth that his day is coming.*
> *The wicked have drawn out the sword,*
> *and have bent their bow,*
> *to cast down the poor and needy,*
> *and to slay such as be of upright conversation.*
> *Their sword shall enter into their own heart,*
> *and their bows shall be broken.*

President Veronica Sayder appears confused at this unwelcome and unlikely commentary from the FBI Director. "Excuse me?"

Jeremy Porter types a command on his keyboard and the President's laptop goes black. With a wide grin, he places his hands behind his head and turns his gaze heavenward. "Perfect."

* * *

She frowns and wiggles the mouse.

"Greetings America," the white words on a black background appear on her laptop screen, and an artificial voice reads the words aloud. "The President of the United States, Veronica Sayder, just moments ago conversed with FBI Director Bill Columbia, and spoke these words . . . "

The President's face flushes. She reaches for the mouse to her desktop computer and taps the mouse to revive the screen. The words are also up on her PC screen.

The last three minutes of her conversation, complete with the video of her speaking into the camera on top of her personal laptop, is broadcast publicly over the world wide web.

The President puts a call through to Homeland Security, but before the Director can answer, her personal phone starts buzzing. The caller ID announces that it is Bill Columbia. She hangs up on Homeland Security and hits a button on the phone to answer it. "Is Jeremy Porter doing this?"

"We don't know who it is, Madame President," he responds via speakerphone, "but I did not just have a conversation with you. This video has completely taken over the whole net and we can't shut it down. We don't know how. This has never happened before. This kind of technology does not exist."

She gasps, and hangs up.

She clenches her fists around the armrests of her chair as she watches herself informing the whole world of her crimes. The planned invasion of Alabama's Statehouse to kill Alabama's leaders, the intent to kill Mary Nell simply to spite Raymond Verity's memory, the admission that she ordered the bombing of the NBS television studio to kill Aaron Little and falsely blame the Personhood leaders—all of it is broadcast to the whole world, and there is nothing she can do to stop it.

* * *

"And that's how your Grandpa saved your life." Mary Nell sits attentively in Tamara's lap, hanging on her every word. "He sacrificed his life for you, just like Jesus."

Tears come to Mary Nell's eyes. "Gwanpaw."

"I miss him, too." Nellie sits on the couch beside Savannah.

"You'll both see him soon," Savannah smiles. Mary Nell gets off of her Aunt Tamara's lap and leaps into the couch to snuggle in between Savannah and her new sister.

* * *

When I twist the doorknob to our townhouse in downtown Montgomery, I am ecstatic at the joy that fills my home.

"Gwanpaw!" Mary Nell runs to me as fast as her skinny legs will take her.

I set my crutches down and ease to my knees. "Wait, wait. Give me a second."

Savannah comes around the couch, smiling, enjoying her daughter's affection for me.

Mary Nell throws her arms around me. "I wuv you, Gwanpaw."

I brush her brown hair away from her eyes with my fingers and gently kiss her eyelids, a tradition showing my appreciation of the distinguishing features of her Trisomy 21. I grab her hands and turn them palms up to kiss her simian creases—the lines in her palm that are unique to Downs. Not to be outdone, she comes up to the paralyzed side of my face and kisses my cheek.

"Thank You, God, for my Mary Nell." I hug her close.

"Tanks," she repeats.

Nellie also comes close to share in Grandpa's affection, as Tamara and Savannah, from their relaxed posture and easy smiles, take pleasure at the tradition that has characterized our greetings ever since I was discharged from the hospital.

"I wuv you, too." Nellie imitates Mary Nell's lisp as she tries to wrap her arms all the way around both of us.

"How was your P.T.?" Savannah asks me.

"Less painful. I'm getting stronger. Slowly." I stand to my feet with the help of my crutches. "Thanks to Frankie."

Frankie—my clone—steps in from the garage, and grins as he sees the affection I share with the girls.

Frankie was freed from the Verity Wing when the elusive Jeremy Porter exposed New Body science's corruption to the world and elicited enough rage to nearly bankrupt the industry. The releasing of clones to their genomic donors was a remedy freely agreed to by industry leaders in order to try to salvage their reputation and decrease the likelihood of government sanction or prosecution, which every day looked more and more likely. Frankie—named so because it sounded similar to his birth name of Fifty—became my assistant at my Montgomery New Body Research Center, where I have begun work on improving health by way of ethical therapies. Frankie freely donated some tissue to correct the gunshot damage to my right lung and esophagus, a fragment of which remains lodged in my seventh thoracic vertebrae.

We have become good friends and workout partners. We read a chapter of the Bible together every day, and finally, I'm beginning to catch on to my sister's ubiquitous biblical metaphors. Believe it or not, I can almost beat Frankie in chess. Almost. I think, though, he sacrifices pieces unnecessarily just to keep me in the game, a kind gesture to his old twin brother, handicapped with half a working face and a bullet in his spine.

"What do you want to do when you grow up?" I asked him at the tail end of one of his slower victories.

He shrugs. "You saved my life, Ray. I, I, I want to serve you."

"Stop it. You're doing that just because I do it."

Frankie smiles widely. "Okay. Just trying to, you know—"

"'In humility, let every man judge others to be better than them,' the Bible says. It's okay if you talk better than, than me. Alright?"

Distracted, he makes a stupid move. I bring my knight back and back his queen. "Bam!" I raise the queen in the air to celebrate. "I got his queen!"

Mary Nell claps and cheers for me, though she probably doesn't even know why.

Frankie crosses his arms over his chest and grins sheepishly. "I meant to do that just to get you to feel better about being such a loser."

"Liar!" I say with a wide grin. "You didn't see it!"

He shrugs and smirks. "Ok. If you say so." He leans forward, moves his bishop halfway down the board. "Mate."

I am numb. He beat me. Again. He comes around and extends a friendly hand to me. I smack it away. He kisses me on the forehead and I push him away with a grin. "Love you, buddy."

He messes up my hair. "Love you too, loser."

* * *

"Mom's not doing well today." Savannah's tone is gloomy and countenance drawn. I hang the crutches on the wall, and with Frankie's help, I hobble to the couch to lean on it.

"Is she in bed?"

Savannah nods and she and Tamara lead me down the hall to the bedroom.

Morgan stands in front of a wall completely white except for a 9 x 11 framed picture of herself from a glamorized photography session several years ago.

"Oh, she's up." Tamara smiles momentarily, but is troubled by Morgan's behavior.

In the two-year-old photograph on the wall, Morgan is wearing a strapless pink dress; her skin is tan, her teeth white, and her hair perfect. Morgan stands in front of the photo, staring at it longingly. With her hair frazzled and unkempt, and her eyes glazed over, she looks as if she is about to speak some profound thought on the tip of her tongue, but she just can't get it out. One hand nervously picks at some sores on her neck, and the other reaches for some invisible object a few feet in front of her between her and the photograph.

I walk to her and wrap my arm around her. "Morgan," I say with a cheerful tone, "what are you looking at?"

She does not even acknowledge my presence. She begins to stutter, "Nuba, nuba, nuba . . . " She turns to glance at me, and then back to the wall. "Nuba, nuba . . . "

Her embarrassing state of intellect makes Frankie blush. He comes and sits on the side of her bed. Morgan points, as if she's asking me to do something for her.

"What is it, babe? What do you want?"

"Nuba!" she speaks more forcefully. "Nuba!"

"She's been saying that all day," Savannah informs me. "I don't know what she means."

"We'll get a new body in heaven." Tamara supports herself by leaning against the dresser. "Soon enough."

"In the meantime," I say, "let's be thankful for what we have and make the best of this special moment." I go to the desk and pick up a wooden cross, something Nellie carved from a chunk of balsa wood as long as my forearm. It is covered with intricate symmetrical markings that Nellie calls the image of Pi at 528 hertz. Mary Nell contributed to the finished product, covering the intricate carving with her handprints in various pastel colors. I remove the glamour photograph from its hook and put the cross in its place. I stand beside Morgan, steadying her with my arm around her waist.

"Ta, ta, ta, ta," she stutters, pointing at the cross. "Ta, ta . . . "

I begin to rock with her gently side to side, staring at the wall, empty of all but the cross. For several moments, we just enjoy a moment together. She grows quiet with our rhythmic sway. I turn to her and think I see the corner of her lips turn up a bit.

"Oh, Morgan." I grieve the irreversible, gradual slipping away of her mind and personality. I draw even closer to her and rest my head for a moment on her shoulder. I kiss her on the cheek. "My dear Morgan."

She is my wife, and I love her.

To the cadence of our dance, I softly sing the song that now means so much to me.

> *Jesus loves me this I know,*
> *For the Bible tells me so,*
> *Little ones to Him belong,*

Tamara, Savannah, Mary Nell, and Nellie join in singing the tune from the open doorway, the girls giggling as they twirl.

> *They are weak but He is strong.*
> *Yes, Jesus loves me,*
> *Yes, Jesus loves me,*
> *Yes, Jesus loves me.*
> *The Bible tells me so.*

Strength stooping to weakness. Tears for pain, laughter for joy. Love.

Perfection.

Author's Note

I hope you enjoyed *Body by Blood*. I need to ask you a favor. Would you help others enjoy this book, too?

Recommend it. Please help other readers find this book by recommending it to friends in person and on social media.

Review it. Meaningful reviews can be tough to come by these days. You, the reader, have the power to make or break a book. Loved it, hated it—I'd just enjoy your feedback. Please tell other readers what you thought about this book by reviewing it at Amazon, Barnes and Noble, or Goodreads. My goal is to have 100 honest reviews on Amazon. Will you help me reach that goal?

Thank you so much for reading *Body by Blood* and for spending time with me.

In gratitude,

Patrick Johnston

Discussion Questions

1. What Bible passages could help us answer the question "When does life begin?"

2. What Bible passages could help us answer the question of how we should treat "the least"?

3. Is it ever right to intentionally kill a human being?

4. What scientific evidence could help us answer these questions?

5. What is the problem with relying solely on science to determine the answers to such questions?

6. What does it mean to be "created in the image of God"?

7. When are we "created in the image of God?"

8. When precisely did God become man? How does this affect your view of when life begins?

9. What New Testament passages describe the duty of civil authorities to protect the innocent?

10. What Old Testament passages describe the duty of civil authorities to protect the innocent, and the consequences if they do not?

11. What is God's inevitable response to nations or communities that shed innocent blood?

12. According to the Bible, what abates the wrath of God on the land for the shedding of innocent blood?

13. What do the Declaration of Independence and the U.S. Constitution say about the "right to life"?

14. When higher civil authorities defy the Highest Power and the law of the land to shed innocent blood, is it the obligation of lesser civil authorities to submit or resist?

15. Describe biblical examples of saints who resisted or rebelled against civil authority and were blessed by God for it.

Resources

For encouraging testimonies of those who courageously loved "the least," visit www.DownSyndrome.love.

For more information on how we should love the least in all circumstances, purchase the video "Pro-Life Without Exception" available on Amazon.

To find a pro-life physician near you, visit www.ProLifePhysicians.org.

To keep up-to-date on local and state attempts to protect the least of God's children and resist federal tyranny, visit www.DefyTyrants.com.

For more information about
Dr. Patrick Johnston
&
Body by Blood

please visit:

www.Johnston.house
www.ProLifePhysicians.org
www.DocJohnstonNovels.com
Email: DocJohnston@yahoo.com

For more information about
AMBASSADOR INTERNATIONAL
please visit:

www.ambassador-international.com
@AmbassadorIntl
www.facebook.com/AmbassadorIntl

If you enjoyed this book, please consider leaving us a review on
Amazon, Goodreads, or our website.